KITCHENS
of
the
GREAT
MIDWEST

KITCHENS

of
the

GREAT
MIDWEST

J. RYAN STRADAL

Quercus

First published in the USA by Pamela Dorman Books, Viking
First published in Great Britain in 2015 by

Quercus Publishing Ltd
Carmelite House
50 Victoria Embankment
London EC4Y 0DZ

An Hachette UK company

A CIP catalogue record for this book is available
from the British Library

HB ISBN 978 1 78429 193 8
TPB ISBN 978 1 78429 241 6
EBOOK ISBN 978 1 78429 192 1

10 9 8 7 6 5 4 3 2 1

Printed and bound in Great Britain by Clays Ltd, St Ives plc

To Karen
Who always did the best with what she had

CONTENTS

LUTEFISK

Lars Thorvald loved two women. That was it, he thought in passing, while he sat on the cold concrete steps of his apartment building. Perhaps he would've loved more than two, but it just didn't seem like things were going to work out like that.

That morning, while defying a doctor's orders by puréeing a braised pork shoulder, he'd stared out his kitchen window at the snow on the roof of the Happy Chef restaurant across the highway and sung a love song to one of those two girls, his baby daughter, while she slept on the living room floor. He was singing a Beatles song, replacing the name of the girl in the old tune with the name of the girl in the room.

He hadn't told a woman "I love you" until he was twenty-eight. He didn't lose his virginity until he was twenty-eight either. At least he'd had his first kiss when he was twenty-one, even if that woman quit returning his calls less than a week later.

Lars blamed his sorry luck with women on his lack of teenage romance, and he blamed his lack of teenage romance on the fact that he was the worst-smelling kid in his grade, every year. He stunk like the floor of a fish market each Christmas, starting at age twelve, and even when he didn't smell terrible, the other kids acted like he did, because that's what kids do. "Fish Boy," they called him, year round, and it was all the fault of an old Swedish woman named Dorothy Seaborg.

• • •

On a December afternoon in 1971, Dorothy Seaborg of Duluth, Minnesota, fell on the ice and broke her hip while walking to her mailbox, disrupting the supply line of lutefisk for the Sunday Advent dinners at St. Olaf's Lutheran Church. Lars's father, Gustaf Thorvald—of Duluth's Gustaf & Sons bakery, and one of the most conspicuous Norwegians between Cloquet and Two Harbors—promised everyone in St. Olaf's Fellowship Hall that there would be no break in lutefisk continuity; his family would step in and carry on the brutal Scandinavian tradition for the benefit of the entire Twin Ports region.

Never mind that neither Gustaf, his wife, Elin, nor his children had ever even seen a live whitefish before, much less caught one, pounded it, dried it, soaked it in lye, resoaked it in cold water, or done the careful cooking required to make something that, when perfectly prepared, looked like jellied smog and smelled like boiled aquarium water. Since everyone in the house was equally unqualified for the job, the work fell to Lars, age twelve, and his younger brother Jarl, age ten, sparing the youngest sibling, nine-year-old Sigmund, but only because he actually liked the stuff.

"If Lars and Jarl don't like it," Gustaf told Elin, "I can count on them not to eat any. It'll eliminate loss and breakage."

Gustaf was satisfied with this reasoning, and while Elin still thought it was a mean thing to do to their young sons, she said nothing. Theirs was a mixed-race marriage—between a Norwegian and a Dane—and thus all things culturally important to one but not the other were given a free pass and critiqued only in unmixed company.

Yearly intimate contact with their cultural heritage failed to evolve the Thorvald boys' sensibilities. Jarl, who still ate his own snot, much preferred the taste of boogers to lutefisk, given that the consistency and color were the same. Lars, meanwhile, was stumped by the old Scandinavian women who walked up to him in church and said, "Any young man who makes lutefisk like you do is going to be quite popular with the ladies." In Lars's experience, lutefisk skills usually inspired revulsion or, at best, indifference among prospective dates. Even the girls who claimed they liked lutefisk didn't want to smell it when they weren't eating it, and Lars couldn't give them much of a choice. The once-anticipated holiday season had become for Lars a cruel month of stench and rejection, and thanks to the boys at school, its social effects lingered long after everyone's desiccated Christmas trees were abandoned by the curbside.

By the time Lars was eighteen, whatever tolerance he'd once had for this uncompromising tradition had long eroded. His hands were scarred from several Advents of soaking dried whitefish in lye, and every year the smell clung harder to his pores, fingernails, hair, and shoes, and not just because their surface areas had increased with maturity. Lars had also grown to become a little wizard in the kitchen, and by his unintentionally mastering the tragic hobby of lutefisk preparation, its potency was skyrocketing. Lutherans were driving from as far away as Fergus Falls to try the "Thorvald lutefisk," and there wasn't an attractive young woman among any of them.

As if to mock him further every year, Lars's dad would shove a forkful of the crap in his face each Christmas.

"Just a bite," Gustaf would say. "Your ancestors ate this to survive the long winters."

"And how did they survive lutefisk?" Lars asked once.

"Take some pride in your work, son," Gustaf said, and took away his lefse in punishment.

In 1978, Lars graduated from high school and got the heck out of Duluth. His grades could've gotten him into a nice Lutheran school like

Gustavus Adolphus or Augsburg, but Lars wanted to be a chef, and he didn't see what good college would do him other than to delay that goal by four years. Instead he moved down to the Cities, looking for a girlfriend and for kitchen work in whatever order, requiring only that no one insist he make lutefisk. That attitude sure left a lot more options open than his father had predicted.

After a ten-year unpaid apprenticeship at Gustaf & Sons, Lars was already skilled at baking—arguably the most difficult of all culinary duties—but didn't want to fall back on that. Because he only chose jobs that could teach him something, and went on dates about as often as a vegetarian restaurant opened near an interstate highway, he gained a pretty decent handle on French, Italian, German, and American cuisine in just under a decade.

By October 1987, as his home state was enraptured by the Twins winning their first World Series ever, Lars had earned a job as a chef at Hutmacher's, a trendy lakeside restaurant that attracted big celebrities, like meteorologists, state senators, and local pro athletes. For years, it was said, a Twins player could enjoy his meals at Hutmacher's unremarked and unmolested, but by the week Lars was hired, jubilant ballplayers were regularly turning the late shift into an upbeat party.

Amid the circumstance of a long-suffering sports team's success, the strange joy of it all spread through the restaurant. It was during these happy weeks when Cynthia Hargreaves, the smartest waitress on staff—she gave the best wine pairing advice of any of the servers—seemed to take an interest in Lars. By this time, he was twenty-eight, growing a pale hairy inner tube around his waist, and already going bald. Even though she had an overbite and the shakes, she was six feet tall and beautiful, and not like a statue or a perfume advertisement, but in a realistic way, like how a truck or a pizza is beautiful at the moment you want it most. This, to Lars, made her feel approachable.

When she came back to the kitchen, the guys would all openly check her out, but Lars refrained. Instead, he'd look her in the face while he told her things like, "Tell them it'll be five more minutes on that veal," and "No, I will not hold the garlic—it's pesto."

"Oh, you can't make a sauce with just pine nuts, olive oil, basil, and Romano?" she asked.

He was a bit impressed that she knew the other ingredients off the top of her head. Maybe he shouldn't have been, but it just wasn't the kind of thing he expected people outside a kitchen to know. He knew he must have communicated this to her when he saw how she was smiling back at him knowingly, like he had been caught in the act of something.

"Well, you know, I can try," he said. "But then it's not pesto, it's something else."

"How fresh is the basil?" she asked. "Pesto lives or dies by its basil."

He admired her decisive way of phrasing that incorrect opinion. It was actually the preparation that determined its quality; proper pesto, he had learned during a previous job at Pronto Ristorante, is made with a mortar and pestle. It makes all the difference.

"It's two days old," he said.

"Where'd you get it from? St. Paul Farmers' Market?"

"Yeah, from Anna Hlavek."

"Oh, you should get it from Ellen Chamberlain. Ellen grows the best basil."

Such wonderfully erroneous food opinions! This was getting Lars all riled up. Still, in his Minneapolis years, liberated from both his lutefisk stench and its reputation, he'd driven women away due to what they called his "eagerness," and he couldn't allow that to happen again.

"Oh, she does, now?" he asked her, continuing to work, not looking up at her.

"Yeah," she said, stepping closer to him, trying to keep him engaged. "Anna grows sweet corn in the same plot as her basil. You know what sweet corn does to soil."

She had a point, if that were true. "I didn't know Anna grew sweet corn."

"She doesn't sell it to the public." She smiled at him again. "And I'll tell my customer yes on the garlic-free pesto, anyway."

"Why?"

"I want to see you work a little harder back here," she said.

He couldn't help it—he was in love by the time she left the kitchen—but love made him feel sad and doomed, as usual. What he didn't know was that she'd suffered through a decade of cool, commitment-phobic men, and Lars's kindness, but mostly his effusive, overt enthusiasm for her, was at that time exactly what she wanted in a partner.

Cynthia was pregnant, but not showing, by the time they were married in late October 1988. Lars was still a chef at Hutmacher's, and she was still their most popular waitress, but despite the storybook romance that had flourished within their establishment, the owners refused to shut the restaurant down on a Saturday to host the wedding reception.

Lars's father, still infuriated that his eldest son had abandoned both the family bakery and the responsibility of supplying lutefisk for thousands of intransigent Scandinavians, boycotted the wedding and refused to support any aspect of it. If Lars was having his mother's first grandchild, she might have been inspired to help, but instead Elin was already busy with Sigmund's two kids; naturally, the one brother who'd never made lutefisk in his life had lost his virginity, and fruitfully, by age seventeen.

The couple honeymooned in the Napa Valley, which was still flush from the shocking Judgment of Paris more than a decade earlier and happily maturing into its new volume of wine tourism. Lars had never experienced a wine tasting before, and while her new husband threw back the one-ounce pours, Cynthia consumed everything on the labels, the vineyard tours, and the maps. It was her first trip to California, and even completely sober, her body swooned at the sight of a grapevine and her soul flourished in the jungle of argot: *varietal, Brix, rootstock, malolactic fermentation*. In the rental car, with his eyes closed while trying to sleep off a surfeit of heavy afternoon reds, Lars could feel her smiling as she drove him and their unborn child through the shimmering California hills.

"I love this so much," she said.

"I love you, too," he said, though that was not what she meant.

They'd agreed, if it was a boy, that Lars would name the baby, and if it was a girl, Cynthia would. Eva Louise Thorvald was born two weeks before her due date, on June 2, 1989, coming into the world at an assertive ten pounds, two ounces. When Lars first held her, his heart melted over her like butter on warm bread, and he would never get it back. When mother and baby were asleep in the hospital room, he went out to the parking lot, sat in his Dodge Omni, and cried like a man who had never wanted anything in his life until now.

"Let's give it five or six years before we have another one," Cynthia said, and got herself an IUD. Lars had been hoping for at least three kids, like in his own family, but he supposed there was time. He tried to impress upon Cynthia the fact that having multiple kids means at least one of them will stick around to make sure that you don't die alone if you fall in the shower or trip on your basement staircase. He pointed out how after he and Jarl had gotten out of Duluth, their middle brother, Sigmund, had taken over both the bakery and the extraordinary demands of their dying parents, and how that was working out super for everybody. This line of argument was not compelling to his twenty-five-year-old wife. Cynthia wanted to get into wine.

. . .

In the same fashion that a musical parent may curate their child's exposure to certain songs, Lars had spent weeks plotting a menu for his baby daughter's first months:

Week One

NO TEETH, SO:

1. Homemade guacamole.
2. Puréed prunes (do infants like prunes?)
3. Puréed carrots (Sugarsnax 54, ideally, but more likely Autumn King).
4. Puréed beets (Lutz green leaf).
5. Homemade Honeycrisp applesauce (get apples from Dennis Wu).
6. Hummus (from canned chickpeas? Maybe wait for week 2.)
7. Olive tapenade (maybe with puréed Cerignola olives? Ask Sherry Dubcek about the best kind of olives for a newborn.)
8. What for protein and iron?

Week Two

STILL NO TEETH, UNLESS WE'RE IMPROBABLY FORTUNATE, BUT WHAT THE HECK ANYWAY:

1. Definitely hummus.
2. The rest, same as above, until teeth.

Week Twelve

TEETH!

1. Pork shoulder (puréed? Or make a pork-based demi-glace?)
2. Vegetable spaghetti squash. What kid wouldn't love this? It'll blow her mind! (How lucky she is to be teething by the start of squash season!)
3. Osso buco (get veal shanks from Al Norgaard at Hackenmuller's).

Week Sixteen

TIME FOR GUILTY PLEASURES!

1. **Mom's Chicken Wild Rice Casserole (recipe below)**

    1 small package wild rice

    2 cups cooked chicken (diced)

    1 can cream of mushroom soup

    ½ can milk

    Salt and pepper

    ¼ cup green pepper, chopped

    Heat the oven to 350°F. Cook the rice according to the directions. Mix the rice, chicken, cream of mushroom soup, milk, salt and pepper, and green pepper. Place in a greased 2-quart casserole pan. Bake for 30 minutes.

2. **Corn Dogs (probably great for gnawing! Find the State Fair recipe.)**

3. **Mom's Carrot Cake (recipe below)**

    2 cups sugar (maybe use less)

    1½ cups salad oil (find substitute)

    4 eggs

    2 cups flour

    2 teaspoons baking soda

    1 teaspoon salt

    3 teaspoons cinnamon

    3 cups shredded carrots

    1 cup chopped nuts (nut allergy risk?)

    1 teaspoon vanilla

Heat the oven to 325°F. Combine the sugar, salad oil, eggs, flour, baking soda, salt, cinnamon, carrots, nuts, and vanilla and pour into a 9-by-13-inch pan. Bake for 45 minutes.

Icing recipe:

¼ pound or ½ cup butter (Grade AA)

8-ounce package cream cheese

3½ cups powdered sugar

Mix and spread on the cooled carrot cake.

This meal plan seemed like a sound strategy to Lars, who remained mindful of what was in season and what had sustained his own family through the long winters in Duluth. His main worry was the chopped nuts in the carrot cake recipe. He'd heard somewhere that a child could get a nut allergy from eating nuts too soon. But how soon was too soon? He had to talk to their obstetrician, Dr. Latch, who had a thick mustache, kind eyes, and what Lars interpreted as a can-do attitude.

In his office, Dr. Latch listened to Lars's question and then looked at the young man the way someone might regard a toddler who's holding a Buck knife.

"You want to feed carrot cake to a four-month-old?" Dr. Latch asked.

"Not a lot of carrot cake," Lars said. "I mean, a small portion. A baby portion. I'm just concerned about the nuts in the recipe. I mean, I guess I could make it without nuts. But my mom always made it with nuts. What do you think?"

"Eighteen months. At the earliest. Probably wait until age two to be safe."

"I could be wrong, but I remember my younger siblings eating carrot cake really young. There's a picture of my brother Jarl on the day he turned one. They gave him a little carrot cake and he smeared it in his hair."

"That's the best outcome in that situation, probably."

"Well, now he's bald."

"Looking over your dietary plan here, I'd have more immediate reservations."

"Like what?"

"Well, pork shoulder to a three-month-old baby. Not advisable."

"Puréed, maybe?" Lars asked. "I could braise it first. Or maybe just roast the bones and make pork stock for a demi-glace. That wouldn't be my first choice, though."

"You work at Hutmacher's, right?" Dr. Latch said. "You do make an excellent pork shoulder. But give it at least two years."

"Two years, huh?" He didn't want to tell Dr. Latch that this conversation crushed his heart, but the doctor seemed to perceive this.

"I understand your eagerness to share your life's passion with your first child. I see different versions of this all the time. The time will come. For now, just breast milk and formula for the first three months."

"That's awful," Lars said.

"Maybe for you," Dr. Latch said. "But your daughter is going to be monstrously satisfied with this diet. Trust me. Now, I'm going to refer you to the most vigilant pediatrician I know."

Back at their apartment in St. Paul, lugging all of the unfamiliar baby gear out of their car, Lars was grateful they could afford a place with an elevator. While waiting for the doors to open, he saw the building's lightly used concrete stairway, which he'd climbed a few times over the years for exercise. Feeling the straps of a diaper bag dig into his shoulder and the plastic handle of the portable baby seat against his palm, he guessed he might never use it again.

• • •

When they weren't sleeping, trying to sleep, or holding their newborn daughter, Lars and Cynthia were usually in the kitchen. Lars didn't want to take his eyes off of his beautiful girl for a minute, so he kept her strapped in the baby seat on the counter.

"Don't you think it might be dangerous to have her in here?" Cynthia asked him the second night, while chopping garlic and parsley for an Alfredo sauce.

"That doctor can take away her right to eat," Lars said. "But she should still be around the smells. Next best thing, you know."

"Yeah. Smelling a bunch of food she can't eat. It's probably frustrating the hell out of her."

"Well, this is where we are, and I want her with us."

"I don't know, putting a baby in a room full of knives and boiling water."

"Where would you like her to be?"

Cynthia shook her head. "Somewhere else."

Lars turned and looked at Eva, who was wearing a pink stocking cap for warmth, and mittens so she wouldn't scratch her own face with her tiny fingernails. He didn't ever intend to stare at her for such long stretches; it would just happen. When their eyes met, bam, there went five minutes. Or twenty.

Cynthia tapped him on the shoulder.

"Water's ready for the pasta."

"Where's the fettuccine?" he asked her, opening the fridge.

She took a green Creamette box out from the lazy Susan by his feet. "I figured we'd try this brand. It was on sale."

"I remember when we used to make our own pasta. I guess those days are over."

"Thank God," Cynthia said. "What a pain in the ass."

• • •

Cynthia was still twenty-five, and bounced back to her skinny frame with color in her cheeks and bigger boobs, while Lars just grew balder and fatter and slower. He had learned, before she was pregnant, that he had to hold her hand or touch her in some way while they walked places together, so that other men knew they were a couple. Now that she was the mother of his daughter, he was even more wary, snarling at passing dudes with confident Tom Selleck mustaches and cool Bon Jovi hair. Cynthia, pushing a stroller as they perused the winter farmers' markets, didn't mind Lars's hulking shadow or the expressions he'd snap at ogling perverts; she was mostly just happy that she could drink again.

"They're looking for a new sommelier at Hutmacher's," Cynthia said one morning, while Lars was changing Eva's diaper. Cynthia's sensitive nose couldn't handle the smell of her daughter's poop, but for Lars, after a decade of making lutefisk, it was easier than flipping an omelet.

"It's only been a month," Lars said. "They said you could have three."

"They said I could come back after three. It's not like they're paying me maternity leave."

"Then take the full three. We have savings." This was not true, after the hospital bills, but Lars didn't want Cynthia to worry about all that.

"I know, but I'm going batshit here. It's the middle of summer and I can't do anything useful outside with that kid strapped on me. And I can't stand what's on TV in the afternoons. And I can't get more than twenty pages through a book before she starts wailing."

"So you want to go back to work early?"

"I've been thinking about it, and I bet we can work out a schedule so that one of us is always home. And Jarl and Fiona are around if we need them."

Lars's younger brother and his girlfriend also lived in St. Paul, a few miles away, and were eager to babysit their niece, but Lars had privately hoped that his baby girl would never be away from both of her parents simultaneously except in an absolute emergency. "Don't you have to take a course or something to be a sommelier?"

"I know the restaurant and its customers better than anyone they could bring in. I also know that wine list back to front. I even picked out a few. The Tepusquet Vineyard Chardonnay from ZD Wines—that was mine."

"I don't know," Lars said. He realized that if he was meeting her that day for the first time, he would've told her to go for it, pursue her dreams, all that kind of stuff. But now, looking at his beautiful, impulsive wife, he thought of his stoic, pragmatic mother. If Elin had ever wanted to be anything besides an unpaid bookkeeper at a bakery and a mother to three boys, Lars sure never heard a peep about it. Was it selfish or realistic to look at Cynthia and want the same, to want to look on in admiration as her arms, legs, hips, and devotion thickened? He didn't know.

"I think you don't want me to do anything with my life besides be a mom. Well, that's bullshit," Cynthia said, and she left the room.

It would be bullshit if it were true, and it partly was. Yes, he just wanted her to want to be a mom, in the same way that he felt, with all of his blood, that he was a dad first, and everything else in the world an obscure, unfathomably distant second.

Lars was lying on the brown shag area rug, reading to his daughter from James Beard's *Beard on Bread,* when Cynthia pushed open the front door. Lars could tell how her meeting had gone from her heavy footsteps. Instead of Cynthia, the restaurant had hired "the famous and respected West Coast sommelier Jeremy St. George" and offered her a job as "supervising floor waitress," which wasn't even a real job, just something they'd made up on the spot to appease her when she started making a scene.

• • •

Cynthia was so furious that evening, she opened a single-vineyard Merlot from Stag's Leap that she'd been saving, and paired it with a bowl of macaroni and cheese from a box.

"Why did he move out here from San Francisco to take this job?" she asked Lars, as if he knew. "He could have any sommelier job in the country!"

She told him that the manager had shown her Jeremy St. George's résumé and headshot, because all of the big California sommeliers had headshots that made them appear both studious and sensual. Cynthia said he was in his early thirties, a graduate of UC Davis, formerly a sommelier in Napa Valley and San Francisco, and he looked like an underwear model. Lars wondered for a moment why she had to say "underwear" and not just "model."

Still, what concerned Lars more was the *box* of macaroni and cheese. It had been a pretty darn brisk slide from their first store-bought pasta to their first processed dairy, and he had to admit that their financial situation was mostly to blame. They were living on just his income, and while everyone outside the restaurant industry seemed to think that being a chef at a nice place was a path to riches, it sure wasn't the case. Even with his working fifty hours a week as a chef at Hutmacher's, there were going to be tight months ahead.

He hated to admit it, but if they wanted to eat better and have fresher, more nutritious food around the house for their daughter—who was finally old enough to be eating mushy fruit and vegetables—Cynthia had to go back to work.

Lars proposed that she demand part-time sommelier duties if she returned, and although Cynthia chafed against the idea of being some West Coast hotshot's "assistant," she admitted that having a job title, any job title, with the word "sommelier" in it could make returning to Hutmacher's more bearable.

The owners of Hutmacher's agreed to the new assistant sommelier title and the job duties, just so long as she also picked up waitress shifts and Jeremy St. George approved of the whole thing. Jeremy St. George said he'd have to meet her first, and after they met, Jeremy told Cynthia that he'd been waiting for an assistant like her all of his life.

The night of her first shift, she came home late, ninety minutes after close, careening through the doorway, singing a Replacements song. He hadn't heard her sing in maybe a year. "How was it?" Lars asked, but he could tell.

At the end of the night, she turned to him and said, "Thank you," before passing out on her side of the bed. Her face, even while asleep, was full of love, and Lars chose to be reassured.

With Cynthia out of town on wine trips as part of her new job, Lars's rounds at the St. Paul Farmers' Market were more logistically difficult, but still just as fun. For some individuals, the process of carrying a two-month-old infant, her diaper bag, and her stroller everywhere could be tiring and complex, but it actually made Lars feel invigorated, even when he had to do it all by himself. With Jarl and Fiona now officially on babysitting detail during the hours that Lars's and Cynthia's shifts overlapped, Lars wanted to make the most of every minute with his daughter.

The late summer heat flooded his body as soon as he stepped outside; armpit stains blossomed in his Fruit of the Loom T-shirt while he was still in the elevator, and he was wheezing by the time he got Eva and her stuff down to the car. But the St. Paul Farmers' Market would, as always, reward their efforts. Mid-September meant the end of peak season for late-harvest tomatoes, and Lars had plans for more chilled soups, sauces, and mild salsas that he knew Eva's young palate would just adore, based on how much she loved the tragically few things that Dr. Latch let him feed her so far.

He'd never realized how couples dominated the farmers' market scene until his wife started going out of town. Saturday morning pairs meandered playfully through the aisles of apples, beets, and lettuces, many with strollers or children in hand. Some were childless, flush from the impulse buy of true love and its heady aftershocks, hands still lingering on each other, as if to make sure the other person was still real. Lars tried to remember what that felt like, but the people stopping to adore his baby daughter distracted him from dwelling on the lone missing member of their little family.

"Do you know that half a cup of marinara sauce has almost eight times the lycopene content of a raw tomato?" he asked his wiggly daughter as he guided her through the slow field of couples that ebbed and pushed around them. "We're going to find some good sauce tomatoes today."

Eva looked up at him, pinching her eyelids against the bright sky, but making happy eye contact with him that seemed to say, *I love Dad,* or maybe, *I just took the runniest shit my father will ever see.* In direct sunlight, it was hard to tell.

Karen Theis's tomato stall, which for close to a decade had supplied the five-county metro area with consistent, handsome Roma, plum, beefsteak, and Big Boy tomatoes—nothing fancy, just the major hybrids— was Lars's first and only tomato stop. But that morning in September, it was gone, and in its place a heavy man and heavier woman sat on purple beach chairs, selling dirt-streaked, unappealing rhubarb (it was way, way past ideal rhubarb season) from a stained cardboard box.

"Oh. What happened to Karen?" Lars asked the hefty woman.

She stared back at him. "Who's Karen?"

"Want some rhubarb?" the big guy asked. "We'll bargain with ya." Flies were landing on the sugary stalks, rubbing their front legs together. The couple made no attempt to shoo them away.

"Karen ran a tomato stall here for the last eight years, right in this location. Just wondering what happened to her, if she moved or is just on vacation or something."

"Oh yeah, that name sounds familiar," the guy asked, and then turned to the woman. "Why does that name sound familiar?"

"People have been asking about her all morning."

The guy nodded. "That's where I know it from."

This kind of exchange was to be expected of people who attempt to sell rhubarb in mid-September. "So, what happened to her?" Lars asked again.

The woman looked at Eva in the stroller. "Well, that's a cutie. How old is your daughter, one?"

"She's about three and a half months. She's big for her age. So you have no idea what happened to Karen's tomato stall?"

As the guy leaned forward in his chair, Lars noticed that one of the armrests was missing, and the man had a series of bright red circles on his left forearm from leaning it against the exposed pole. "Sir, if I know one thing," the man said, "it's never call a woman fat. Especially at that young age where it seeps into their unconscious."

"Can anyone help me find Karen Theis?" Lars shouted, looking around at the nearby vendors.

"Out of business," a nearby vendor of Nantes-type carrots said. "The Orientals chased her out."

Anna Hlavek, the herb vendor one stall over, yelled, "The Orientals didn't chase her out, the Orientals grow better tomatoes."

Lars met Anna's gaze, and it apparently gave her license to continue her argument.

"What's-his-name Oriental fella over there. That's where the New French Café gets their tomatoes now, y'know," Anna said, referring to the trendiest of the new Minneapolis restaurants. "How's your little girl?" she asked, stepping out from behind her stand to touch Eva's hands and lift them in the air. "Sooooo big! Soooo big!"

Lars liked Anna, but people touching his daughter without asking him first got his blood up a little bit.

"Tell me again," Anna said. "Is she one, one and a half?"

"No, three and a half months. She's just . . . ambitious for her age."

"Where's that cute wife of yours? Still in California?"

"Yep," Lars said. "It's harvest time, for certain varietals."

"Oh boy, how long is that going to take her?"

"Two weeks, I think." It had been four already, but Lars knew that sounded bad.

"I can't imagine a mother being away from her child for that long. My Dougie goes everywhere with me. I never let him out of my sight for a minute." Lars saw a sullen, towheaded four-year-old sitting a few feet away, stabbing pavement cracks with a plastic knife.

"It happens in the wine business," he said. "So where can I find a few tomatoes?"

The Southeast Asian vendor sat on a blue Land O' Lakes milk crate, his body broad and oblong like an Agassiz potato, his fat tan legs splayed. He stared ahead—unsmiling, through Ray-Ban sunglasses—at everything, or nothing. Beside him, shimmering in the livid heat, sat platoons of beautiful, alien tomatoes, in heartbreakingly bright orange, red, yellow, purple, and stripes, in precise, labeled grids across a trestle table covered with a clean gingham tablecloth.

As Lars pushed his daughter's stroller toward the stand, Eva reached in the direction of the tomatoes, her chubby fingers grabbing the air between herself and those brilliant little globes.

"Hi. Do you have samples?" Lars asked the vendor.

"No samples," the man said, not taking his gaze from Eva's outstretched hands. "You try, you buy."

"Maybe I will, then," Lars said. "I'm looking for a sauce tomato, something high in lycopene, like a Roma VF. What do you sell that's like a Roma VF?"

"I don't sell anything like a Roma VF. I sell tomatoes."

"OK. So what's a Roma VF, then?"

"Made in a lab by scientists."

"OK."

"Sir, if you want a lycopene-rich tomato, you want a Moonglow. Highest amount of lycopene. Of any heirloom."

The vendor picked up a small orange globe, between a golf ball and a baseball in diameter, and showed it to Lars, not handing it to him. Lars reached for it, and the vendor set it back with its sisters again.

"The Moonglow is for slicing and salsas," the vendor continued. "If you want a sauce tomato, you want San Marzano. Best in the world for paste and sauce." He held up a long red tomato shaped a little like a red pepper and gently laid it in his own palm.

"I'll buy a Moonglow, to try it."

"Thirty cents," the vendor said.

"Well dang," Lars said. "At that price, it would cost me two bucks to make anything."

"Cheaper by the pound. Individually, thirty cents."

Lars sighed, but then exchanged a pair of gray coins for a soft, gleaming orange ball. He just had to. He bit into it like an apple, and orange water flung across his mouth and stuck to his beard. The sensation bothered him just for a moment before the flavor of the heirloom broke across his palate.

The approach was wonderfully sweet, but not sugary or overpowering; there was just a whisper of citric tartness. As he chewed the Moonglow's firm flesh, he closed his eyes to concentrate on the vanishing sweetness in his mouth. He thought of Cynthia and how the last time they were here, they bought Roma VFs for a dish to pair with a light-bodied Corvina Veronese. He thought about how much she'd love this—how she'd be coming up with wine pairings for each of this guy's tomatoes—and wondered where she was in California right then. He thought about how this trip had been the longest yet and how it had been three days since he'd heard from her.

Lars shook himself from these thoughts and knelt to hold the other half of the Moonglow to Eva's mouth. Grinning, she smeared its bright carcass across her radiant face.

He introduced himself to the vendor, told him what he did, and asked the man his name.

"John," the vendor said, not smiling, shaking hands firmly but briefly.

"Best thirty cents I've ever spent in my life, John," Lars said. "I had no idea that the Hmong grew such brilliant tomatoes."

"They don't. But if they're lucky, maybe I'll teach one of them how."

"Oh jeez, I suppose I thought you were Hmong."

"Christ, you people. I'm Lao, from Laos. Big difference. The Hmong, we let them in from Mongolia. Never should've done it. They were trouble from the beginning. Their Plain of Jars? Lot of poppy fields up there. I don't have to tell you what they kept in those jars. It wasn't water."

Lars was taught always to listen politely, but the prejudices of this heirloom tomato grower—a sharply opinionated lot regardless of national origin—began to make him feel a tad uncomfortable. Because of this, his awareness clouded, and he only saw Eva out of the corner of his eye as she grabbed the corner of the tablecloth and pulled her way over to the tomatoes. The soft thud of massive amounts of fruit hitting the ground was unmistakable to anyone who's ever worked with food.

"Oh crap!" Lars said, taking in the pile of tomatoes on the ground. "Oh crap, oh crap, oh crap."

John pushed past Lars with the decisive force of a first responder at the scene of an accident, and knelt over his tomatoes, unsentimentally sorting the resellable from the irretrievably broken.

When Lars pushed the tomatoes aside from his daughter's face, he was shocked to find that she wasn't crying, but rather trying to cram a broken Moonglow into her tiny mouth.

While Lars and John were able to save most of the San Marzanos, about half of the Moonglows and almost all of the pink Brandywines were bruised or splattered from their impact with the ground, the stroller, or baby Eva.

"How much do I owe you?" Lars asked, afraid even to look John in the face.

"Accidents happen," he said. He put the broken fruit in a box under the tablecloth and sat back on his milk crate.

Lars removed a twenty and a ten from his billfold and held them out to John. It hurt him to do it; it was almost half a day's wages.

"Here," he said. "Please take it."

The vendor didn't speak or acknowledge the cash. As passersby and other vendors stared at him, Lars's face burned with shame. After fighting through several seconds of silence, he had to put the bills away and understand that the depths of this debt might occupy a different space than money could fill.

On the fourth day without hearing from Cynthia, Lars started to call around. Their manager, Mike Reisner, had heard nothing, and neither of the owners, Nick Argyros or Paul Hinckley, had heard from either Cynthia or Jeremy. By the afternoon, he was calling wineries he knew they might have visited: Stag's Leap, Cakebread, Shafer, Ridge, Stony Hill, Silver Oak. He even tried a few of the Rhone Rangers, like Bonny

Doon and Zaca Mesa; they all knew Jeremy St. George, but no one had seen him or Cynthia.

"Are you sure?" he asked the guy at Shafer. "They'd be there for the harvest."

"Our harvest isn't for several weeks," the guy said.

Lars's brother Jarl didn't seem alarmed. "They're probably driving back," he said, lying on Lars's shag carpet, still wearing the white dress shirt and tie from his job as a paralegal. Once Jarl had left the tyranny of their father's empire, he'd wanted a job that required him to wear a tie every day; in Jarl's world, people wearing ties would never have to make lutefisk or stick their hands in a hot oven or lift pallets of pullman loaves or otherwise suffer physically on the clock.

"But they flew out there," Lars reminded him.

"Aren't there wineries in Arizona and Texas, and places like that?"

"None of the big places in Napa saw them," Lars said from his easy chair. Eva was on his lap, sucking on the end of a turkey baster.

"Maybe they didn't go to the big places," Jarl said. "Or maybe they're somewhere good, like Riunite."

"Riunite's not a place."

"Yeah it is. It's in here," Jarl said, pointing to his heart. "Get over yourself and like something that normal people like for once."

"I like normal things. I just also like quality healthy things."

"I like quality healthy things sometimes," Jarl said.

This was not true. For a guy who insisted on dressing nicely all of the time, Jarl had terrifyingly provincial taste in food and wine.

"You, I haven't even seen you eat a vegetable since the early eighties." Jarl seemed surprised. "Where was that?"

"And it hardly counts. The coleslaw at Charlie's Café Exceptionale."

"That was the best place in town. Not someplace snooty like Faegre's." Lars shook his head. "Best Caesar I've ever had."

"Christ, you're a snob," Jarl said, and looked at Eva. "Admit it. And you're going to raise her to be a snob, too. She's going to be the biggest snob of all time. Between the two of you, the fancy food chef and the fancy wine drinker. Next time I babysit her, I'm feeding her Cheetos."

"Don't even think about it."

"Cheetos and Hi-C."

"Please, don't."

"*We* ate that kind of stuff as kids. What's your problem with it now?"

"I just want my children eating stuff that's actually nutritious."

"Children?" Jarl asked. "Got some news?"

"Yes, we're having another kid."

"When? I thought you guys were going to wait five years or something."

"No, last time I talked to Cynthia, I told her I want another one now. I don't want to be a fat old man chasing around a toddler."

"Then lose some weight, lardo," Jarl said.

Lars's phone rang.

"Can you get it?" Lars said, pointing to the baby on his lap.

"Oh sure," Jarl said. He did four push-ups, with a clap between each one, his tie hanging to the floor like a long striped tongue, and rose to pick up the receiver in the kitchen. "Hello, Thorvald residence," he said.

"Who is it?" Lars asked.

"It's your work. Paul somebody."

"One of the owners," Lars said, setting his daughter on the carpet before running into the kitchen. "Keep an eye on Evie," he told Jarl as he put the phone to his ear.

"Hey there, Lars," Paul Hinckley said. He'd previously been a big-time lawyer in the Cities, and he didn't know much about food, but he was more than a tad detail-oriented as a restaurant owner. He didn't hire a graphic designer or an interior decorator for anything; he chose the logo, the typeface on the menu, the dining room's color scheme, the design of the flatware and stemware, and even the names of some of the dishes.

He also liked to know what was going on with everyone on his staff all the time.

"Hello, Paul. What's happening?"

"Well, hi, Lars. Say, just have a quick bit of news for ya here."

"Sure, what's going on?"

"Just wanted to tell you, we had a staff parking space open up, and we thought maybe you'd want it—you know, for all the hard work you've done for us."

"Yeah, sure, it'd be nice to park on the property there."

"That's what we were thinking—you know, me and Nick. We thought, who deserves it? And your name came right up, so."

"So yeah, is that it, then?"

"Yeah, pretty much, I guess. But I thought, maybe you'd want to know, the reason the spot opened up is because Jeremy St. George tendered his resignation today, effective immediately. So, you can have his spot when you come in this afternoon already."

"You heard from Jeremy St. George?"

"Yep, he called us from the airport, and said he was quitting, so."

"What did he say about Cynthia? Did he say anything about Cynthia? She's with him, you know."

"Oh, I figured she talked to you. Well, we asked, we did ask, and he said that she had her own decision to make, so I guess we'll see. We'll see on that. Oh, I got a call on the other line. Can you hold, please?"

"No, that's all right," Lars said. He hung up the phone and stared out into the living room at his daughter, who was lying on her back, sucking on an egg separator, as her uncle tried to make her smile.

Three days later, Lars opened his lobby mailbox to a letter, postmarked San Francisco. He saw the swoops and curls of the hand behind the blue pen that had written their address, and he tore open the envelope right there.

My Dear Lars,

I don't know how to say this. I suppose I should've called, but every time I picked up the phone and started to dial our number, I started to cry. Plus I knew you would try to talk me out of this, and at this point, you can't. Since I last saw you five weeks ago, I've had experiences and made choices that would make it impossible for me to return to you with a whole heart. You could argue for me to come back, but the person you want no longer exists, and maybe never did.

You are the best father the world has ever seen. But I wasn't cut out to be a mother. The work of being a mom feels like prison to me. I know this might sound horribly selfish to you, but out here in California, I found a sense of happiness that I haven't felt since before I was pregnant. If you truly want me to be happy, you must try to understand this. I will never be happy being a mother. Having a child was the biggest mistake of my life and I honestly believe that our daughter will be better off having no mother instead of a bad one.

I'm leaving today for Australia or New Zealand. I haven't decided which yet, but by the time you read this, I'll be in that part of the world. You're free to keep, give away, or throw away anything of mine I've left behind. Don't try to send anything to me and please don't come looking for me.

A lawyer will be serving you with divorce papers. I'm giving you full custody of our child and complete ownership of our shared property. Please sign it as written. Otherwise, it will only lengthen the process, because I will not return to the U.S. for any reason, perhaps for a very long time.

Maybe it won't seem like it to you, but the reason I have to make such a clean break is because this is absolutely heartbreaking to me. I love you so much and I will think of you every day for the rest of my life. You have made me a better person, a person brave enough to know what she is and what she is not.

I am so sorry to put you through this. I didn't mean to lose you. But you are just so passionate about being a father, I feel that the kindest thing I can do is to free you from our marriage so you can find a woman who's equally committed to being a mother. I know she's out there for you. You're an incredible guy, the kindest man I've ever met, and any woman would be lucky to have you. I want you to actually have the life, and the family, you thought you had with me. If I come back to you, you will not have that.

I have to go. I will miss you so, so much.
All my love, forever,
Cynthia

Lars unlocked the front door of his quiet apartment. He'd intended to just leave Eva alone for a moment while he checked the mail. She was still sleeping on a blanket in the middle of the living room floor, as if he'd never left, and what he'd found in the mailbox never existed. He walked the letter into the kitchen, softly opening a child-locked drawer under the counter. His daughter should never see this letter or know the words inside it, he decided, so he would burn it, right now, in the sink, but now he couldn't find his butane BBQ lighter. Or even his crème brûlée torch. He wanted to burn the letter now, so that maybe all of the bad thoughts would be burned along with it.

He heard his daughter stir and start to cry. He ignited a gas burner on his stove and held the letter to the flame. It caught fire so fast that he dropped it on the kitchen floor and watched it whisper out on the brown vinyl.

His daughter started to wail.

"Just a minute," he called out. He picked up what was left of the letter and held it to the gas flame, leaving it on the burner this time. He watched as it caught fire and curled, and once it was aflame, the heat lifted it into the air and dropped it perfectly into the crack between the stove and the kitchen counter.

"Shit," he said. He picked up a coffee mug full of tepid water in the sink and dumped it into the crack, onto the irretrievable, smoldering envelope.

Satisfied that the kitchen wouldn't catch on fire, he ran into the living room to lift his daughter into his arms. She would never hear that she was a mistake, he decided. She would never read a letter in which her mother abandoned her without even saying *I love you.* In fact, she would never even hear a bad word about her mother, not one—at least not from him—as long as he lived. What he would tell her instead, he hadn't yet decided, but now was not the time to think about such things. Now was the time to sit with his little family of two people, and cry.

Jarl lifted his brown necktie and yellow polyester shirt and scratched his hairy gut. "What do you mean she left for Australia because you're fat and ugly?"

Fiona, sitting next to Jarl at Lars's kitchen counter, put her hand over her thick, cherry-lipsticked mouth. "Oh my God," she said, her eyes bulging beneath fake eyebrows that looked like cartoon mountains. "I'm so sorry, Lars." She got up and hugged him. It occurred to Lars just then that he hadn't been touched by a woman in several weeks. It felt disorienting, like waking up from a car nap, but her sweet, lumpy, perfumed body next to his was comforting.

Jarl took a sip of his Grain Belt Premium. "This is where you're supposed to say he's not fat and ugly, Fiona."

"But I am fat and ugly," Lars said. "I've never looked worse in my life."

"We need to get you in shape. It's what I've been saying," Jarl said. He turned to Fiona. "It's what I've been telling him."

Lars shrugged and lifted his beer, but Jarl grabbed it from him before he could raise it to his mouth.

"Let's start right here," Jarl said. "No more beer."

"You brought it over."

"I can't believe a mother could just abandon her child like that," Fiona said. "She can't be serious."

"She didn't abandon our daughter," Lars said. "She was very clear about that. She abandoned me. I wasn't making enough. I let myself go physically. It's all on me."

"When she comes back," Fiona said, "maybe we can knock some sense into her then."

Jarl nodded. "And drag that Jeremy St. George behind a car, that's what I'd like to do. He seduced her, I bet. I bet you it was all his idea."

"We're going to leave them alone, Jarl," Lars said. "I gotta get on with my life."

"That tall skinny bitch," Fiona said.

"Please," Lars said. "Don't ever talk about her like that, especially around my daughter."

Jarl looked over his shoulder. "She's sleeping."

"I mean, ever. All right?"

"But she did a terrible thing to your family," Jarl said.

"Maybe her mother did a bad thing to me," Lars said. "But not to Eva."

"But she abandoned her."

"Her mother loves her very much," Lars said. "She just has to find her own way in life."

"That's so selfish," Fiona said. "Forget her. She's dead to me."

Lars leaned forward across the counter. "What's more selfish? Working a job you hate just to come home and be an exhausted, frustrated, unhappy mom? Or following your dreams and becoming a successful woman that our daughter could feel proud of?"

"I think a baby wants to be with its mom," Fiona said. "And the mom should want to be with her baby."

"What if the mom doesn't want to be with me?" Lars said.

"I agree with Fiona," Jarl said. "Screw her."

"Yep, screw her," Fiona said. "And I mean the other word, by the way."

"Oh, and besides," Jarl said, "Fiona has a ton of single lady friends. They're younger than you, mostly, but some of them are super cute. And they wouldn't mind a bald guy, right?"

Fiona shook her head. "Just whenever you're ready."

Lars nodded.

Fiona turned to Jarl. "Which ones do you think are super cute?"

Jarl ignored her and sipped his beer. "So, can we stay here tonight, or should we take her back to our place?"

"Whatever you want."

"And, uh, I've been meaning to ask you," Jarl said, standing up. "Maybe now's not the best time to bring this up, but, I was actually wondering, because she sleeps in your room every night, and there's that empty room—we could move in for a while, split the rent with you."

Fiona nodded. "It would really help."

At the time, Lars didn't want to admit that he might have needed them even more, so in his classic Lars way, he just told them he'd think about it, and he walked to his room to get dressed for work. As he buttoned his white shirt, he was already thinking where he'd move furniture around, already thinking about the good and the bad and the deep human necessity of it all, and how anybody ever got anything done without family, and how someone could give that up in the amount of time it takes to seal an envelope, with the same saliva once used to seal a marriage.

Christmas is only exciting when there's a child in the middle of it, and it's lovely and sad how three adults with about one and a half jobs between them will pile presents under a tree for a six-month-old baby. Fiona was particularly intent on getting little Eva up to date with some modern fashions, such as baby leggings, a My Little Pony onesie, and some pink Stride Rite shoes.

The adults didn't have wish lists, but Lars was working on a surprise for Jarl. He absolutely didn't want to make it himself, but he had a lead on a butcher down south of the Cities who apparently sold the freshest lutefisk in the metro area, at some old family-owned shop that had been in operation for eighty years. While he was at work, Lars would make the accompanying cream sauce—which softens lutefisk from being a hostile sensory assault to merely a disgusting one—and he would surprise Jarl with the whole shebang as a big practical joke on Christmas Eve night.

There was a lot to think about on Christmas Eve. The restaurant was closed, thank goodness, because Lars had planned a five-course meal for Eva, Lars, Jarl, Fiona, and the four people who would drive up from West Des Moines: Fiona's sister Amy Jo, Amy Jo's art professor husband, Wojtek, and their kids, Rothko and Braque. Wojtek and Amy Jo were really into food and culture, or so Lars was told. They were attracted to the idea of having their Christmas Eve dinner prepared by a professional chef; that seemed to be Fiona's selling point. Lars hadn't met them yet, but being that they were driving so far out of their way and staying the night in a hotel, he felt inspired to pull out all the stops—pork shoulder, winter squash, venison meatballs, wild rice salad, crème brûlée, and, of course, the surprise for Jarl.

It was ten in the morning, and Lars was just about to make the drive to the old butcher shop to acquire the key ingredient for the surprise when Amy Jo and Wojtek Dragelski's Mazda 626 pulled into a guest parking space outside. Lars watched from his living room window as the family, who must've left Iowa around 6:00 a.m. to arrive here so early, trudged through the snow toward the lobby of his building.

"They're here, Fiona," Lars called out to his brother's fiancée. Fiona and Jarl had gotten engaged a few weeks before, on Black Friday. Jarl thought they could get a better deal on rings that way.

Fiona set down her magazine and leapt from the sofa; he'd never seen her move so quickly. "Let's go down and greet them at the door," she said, already putting her shoes on.

The Dragelskis looked like one of those odd families where, but for some vague physical resemblances, no two people looked like they belonged together. Amy Jo, the mother, had the dress and demeanor of a museum docent; Fiona had described her older sister as "fancy" and "uptight"—surely she was the one to rouse a family before dawn for a four-hour drive in the dead of winter. Wojtek, the father, had a full black beard, wore a brown leather jacket over his thick torso, and the tired, glazed-over face of a man on autopilot. The thirteen-year-old son, Rothko, or "Randy," as he apparently preferred to be called (and who could blame him), had curly rocker hair, a dangling silver earring, steel-toed boots, and a long-sleeved Guns N' Roses *Appetite for Destruction* shirt. Braque, the eight-year-old daughter, was a tall, stunning blond child in an Iowa Hawkeyes Starter jacket and bright new Nikes.

Lars watched while Fiona hugged them all, some reciprocating more willingly than others. Lars knew by now that Fiona loved her older sister and viewed Amy Jo's family as a paragon of sophistication. As Lars was introduced to them, he felt as if he was being shown off as an example of how Fiona could be sophisticated as well.

"I need to take a piss," Randy said, looking down at the skulls on his shirt.

"Randy!" said his mom.

"Well, I do," Randy said, as if the facts and not the language had been called into question.

The elevator door opened, and Jarl walked out holding Eva with one hand and a Grain Belt Premium in the other. Although she was fast asleep, she cast a spell over the six people in the lobby, in the manner of most infants.

Fiona frowned at the beer bottle in Jarl's hand. "You sure you're OK with her?"

Jarl frowned back at the dumb question. Everyone knew that he was great with the baby, so far, and everyone knew that the baby just loved him; even when Eva was bawling her head off, for some reason she quit crying instantly whenever he picked her up. It was one of those things.

"Can I hold her?" Braque shouted, lunging toward Eva, not even waiting for confirmation. Dang, she was an assertive little thing.

Lars noted that Jarl easily managed to hand the baby over to Braque without setting his beer down. He was a little concerned about his baby in the arms of that brash little girl, but decided not to make a big deal out of it; he had somewhere to be.

"Hey," he said. "I gotta run an errand south of the Cities. I'll be back in about an hour or so. Fiona, you give 'em the tour. Got coffee and venison meatballs up there."

As the Dragelski family followed Fiona and Jarl to the elevator, Lars glanced at Randy. "Oh, and no one's in the bathroom, last I checked."

"Thank you, sir," Randy said, which was not what Lars had expected to hear, for some reason, and on the way to his car he felt reassured about his strange new guests.

The man behind the counter at the old small-town butcher shop had a handlebar mustache and signs on his walls that read things like BUTCHERS DON'T GET OLD—THEY JUST LOSE THEIR PRIME. When Lars explained that he wanted only a pound of lutefisk, the guy acted like it would be a waste of his time to get off his ass for that small a sale.

"That'll hardly feed a family," the butcher said.

No one else was in the shop to help counter this argument. "Frankly, it's excessive," Lars said. "It's kind of an inside joke. I can't in good conscience make people actually eat it."

"Yeah you can," the butcher said. "Who's in charge at your house?"

Somewhere, somehow, Lars thought, *this man is a blood relative of Gustaf Thorvald.* "Just a pound," he said. The butcher shook his head and sliced off a chunk of snot-colored whitefish about the size of a hardcover book. The smell was nearly giving Lars PTSD, but it was worth it; he couldn't wait to see the look on Jarl's face.

"Have a good day," Lars said as he left the shop.

"If I have to," the old butcher said, sitting down again, relieved to be rid of a city-slicker lutefisk tourist.

As Lars drove back to St. Paul, it began to snow, and on the radio he heard reports of "glare ice" and an accident on westbound Crosstown between Minneapolis and St. Paul. He thought about Cynthia in Australia or New Zealand and how it was summer in that part of the world. Jarl and Fiona were so incensed that Cynthia didn't send Eva a present for Christmas that they were threatening to hire a private investigator to find out where in Australia she was.

But Lars didn't want that. He'd viewed Cynthia neglecting Eva's first Christmas as a litmus test, confirmation that she was serious, that she was forever done with being a mother and would never come back. On the drive, he thought of a story that he'd maybe tell on Christmas: that he'd gotten a call from the police in Sydney and they'd told him that Cynthia had died alone in a one-car accident, and they were going to just bury her out there. Cynthia wasn't close to her own mom, and her dad had died when she was a teenager, so it was perfectly feasible that no one would blow the lid off of this story; he couldn't think of anyone left in the United States who would hear the news and buy tickets to Australia for the funeral.

As he climbed the stairs to his apartment—he always took the stairs now—he wondered about Cynthia's friends at the restaurant. Did she still keep in touch with any of them? With Allie, Cayla, Amber, Amy, or Sarah? He hardly spoke with them anyway. Maybe he wouldn't tell them.

The concrete stairway was cold, but Jarl was right, getting into shape was important. He'd lost four pounds in two weeks and the stairs were a big part of that. If he was ever going to attract someone who could be a good mother to his daughter, he thought he should probably at least get below two-sixty. A person had to start somewhere.

He was on the third-floor landing before he realized he'd forgotten the lutefisk in the trunk and had to go back down to get it. Well, it was an excuse to get a little bit more of a workout. Maybe he had even forgotten it subconsciously, knowing what a calorie explosion the holidays were. He jogged down the stairs, his breath clouding in his face, and kept jogging toward the rusty blue, salt-streaked Dodge Omni, where he retrieved his surprise for Jarl out of the back.

Halfway up the third flight of stairs, he felt a pain in his shoulder, and he gasped for air in the cold, opening his mouth. He sat down in the middle of the staircase to take a rest and felt a stabbing pain so intense, he felt tired. He closed his eyes, dropping the lutefisk, leaned his head against the railing, and felt his body tumble down to the landing without him.

CHOCOLATE HABANERO

It was 7:00 a.m. on the day before her eleventh birthday, and Eva was on her knees in her favorite stretchy blue jeans, hard at work in her closet. She was checking the dryness of her hydroponic chile plants when her mom knocked on her door.

"Come in." Eva straightened her back and turned to look at her mom, Fiona, who was wearing a pantsuit the color of a serrano pepper with matching shoes and big silver hoop earrings. She looked like a shorter, wider Hillary Clinton, but with the posture and attitude of someone fifty-eight hours into a sixty-hour workweek.

"What kind of treat do you want to bring your class for your birthday?" Fiona asked her daughter. "I'll pick it up after work tonight if I have the energy."

According to Eva, the worst birthday tradition ever in world history was the one where *you* had to bring some treat to class when it was *your* birthday. Well, she figured, if she had to feed the entire sixth grade, she might as well feed them something she'd actually eat.

"I was thinking, vegan blueberry sorbet from New City Market."

"Oh Christ. Really?"

"Do you know what they put in ice cream—especially chocolate ice cream?"

"You've told me."

"I'm adding years to their lives, which is more than those sewer rats deserve."

Fiona shook her head. "They can't all be sewer rats. What about that nice Bethany Messerschmidt?"

When it came to Eva's life, her mom had the awareness of a fifty-cent guppy; there were sad-eyed janitors at school who seemed to have more insight into Eva's heart than her own parents did. At least her parents had moved the family down here to West Des Moines, Iowa, so they could be close to Eva's cool uncle Wojtek Dragelski and aunt Amy Jo and her awesome older cousins Rothko (who everyone called Randy) and Braque (who everyone called Braque). Bethany Messerschmidt made fun of people behind their backs all the time, and had no interest in cool things like food or art or books or cool music, like Randy did, though she once said Randy was a "hottie," which was super weird.

Worst of all, however, Bethany had called Eva a "fucking sasquatch bitch" in front of everyone when Eva wouldn't lend her five dollars after school at McDonald's. Even though Eva drank coffee and two or three times had tried a cigarette and did other things that were supposed to stunt her growth, she was a not particularly skinny five foot seven, and there was nothing she could do about it. The kids at this new school already hated her for being younger and smarter, but since that day, she was only Sasquatch to them, and it hurt worse than anything. She didn't cry about it anymore, but the word still stabbed her brain.

"Bethany Messerschmidt is dead to me," Eva said. She also didn't want to tell her mom that even the smell of McDonald's brought back this memory, because her parents loved fast food, especially McDonald's. To announce its correlation with her trauma would only make them seem thoughtless every time they brought it home, and they loved it too much to ever give it up.

"Well, you need some friends your own age for once. Randy and his Mexican chef friend don't count."

"The kids my age are awful. They aren't even human."

"Anyway, I want you to give Randy some space until he's off probation."

"But nobody else in the whole family even talks to him."

"You know, you only got a few years left of being a kid. You should enjoy it. You have the rest of your life to be on your hands and knees working like a slave. Now hop to it. The bus will be here in fifteen minutes."

One of the things that Eva hated the most about being a kid was how everyone always told her that childhood was the best time of their entire lives, and don't grow up too fast, and enjoy these carefree days while you can. In those moments, her body felt like the world's smallest prison, and she escaped in her mind to her chile plants, resting on rock wool substrate under a grow light in a bedroom closet, as much a prisoner of USDA hardiness zone 5b as she was.

Unlike her, they were beautiful in a way that God intended. The tallest chocolate habanero plant came to her waist, and its firm green stalks held families of glistening, gorgeous brown chiles at the end of its growing cycle. Holding them, tracing her finger around their smooth circumference, she could feel their warmth, their life, and their willing-ness to give.

To preserve her habs for the rest of the year, she made most of them into chile powder—her parents had learned to avoid the kitchen and order pizza when she did this—and with her first harvest this year, she made chile oil with this hot infusion recipe:

1 cup dried chiles

2 cups grapeseed oil

Cut the dried whole chocolate habanero chiles into small pieces and put into a pan with grapeseed oil. Heat slowly over low heat until bubbles start to rise. Turn off the heat and allow the oil to cool to room temperature. Pour the chile and oil mixture into a glass bowl and cover. Store in the refrigerator for 10 days. Strain through a wine strainer into sterile bottles.

• • •

She couldn't wait to try it in a recipe herself, but first wanted to bring it to her friend Aracely Pimentel, the co–executive chef at Lulu's, the best Mexican restaurant in the greater Des Moines metro area and probably all of Iowa. But before then, she had to make it through another day.

The morning bus ride was the most excruciating part of every day. Not everyone left school at the same time—many of the worst boys stayed after to play sports—but everyone arrived at the same time, and other transportation options were scant. Just to set up her mom's fashion advice for failure, Eva wore one of the two feminine outfits she had: a navy blue dress that had two bald eagles fighting on the front. Her cousin Randy had given it to her for her birthday last year, right before he relapsed again, and she still just fit into it. Since the Bethany Messerschmidt incident at McDonald's, some of the boys, and many of the girls, repeated that one awful noun whenever she walked down the center aisle. To cope with it, Eva put on her Walkman and played tapes made by Cousin Randy—that day it was Tom Waits, who sang about cool stuff like hookers in Minneapolis—and reminded herself that all of these boys would be changing her oil someday.

"Hey. Sasquatch. I'm talking to you," said Chadd Grebeck, a beefy soccer dolt in her class. Eva turned her head and stared out the window, but he yanked the earbud out of her left ear and whispered into it. "Sasquatch. Sas-quatch. Sas-quatch."

One of Chadd's buddies, a tall zit-faced oaf named Brant Manus, the kind of boy who liked to pop his pimples at recess and rub the pus on other kids, said, "Hey dude, why don't you just make out with her?"

"You make out with her, ant-anus," Chadd said.

Dylan Sternwall, another friend of theirs, chimed in from behind Eva. "I'll pay either one of you dick lickers five bucks to kiss her. On the lips."

"You kiss her, sperm-wall," Chad said.

"Give you five bucks."

"No fuckin' way."

"Ten."

To the extent that this creature could think, Chadd seemed to consider this for a moment. "The money first, ass-munch."

"No, the money second. All fees paid for services rendered."

"Shit," Chadd said. He leaned his face over Eva, who struggled to turn away from him. "She smells like dirt." Chadd then moved in and briefly hit her cheek with his face. "There, now pay up."

"It's gotta be on the lips."

"Hold still, Sasquatch," Chadd told Eva. "I don't like this any more than you do, trust me." He smelled like cheap apple juice and was gross like mayo oozing out of the side of a free sandwich. But there was also a coldness—an almost adult male menace to him—and perhaps only the thin decorum of this public setting prevented him from doing much more, much worse.

By now, the entire back half of the bus was transfixed, and the driver, a no-nonsense middle-aged lady, figured something was up. "What's going on back there? In your seats, face front!"

The kids leaning against the backs of their seats, watching the action, were shielding Eva and Chadd from the bus driver's mirror. The driver couldn't see Chadd grab Eva's head in his hands, turn it around to face his, lick the front of her closed mouth like a popsicle, and vigorously spit out the window afterward.

"Sit down back there!" the driver yelled. Amid the jeering and the laughs, the kids obeyed.

Eva's tall spine rattled in her body and her hands shook as she put her earbud back into her empty left ear. She felt the mean hardness of Chadd's hands linger against her skull, and tears welled up in her eyes. Still, she held them back, rubbing his touch off the sides of her head, wiping her lips, taking deep, shaky breaths.

"So where's my ten bucks?" Chadd asked Dylan.

"Pysch, dude," Dylan said. "I just wanted to see if you'd kiss her."

Chadd left the seat he shared with Eva to climb over to Dylan, attempting to put him in a headlock, and the driver yelled at them.

That, as she would remember it, was Eva Thorvald's first kiss with a boy.

Eva's mom didn't know this, but Randy often picked her up after school in his cool black Volkswagen Jetta. He'd roll up to the white curb five minutes before the final bell, blasting Nick Cave or Nine Inch Nails or Tool out of the open windows. He had long dyed black hair, and always wore black T-shirts and ripped jeans and sunglasses, making him look like a scarier Trent Reznor. To Eva and the kids her age, it was a look that spelled *cool* and no one messed with Eva within five hundred feet of this guy.

The first time Chadd and Brant and Dylan followed her out of the school, Randy just flicked his cigarette to the ground and took a hard step toward them and those little pricks scattered like dropped gumballs. Now they didn't even leave by the same exit anymore. To Eva, Cousin Randy was an untouchable demigod—an angel's wing broken from an ancient statue, sent here to help her hover above all things insipid and heartbreaking.

One morning, after seven years of excessive hydroponic indica intake— and he'd never told Eva why, exactly—he had dumped his final three pounds of weed into the Des Moines River. For her birthday that year, against Fiona's and Jarl's initial resistance, he'd bestowed on her his expensive grow lights and gardening hardware. He went to a place called Hazelden, a word Eva remembered from when people suggested her dad should go there after he was fired from the law office back in Minnesota. That kind of place was for people like Randy, people with real serious issues, Eva overheard Jarl say to Fiona once, not for "functional guys" like himself. Eva wondered if that was why Jarl didn't want to have anything to do with Randy; maybe people who drink look down on people who use drugs, just because drugs are illegal. To Eva, it was like a one-legged person being mean to a no-legged person, and she didn't understand it.

In the intervening years, however, with the help of Randy's gift, Eva had evolved from a slightly tall eight-year-old struggling to grow her first jalapeños in her bedroom window box to a giant almost-eleven-year-old who supplied the city's most popular Mexican restaurant with the exotic peppers for its signature dishes. She didn't need her parents to be proud of all this if Randy was, and when she was with him she felt part of something adult and sophisticated. His love for her made her feel like she was wearing sunglasses even when she wasn't.

Eva threw her arms around Cousin Randy when she saw him leaning against his car, and she hit him so hard with her embrace that he dropped his unfiltered Marlboro Red on the sidewalk.

"Oh, shit, dog," he said, laughing. "Get in, we're going to Lulu's."

"Yeah," Eva said, smiling for the first time that day since she was alone in her room that morning.

In the car, speeding out of the school grounds to the music of Nick Cave and the Bad Seeds, Cousin Randy asked whether she had her dried ground peppers with her.

"Just wanted to make sure that we had a legitimate reason to stop by," he said. "I told Aracely the last time I saw her that you'd have something for her."

Aracely Pimentel's cooking attracted regular customers from as far away as Fort Dodge and Ottumwa, and recently even two people who drove all the way from Minneapolis. This was amazing to Eva, to have people drive that far to eat something you made! She couldn't imagine it. Eva liked to fantasize that Randy and Aracely would get married and she could move in with them and grow ingredients for the restaurant all day. Anything, to be a part of it all. She told that to Randy once and he said, "One step at a time."

As they drove from West Des Moines into Des Moines, Randy asked how her day was, and Eva told him the story of what had happened on the bus. Randy swore and pounded the steering wheel and said he wished he were in sixth grade again so he could shove a fist up their asses. This was the kind of thing that her parents would never say in a million billion years, and it was exactly what Eva wanted to hear.

Driving with just his left hand, Randy put his right arm around her shoulder. When his hand touched her back, the strength that had willed back her emotions for the last seven hours blew away, and tears welled up in her eyes. As she repeated what the boys on the bus had called her, she sobbed, and she wasn't even sure why she was crying. She hated those boys and knew that they were stupid and hence their opinions were baseless and the impact of their lives on the planet would be measured only in undifferentiated emissions of methane and nitrates . . . but still. It hurt, and it hurt that it hurt, and she covered her eyes and buried her face over her chest and her body shook under Randy's warm, steady hand.

"Dude," he said, "you're gonna get snot all over the eagles!" At a stoplight, he looked around his car for a tissue, which of course he didn't have, so he leaned over and wiped her face with his black T-shirt. "There," he said. "You gotta keep the eagles snot-free, or they're gonna fly somewhere else." This made Eva laugh a little bit.

"You know what?" Randy said. "I got an idea for those boys."

"What is it?"

"Gotta make sure they have something in stock first. Just don't sell Aracely all of your stuff."

At 3:10 p.m., the restaurant was still about two hours from opening, which was how Randy liked it for their visits. As they passed by the wooden benches and coat racks in the lobby, Eva liked to stop and look at a sepia-toned portrait of the owners, Jack Daugherty and Ishmael Mendoza, and a framed "Story of Lulu's" that was meant to help pass the time for customers willing to tolerate a substantial wait.

When she owned a restaurant, Eva decided, she was going to have the same thing in her lobby, and in her story, she was going to mention Cousin Randy and Aracely and her cousin Braque, who got a softball scholarship to Northwestern and said that Eva could visit Chicago anytime. But probably nobody else. It wasn't that she hated her parents or anything—they meant well, she knew that. But Eva just belonged somewhere else, somewhere with real important chefs like Aracely Pimentel, who didn't make time for stupid friends or stupid social events, and didn't view those choices as compromises that would ruin your life, like Eva's mom did.

Aracely was sitting at the bar in her chef whites and striped pants, drinking coffee and reading a magazine, her gray-streaked black hair pulled back into a tight, kitchen-ready bun. Her beautiful makeup-free face emanated the kind of don't-mess-with-me aura of Secret Service agents and British rock stars, but she was always happy to see Eva.

"Hey!" Aracely said with a wide smile, shoving the magazine into her bag and slapping the barstool next to her for Eva to slide onto. Randy went in for a hug but realized that he had snot all over his shirt just as he saw Aracely's eyes fall on it.

"Allergies?" Aracely asked him.

"Aw, crap. I'll be right back," Randy said, already on his way to the men's room.

"Let me show you something we had to do because of you," Aracely said, rising from her stool and walking around the corner to the maître d's station. Eva was fascinated by the empty bar, with its exotically shaped colored bottles with names like Galliano and Cynar and Midori. Randy had told her that these bottles were full of poison that ruined lives, but they looked so gorgeous, they couldn't only be evil.

Eva also loved the painted WALL OF FAME banner opposite the bar, meant for the "survivors" of the "Caliente Combo." The deal was, if you spent a lot of money, like forty dollars, and ate everything on the Caliente Combo plate—which was a chicken burrito, a cheese enchilada, a chile relleno, two carne asada tacos, and rice and beans, all infused with scant amounts of Eva's hot peppers—you got a T-shirt and your picture on the Wall of Fame. Eva was told that that Caliente Combo would not exist without her chocolate habaneros. It must've been a tough plate for adults to finish because it had been on the menu since her last chile harvest and there were only nine pictures on the wall. The newest one was of a guy named Edgar Caquill, who came all the way from St. Paul, Minnesota. Eva had finished the plate twice—it was a challenge to eat only because of the amount of food, not the spiciness quotient—but the owners hadn't gotten around to putting her picture on the wall or even giving her a T-shirt yet.

When Aracely returned to the bar, Eva opened a menu and pointed to *Abuelito Matias's Chimole—PELIGRO! MÁS CALIENTE!*

"Why did you add the warnings?"

"People were sending it back," Aracely said. "Only about one in five customers can finish it. That many Scoville units is really tough on most people."

Eva's last batch of chocolate habs was just over 500,000 Scoville heat units, according to Aracely's friends at the Iowa State Food Science Lab, and that number was unbearable for most people. This new crop Eva estimated at close to double that, giving her chiles a heat index almost halfway to Mace.

"I can do better than five hundred thousand."

"It's a lot. I don't let my cooks handle them without gloves on."

Eva dug around in her backpack. "I've stressed them out even more this year. Why don't you bring Iowa State some of this stuff?" She held up a glass pint jar a little more than halfway full of a dark brown powder, and a four-ounce bottle filled to its cap with a tannish liquid. "I have more oil at home," she said. "I just wanted you to give me notes, because it's the first time I've made it through hot infusion, like you told me to."

Aracely studied the jar. "So what you're saying is, this stuff is stronger than what we currently use in the chimole?"

"Oh, unequivocally."

"How much can you sell me?"

"Whoa," Randy said. "Don't sell all of it."

"Why not?" Eva asked. "I have lots of overhead costs. I don't exactly plant my habaneros in dirt from the backyard, you know. Plus I have to buy my own distilled water and special kinds of nutrients and stuff."

"I had an idea. Aracely, those churro bites you make, do you have like thirty of 'em I can buy?"

Aracely seemed wary. "What are you going to do?"

"It's a birthday surprise," Randy said, with confidence, and then he noticed that Eva had opened the bottle of chocolate habanero chile oil and was applying it to her lips with an eyedropper. "Whoa, hey!" he shouted.

"Hey, I'm fine," Eva said, the chile oil dripping from her mouth.

"Oh, Christ, no!" Aracely said, and grabbed Eva by the arm.

"I'm fine," Eva said.

"We gotta get you some dairy," Aracely said, yanking Eva in the direction of the kitchen. "Oh no, oh no."

"I'm fine," Eva repeated, as she disappeared around a corner.

Twenty minutes later, after the adults were calmed down from shock into mere amazement, and even asked Eva to do it again, Randy reminded everyone they had to get her home before her parents got off work.

First, Eva and Randy sat in his Jetta in Lulu's parking lot with the box of churro bites, the pint jar of chocolate habanero chile powder, and the eyedropper. For ten minutes, they tried to inject a few flecks of the corrosive powder into a piece of churro the size of a Tater Tot without the latter falling apart or leaving an obvious wound. In that amount of time, they got one done decently well and screwed up two beyond repair.

"Recognizing that this was my idea, I raise a practical question at this point," Randy said. "Do sixth graders even like churro bites?"

"Sure," Eva said. "Bethany Messerschmidt brought them once. They were as popular as anything that's basically sugar and fat."

Randy looked at his dashboard clock. "Crap. Can you finish the other twenty-nine of these at home tonight?"

Eva could see that he felt guilty about leaving her with all of the work. She loved that about him. They were each outcasts in their own way, and even though he was way more fearless and tough than she'd ever be, he looked after her, and she knew nothing bad would ever happen to her if he was around.

The first thing Eva did every day when she got home was go to her closet and make sure that the grow light was still on. Once or twice a year one of the bulbs would go out, which was devastating. Every morning at 6:30, to simulate the long, hot days of tropical climates, Eva turned on the two-foot Hydrofarm fluorescent lamp over her plants, and kept it on until ten at night. Her parents didn't like the effect on the electricity bills, but usually only complained, and rarely threatened.

By the time her parents got home from their jobs, Eva was sitting at the dining room table, doing vocabulary homework—the one where they teach you a new word and you have to use it in a sentence. She was writing all of her sentences in iambic pentameter to make it more interesting for herself.

These people didn't know what to do with someone like her. Her teacher, Mr. Ramazzotti, was a sweetheart, but spent 90 percent of class time managing the five stupidest little bastards in class, who chose to create a battle out of everything, making even something as rote as taking attendance twice as long as it ought to be. Where does that leave someone who wants to have the largest pepper garden in Iowa? Did she really have to wait out seven more soul-shredding years? It was like being told you can run free one day—in June several years from now—but during every second of the intervening time, you'll be getting run over by the world's slowest steamroller, and every day it cracks a bone, and re-cracks it, and recracks it, and when you're eighteen all you're going to have is a body full of dust, lifted and carried into the future like a flag loose from its mast.

Eva beat her parents home, thankfully, and even had a birthday package come in the mail from her cousin Braque at Northwestern—a T-shirt of something called "Bikini Kill." She didn't know what it was—probably a band? But it was from Braque, so it definitely was cool.

She was finishing the second-to-last sentence of her homework when her mom came home and walked into the dining room, green pantsuit and Hillary hair disheveled from a day doing who knows what at the temp agency, lugging two heavy grocery sacks, dropping them on the floor of the kitchen.

Eva glanced up. "How was work, Mom?"

Fiona was moving milk, butter, and ice cream from the grocery bags to the refrigerator and freezer. "Good, now that it's over. Here, I picked up some chocolate chip ice cream, and some little pink cups and spoons at the gas station."

A frosted plastic tub of Blue Bunny ice cream thudded onto the kitchen tile. At least it was a local brand. "Sounds fine, Mom."

"I'm sorry I couldn't get you that organic stuff for your class," Fiona said. "I know it's your birthday."

Eva knew that her mom hadn't gotten the vegan sorbet because it was too expensive. In their home, cost was the main reason why something good didn't happen.

Fiona set a small white paper carton of N. W. Gratz brand Vegan Blueberry Sorbet in front of Eva. "So I just got a little one, just for you."

Eva couldn't believe it. Her mom had driven into the city just to get it for her. She sometimes forgot that her parents were actually capable of doing nice things. Too often she could focus only on the horrifyingly unjust occasions when they prevented her from doing stuff, like when they told her that she couldn't go to the downtown farmers' market alone until she was ten, and even then didn't let her go until she was ten and two months. Or their stupid rules regarding Randy.

She reached for the carton, but her mom grabbed it back.

"Tomorrow," Fiona said. "Save it for your birthday."

Her dad, Jarl, still in his collared shirt and necktie after his day of work in the mailroom at Pioneer Seeds, grabbed a Busch Light from the door of the fridge.

"Hey, Dad," Eva said, and Jarl opened his beer as he sat down at the dining room table.

"Blueberry sorbet," Jarl said to no one in particular. "Is that something you could make at home?"

"Yeah, I guess," Eva said. "I hadn't thought of it."

"How was school?" her mom asked. She was reheating the leftover morning coffee in the microwave; she always did that instead of making a new batch.

"Fine," Eva said.

"What'd you do after school?"

"Nothing."

"Did Randy pick you up?"

"Yeah, but he just brought me straight home."

"Look, I can't stop you from going to Lulu's if you want. I personally don't see what's so damn special about Randy and that Mexican chef, but I know they're your favorite people in the world. Not that they buy your food or put a roof over your head or anything."

"They sure don't," her dad said, nodding as he drank his beer.

Eva rested her forehead on the dining room table and shook it back and forth as her mom spoke. "They're nice people," she said. "And they like the same stuff I like."

"Randy didn't give you cigarettes or weed or anything?"

"No! God, Mom."

"Well, still, maybe you should take a little break from Randy for a while."

"But, Mom."

Jarl picked at the tab of his beer can. "He used to drive while high, you know. That's how he got busted. He coulda killed somebody. Coulda killed himself."

"I know that," Eva said. "He doesn't drive stoned anymore."

"Y'know, I don't think he's out of the woods yet," Jarl said. "With his drug problems."

"How would you know?" Eva said, gathering her homework from the table and bolting off to her room, away from this awful conversation. "You never even talk to him."

Eva thought maybe she heard Jarl say "I just don't wanna lose you" at her, before she closed her bedroom door, but she wasn't sure.

• • •

Alone at the too-small child's desk in her room, Eva finished the last line of the most pointless assignment ever, and though she wanted to start on the evening's true mission immediately, she kept the box of churro bites closed under her bed. Her parents went to sleep at ten o'clock on weeknights. Only three and a half more hours to wait out.

After a brazenly lifeless dinner of fish sticks and frozen peas, Eva scurried back to her room. Fortunately, neither of her parents had brought up Randy again. If they had, Eva would've gotten up from the table that second.

She was sitting on her bed reading recipes in an old copy of James Beard's *Beard on Bread*—she found that book comforting for some reason—when her dad, smelling like sweat and warm beer, knocked on her door and opened it. He was still wearing a tie, but now also had on sweatpants cut off at the knees. Probably the dorkiest outfit of all time.

"Yes?" Eva asked, looking at her dad's face as his wide, soft body filled up the doorway.

"How's it goin'?" Jarl asked. "Is everything OK?"

Eva nodded, not setting down her book. "Yep," she said.

"You don't seem very excited about your birthday tomorrow, is all. Are things still better at school?"

A month ago, after some girls dumped a thirty-two-ounce Pepsi on her head during recess, she had made the mistake of telling her dad, who called the school, who talked to the girls, and this made things even worse, because now she was a "narc" and a "snitch bitch" in addition to being Sasquatch.

"Yeah," Eva said.

"You can tell me. You can tell me anything. You come to me first, not Randy."

Ah, that's what this was about. It was as much an anti-Randy message as a pro-Dad message, even if her dad did somehow believe he could actually protect her from that horrible world that started where their driveway stopped.

"I will," Eva said.

"OK," Jarl said. He suddenly looked sad and bewildered, like an elephant that had been fired from the circus and was wandering down the side of the highway with nowhere to go. The thought occurred to Eva that if her dad confronted those boys face-to-face, they'd make fun of her weak, fat, kindhearted father as brutally as they made fun of her, and she needed to protect her dad from that; his ego was already so fragile.

"Everything's better, Dad. I promise."

"Happy day before your birthday," he said, and smiled at her as he closed her bedroom door. "I love ya, you know. We love you."

"Yeah, I know that," Eva said in reply.

They did, she knew that. Eva knew that Jarl's big brother Lars had died of a heart attack a few months after she was born, and it probably made them both paranoid about losing another family member. Eva didn't remember Lars, because obviously she wouldn't, but apparently he was a super nice guy who really helped out Fiona and Jarl a ton when they were just starting out. And he'd been a chef, which was awesome. It was incredible knowing she'd actually been related to one. Her other uncle on that side also used to run a bakery way up in Duluth, but he sold it about six years ago, and they never saw him anyway. But Lars Thorvald, everyone said, was a legend in the kitchen.

Her parents, on the other hand, worked about as far away from a kitchen as you could get. Until a couple years ago, Fiona was an independent sales consultant for Madison May Cosmetics, but lately had been temping because she said she wanted to work in an office environment, and it seemed like a good way to try out different ones. Jarl, meanwhile, had been at the same mailroom job at Pioneer Seeds for three years now, a record. They each worked hard and barely seemed to spend any money on stuff just for themselves, and noticing the kind of stuff that the parents of other kids bought, and hers didn't—snowmobiles, camping trips, cruise ship vacations—Eva wondered if they ever would. What happened to all of the money her parents earned, Eva wasn't sure. Maybe it was true; maybe it was, as her mom said, all just going to the house and car payments and barely keeping them afloat, and that was why the dryer was loud and the deck wasn't going to be repainted anytime soon and why there was no handle on the toilet and you had to reach inside the back part to flush it. Fiona said they were one emergency from everything falling apart. But it didn't feel like it to Eva. Their home felt safe. She could have a pepper garden in her closet and take buses around the city alone and sneak time with Randy if she was careful. And when things did go bad, like they often did at school, she could decide for herself how to respond. Sure, maybe the churro bites were Randy's idea, but it was up to her to execute it. And she would.

After she was sure that her parents were asleep, Eva got up and sat at the vanity in her room with the box of churro bites and the pint jar of crushed peppers. She remembered Aracely saying that half a teaspoon spread over an entire meal was still too much for 80 percent of full-grown Iowan adults who ordered the chimole dish; it sent them coughing and gasping to the bathroom or downing whole glasses of milk after two bites. Half a teaspoon over maybe two pounds of food. She thought about Chadd Grebeck and Dylan Sternwall and Brant Manus and Bethany Messerschmidt as she carefully injected a full teaspoon of chile powder into the sugary guts of each one-ounce churro bite, again and again. She stopped once to consider whether a straight full teaspoon was excessive; although she had no friends in the class, perhaps not everyone deserved to have the sensation of their taste buds seared off, let alone burning diarrhea. All she knew was that there was no way that Chadd or Brant or any of those assholes should accidentally end up with one that had no chocolate hab in it, so therefore she had to severely doctor them all.

When she was done, a little before midnight, she licked the cinnamon and sugar and her chocolate habanero pepper powder off of her fingers all at once, feeling the severe, pleasant burning on her lips and mouth.

She was pretty sure that in her three-plus years of handling and eating extremely hot peppers, she had exhausted most of the substance P from the soft tissues in her mouth and hands, which didn't replenish, even as she got older; the main reason she began growing increasingly hot exotic peppers was to find something with enough capsaicin to release the endorphins that became more and more inaccessible with increased heat tolerance. She wanted to feel lava blossoming in her eyes and nose and mouth again, like the first time she ate a regular habanero with Cousin Randy, back when he was still allowed to babysit her. She cleaned out her last teaspoon of chile powder in the jar with a wet finger, put it on her tongue, and let the graceless heat savage her soft tissues as she lay on her bed, closed her eyes, felt the angels in her blood begin to sing, and officially turned eleven.

Her mom offered her a ride to school the next morning, which was rare, and normally Eva would've jumped at it, but that would mean revealing the churro bites and not being able to accidentally forget the ice cream, so she took the dreaded bus instead. She sat two seats behind the driver, which she hated doing because it was dorky and fearful, and only the little kids sat way up front.

That day, there was no escaping the awful boys either way.

"Hey, scrotum-breath," Dylan Sternwall, seated four seats behind Eva, said to Chadd. "Ten bucks if you kiss Sasquatch again."

"Give me the money first, gerbil-dick."

Dylan took a crumpled twenty-dollar bill out of his pocket. "I'll pay you for this time *and* the last time. After services rendered."

"You hear that, Sasquatch?" Chadd said. "I'm gonna get you again to-day. Outside. If you go running into the school I'm going to de-pants you."

Eva could only nod in response and look at the bus floor. De-pantsing was the highest of the high-level threats. Even if they succeeded, Eva knew that punishment would be elusive for these boys, especially when their dads were high school coaches and managed car dealerships and were far richer and more popular around town than her own little fam-ily. Once or twice, she had overheard people calling her parents "white trash," and she had quickly figured out that no one protects or stands up for white trash, and no one on the outside ever would. To be called white trash is to be told that you're on your own.

"Meet us at the end of the fence around the corner."

That was off school property. Eva nodded again. She saw him stare at her box of churro bites.

"Is that Mexican crap for school?" he asked. "That shit sucks."

Chadd grabbed the box from her in one move with his greasy boy hands and held it over her head.

Eva leaped to her feet. "Give it back!"

"What was that?" the bus driver yelled.

Chadd slid to a seat across the aisle, crushing a couple of third grad-ers with his chunky body, and slid the box out an open window. "Whoops," he said.

"No!"

Eva pulled down her window and looked out to see just the faintest glimpse of a lavender box tumbling on the road.

The bus driver stopped the bus and turned around, looking right at Chadd. "You. After I drop you off today, you are suspended from this bus."

"You can't do that." Chad smiled. "How am I gonna get to school?"

"Come up here," the driver said, pointing to a seat right behind her.

Chadd's friends made hubba-hubba noises as Chadd took his time getting to the front of the bus. He paused only to flick his tongue at Eva, who had her head in her hands and saw hardly any of it.

After a minute, a block before the bus arrived at school, Eva removed the little bottle of concentrated chile oil from her backpack. She first smeared some on her fingertips and then poured the rest in her mouth, holding it there like mouthwash. Even with her heat-ravaged mouth and hands, this stuff was special; it felt like the skin on her fingers and the inside walls of her mouth were searing off. She even glanced down once to see whether the skin on her fingers was actually peeling. She held a placid expression as she stepped out of the bus and made a right when every other student was making a left. She walked to the end of the block and turned at the fence, hearing Dylan, Chadd, and Brant laughing behind her, closing the gap. Then, by the fence at the official edge of school property, she waited.

As the boys surrounded her, she stood as still as a pot of dry soil, holding the fire in her cheeks. Maybe things would've gone according to plan if Chadd hadn't come up to her from behind and whipped her around, the shock of which made her spit the entire mouthful of searing pepper oil onto his face before he even kissed her.

As Chadd fell on the grass screaming, Eva stared at him for a second. It was really working. She reached over and grabbed Dylan's head and wiped her chile-oil-dripping fingers across his eyes, actually feeling his eyeballs under her fingertips. Screaming, he shoved her off and fell against the pole on the edge of the chain-link fence, shouting, crying, and grasping Oedipally at his face.

Brant got one look at Eva, her mouth and fingers red and swollen from the oil. Between that and hearing the cries of his friends, his flight instinct kicked in, and he ran toward the school as fast as Eva had ever seen a boy run.

Chadd was kneeling in the open lawn, fists uprooting handfuls of grass and dirt to wipe against the fire consuming his face, and was screaming—as was Dylan, who was still clawing at his eyes and weeping, long since having dropped his twenty-dollar bill, which Eva picked up, folded, and shoved in Chadd's fat back pocket. She then collected herself and walked toward the school.

Eva didn't even make it more than two feet into her classroom before she was once again approached from behind, this time by stern adults, and whisked to the principal's office. The look on sweet old Mr. Ramazzotti's face seemed to say, *Why her? She's one of my good ones.*

As she was escorted past the secretarial pool area of the front-desk administrators, she heard an ambulance being called. The principal opened a heavy wooden door to what Eva judged to be the second-fanciest office she'd ever seen after her dad's boss's office that one time, and followed the principal's stern orders to sit down in a chair facing the desk.

Just when the principal asked, *What did you do to those boys,* Eva could hear Dylan Sternwall, crying—wailing, really (she'd never heard a boy her age cry so loud)—as he was brought to the nurse's office. What a fantastic noise. She curled her hot, swollen lips over her teeth to fight back the smile and look contrite. There was no going back from this— she had just pushed her life forward in a particular direction—and as the principal lifted her cordless desk phone to call Eva's mother, Eva saw that not all of it was going to be as pleasant as this moment. So while the phone rang at her mom's work, she leaned back in her chair, listened to the astonishing sounds of justice, and no longer pretended to look sorry.

SWEET PEPPER JELLY

Braque Dragelski's Schedule for June 2:

5:30 A.M.—Off my ass and out of bed; hot lemon water (~0 calories), morning ablutions

5:50 A.M.—Breakfast (almond butter, avo & banana sandwich, egg whites; ~800 calories)

6:20 A.M.—Shower (water temperature ~110°F)

6:30 A.M.—Study for 210-2 U.S. History final

8:10 A.M.—Meet Patricia at SPAC; 20 min. of cardio, 70 min. of core & weights

9:40 A.M.—Shower (water temperature ~80°F)

9:50 A.M.—Leave SPAC; drink protein shake (~200 calories)

10:00 A.M.—Lunch at Whole Foods hot bar (~600 calories)

10:30 A.M.—310-1 Micro 1 discussion group

11:50 A.M.—Leave Micro 1 discussion group

12:00 P.M.—U.S. History discussion group

12:50 P.M.—Leave U.S. History discussion group

1:00 P.M.—Second lunch (grilled chicken, brown rice, steamed veggies; ~550 calories)

1:30 P.M.—Study for 203-0 French oral final presentation

3:00 P.M.—French oral workshop

3:50 P.M.—Leave French oral workshop

4:00 P.M.—Change; short jog around lakefill

4:40 P.M.—Small dinner (mixed greens, quinoa, protein shake; ~350 calories)

5:00 P.M.—Study for 215-0 Economy & Society final

7:00 P.M.—Snack (apple, raw carrot, kombucha; ~200 calories)

7:15 P.M.—Study for Micro 1 final

9:15 P.M.—Final snack (⅓ cup avocado on six whole wheat crackers;
          ~200 calories)

9:30 P.M.—Return outstanding e-mails, texts, phone calls; write schedule
          for tomorrow

10:30 P.M.—Lights out, no exceptions.

8:03 A.M.

People in Evanston moved so goddamn slow. It was one thing when the sidewalks were covered in ice and lake-effect snow. But this was June, the day after Braque's cousin Eva's birthday, which used to mean a big family party marking the beginning of summer, at least before her dad left and her brother Randy went into rehab. Back then, when they were all together, Braque's mom used to say that Iowans knew how to appreciate the two most precious things in life—family and warm weather.

Given that summer in Iowa was often fleeting, her mom was making one hell of a poignant juxtaposition, especially considering what had happened, and what that batshit crazy woman had done, and still did, to everybody. Still, once in a great damn while Braque did hear those words as her mother intended, and in particular they came to mind today, in this dismally temperate Chicago suburb, as the lumpy assholes on Clark Street refused to move aside for a runner who was out taking full advantage of the first beautiful day of the year.

The slow, sad-faced suburban ass-clowns weren't even the worst part about the morning so far. Across the street, on the corner of Clark and Orrington Avenue, the greasy egg-fart odor of the Burger King made Braque cover her face. It always smelled like ass, but today it was so overpowering she wanted to puke. Worse, the damn smell was also somehow alluring; she had to beat back memories of visiting her aunt Fiona and uncle Jarl and getting bags of delicious, slimy fast food for lunch. Shit, she used to love that BK Big Fish sandwich. Thirty-two grams of fat and 1,370 milligrams of sodium—91 percent of your recommended daily intake. Awful, feeding that to a kid. At least now, in the year 2000, those places also had supposedly healthy menu options, but still. That smell.

She could detect fish in the greasy breeze, she swore. Ha, what if she had one, just one time? Or half of one. But fuck that! Fuck that in the face! Bad fat, empty calories, and they put HFCS in everything, even the bun. She'd kill her gut and as a bonus have a goddamn sugar crash. No thanks, Hank. Jogging onto the campus, she washed out her olfactory system with the smells of wet sidewalk, the freshly mown grass of Deering Meadow, and the explosive lavender of the Shakespeare Garden. The lavender was bloomy as fuck and did the trick; all better.

After she swiped her WildCARD student ID at the gym's front desk, she noticed that everything at SPAC seemed doused in the citrusy alcohol-based cleaner they used to wipe down the equipment. People were so anal about each other's sweat and germs, especially the weekend warriors and noncompetitive athletes. Braque was a softball player. That's a life in the dirt, a life touching dirt, a life touching things that touch dirt. Did Dot Richardson sterilize everything she touched until she was handed a gold medal? As if. Braque waited until she knew people were looking at her, then spat in her hands and lifted a 17.5-pound kettlebell from the rack. Patricia Bernal, her workout partner and fellow Academic All-American award-winning softball player, would be here in thirty minutes to spot her, and she'd do k-bell swings and stairs until then.

It was hardly more difficult to do swings with a 17.5-pounder as opposed to her usual 15, but today, ugh. It didn't feel like abdominal tightening. It felt like a fist had broken through her intestinal wall and extended its fingers inside her. She felt the bile chuckling in her throat. The kettlebell clanked to the floor.

She stood facing the toilet, tasting the bile she spit into the water. She could hear another woman vomit a few stalls down, and another woman take a dump, and the goddamn smells of shit and bile were just too much. She covered her nose with the back of her left hand and let the vomit burst from her mouth. She puked so much, her eyes started to tear.

Afterward, she wiped off her face and washed her mouth out several times, so the stomach acid wouldn't chew up her enamel. It sucked having to bail on her weights partner, but it also sucked having probable food poisoning. She wondered if Patricia had the same bug. They had eaten the same thing at least once yesterday—grilled chicken and vegetables, which had never made them sick before, but who knows. As her second baseman—her partner in the middle infield—they often thought and moved in tandem.

8:51 A.M.

Braque had never been at Whole Foods this time of morning before. It was way less slammed with rubes than at lunchtime. It sucked balls having to skip weight training, but after vomiting, she needed two bananas, reverse-osmosis water, and a protein shake to replenish, along with an extra protein shake for Patricia to make it up to her.

While she was reading the ingredients on an N. W. Gratz brand Vegan Protein Smoothie, she saw something weird written amid the Nutritional Facts: the phrase SWET PEPER JELY, all caps, large type.

Something about it made her shiver. As she set the protein smoothie back on its shelf, the three strange words leapt out at her; she turned the bottle around so the front faced out instead. This was some creepy-ass bullshit, for sure. Still, fear is a choice, she reminded herself, and why choose it? She made up her mind that the strange words on the bottle didn't exist and never existed. It was just her nutrition-starved brain shorting out on her.

After a moment, she picked up the bottle and looked at it again. The bold text was gone, replaced by the usual crap about soy protein isolate and organic cane sugar. Sure as shit, she was going hypoglycemic from the food poisoning and not having eaten. Her temples began to ache; she needed to get something in her system, stat.

Then Braque saw someone down the aisle who she hated, and it gave her a huge sense of relief. There were Lolo McCaffrey's thick braids and patchouli-oil smell, crouched down by the nutritional bars, her moon face staring at the label of a Clif Bar like someone who can't read. Lolo was the strength and conditioning coach for the team who made every-one do hot yoga and meditation and was covertly seeing senior shortstop Tarah Sarrazin, the player who incoming first-year Braque Dragelski had beaten for a starting job. Seeing Lolo, right here, in the same store at the same time, Braque considered the possibility that either she or Tarah had somehow poisoned her dinner yesterday. She wouldn't put it past that pair of jealous skanks, that's for sure.

"Lolo," Braque said, looking down at Lolo. She was easy for Braque to intimidate, and Braque felt it was good for her soul to intimidate coaches who preached loving kindness and mindfulness; her headache and confusion instantly disappeared as she approached the shorter woman. "How's it hangin'?"

"Hello, Dragelski." Lolo nodded, not looking up from the Clif Bar.

"So," Braque said. "What do you and Tarah think you're doing?"

Lolo looked at the ground; she could never look Braque in the face. "I know what you're going to say, and I don't see how our wedding af-fects the team in the slightest," she said, looking Braque in the face for the first time.

"Wedding? Wow." First Braque had heard of this. She'd only just heard a few weeks back that they were dating, not that she cared. "Don't you have to go to Vermont or something?"

"Well, that's the plan," said Lolo, who seemed to realize that she had just volunteered more information than she intended.

"If you kids are planning to elope, why is Tarah on my dick all of a sudden?"

"Tarah is in Wyoming right now, having a very important conversation with her family. I seriously doubt she has given one thought to anything you're doing."

"Then why are you here, you stalking me?"

"I didn't even notice you there until you came over and initiated your unbalanced discourse about dicks—which has totally uncentered me, so thank you."

"Christ," Braque said. These hippie yoga chicks were the goddamn worst, no matter who they fucked.

"You should think on what you're saying and doing," Lolo said. "You're putting negative energy into the world that's cycling back. That's what happens, it cycles back."

Yawn. Now that she was close to 100 percent sure that Lolo and probably Tarah had nothing to do with this, she wanted to wrap this shit up and get on with her day.

"You would know," she said. "Now if you'll excuse me, I have to replenish my GI tract."

"Morning sickness?"

"Ha. Fuck you."

Lolo looked at Braque and smiled a little bit. "I've been a doula for five years. You seem pregnant to me. I'd guess five or six weeks."

"Bullshit," Braque said, and walked to the checkout. Crunchy little moon-face bitch actually got under her skin. Braque almost admired her for it; it was the first time since she'd met Lolo that she'd felt in her gut that the woman had any authority. And now it scared her a little.

9:39 A.M.

Braque was in the ground-floor women's bathroom at Chapin Hall with her pants to her knees, but her whole day wasn't fucked yet. Yes, this was a substantial detour, but she still had an hour to make it to her last Micro 1 discussion group before the final. According to her schedule, it had been thirty-three days and sixteen hours since her last period, so a worst-case scenario was possible, and she needed to figure that out, stat.

The bathroom was one of those white-on-white jobs with white tile on the floor and a frosted window that had been painted shut. The toilet paper was so cheap, you could read a magazine through it, and the place smelled like mildew because of the self-conscious dipshits who took a shower in there every day and trapped all the humidity inside a room where the window couldn't open. But it was just the place for an operation as stupid as a secret pregnancy test.

Patricia, of course, freaked out when Braque texted her about what was happening and insisted on skipping her own weight training just to help Braque with the lame-ass pee stick. This was unnecessary but fine. In the road games against Michigan and Purdue, Patricia had seen Braque do far more embarrassing things, like overthrow the catcher on a play at the plate and call off the left fielder on a fly ball that ended up going halfway to the warning track.

"Wow, Tarah and Lolo are getting married," Patricia said, watching Braque take the pregnancy test from Osco out of its box. "Sure didn't see that coming."

"Who gives a shit?" Braque said. She held the white plastic stick under the light. "I'm gonna get pee all over my hand. Can I just pee in a cup and put it in the cup?"

"You ever been to a lesbian wedding?"

"Nope. I hate all weddings."

"I like the dancing part. Even the Chicken Dance. I will totally dance the Chicken Dance."

"Ugh. Get the gun." Braque was down on her hands and knees, looking through the white cabinet under the sink, which was cluttered with waterlogged rolls of single-ply toilet paper and cheap, non-organic cleaning supplies. "I wonder if there's like a paper cup somewhere in this bathroom I can pee in."

Patricia gently kicked the back of her friend's shoe. "You'll touch a bathroom floor, but you won't pee on your hands? Urine is sterile, you know."

"OK, fuck it," Braque said, pulling her underwear to her ankles and sitting on the toilet. "Hand me the goddamn stick."

There was a knock on the door. It was the only private bathroom in the entire building, so it had its regulars.

"It'll be a little while!" Braque called out.

"It's OK, I'll wait," the tiny female voice answered. It was Braque's roommate Katelyn Pickett. She only ever used this bathroom.

"Wouldn't if I were you," Braque said, but she could see from the shadow in the opaque door glass that Katelyn hadn't moved.

Braque thought she heard a burst of music from the pocket of her balled-up sports pants just as she began to pee.

"I think it's my phone," she said.

Patricia looked surprised. "Is it that French guy?"

"Tuna Can? I doubt it."

"Let me pick it up," Patricia said, reaching for Braque's pants at her feet.

"No, don't," Braque said. She stood up and leaned forward as she was peeing, getting urine all over her hand, the stick, and the toilet seat. "Goddamn it! I told you not to touch that," she shouted as she stood, set the stick down on the sink, pulled up her underwear, and grabbed the phone from Patricia.

The phone buzzed in Braque's hand. It read INCOMING CALL: AMY JO DRAGELSKI.

"Not a good time, Mom," Braque said as she answered.

"Your niece is missing," her mom said.

"Sure she is."

Braque was used to this kind of crap; her mom had been a master choreographer of anxious micromanagement since Braque could remember. When Braque and her brother Randy were kids, their mom used to wake them up at 5:30 in the morning for family road trips, to avoid traffic; there were safety latches around the house until she was eleven; there was no TV and sure as shit no candy, pop, alcohol, or smoking; she ironed bedsheets and bleached underwear and cleaned the bathrooms at least twice a day. The menace of her manic perfection made it impossible to relax—and fucking forget having friends over, unless they enjoyed being bum-rushed by a Sears vacuum. Braque was sure that was why their art professor dad Wojtek cheated on their mom once when they were little (who wouldn't!) and ultimately went on an indefinite sabbatical to Malta, why Randy escaped into music and drugs, and maybe even why Braque signed up for every sport and pointedly excelled at the dirtiest one. Braque was, by careful design, nothing like her mom.

But with her mom's own family out of her grasp, she now meddled with her relatives instead, and the struggling little Thorvald clan was less than two miles away, helpless against the force of her help.

"Eva ran away last night. Nobody knows where she is. Fiona and Jarl are losing their shit."

"How do you know she ran away?"

"Because Fiona threw away all of her habanero plants."

"Holy Christ."

"I guess she made some kind of oil out of them that she was using as a weapon at school. She sent two boys to the hospital."

"Do you know what happens to her at that school, Mom? Those little shits probably had it coming."

"She got suspended by the principal. Well anyway, Randy thinks that there's a chance that she might be coming out your way, so maybe you should go out and put some signs up or something."

"I kinda got my hands full right now."

"But your cousin is missing!"

"Kids do this kinda shit all the time, I'm sure she's fine."

A small fist pounded on the bathroom door. "Are you just talking on the phone in there?"

"*Ahh, shaddup!*" Braque said. Patricia got up from the floor and returned a volley of slaps on their side of the door.

Braque returned the phone to her ear. "Sorry, not you, Mom."

"I think you're being selfish and lazy," Braque's mom said. "When I get a hold of your dad in Malta I'll tell him that you're not helping the family."

"Look, I'll help as soon as finals week is over. OK? I can't fail spring quarter and lose my scholarship because my cousin ran away from home for a couple hours."

"I can't believe I raised such a selfish daughter."

"Keep me posted, Mom. Love you." Braque pressed her phone's keypad, ending the call, and shook her head. "Christ. Neediest goddamn chick in the world."

She looked at Patricia, who was standing by the sink with a sad, scared look on her face.

"What is it?"

Patricia handed Braque the pregnancy test. Braque stared at the two pink lines in the result window.

"Well, fuckin' A, Patty."

Patricia put her hand on Braque's shoulder. Braque leaned against her friend's waist and let her friend cradle her head.

"Holy fucking shit," she repeated, as Patricia held her and squeezed her shoulder.

A limp, tiny hand slapped the bathroom door. The small shadow at the foot of the doorframe was now joined by a larger one. "I got the RA with me!" Katelyn said.

10:01 A.M.

Goddamn cataclysmic devastation, pretty much.

Braque threw the pregnancy kit and the box it came in into the trash of the dorm across the street from Chapin. Her head was absolute pudding; she could hardly remember where her Micro class was, or what day the final was on, or anything else imminent and relevant. She tried to recall her schedule and where she was supposed to be at that moment, but her thoughts separated and vanished like April snowflakes.

She would terminate her pregnancy. No question. She didn't have time for this. She was a scholarship Division I athlete and a 4.0 student. Her job was to lead Northwestern to the Big Ten title, qualify for the 2004 Olympic team in four years, and then go to the Kellogg School of Management for a business degree. That was the plan. No time for serious boyfriends, and no interest.

Which didn't mean that she didn't have the scorching desire for a halfway decent fuck every once in a while. But for starters, she couldn't even remember which of her two spring quarter sex partners could've been the father. Luc-Richard, the French tennis player whose junk was wider than it was long? He went back to France and who cares. Or was it Yuniesky Cespedes, the shortstop for the Kane County Cougars, who just got promoted to Daytona in the Florida State League? It's not like she wanted to call either of these dudes and be like, hey, are you sitting down? They didn't sign up for this. And neither did she.

Did a condom break? She couldn't be on the pill because it messed with her system too much, so she compensated in other ways. Once she made a guy wear two condoms. Of course he hated it, but give a male animal a choice between wearing two condoms and going home with blue balls, and imagine what they do. Could a guy not notice when a condom breaks? Could she? There were times she took the Plan B pill just because she thought one might have broken. That Yuniesky dude always flushed his condoms afterward. Was it him?

As she entered the lobby of Chapin, where some lame-ass freshman boys were setting up a beer pong table, her phone buzzed.

It was a text message.

SWET PEPER JELY, the screen seemed to read.

Braque stopped walking and took a deep breath. She glanced away from her phone and looked back. The words were gone.

Some oaf in a *Star Wars* shirt was trying to get past her with stacks of blue plastic cups. "Excuse me," he said.

"No," she replied, not getting out of his way. She looked at her phone again. A brand-new Nokia 3210. Almost everyone on the team had one; text messaging was way easier than calling. It couldn't be busted already.

She looked through the message history. No SWET PEPER JELY. Whatever that was about. As the big nerd with the plastic cups finally tried to squeeze past her, she put away her phone and shoved past him toward her dorm room.

10:10 A.M.

To Braque, the Humanities dorm was like an icicle up the glory hole. She'd put it down as her fifth choice of five. Only after getting to school did she learn that anyone who'd put it down as *any* choice got stuck there. Some had it as their first choice. Every one of those dorks was as big a rube as Katelyn, who was wearing a stupid combo of a pink Chicago Bears T-shirt (she probably couldn't name even one player on the Bears) and white high-waisted shorts. She was lying on her bed reading some dumb piece of Victorian literature.

"Just to give you a heads-up," Katelyn said, not looking up from her book. "My sister Elodie's coming here in two days, and I told her she could have your bed."

"Fuck that," Braque said, tossing her Micro notes into her old JanSport bag. "Your sister's not staying in our room, and sure as hell not in my bed, end of discussion."

"The RA said it's OK, after you locked me out of my bathroom."

Braque dropped her bag on the floor. "I have so many problems with that statement, I don't know where to begin. For starters, Katelyn, you're rich. Put her in a hotel." This was true; her dad was a corporate lawyer in Minnesota and they lived on a lake in Orono, which were facts Katelyn seemed proud of when boys were around.

"I'm not rich. My family is relatively successful, but I am not personally financially capable of buying hotel rooms for my guests."

"Well, maybe she can spring for it herself. It's what adults do."

"You're just being selfish because you're being inconvenienced. You can't stand one tiny little inconvenience in your life, ever."

"This isn't tiny," Braque said, standing in the open doorway. She was running late, which meant that she was not going to get to class as early as she usually did. "You're trying to kick me out of my bed during finals week. How about I kick you out of your bed?"

"You already owe me four nights in here alone for the four nights I had to sleep outside in the hall because you were boning some dude in here."

"To be continued," Braque said, stepping out of the room and closing the door behind her. The entitled little twat kind of had a point. But whatever her past grievances, however, there was absolutely no reason Katelyn's sister couldn't stay in a hotel during finals week. And who visits during finals week anyway? The sisters of rich girls who don't give a shit about their grades, because they'll never have to worry about money in their entire lives.

Northwestern's roommate assignment policy was sadistic: Incoming first-year students on financial aid were always paired with someone not on financial aid, and it only served to teach Braque how cheap rich peo-ple were. Katelyn went to Vail over spring break and she didn't even ski, but then she came back a week later and used all of Braque's Seventh Generation detergent without asking. And now she was giving away Braque's bed like it was hers to give. Fuck these rich kids in the face.

12:50 P.M.

To Braque, both the Micro 1 and U.S. History discussion groups were an ambient fog of vaguely familiar nouns. She could concentrate on only about every fifth word. Walking out of Kresge Hall, she felt even worse than before.

Braque sort of didn't want to turn her damn phone back on after the weird thing that happened earlier. But if her cousin Eva had actually run away from home, which seemed likely, Braque knew she might get a call from her—especially if she wasn't with Randy.

She had one text message and two missed calls. The voice mails were from Mom; she'd endure them while walking to the Stucco Palace to have lunch with her teammates.

The text was from Patricia: hey BD, every1 here supports & luvs u. C U soon <3

She thought about texting back something smart-ass like *tell every-one to think of me when they rub one out*, or something equally profane and Braque-ish, like she normally would when confronted with sincere sentiment, but this time, she just went with: thx.

12:59 P.M.

After missing both her morning workout and her first lunch, Braque felt her blood sugar falling off a goddamn cliff, and she could smell the tur-key grilling even half a block from the Stucco Palace. Ann Richards—their six-foot-three starting pitcher from Texas, no relation to the former governor—opened the door. "Pony" by Ginuwine was playing on their stereo, and Ann instantly started dancing alone on the hardwood floor as Braque followed her inside.

"Come on, B.D.!" Ann said, as Maya Cromartie, their junior center fielder, joined Ann in the living room. The best players on the team lived in the Palace, and it had been that way as long as anyone could remember. Braque would be living there now if Northwestern didn't have that dumb rule that first-years had to live on campus.

"I can't, I've been sick all day," Braque said. She waved at first baseman Tangela Bass, who was typing on her laptop with headphones on, and walked into the kitchen to put her arm around Patricia, who was standing over the stovetop, sprinkling a tiny pinch of pungent diced garlic onto the almost-done turkey patties.

"So, what's the latest?" Patricia asked.

"I don't even know where to start," Braque said. "But I made up my mind. I wanna get rid of this thing."

Patricia put her arm around her younger friend. "You're a hundred percent sure?"

Braque nodded.

"Eat something," Patricia said, and handed Braque a plate and lifted the lid over a steamer basket full of broccoli and carrots. The fresh garlic on the turkey burger smelled to Braque like the most amazing garlic in world history, and at the table, Maya Cromartie was pouring habanero sauce over all of it as if it were gravy on mashed potatoes.

Braque winced just watching this perverse offense to the sanctity of a healthy lunch. "Do you hate the taste of food all of a sudden?" she asked.

"We're going to the Hell Night tonight," Maya said. "Gotta prime myself."

It sounded to Braque like a stupid frat theme party, but no one in the Stucco Palace, to Braque's knowledge, had ever been in a fraternity house in their lives. "Explain," she said.

"It's at The Truth down in Wrigleyville. They have a Hell Night where they put ghost chili into everything. We are all over that shit this year."

Ann Richards twirled into the dining room and grabbed Braque by the shoulders. "Are you coming? You should totally come!"

"You gotta sign a waiver just to order the food," Maya said. "People had to go to the hospital last time."

"It sounds awful," Braque said, taking another bite of her plain brown rice. "Besides, I got a French oral final at nine. While I'm standing there trying to remember verb conjugations, I don't want my sphincter to feel like a ditch fire."

"I heard spicy food can cause a miscarriage," Patricia whispered to her. "Sure's cheaper than the alternative."

"Nope," Braque said. "I want some dude's hairy knuckles up inside me, ripping that thing out for real." She looked over her silent teammates. "Anyone know a cheap clinic off the Red Line?"

1:26 P.M.

As she walked down Noyes toward campus, past the giant chirping trees and sturdy hundred-year-old homes full of twenty-year-olds, the sky was the bright, eye-stabbing silver that she hated on game days. The beautiful morning had evolved into a classic midwestern scorcher and there was no relief from any incoming low-pressure front from Minnesota. She felt that stupid unborn thing turning around in her belly, or she thought she did. Would it get heatstroke if she did?

Oh, fuck that, though. There was no easy way out of this. Ann Richards knew a clinic that charged $445 for a medical abortion done prior to nine weeks of pregnancy; of course, Braque's blood type was O Rh negative, so she'd also need to spend an extra $65 for Rho-Gam. Problem was, even if she totally scrapped her diet and regimen for the next two weeks, which she was *not* doing, she still wouldn't have 510 bucks. She would get some stupid evening restaurant job in downtown Evanston and work however many days in a row she needed to to make the cash. She'd just crash on the couch of the Stucco Palace until then. There was no way she'd take this fetus home to Iowa. If her mom found out, that'd be the end of everything.

In the lobby of Chapin Hall, twenty people were clustered around the ping-pong table like ants on a wet Dorito; the finals week Beer Pong Classic was in full swing. The kids inside acknowledged her, but no one invited her to play. Not that she would've. She hated beer, even so-called good beer, and the prospect of drinking warm Keystone Light with a dirty ping-pong ball floating in it had about as much appeal as eating gum off the floor of a bus. But why didn't they at least ask? Buncha space dockers.

The door to her room was ajar, which was weird. As Braque nudged it open with her foot, her roommate stared at Braque from her bed, eyes as big as catcher's mitts, and held a finger to her mouth and said, "Shhhhhhh!" as she pointed to Braque's side of the room with her other index finger.

"You shh, camel-toe," Braque said, because Katelyn did have serious camel toe in those dumb high-waisted shorts. Then she saw what Katelyn was pointing at.

Braque's cousin Eva, eight years younger but taller than Braque, was curled up, sleeping on Braque's bed, wearing black jeans and the Bikini Kill shirt that Braque had just bought her for her birthday.

1:35 P.M.

Katelyn stood in the hallway, her hands on her hips, enjoying the hell out of the moment. "So I see how it is," she said. "Your cousin can visit during finals week but my sister can't."

"I didn't even know she was coming here," Braque said.

"Maybe you should check your e-mail. The poor girl takes the bus all the way from Iowa and you're not even here to let her into the building. Do you know who let her in? I let her in. That's the kind of person I am."

"No it isn't," Braque said.

"I don't suppose she came out with enough money for a hotel room, did she?"

"She's ten. No, eleven. So no, let's assume she didn't."

"Well, then, if she gets to stay here, then Elodie does for sure."

"Look, I'll talk to her. It'll be one night, tops. And maybe not even."

"That's not what she said."

A wet ping-pong ball rolled down the hall toward them. A guy in horn-rimmed glasses and a red pearl-snap shirt ran after it, but he stopped when he saw the women talking. "Oh hey, Katelyn," the guy said. Braque recognized him; it was Brian something, or maybe Brady something. He appeared to be staring at Katelyn's camel toe.

"Is this your game ball?" Braque asked, walking over to the wet ping-pong ball and crushing it under her right foot.

"Fuck you!" the guy said. He looked past them, took an unsteady step back, quickly said, "No, not you! Sorry!" and scrambled off.

Braque looked in the direction of the guy's apology. Eva was standing in their doorway, watching the guy dash down the hall as he complained to his buddies about the bitch who had busted their ball.

"I've heard worse," Eva said.

Braque walked over and hugged her. "You know you're in deep crap, right?"

"Yeah, I don't care," Eva said. "Let 'em sweat it out for a few days."

"See?" Katelyn said. "A few days?"

"We're going on a walk," Braque said, leading Eva down the hall. "Now."

The beer pong game went silent as the cousins walked through the lobby.

1:42 P.M.

Behind Chapin Hall was the official campus rehearsal and practice space building for music students. Everyone called it the Beehive, because during school, the building emitted an atonal assemblage of strings, horns, and keys through its windows; Braque guessed that some imaginative people once likened it to the pleasant buzzing of insects. But to her the racket sounded like ass, so she called it the Ass Clown Palace.

Today the milieu of the Ass Clown Palace was ideal for drowning out their conversation so none of the nosy dorks in her dorm would get the dirt on her. She and Eva sat in the grass on the south side of the building, and in her head, Braque tried to rationalize getting only forty-five to sixty minutes of study time today for tomorrow's French oral final. She was already getting an A in French; the oral final was only 20 percent of the grade, and she could probably ace it with minimal prep. The U.S. History one was going to be much harder because it was 50 percent of the grade and she had to memorize a bunch of shit for it.

She tried to put it out of her mind as she watched her tall cousin uncurl on the grass, staring into the punishing white sky like she was watching a movie. What a fascinating creature. How were they even related?

"Shirt looks great on you," Braque said.

"Thanks," Eva said. "What's Bikini Kill?"

"A punk band from Olympia, Washington, you'd like them. Our head coach listens to them."

"Cool. And thank you."

"So when did you get here?" Braque asked.

"The Megabus dropped me off at Union Station at 6:50 a.m. I wasn't sure if you'd be up yet so I took the train up to Ann Sather and had Swedish pancakes with lingonberries."

"How did you know about Ann Sather?"

"I read about it on the Internet and it sounded cool. There's this other place I want to go to as well but it's not open yet. Have you ever been to a chili bar called The Truth? Can we go there later?"

"Yeah, I've heard of it. Anyway, look. I love you, and I know you want to piss your mom off, which is fine with me, because I know what she did to your plants," Braque said. "But this is not a good time for me."

"I didn't know where else to go," Eva said. "Anyway, you also told me a couple months ago I could come visit you in Chicago sometime when it wasn't softball season."

"Oh yeah, I did say that, didn't I? Well, you've happened to come during finals week. And things are kinda nuts right now. And also, I'm sorry, but I don't even know how I'm gonna feed you or anything. I got some avocados and organic almond butter and other random stuff, but not a ton of it."

"It's all right. I got a hundred and sixty-eight bucks, I can figure out my own comestibles."

"Wow. That's a chunk of change. Birthday money?"

"Birthday money and chile sales. And then I won ten bucks from a guy at the bus station."

"How'd you do that?"

"He wasn't eating his jalapeño peppers that came with his sandwich, and I said I'll eat 'em, and he said I bet you can't, and I said I bet you ten bucks I can eat 'em all, and I did." She dug around in her pocket and pulled out a ten-dollar bill. "See?"

"Nice. Have you done that before?"

"No, but I could. I can eat things way hotter than jalapeños."

"For money?" Braque asked.

1:56 P.M.

Happily, Katelyn was out of the dorm room, off doing whatever the hell she did on campus, so Braque could type her computer passwords for Eva without worrying about her cooze of a roommate getting them. Eva was looking around the room as she waited, taking in the décor on Katelyn's side of the room. It was the usual college girl bullshit: clever and inspirational quotes pasted onto pastel-color strips of construction paper and taped to the wall, along with a framed poster of Robert Doisneau's *Le Baiser de l'Hôtel de Ville* that Braque had seen in no fewer than three other dorm rooms.

"Dormitories are even cooler than I thought they would be," Eva said.

"They're like a prison, but the sex is worse," Braque said.

"How come you don't have anything like this on your side of the room?" Eva asked. Braque did indeed have something on her side of the room—that year's Big Ten softball schedule.

"Because I don't want my room to look like a Hallmark store, that's why," Braque said.

Eva walked over and looked at one of the cutout quotes taped on Katelyn's side. "'The only thing necessary for the triumph of evil is for good men to do nothing—John F. Kennedy,'" she read.

"Total bullcrap," Braque said, getting up from her computer and turning the chair around for Eva. "OK, I gotta study for a final and go to a class. Go ahead and look up a bunch of places where you can work the crowd."

"Do you have Netscape?" Eva asked.

"Netscape is for dorks. Use Google. Maybe search for 'spicy food Chicago,' or something. Just log out of everything when you're done. I'll be back around four."

"OK," Eva said, smiling at her older cousin.

Braque gave the back of Eva's head a light slap and dashed out. She decided to go to the main library, a giant concrete thing built on Lake Michigan shoreline marshland, which—because they didn't account for the weight of the books inside—was sinking into the ground by a few inches every year. Too bad it had the best study alcoves outside the business school.

1:59 P.M.

Walking through South Campus, down a chalked-up sidewalk that hyped campus a cappella groups and a stupid Battle of the Bands, she passed the Rock, a five-foot boulder on a patch of dirt boxed in by a hedge and a foot-high retaining wall. The Rock was one of those shitty campus traditions, repainted every couple of days by some student special interest group. Braque liked this school for its softball team and its academics, but hated typical college stuff like this. She wouldn't have given it a second thought today either, but except for what the Rock said: SWET PEPER JELY.

Braque stared at it, looked away, and stared again. This time the message wasn't going anywhere. She turned her head and looked back again, and there it was, still. SWET PEPER JELY.

Was it actually there, this time?

She waved at a woman passing by—a hunched-over, frumpy English-major type with thick glasses. Braque demanded that the woman tell her what was on the Rock, which freaked the frumpy chick out; she instantly assumed that it was a hidden-camera joke set up to make her look stupid, and scuttled away. How did people like this get through life, viewing the world as something that was constantly out to get them? What was in it for them to think like that?

Braque stopped a too-handsome jock-looking guy wearing a pink polo shirt and board shorts. These confident types were usually straightforward in a pinch. He sighed, like he was disappointed to be stopped on the street by a woman who wasn't his type, but at least he was helpful.

"Sweet Puma Belly," Polo Shirt said.

Braque looked again. It did indeed say SWEET PUMA BELLY.

"What the fuck is that?" Braque asked.

"It's a jam rock band. They're in the Battle of the Bands," Polo Shirt said, walking away. Now she noticed that the phrase BATTLE OF THE BANDS was painted on the front of the short retaining wall. "Get some glasses, babe."

. . .

She stared at the stupid rock again, just to make sure. Up until now, she didn't think she was going nuts, but she was beginning to suspect that perhaps she was, and it made her deeply sad.

Her phone buzzed.

It was her mom.

"Yeah, what?" Braque said.

"Have you heard anything?" her mom asked.

"No, I haven't."

"Your dad's coming back from Malta to help the family."

"Have you spoken with him?"

"Well, I can't get a hold of him yet. But when I do, I'm going to make sure he's on the next plane outta there."

"Do you even know if he's in Malta?" Braque's father had left on a yearlong sabbatical when Braque was fifteen. That was four years ago.

"Don't. Don't go there again with me."

"Whatever. Look, I'm sure Eva is fine. Give it a few days, she'll come back."

"She could be raped and murdered in a few days. You're just trying to get out of helping me. It's all about you, isn't it? It's all about you, all the time."

Braque hung up.

She reached into her backpack, pulled out half an avocado from its plastic wrap, hurled a perfect strike at the u in PUMA, and walked to the damn library, the sun burning the top of her blonde head.

4:15 P.M.

Viewed through the window of the Purple Line train, the southbound Howard stop on the El was crowded—but less so than the northbound side, clustered with the first bloom of suburban commuters, weary from their early mornings and afternoon caffeine and blood sugar crashes. It was ninety-three degrees outside, which meant it was like a hundred and ten on the train, but Braque didn't mind her cousin's head leaning on her shoulder. The sincerity and plainness of the gesture was so rare and wonderful. It reminded Braque of the day she first met Eva, a day that her mind otherwise left alone. Braque was the one who'd held Eva for hours as all of the adults cried and ran around and made phone calls. No one thought to comfort Braque, but it didn't matter. That day, she poured all of her strength into that little baby, and she'd held on tight to her, whispering again and again that it would be OK, and Eva didn't cry once the whole time Braque had her.

Eleven years later, her cousin's head on her shoulder, she could've held her like that again; even on a train that smelled like hot metal and strange male sweat, she could've put her arm around Eva and kept her close and safe, all the way to 95th/Dan Ryan and back again, on an infinite, silver loop.

As they clattered into the Argyle station, Eva raised her head, looked around, and began digging in the giant black backpack at her feet. What was in that thing?

"I want to go to this place," Eva said, pointing to a name on a list of restaurants, ranked in order of their inhumanly hot cuisine. "Hell Night at The Truth."

After already telling her teammates there was unequivocally no way she'd ever set foot in The Truth, Braque really didn't want to run into them there, especially when she was with her kid cousin. One of them might accidentally bring up the pregnancy or the abortion. Braque knew that she could deal with this fetus thing quickly and efficiently and Eva, who looked up to her so much, would never have to know. A big part of her was afraid that Eva would think less of her if she found out—maybe because that same part of her now thought less of herself.

"That'll be open late. Let's go to a few other places first. What's next on your list?"

"Jack Cermak's Tap Room. It's off the Logan Square stop. They have something called Circle of Hell Wings. When they bring them to your table they ring a bell and play a song. And if you eat an entire order, you get your name and picture in the Ring of Fire."

"How do you wanna play this, then?" Braque asked.

"Well, we order them and then bet someone that I can't eat them."

Braque shook her head. "Nope. You're gonna get full from wings after one bet. We gotta get several bets out of each location."

"I can probably go vomit somewhere, or something."

"No, screw that. You said there's a bell that rings every time there's an order. We'll just go to the table with the bell, watch them try to eat one, and then say, 'I bet this little girl can eat one.' That way we don't have to spend any money."

"I detest being called a little girl, FYI," Eva said, moving slightly away from Braque.

"I know, you're eleven now, but you should try to play younger. It'll work to our advantage."

Eva looked at the dirty floor. "I suppose."

"So what's my cut?" Braque asked. "Fifty percent?"

"Maybe forty percent," Eva said.

Braque laughed. "What do you need sixty percent for?"

"Well, I'm the one actually eating everything, right?"

She had a point.

Eva stared out the window as the train whipped by the windows of a brick apartment building. "And back home, I need lots of stuff. New plants for sure. My mom said she'd let me grow anything except hot peppers."

"Are you OK with that?"

Eva shrugged. "I don't know. I said no at first. But I was thinking about it on the bus, and I was like, how much hotter can I make them anyway? It's like something dumb a boy would do, you know? Just try to grow the hottest pepper that no one can even eat. I mean, I want to ac-tually use them in recipes. And this last batch I made, I don't know. I do kinda want to grow other things."

"Like what?"

"Maybe fruit. I'm thinking about trying to make my own homemade vegan sorbet, or something."

"That'd be cool. Where'd you get that idea from?"

"My dad actually mentioned it."

"They being good to you?" Braque realized that she had uttered the awkward and potentially revealing question without thinking. There was an agreement among the family never to discuss Eva's origin; her birth mother was apparently the worst woman in world history. But Eva, staring out the window, didn't seem alarmed.

"Sometimes, I guess. When they're not throwing away my plants," she said. "They're just so, I don't know, normal. They're too tired all the time to do much. But we hardly like any of the same stuff anyway. Their tastes are so just so plebeian."

Braque smiled; she loved her young cousin's vocabulary. "Pretty much everybody feels that way about their parents," she said, hoping it canceled out the earlier statement. "But you know, they did get you that new grow light for Christmas. And didn't your dad drive you to that hot pepper convention in Madison?"

"Yeah, I guess."

"You know, for a kid, you're really smart and motivated. I think it kind of intimidates them sometimes, to be honest. But I know they love the hell out of you."

"Yeah."

Braque was seeing Eva at a low point, absolutely, but she remem-bered the previous Christmas. Eva didn't see it, but Fiona and Jarl were so happy while they watched their daughter unwrap the grow light they'd bought for her. When Eva saw what it was and squealed in de-light, Jarl started crying.

Braque knew how expensive that gift was for them. Amy Jo had tried to give them some money to help pay for it, but Fiona and Jarl refused. They wanted to earn and be accountable for the happiness of that wonderful, strange little girl they were raising. They wanted to know for themselves that they could make Eva overjoyed.

"I guess I still love them," Eva said. She suddenly turned and looked at Braque. "What are you going to buy with your share of the money?"

Braque shook her head. "I'm not even gonna get into it right now."

The rush-hour express train whipped through an unfamiliar North Side El stop. The car rattled, and its violent motion caused the bodies of the young dudes in the aisle to absorb the shock into their nonchalant sways, making them look like people who were about to dance and instantly changed their minds.

5:15 P.M.

Yep, Jack Cermak's Corner Tap was the eighth circle of hell. In a gentrifying neighborhood like Logan Square, setting up a sanitized, overpriced bar to look like a cheap small-town dive was just plain sick. They even had old signs on the walls for beer that they didn't serve (and Braque asked): Old Style, Grain Belt, Schmidt, Special Export.

Of course, the place was still filled with flat-screen TVs, each tuned to sports, and it smelled like french fry grease, beer vomit, and orange-scented disinfectant. This all made Braque feel like retching, which made her think of the last time she vomited, which made her think of her damn fetus.

They sat down in an oversized wooden booth and ordered a vanilla milkshake (Eva) and a side salad with no dressing (Braque) from a waiter in bib overalls. They waited for the bell, which didn't take long. As the trumpets of Johnny Cash's "Ring of Fire" burst over the loudspeakers, two members of the wait staff came out holding sparklers, and a chimney-red platter of steaming bright orange chicken wings was brought to a table where two pudgy adult men sat, ties loosened, shoes shiny. Braque knew their kind from Des Moines and around Evanston: just two more people who didn't try hard enough at anything in life to make any kind of difference to anybody or anything. Ordering these chicken wings would probably be their highlight achievement for the month.

Almost everyone in the restaurant was watching their table, so Braque felt certain that they hadn't noticed her sizing them up. The dude who ordered the wings took one bite of the first one and dropped it on his pants, chugging water as everyone laughed.

The man was crying and shoving a napkin in his mouth when Eva walked over to the table by herself.

"Excuse me," she asked. "Are those really hot?"

The guy spat the orange-and-white napkin from his mouth and nodded. "These wings are from another planet, kid."

Eva tried to keep her expression steady. "I bet I can eat one."

The two guys looked at each other and laughed. "No way," one said. "Where are your parents?" asked the other.

Braque saw Eva point to her and waved back from her seat a few booths away. The two guys smiled at Braque, and she took it as her cue to walk over.

"How much would you give me to finish one?" Eva asked Napkin Guy.

"I think you should leave these nice men alone," Braque said. "Those wings actually look really hot."

"Yeah, they're no joke," Napkin Guy said.

"I'm serious, how much?" Eva asked.

Braque tugged on Eva's arm. "Come on. These aren't like the ones Mom makes at home."

"I'll put down ten bucks," Napkin Guy's friend said. "But you gotta eat the whole thing."

"Twenty for two?" Eva asked.

"No way she gets past the first one," Napkin Guy said, looking at Eva.

"I'll even eat more than two," Eva said.

"No you won't," Braque said. "You're gonna get sick and they're gonna take all our money."

Their strategy was working; Napkin Guy now looked like a man who thought he smelled blood. "OK, then. Let's do forty for four. You girls got forty bucks?"

"Forty bucks?" the guy's friend asked him.

"It'd cover our tab," Napkin Guy said, and his friend nodded, pleased with the reasoning.

The waiter, a skinny young dude with a dark beard and a red plaid shirt, walked over and positioned himself between Eva and the table. His nametag read DANE.

"How's everything over here?" Dane asked, smiling professionally, putting his hands on the table. "You enjoying the Circle of Hell Wings?"

"You ever see this girl in here before?" Napkin Guy's friend asked Dane. It was a savvy question, Braque thought. Dane shook his head.

"We don't typically allow minors to eat these wings," Dane said. "Where's her parent or legal guardian?"

"Here," Braque said, stepping forward.

Dane seemed impressed. "Are you willing to sign a waiver?"

Braque shrugged, and put forty dollars on the table. "If she is. This is all on her. She's gotta learn one way or another."

"OK," Dane said. He pulled a piece of paper and a pen from the front pocket of his apron and handed it to Braque. "She doesn't need to sign it, just you."

Afterward, Dane took the signed waiver back, folded it, and picked up the money from the table. He'd evidently done this kind of thing before. "And this is the pot, right here? Eighty bucks? What's the bet exactly?"

Napkin Guy pushed the plate of wings in Eva's direction. "She has to completely eat four wings. If she does, she gets the money. Otherwise we do."

"I'm gonna go grab her milkshake," Braque said.

"Nope," Napkin Guy said. "Nothing, until she's done with the wings." Now the two guys were getting edgy. The sooner they started this the better. Eva climbed into the booth as Napkin Guy made room.

Eva looked at the assembled adults. "Just tell me when," she said, looking at the plate of simmering orange chunks.

"OK, go," Dane said.

Eva picked up the four wings in turn, and with the beautiful focus of a woodpecker boring a hole, she completely cleaned them back to front in just over a minute, setting down the fleshless bones in a neat little row.

"Holy shit," Braque said.

"No kidding," Napkin Guy's friend said.

"They were a little hotter than I expected," Eva said, turning to Napkin Guy. "I'm sorry for doubting you. These were the real deal."

Napkin Guy stared at Eva. "Hustler," he said, not being funny.

Dane handed the eighty bucks over to Braque. "I think this belongs to you guys."

Braque took the money, nodded, thanked everyone for their tolerance, and pulled Eva safely away from the unhappy men and back to their own table.

"Jesus," Braque said. "I had no idea."

"You didn't think I could win? I thought you were just being a real good actor."

Braque handed Eva fifty dollars. "Well, here's your sixty percent. You owe me two bucks."

"Those wings weren't actually the real deal," Eva said, pocketing the money. "I was just trying to make him feel better."

7:39 P.M.

Eva and Braque made $180 at Jack Cermak's before complaints from the nosy wait staff and whiny-ass sore losers forced them out. Then they made a quick five bucks at the famous Every 1's A Wiener hot dog stand in Andersonville just for taking a bite from a Fire Dog. Eva actually took two bites, because that's just who she was.

After travel and expenses, Eva had almost ninety dollars, and Braque made about seventy dollars, and the big score still awaited them. For an hour, Eva had been begging to go to Hell Night already, but Braque wanted to wait until it got closer to eight, figuring it would be late enough to miss her teammates. Those girls were just like she was: early-to-bed types who were up doing squats at 6:00 a.m. because they were focused on what mattered. Which reminded her.

On the way to the Berwyn El stop, and on the train all the way to the Addison stop, and while walking to The Truth on Clark, Braque made Eva quiz her for the Nineteenth-Century U.S. History final, using flash cards she'd made.

"President from 1853 to 1857?" Eva asked.

"Franklin Pierce, Democrat."

"Who did he defeat in the election of 1852?"

"Winfield Scott, Whig Party."

"Vice president?"

"William Rufus DeVane King."

"Are they really going to ask you that tomorrow?"

"It's a final on the whole century, I have to be prepared for everything."

"I think you're gonna do OK on this final."

"Ask me another one."

"What's this line of people for?"

A ribbon of people, mostly husky white dudes, lined one side of Clark Street. Braque looked up ahead. The line wound into the doorway of The Truth Kitchen & Barbecue Pit.

Braque looked at a guy standing near the front. He had dirty leather clothes and beady eyes and looked as if he stress-tested motorcycle helmets for a living.

"This the line for The Truth?" Braque asked.

"The hell you say?" the beady-eyed man said.

Behind him, an eager-eyed frat-boy type in an American Eagle polo was more of a help. "Yep, sure is," he said. "Been here two hours already. Sign up in there and get in line."

Someone behind him said, "The line goes all the way to Grace Street!"

Braque turned to Eva and was about to say, "Looks like we're screwed," but Eva was already bolting into the restaurant, past the maître d's station, and into the crowded, sticky mayhem of The Truth on Hell Night.

8:10 P.M.

Even on a regular night, The Truth was intolerable. The floor was coated in sawdust, music that could only be described as cock-metal blasted on the sound system, Christmas lights flashed out of sync at a headache-inducing pace, and the walls were covered with faux-homey wooden signs that said shit like:

YOU ARE NEVER

2 OLD

2 DRINK

2 MANY

6 PACKS

And:

FREE BEER: TOMORROW

And:

LADIES 18–30:
NO SHIRT, NO SHOES, NO PROBLEM!

And now the place was at, or quite possibly in excess of, the fire marshal's maximum capacity, the majority of whom were men—loud, beefy, tattooed, openly leering men—choking down their first bites of The Truth XXX ghost pepper chili, pummeling their open mouths with full steins of pissy lager, screaming, bellowing, swearing, gasping, crying.

Eva was calm, surveying the room like a walk-on first-year outfielder looking for her parents in the stands. Braque grabbed her cousin's arm.

"We're gonna get thrown out of here," she said.

"The line is for a table," Eva said. "We don't need a table for what we're doing. Oh, look, I recognize those people. From your wall calendar."

Braque looked where Eva was pointing. Patricia, Tangela, Maya, Ann Richards, Ann's gay friend Nate, and starting junior catcher Rachael "Thunder" Rhodes—a wide-hipped Nebraskan with a left arm that nailed 46 percent of attempted base stealers—sat around five mostly untouched Styrofoam bowls of chili, cramming bread into their mouths and drinking milk and water.

"*You made it!*" Patricia said, running across the room to hug Braque. "Is this your cousin? Come join us!" And so Braque had to. She introduced Eva to everybody, and, once they had jammed into the booth, withstood a volley of questions about why she had changed her mind and joined them, and wasn't she supposed to be studying, and all of that shit.

"I didn't know your cousin was finally visiting. What have you been doing?" Patricia asked.

"How much will you give us to watch her eat some of that chili?" Braque asked.

"This chili?" Maya asked. "I can hardly eat a bite of this chili."

"Yeah, how much would you bet that Eva can't eat two spoonfuls of it?"

"Two spoonfuls?" Maya said. "Better have some milk ready."

"How much?"

Maya looked at the chili. "I'd pay ten bucks to see her try, but I don't think anyone that size can handle that."

"I don't know," Tangela said. "I'm out."

"Twenty bucks," said Rachael Rhodes. "To eat, chew, and swallow."

"I'll do five," Patricia said.

"I think she can do it," Ann Richards said. "I'm not betting against her."

"I don't gamble," said Nate.

"Money on the table?" Eva said, putting thirty-five of her own dollars down.

Maya passed a white Styrofoam bowl over, and Patricia grabbed a clean spoon from the cylinder in the middle of the table. Eva took it and immediately scooped up a spoonful of chili.

"Oh my God, I can't believe she's actually going to do this," Patricia said.

"How old is she?" Tangela asked.

"Eleven," Eva said.

"Get a big, heaping pile on your spoon," Rachael said. Christ, Rachael could be a bitch.

To Eva's credit, she plunged the spoon back in without protest, presented a mound of steaming red and brown chunks, and thrust it into her mouth.

For the first time all night, Braque saw that Eva was in evident pain. Eva pulled the spoon from her lips as color ran to her face, and she slowly moved the chunky chili around in her mouth. She closed her eyes and the lumps disappeared from her cheeks and crawled down her throat. Her tongue poked from her mouth and did a full, slow circuit around her lips. She opened her mouth and her eyes, exhaled, and immediately ate another heaping bite.

"Fuckin' A," Rachael said.

"I told you! I told you bitches!" Ann Richards said, leaning forward to give Tangela Bass a high five, and both women who hadn't bet against Eva high-fived her in turn. Other than that forced show of solidarity, Eva gathered the money without a word or change in expression.

"How was it?" Braque asked.

"Whoa," Eva said.

"Could you eat more?"

Eva nodded enthusiastically. "But gimme a minute."

Then came the barrage of questions about where Eva developed her tolerance for hot spices, where else they'd been that night (everyone was somehow equally amazed that she ate the Circle of Hell Wings at Jack Cermak's), and how much more she could eat, because the team totally wanted to soak this room of gross, cocky men for everything they had.

"Before we start," Braque asked, "where's the crapper in this hellhole?"

"Through the gift shop," Maya said.

Of course it's through the fucking gift shop.

8:31 P.M.

The Truth's gift shop was worse than Braque had imagined. First of all, there wasn't a straight path through it; it zigzagged like a duty-free store in an international terminal, forcing you to reckon with the words THE TRUTH on every conceivable piece of Made-in-China crap known to humanity—shirts, caps, mugs, steins, keychains, license-plate frames, trucker hats, vests, and belt buckles. They also had a full line of Truth Sauce, Truth Rub, Truth Spice, and something else that caught Braque's attention.

Braque walked to the register. "How is this sweet pepper jelly?"

The young tattooed woman behind the counter nodded. "All of the food products here are actually pretty decent. They're made locally in Batavia."

"Have you had this?"

"I've only tried the green. The green is awesome."

"OK, I'll go back and get the green."

By the time she returned to the register, there was a line. The guy right in front of her was the American Eagle polo guy from the line outside. His face was flushed and sweaty, his eyes looked bloodshot, and he was holding a golden ticket in his hand. Braque wasn't going to say jack shit to this weirdo, but he turned and looked at her.

"Oh, hey, Miss Cut-in-Front-of-Everybody," he said, not unfriendly.

"I was meeting a group of people here," Braque said.

"Oh. Well, why didn't ya say so? I thought you were gonna start a riot out there after you bolted in here like that."

"I don't fuckin' care," Braque said.

"I like your attitude," the dude said. He stepped forward to the now-empty space in front of the register and handed his ticket to the woman behind it.

"How quick did you finish it, Benny?" the woman asked, taking the ticket.

"Three minutes, four seconds," Benny said.

"What's your size?"

"Men's large," Benny said, and when the woman handed him a black T-shirt, he put it on over his polo. The shirt read I CAN HANDLE THE TRUTH'S HELL CHILI on the front in a garish font, and HELL NIGHT, THE TRUTH, CHICAGO ILLINOIS on the back.

"You just got here," Braque said. "You've already finished a whole bowl of that chili?"

"Ah, it's way weaker this year. What are you getting? Aw, that stuff is the bomb."

"Glad you approve," Braque said, handing the green sweet pepper jelly to the woman. It was then that it occurred to her that she should've just stolen this shit; why was she buying it and supporting this awful establishment?

"Do you know who makes the best sweet pepper jelly in the world?"

Braque hated it when people, guys especially, asked the kinds of questions that only they evidently knew the answers to. "I don't care," she said.

"It's this woman down in New Mexico. But you gotta go there in person. She won't let you order it online."

"I'll be sure and ask you all about it," Braque said.

"That'll be $5.10," the woman behind the counter said.

"Have you handed out a lot of those T-shirts tonight?" Braque asked.

"No, that's the first," the woman said.

Braque was actually going to turn and congratulate Benny, sort of, but he was gone.

8:37 P.M.

Braque sat in a Pepto-Bismol pink toilet stall in the otherwise empty women's bathroom and opened the jar of green sweet pepper jelly. Even with the sound of AC/DC playing and the smell of cheap bleach rising to her face, the scent of the jelly overwhelmed her senses. She realized that she had forgotten to bring a spoon or fork with her, but then she realized that she hadn't forgotten at all; this was an impulse buy. Why wasn't she offered one at the register? Probably because the woman didn't assume that she was darting off to eat it in the bathroom. So, OK, fine. She plunged her fingers in and drew a handful of warm green goop to her mouth.

Oh, wow. It was the best thing she had ever tasted. This was the best thing she'd ever done in her life, maybe. She smeared another handful across her tongue. It was incredible. What had she been waiting for? What *had* she been waiting for?

Her phone buzzed. She wiped her hands on the single-ply toilet paper and pulled the phone out of her bag. It read TOLD YOU.

She had to sit and think about this for a second.

Braque was still pretty damn sure that what she'd been seeing around all day—the ephemeral SWET PEPER JELY on a protein bar, on the campus Rock, on her new phone—was some kind of madly subjective fever dream. She didn't even bother to tell Patricia about it, and she told Patricia everything. She might have been making it all up.

So, that confirmed, she didn't see the harm in writing back.

YOU WEREN'T FUCKING KIDDING, she typed. THIS SHIT IS AMAZ-ING. WHY DO I LIKE IT SO MUCH?

BECAUSE I LIKE IT, it wrote back.

Braque typed, WHY CAN'T YOU LIKE SOMETHING NON-PROCESSED AND LOW-CALORIE?

ARE WE GOING TO NEW MEXICO RIGHT NOW, it wrote.

NO, WE'RE NOT GOING AT ALL, Braque typed. TOUGH TITTY.

BUT THE BEST SWET PEPER JELY IS IN NEW MEXICO THE GUY SAID.

SCREW THAT GUY, Braque typed.

NO WERE GOING, it typed back.

Bile rose in Braque's throat, and she vomited up her side salad and the recent green pepper jelly all over the tile in front of the toilet.

DID YOU JUST MAKE ME DO THAT? she typed.

YEP, it wrote.

WELL FUCK YOU, Braque wrote. If this wasn't happening, and she was hallucinating or dreaming this, she might as well take a hard line.

WERE GOING TO NEW MEXICO, it wrote. IT WIL CHANGE YOUR LIFE.

Braque threw her phone in her bag. She left the stall, and even though two excessively perfumed chicks were staring at her from over by the sinks, she stood there and shoved the last fistfuls of amazing, beautiful jelly into her mouth.

When she was done, she cleaned out the last flecks in the jar with her tongue as they watched, and threw the empty thing in the bathroom trash.

8:48 P.M.

There was an immense noise coming from the main part of the restaurant, like what happens in sports bars during the Stanley Cup or World Series or Super Bowl or that kind of thing. Cheering and thumping and then a huge applause. The woman who was supposed to be behind the register wasn't there; she was standing on the border between the gift shop and the restaurant, watching whatever was happening in the dining room. Everyone that Braque could see had their backs turned to the gift shop.

Braque made her move. She grabbed all of the jars of green sweet pepper jelly and a few reds and crammed them into her shoulder bag. As she shoved two more into her pockets, she thought maybe she'd have one now. Why the hell not?

The roar of the crowd noise got closer, and Braque rose, fist and mouth full of delicious green sweet pepper jelly. She peeked over the top of the aisle just in time to see her cousin being carried aloft by her softball team and set down on the counter by the register. Benny took off his own HELL NIGHT T-shirt and slid it over Eva. Ann and Tangela raised Eva up again, and the crowd roared.

When it finally hit Braque what was happening, she shouted and raised her green-stained fist in the air. Catching her cousin's eye, she pushed toward Eva, reaching for her hand, just as Eva bent at the waist and vomited a flume of steaming brown and red chunks all over the cash register. It smelled like a cross between a fart and a burning tire.

The smell made Braque's throat open and evacuate a full eight ounces of undigested green slime onto the floor. What a scene! People backed away groaning and shouting. Someone called for a janitor. In the midst of it all, glowing with rude joy and shining with vomit, Braque at last grabbed her little cousin's hand, and raised it to the sky.

WALLEYE

It was not just Will Prager's opinion, but also unbiased fact, that in order to get girls in high school you had to have a *thing*. Maybe your thing was that your mom or dad was a lawyer and you lived in a nice house with a pool. Maybe it was rock-hard abs. Maybe your thing was that you were a computer nerd and you spent Prom Night in your parents' basement, listening to Rush and thinking about string theory. There was someone for everyone, just so long as you *were* someone.

Until freshman year, Will Prager didn't have a thing. He was smart, but not a super-genius, and played sports, but not well enough to ever get a scholarship somewhere. Then some seniors who were in a band called Smarmy Kitten invited him personally to one of their shows. Their lead guitarist, Brandon Spencer, who always wore T-shirts of really obscure stuff like Merzbow and Tzadik Records, and was the coolest guy in the band, looked Prager in the eye and said, "Hey man, you should come to our gig. You'd like it." Well, he did, and that was it. Ever since, Will Prager's thing was music.

In the summer of '05 alone, he drove the forty-five minutes from River Falls, Wisconsin, to Minneapolis ten times, and saw Built to Spill, Drive-By Truckers, Spoon, Heiruspecs, Dillinger Four, Boiled in Lead, Maitiera, Tapes 'n Tapes, the Owls, and Atmosphere with Brother Ali, mostly with his friends Vik Gupta and Ken Kovacs. He also started a band called the Lonesome Cowboys, with Vik on drums, Ken on bass, Zach Schmetterling on pedal steel, Erick Travis on violin, and Will on lead guitar and vocals. Their thing was that they played sad cowboy music, and played cover songs in the style of sad cowboy music. Their cover of "No Diggity" was off the chain! It made hot girls forget you were a dork, which is the point of all music. Girls were lucky, they didn't have to have a thing. They just had to look nice and come to your shows and not call you all the time about stupid stuff.

But the new girl in the back of Killer Keeley's fifth-period American History class, first day of school, junior year—she for sure had a thing. She had on oxblood Doc Martens, black nail polish, a black miniskirt, bright red Manic Panic hair, and a white T-shirt that read THE SMITHS and MEAT IS MURDER. Total Goth.

"What was North America like before the Europeans arrived?" Killer Keeley asked. Will Prager raised his hand, and Killer Keeley continued looking around the classroom. It was time for Prager to set the tone for how the year was gonna go.

"Anyone else?" Mr. Keeley asked. He somehow already knew better than to call on Prager, but no one else had his hand up. It was fifth period, right after lunch, so everyone was in a food coma, and it was eighty-five degrees outside, and the question was insultingly broad.

"I just want to be in love," Prager said. "Will you help me or not?"

"I didn't call on you, William," said Keeley.

Prager sang the first lines of "Where Is the Love," and the cute new girl in back, the Goth, laughed.

Rumor was Killer Keeley had gone soft over the last couple years. Now, thanks to Prager, he was losing his new batch of juniors in record time.

• • •

At the end of class, Prager got a good look at the girl who'd laughed at his heartbreaking rendition of the Roberta Flack/Donny Hathaway soul classic. She was even hotter than at first glance. She had boobs and an ass that looked too amazing for mere Wisconsin boys and their cold, jittery hands; he imagined her in Miami, riding a dolphin while wearing a bikini, capsizing sailboats full of horny men. Plus she was tall, at least six-two, which was cool with Prager, because he was six-four. And she thought he was funny, which was also pretty sexy.

An hour later, walking into Madame DuPlessis's seventh-period French class, he saw her seated in the back, and probably smiled when he saw her, but tried not to in case she saw him. The seat to her left was open, and even though he didn't like sitting in the back row because his vision wasn't so good, he took it.

"Hey," he said, glancing in her direction.

"Hey," she said brightly, and even welcomingly, he thought.

"What's your name?" he asked.

"Eva," she said. "You?"

Uh-oh. He had to think for a second how to phrase it in a way that sounded memorable. "Will, Will Prager," he said. Now he had to keep the conversation flowing somehow. "So, you like the Smiths?" he asked, looking at her shirt while simultaneously trying not to stare at her chest.

"Yeah, they're OK," she said.

"You a vegetarian?" he asked.

"No," she said. "I just wanted a Smiths shirt. You?"

"Yeah, just started," he said. He'd seen a documentary about chickens at Ken Kovacs's house the week before that had converted both him and Ken. It was now another thing they both had, in addition to their band.

Madame DuPlessis stood in front of the class, dressed for the heat in a sleeveless sundress, straight brown hair glistening under the fluorescent lights. She was kinda cute but she was also the mom of a kid who was a freshman, so that was weird.

"*Regardez ici, s'il vous plaît*," Madame DuPlessis said.

"*À bientôt*," Will Prager said to Eva. Damn, that was smooth, he thought, as he turned his attention to the teacher.

They had to speak and write things in French for the next fifty minutes and there was limited time for meaningful interaction until the bell rang, which, after a burning eternity, it finally did.

"You like Radiohead?" Will asked Eva. He was hoping that she'd linger and talk with him, but she was clearing her desk too quickly, sweeping her books into a black shoulder bag.

"Yeah, they're cool," she said. She seemed to be in a hurry.

"My band does a couple Radiohead covers," Prager said. He had to work in the fact that he was in a band before it was too late. "We have rehearsal tonight."

"What's the name of the band?" she asked, standing up.

"The Lonesome Cowboys."

"Cool, maybe I'll check you guys out sometime," she said. "Nice to meet you."

"What are your plans tonight?"

"Going to make French onion soup with my dad," she said. "Catch you tomorrow." And with that, she was gone.

That night when he got home, Prager found this recipe in a cookbook in his dad's kitchen:

French Onion Soup (Serves 8)

¼ cup unsalted butter
5 medium onions, thinly sliced
1 bay leaf
½ teaspoon dried thyme
2 tablespoons dry sherry
3½ cups beef stock
1½ teaspoons kosher salt
½ teaspoon black pepper
8 slices of French bread, toasted
1½ cups Gruyère cheese

Heat the butter in a soup pot over medium heat until it is melted. Add the onions, bay leaf, and thyme. After 15 minutes, or as soon as the onions begin to brown, reduce the heat to medium low and cover, stirring frequently, until the onions assume a deep brown hue, about 30–40 minutes. Take care to not overcook the onions; patience is essential for perfect caramelization. Stir in the sherry.

Increase the heat to high, stirring vigorously, until all the sherry has cooked off. Stir in the beef stock, bring to a boil, and then simmer for 20 minutes while partially covered. Sprinkle with salt and pepper. Remove the bay leaf before serving. Place eight ovenproof bowls on baking sheets. Fill each bowl with soup, top the bowl with one thin slice of toasted French bread, and gently cover each with 3 tablespoons of cheese. Bake in an oven at 450°F until the cheese is melted and becoming just a bit brown. Use Gruyère from Switzerland, or you'll be wasting your time.

It was so beautiful, and strict, and complicated! Prager could never conceive of making such a meal. That someone his age would make this, a hot girl he liked, no less, made him feel inadequate and lustful.

• • •

Will Prager's father, Eli, was in the living room, watching the first *Monday Night Football* game of the season, while Prager sat on the kitchen floor, about ten feet away, on the linoleum, still poring over the recipe. Eli was shorter and skinnier than his son, but somehow took up more space in a room; his scarred face, long biker beard, and the sharp greasy smell from his motorcycle shop had the effect of wet wood tossed on a campfire, and no one blocked his path, even at home.

"Hey, Dad," Prager asked, "can we make French onion soup sometime?"

"French onion soup?" Eli asked. "What the hell you want that for?"

"I don't know, something different," Prager said. "But what's the deal with Gruyère from Switzerland? This recipe is super anal that the cheese has to be from Switzerland."

"Who the hell knows? That cookbook's from the early seventies. I don't think farmers in Wisconsin made that kinda cheese back then."

"Who got this cookbook?"

"The damn thing belonged to your mother," Eli said. He sometimes talked about her as if her death were a jackknifed semi on the road ahead. Will viewed it more like the giant crack in their concrete driveway; he felt it, saw it, and walked over it every day, but it was too big and strange to fix.

"Then we should keep it," Prager said.

His sister, Julie, jogged into the kitchen and took a protein shake out of the fridge. She was in her usual summer outfit of cotton T-shirt with the neck and sleeves cut off, sports bra, and running shorts. It had been six months since their mom's death, and Prager was a little worried about how his little sister was handling it. She and their mother hadn't been getting along when their mom died. Since then, Julie had quit the softball team, which was weird, and now only did cross-country running, and hardly had friends over anymore. People kept asking Prager if his sister was depressed, and he wasn't sure what to say. She was a thirteen-year-old girl, the most puzzling and mutable creature in the known universe.

"Dad, you make anything, or are we on our own for dinner?" Julie asked.

Eli didn't look up from the game. "If you want to order something, knock yourself out."

"God, Dad," Julie said. "You can be so indolent." She was super into big words all the time, for no reason.

"If you don't like it, you can skedaddle," Eli said.

"What are you doing for food?" Julie asked Will.

"I'm gonna heat up a microwave burrito," Prager said. "Then I'm gonna eat it over the sink like a total baller."

"You're so frickin' lazy it kills me. You won't even wash one stupid plate."

"Nope," Prager said, watching the three-minute digital timer start its countdown.

He couldn't stop thinking about Eva for some reason. Her face. Her awesome, beautiful height. The things she said and the way she said them. Damn. Will Prager liked a girl. And her thing was cooler than just being a Goth. It was food.

Hanging out by the vending machines before school the next day, Prager asked his drummer, Vik Gupta, where to take a girl out to eat in Minneapolis, if she's into food. Vik's dad was a tenured professor at UW–River Falls and took his family to some real nice places.

"Let's see. I liked Goodfellows," Vik said. "Café Un Deux Trois. Hutmacher's. Locanda di Giorgio. But they're all *très cher*." The French sounded fine coming from Vik. He was one of those guys who wore a tie to school, and the Nils P. Haugen Senior High standards of taste only required that you wore a shirt with no swear words on it. "Who's the girl?"

"She's new, her name is Eva Thorvald."

"New blood," said Vik. "Go big, Prager, blow her away. A first date calls for the most opulent luxury."

"Well, that's kind of the opposite of what I've been doing my whole life," Will said. "I thought you didn't want to set the bar too high right away."

"You're single now, right? That means that all of your previous plans have failed. Do you like this girl?"

"I think the most ever."

"Then you, sir, have no choice."

It took forever for fifth period to come around. She looked even more amazing than he remembered. She had almost the same outfit on except a Nick Cave shirt this time.

"How was the French onion soup?" he asked. He had figured this out with his last girlfriend—women love it when you remember shit they tell you, and love it more when you repeat it back to them. But in this case, he was genuinely curious about the soup.

"Oh, it was OK, thanks for asking," Eva said.

"Just OK, huh?"

"Yeah. My dad bought me blue cheese by accident instead of Gruyère, because it was cheaper. So it wasn't exactly how it's supposed to be, I guess. The cheese really overpowered the broth."

"You know, for French onion soup, the Gruyère from Switzerland is the best."

"Wow," she said. "I wouldn't know."

Will had thought for a long time about how he was going to phrase his next question, the big one. He wasn't dealing with his freshman ex-girlfriend anymore; this girl was a sophisticated junior, and she was seriously into food. He took a deep breath. "How'd you like to go on a culinary adventure?"

"With you?"

Killer Keeley rapped Prager's desk with a ruler. "William," he said. "Front row." Damn, Keeley picked a crappy time to get his groove back.

"Yes," Prager said, looking back at Eva as he moved up four desks.

"Sure, sounds fun," she said, and her smile scattered every other thought in his mind. He spent the rest of the class entranced, watching Keeley's mouth make noise, as he luxuriated in the hopeful blood shimmering through his veins.

Eli was eating Fritos out of the bag and reading the sports section when Will walked into the kitchen and leaned against the counter.

"Dad, I really need to use the car Friday."

Eli didn't look up. "Why, what's happening?"

"I got a date with a girl."

"Ah, that's funny, I have a date that night myself."

"You have a date?" This was the first Will had heard of his dad dating anyone since their mom died. It had never even occurred to him that his dad would ever date anyone again, much less have sex, or even want to.

Considering how his mom died, hurled from the back of his dad's Harley Panhead, in an accident that left Eli with just a sprained ankle, and also considering that Eli had not been on a motorcycle since then, it seemed to follow that his dad would be in a state of perpetual mourning, and this course of action had Will's and Julie's approval. Anything else felt like hateful treason.

"Yeah, a woman I met at church."

That was another thing, much less devastating, but dumbly annoying: Eli had started going to early services at a Lutheran church after the funeral. Prager totally didn't get this at all. Prager's grandpa on his dad's side was a nonpracticing Ashkenazi Jew named Frank who had had the misfortune of marrying a devout Lutheran woman named Greta who raised all of their kids, including Eli, strict Missouri Synod Lutheran. And even though Will wasn't technically Jewish because neither his mom nor his grandmas was Jewish, being raised Jewish would have been a thing, and Prager knew he would've loved it.

Eli, meanwhile, refused to recognize any of the traditions, mostly because he didn't know them, so it was up to Prager to hold his own Passover Seder and observe the High Holy Days and set out a menorah on Hanukkah and get noisemakers for Purim. Eli neither encouraged nor prevented any of this.

Prager, however, totally disapproved of his own dad's religious practices, especially if it meant that he was using Lutheran Bible study class as a meet market.

"Oh," Prager said. "Where are you going?"

"Just Luigi's, downtown there."

"Oh," was all he said. It was too much to take in.

"You can have the car that night, if you don't mind dropping me off."

"Oh," Prager said. What an awful bargain; what a shadow cast over what could've been such an incredible night.

"Hey," Eva said before fifth period the next day. "Just letting you know. My dad wants me home by nine at the latest."

"Oh," Prager said. That was sure some overprotective dad bullshit right there. It just about killed having dinner in Minneapolis, unless they ate at six or something. What a better world it would be without people's dads.

"And he wants to meet you," Eva said.

"Up here, William," said Killer Keeley, pointing at Prager's head. "Now."

Prager turned up The Current 89.3 as he drove his dad down Main Street toward Luigi's. They were playing "Ashes of American Flags," by Wilco. His dad turned down the volume without asking.

"Hey, so who you going out with tonight?" his dad asked, unnervingly chipper.

"Just this new girl." Prager didn't feel like talking. He felt almost like his mom was still alive and he was driving his dad to meet his dad's mistress. He thought for a second about rear-ending the car in front of him, just to put the kibosh on his dad's awful plans, but the fact that he had his own wildly anticipated date greatly overrode any impulse to sabotage his father's.

"What's she like?"

"I don't know yet."

"Well, I'll tell you about the woman I'm meeting. Her name is Pat. She's a widow, her husband died three years ago. She's got one kid, a little boy named Sam. And she's younger than me, thirty-five."

"Sounds great," Prager said. He hoped that his dad came across like how he really was, not how he was behaving tonight, all bright-voiced and interested, and would drive this woman, and all women, away screaming forever. There was reason to be hopeful for this. He stopped at the curb down the block from Luigi's. "Is right here OK?"

"Sure," Eli said. "Well, good luck on your date, and we'll swap notes in the morning, huh?" Eli raised his eyebrows in that *hubba hubba* motion. Mortifying.

"See ya," Prager said.

"Love ya, kid," Eli said, and walked to the front door, fifteen minutes early for his horrible date with the Lutheran widow.

Eva and her family lived in a stout tan-colored apartment building farther down Main, near the Knowles Center. The paint on the sides of the building was chipping and faded and the parking lot was mostly filled with cars that looked like they were abandoned at an impound lot: old, but none old enough to be cool. It was not the sort of place where you'd ever guess someone as amazing as Eva might live. Prager had probably passed this place a million times and never really noticed it. Now he was here, parking his dad's Ford Taurus in the lot, his heart punching his sternum, walking across fast-food wrappers and cigarette butts to reach her door. There was an RC Cola vending machine outside the lobby under an overhang; someone had taped a handwritten sign to it that read BUSTED.

"Hey, Will," she said. He didn't even see her standing there, watering plants on a first-floor patio. She was wearing a black babydoll dress, a German army jacket, and fingerless gloves. That outfit, and her smile, made him want to throw himself at her feet.

"Oh, hey," he said, not taking off his sunglasses. "I guess we'd better skedaddle." Did he just say that? God, he was a dork sometimes.

"Hey, come in for a sec, my dad wants to meet you."

He was hoping she'd forgotten this part.

The man introduced as Jarl Thorvald sat in a poofy navy blue lounge chair, watching the game show *What a Life* and drinking Old Style out of a can tucked in a bright blue beer koozie. He stood up after Eva and Prager closed the door behind them. Prager's first impression was that he hardly looked like Eva at all; this guy was short, fat, bald, and wearing a half-buttoned short-sleeved shirt, a loosened blue tie, and stained sweatpants. He did not look like a man capable of cooking, or even eating, French onion soup with blue cheese, let alone with Gruyère from Switzerland.

"How do you do?" Jarl asked, after they were introduced from afar. He buttoned his shirt to the top and straightened his tie.

Prager took in the small, dim apartment as he walked over to the living room. Even with the porch drapes closed and only the kitchen light on, he could see how underfurnished the place was; the living room had no couch, just a lounge chair and a folding chair, a black TV and DVD player on a cheap particleboard stand, a glass table in the dinette with two padded folding chairs that was stacked with sports magazines and beer cans, and nothing on any of the walls except a giveaway wall calendar from a local bank. It looked like the apartment of a man who lived alone; there was no evidence of a teenage girl anywhere.

"So I hear you're in a band," Jarl said, and took another swallow of Old Style. His beer koozie said KEEPIN' IT REEL and had a picture of a fisherman on it. "What kind of music?"

"Sad country ballads," Prager said.

"You like Jimmy Buffett?"

Weird question, Prager thought. Jimmy Buffett wasn't close to what he would call country. He thought that Jimmy Buffett was music for people who hated music. But he looked at Jarl there, the father of the object of his affection, considered the man's decisive way of phrasing his opinion, and said, "He's OK, I guess."

"OK? He's the most influential musician of the twentieth century. That's what he is."

Not even close, Prager thought. Not even in the top one thousand. Maybe he was somewhere in the fourteen hundreds, between Poco and Edison Lighthouse.

"So, your parents OK with you being a *country* musician?"

"Yeah," Prager said. "My dad doesn't mind, and my mom, she, uh, she passed away, but I like to think that wherever she is, she's a fan." Prager nodded and pursed his lips. He didn't talk about her often, but when he did, he badly wanted to bring her up in conversation like he was over it, so he could put other people at ease.

"We should go, Dad," Eva said.

"Oh yeah, that's right," the old man said, exuding the enthusiasm and authority of a school custodian. "Be back by nine."

"I know." Eva kissed Jarl on the cheek and led Prager to the front door.

"Hey," Jarl said. "Where are you two going?"

Eva looked at Prager, as if to say, *Better tell him.*

"Steamboat Inn, down in Prescott," Prager said. It was the nicest restaurant he could find nearby. He'd wanted it to be a surprise.

• • •

Eva looked at Prager as he unlocked the passenger-side door for her.

"I'm sorry about your mom," she said. "I didn't know."

"It's sad, but it happens," he said, repeating the line he always said in this situation, staring past her at the grocery store across the street.

"My mom died too, two years ago," Eva said.

"Really?" he said. "Of what?"

"Lung cancer. Yours?"

"Motorcycle accident."

"Come here," she said, and hugged him, right there in the parking lot, in front of everybody letting their kids out of minivans and hauling bags of groceries and driving by in sports cars. When, after at least ten seconds, they let go of each other—him first—Prager looked at her. She now looked older, like a woman, a woman whose hand he could take and stride into the darkness with, because she was a woman whose darkness matched his own, and they could fix each other without even trying. They wouldn't even have to talk about it.

In the car, Eva explained that she and her dad had moved to River Falls from Mankato, where Jarl had been working as a parking lot attendant before he was let go after some misunderstanding. Through no fault of his own, she said, it had taken him a long time to find work. A company in River Falls called Loomis Home Products that made novelty beer koozies for truck stop gift shops finally hired him part-time last month to work in shipping. She asked Prager if he wanted a beer koozie and he said sure, so she dug around in her black bag and, laughing, gave him one that read SEXY GRAN'PA.

"I will treasure it always," he said. He realized that might have sounded sarcastic, but even if it sounded cheesy, he meant it. She'd given him something, something of hers, and it felt like a piece of her heart, and confirmation that she liked him. He didn't know where else to put it for the moment, so he placed Sexy Gran'pa on his dashboard, between his eyes and the road, and it glowed under the passing lights.

The radio was playing "Super Bon Bon" by Soul Coughing. He turned up the volume way past where his dad had left it. He rolled down the driver's side window and stuck his hand out into the night air, the song's deep upright bass riff blasting through their bodies and bouncing off the passing trees and fenceposts and mosquitoes toward the sky. Then she rolled down her window and stuck her arm out as well, and he smiled, and maybe she smiled at him, too.

The Steamboat Inn, a docked steamboat attached to a full restaurant on the shoreline of the St. Croix River, was even fancier than he expected; they had cloth napkins and candles on the tables and no TVs anywhere. He had made a reservation, which he had never done before, and he'd hoped that was as impressive to Eva as it was to him.

It came out while they were parking that Eva had only eaten out twice all year until then, both times during her family's move from Mankato to River Falls, while their kitchen implements were packed in a box in a U-Haul. She had rarely even eaten in restaurants while growing up—just for birthdays and special occasions, she said—except for a trip to Chicago she'd taken at age eleven where she ate out for almost every meal. The way Eva's eyes glimmered when she recounted that memory assured Will Prager that he'd done the right thing for their first outing and certainly taken her to the right place.

They got a nice table not too far away from the windows with a view of the river, though at dusk they could mostly just see the reflection of the interior of the restaurant. They were definitely the youngest people there who weren't there with their parents, and that felt positively badass.

The menu, though, was really expensive, like over fifteen bucks just for most of the dinners, so it was a good thing he'd saved money from his summer job at Sam Goody. One of the cheapest things was the Caesar salad for seven bucks.

"The Caesar salad looks interesting," he said.

"Grilled walleye pike," she said, noting a menu item that cost eighteen bucks. "With dinner salad and your choice of potato."

Prager was used to restaurants where college students or even high schoolers worked as servers. At the Steamboat Inn, they got a woman who was probably in her mid-twenties; an official adult. She came to their table and asked if they wanted anything besides water. "Do you have root beer?" he asked. They did.

"I'll stick with water, thanks," Eva said.

"Do we order now?" he asked the waitress. She said sure, if they're ready, and asked them if perhaps they wanted to hear the specials first?

"Absolutely," Eva said.

The special was roasted maple-glazed Canadian duck over a bed of saffron wild rice, served with Savoy cabbage, for twenty-eight dollars. Prager's palms were sweating. His dad didn't let him have a credit card, and he'd only brought thirty-five bucks with him for the whole date.

"Sounds good," Eva said. "But would you recommend the walleye pike?"

Absolutely, the waitress said, noting that it was freshly caught in Mille Lacs Lake.

"Wow, so you know the specific lake the fish is from?"

The waitress nodded.

"That's cool," Prager said. "Never heard of that."

Eva ordered the walleye, with a baked potato and no dressing on the salad.

The waitress asked Prager if he wanted chicken on his Caesar salad for an extra $3.99.

"Absolutely not," he said. "It's a moral issue."

. . .

When the waitress left, Eva looked Prager in the eyes, all serious.

"Can I tell you why I agreed to all this?"

"Uh, sure," Prager said. The question jolted him; she hadn't even seen his band yet. What else could it be? Was it because he was cute and funny? That'd be nice maybe.

"That thing you said the first day of history class. When you said, 'I just wanna be in love.' Did you mean that?"

He'd said it to be funny; he hadn't really thought whether he meant it or not.

While he was still thinking of how to respond, she leaned in toward him. "Because I thought it was the coolest, most vulnerable, most honest thing I've ever heard anyone say in a classroom, ever."

"I guess I did mean it," he said.

"Good," she said, and leaned back in her chair. "You show promise."

"Do you have a favorite variety of cuisine?" Prager asked, after a time. What sophisticated phrasing, he told himself. If someone was listening to this dinner conversation on the radio, they could seriously be mistaken for adults.

"Nah," she said. "I'll eat pretty much everything. I used to really like spicy food, but not so much anymore."

"Why not?" Prager asked.

"I ate too much one time, and after that I had to give it a break for a while."

"I love spicy stuff. I put Tabasco sauce on almost everything. I put it on yogurt, even."

For some reason, she looked at him the way a mom might look at a teenager who had just bragged about being able to dress himself.

"What?" he asked.

"You shouldn't want to do that," she said. "You should want to taste the actual flavors of what you're eating."

"You have a point," he said. "I'll never use Tabasco sauce again." He'd read that being in an adult relationship means having a willingness to change. Knowing when you're wrong and owning up to it—that's the definition of being a man. He was thrilled for the opportunity to mature before her eyes like this.

"OK." She shrugged.

When the food arrived, the waitress asked if he wanted pepper on his Caesar salad, and held out this long wooden pepper mill thing, which he'd seen before at places once or twice, but never really tried.

"Just a little," he said. "I want to be able to taste the salad."

Eva took one bite of her grilled walleye. Prager watched her as she chewed the fish but didn't swallow, instead moving it around in her mouth. Was this how people who were into food behaved? It was fascinating.

"How is it?" he asked.

"It's very good. Just a little heavy on the rosemary, maybe."

Prager hadn't even remembered seeing rosemary in the description of the dish. "Where's the rosemary?" he asked, pointing at the pine-colored flecks on the filets. "Is it that green stuff?"

"No, that's parsley," she said. "They probably got rid of the rosemary. But if you've had it before, you know the taste." She put a bite on her fork and held it out.

Prager considered reminding her that he was a vegetarian, but with Eva Thorvald about to feed him at the table, from her own fork, he felt he could make an exception one time.

"Yep, absolutely," he said. He had no idea what rosemary even tasted like.

. . .

A few minutes later, the waitress came by with the water pitcher and asked how was everything.

Prager said, "Good, just a shade too much rosemary in her walleye."

The waitress stared at Prager as if he was talking in code. OK, she said, she'd let the chef know.

"Otherwise, it's real good," Eva said as the waitress walked away.

"Want to try some of my salad?" Prager asked.

"No, that's OK," she said, slicing her walleye into small bites, spearing one with a fork she dangled from her grip in the style of an old-timey flapper with a cigarette holder. Prager found her effortless elegance almost heart busting. "You didn't have to volunteer that information. I haven't had a lot of walleye in my life, but this is probably the best I've ever had."

"Weird that it's from a specific lake," was all Prager could think to say.

"I know, right? I wonder how much of it has to do with the lake where the walleye's from, if that's such a big deal?"

Neither of them noticed the wiry old Native American guy in white clothes and a gray ponytail standing next to their table until he spoke.

"Pardon me, I'm Jobe Farnum, I'm the head chef here."

"Hi," Prager said, his mouth full. He and Eva looked at each other. Were they in trouble? Now Prager felt like an idiot for complaining on her behalf. He'd just ruined the entire date, he knew it.

"It's a slow night," the man continued. "So I just wanted to get a look at who's giving me notes on my grilled walleye."

Eva looked up at him. "Oh my God, I'm so sorry," she said. "It's real good. It's probably the best fish I ever had."

"Don't be sorry," Jobe said. "I'm gonna ask you this. Normally, the customer who orders this dish pairs it with a sauvignon blanc. Which pairs well with rosemary. So, let's say I'm curious how this dish can be better prepared for someone who is unable to partake in the wine pairing. What would you do differently? I'm all ears."

"Uh, maybe just a tiny bit less rosemary?" Eva said. "I think everything else in here is real good."

"You perceived the rosemary, which isn't even on the plate. What else do you think is in this dish?"

"You want me to taste it and tell you what's in it?"

Prager quit eating and crossed his arms. Now this chef guy was getting real annoying. The conversation had been going flawlessly until he showed up.

"Give it a shot," Jobe said.

"Oh, boy." Eva swallowed a bite and looked up at Jobe. "Let's see. Parsley. Lemon. *Rosemary*. Black pepper. Salt. And I think it's cooked in butter and something else, some kind of fat or tallow, maybe, I'm not sure."

"Duck fat. Would've been shocked if you got that one. But very good. That was everything."

"It was? It's that simple?"

"It doesn't have to be complicated. This dish won the silver medal at the Taste of Wisconsin last year."

"Wow, really?"

"It's mostly dependent on how fresh the ingredients are. Oh, and that said, you did forget one thing."

This was starting to make Prager want to kick the guy. He caught the waitress's eye, raised the bread basket (they had given them a whole basket of free bread for no reason!), and requested more free bread.

"Oh, duh, the walleye," Eva said.

"Do you make walleye at home?"

"We can't really afford that kinda stuff," Eva said, averting his gaze.

"How often do you cook at home?"

"Every day, usually twice," Eva said, looking back up at Jobe. "It's just me and my dad, and he doesn't cook, so someone's got to."

"And so what do you make at home?"

"I try to do something different every day. I work part-time at a health food store so I get a discount on stuff."

Prager finally had an in. "She works at Whole Earth," he said.

Jobe nodded. "What was the last thing you made?"

"Last night I made a vegetarian lasagna with quinoa pasta."

Prager perked up. "I like quinoa. It's got a lot of protein."

Eva took another bite of her walleye. "I'd love to see how you did this sometime, it's really an amazing piece of fish."

"If you can come by around three or four on a weekday, sure," Jobe said. "Just call me and we'll figure something out."

"What? You're kidding."

"Sure, if you can bring me a few things from Whole Earth. The restaurant will pay you back. "

"Oh my God, sure," Eva said. "Whatever you want. I'll use my employee discount."

It was weird for Prager to see Eva so in awe of somebody.

"I should get back to the kitchen. Nice to meet you," Jobe said, shaking Prager's hand. "And very nice to meet you, Miss?"

"Thorvald, Eva Thorvald," she said.

"Hope to see you soon," Jobe said, and walked away.

"Wow, it was cool for you to know those ingredients," Prager said, but Eva wasn't finished with this moment yet. She was still glowing for at least a minute afterwards.

Prager dug back into his salad. "Just a shade too much lettuce in this," he said.

At the end of the meal, the waitress asked them if they cared to see the dessert menu, and set it down in front of them anyway.

"Nope, I'm totally full," Prager said. "Full, full, full."

"You had too much bread," Eva said. "Yeah, I'll order the blackberry sorbet," she said.

That was a five-dollar dessert. With the walleye, the salad, and the root beer, they were now at $31.92, before tax and tip. He held up his flip phone for her perusal. "Are you sure? It's 8:26 p.m.," he said, now grateful for her curfew.

"Oh, we can fudge it a little," she said. "My dad likes you. He won't mind."

The waitress brought the bill over: $33.52.

"I got it," Prager said. Wasn't the tip supposed to be like 15 percent? This was gonna be like 5 percent. Which was probably real bad. Or were waitresses just happy to get a tip at all? He'd been watching the people who'd finished eating and they all were leaving cash on their tables.

"Well, thank you," Eva said, putting her bag back down on the floor. "I actually forgot my wallet anyway."

Prager wondered if there was still change in the ashtray of his dad's car. Then he saw the waitress walk down the hall toward the restrooms.

"Let's skedaddle," he said, cramming the contents of his wallet under the bill as he stood to pull out Eva's chair for her.

"Well, what an amazing culinary experience," Eva said at 8:59 p.m., when Prager's car parked in front of her apartment.

"Yeah, thanks for coming," he said. He didn't want to risk even The Current playing a vastly inappropriate song in this moment like, say, "The Distance" by Cake, or something by Rage Against the Machine or something, so he had his Built to Spill mix CD playing, and the song "Car" was on, the absolute perfect soundtrack for how he had premeditated this moment in his head.

"No, *thank* you," she said, still sitting in his idling car, not moving.

"No, thank *you*," he said.

"It was a great night," she said.

"Yeah," he said.

She sighed. And then she kissed him. And they kissed for a long-ass time.

On the way home his lips hurt and his hard-on wouldn't go away and he had to turn the defroster on and roll down the windows as he drove home, they'd fogged the car up so bad.

Prager lay down on top of his bed that night, in his clothes, staring up toward the Radiohead poster tacked to the drop ceiling in his bedroom, and he put on the song "In the Aeroplane over the Sea," by Neutral Milk Hotel. Ever since he first heard this song, he wanted someone to think of when he heard it, and now he had her, he had the beautiful face he had found in this place, and he turned off the lights and put the song on repeat, a more complete man than he was that morning, lying there in the dark, falling in love with somebody.

"So why didn't you have sex with her all night long?" Vik Gupta asked him. "If you miss band practice to be with a woman, you should be having sex all night long. In fact, you should be late for school today because you should still be banging her."

Prager leaned against the wall opposite the Pepsi machine. "The night was almost perfect the way it was."

"I should be able to hear you from here. You should be having sex so loud right now, I should start to wonder if I'm the one having sex."

"The only problem was the chef. He came out of the kitchen in the middle of our meal, and totally hit on her."

"Why, that's rather gauche of him."

"Yeah, he was telling her, like, I'll teach you to cook walleye, like right there in front of me."

"You should be the one cooking walleye for her, my friend."

"Well, yeah. But one of their deals is, their walleye is super fresh, like right out of Mille Lacs Lake. Nothing I can just go buy in a store is gonna compete with that."

"Then I know what you do, Prager. You go straight to that lake."

Prager had to make the most of his few moments in fifth period before Killer Keeley moved him to the front row. He saw Eva, wearing a plain black V-neck T-shirt and skinny black jeans, and her presence suffocated all of his big plans to say the cute things he'd practiced in the bathroom mirror. He hadn't even texted her since last night, and even though he'd assembled a perfect image of her in his head, it still paled beneath the force of her face and body in real life. Even as she sat slumped in her desk, writing something in pen on the side of her hand, everything about her seemed fragrant and American and glowed like neon. He walked up to her, unaware of just how much he was smiling. She was smiling too, maybe back at him, maybe because he was.

"Hey," he said. He looked at what was written on her hand. It was the word "Moonglow."

"Hey." She smiled.

There wasn't much time to act, but in twenty seconds he'd secured a decisive yes for an all-day fishing date that Saturday. He was getting better at this.

Prager waited until Wednesday to ask his dad permission to put a canoe on top of the car and use it for a full Saturday. His dad was in the garage, underneath the Ford, his legs sticking out toward the doorway to the kitchen where Prager was standing. A transistor radio in the garage was playing "In the Mood for a Melody" by Robert Plant. It was another beautiful September day outside, but the garage door was closed and the air had the warm sweet stink of oil.

"Dad, is it OK if I put a canoe on the car?" Prager asked.

"What the hell you want to do that for?" Eli said. "Some kinda joke?"

"No, to drive it up to Mille Lacs Lake on Saturday to go fishing. What are you doing to it right now?"

Eli pulled himself out from under the car. His face and hands were smudged with black. "Just changing the oil. Who are you going fishing with?"

"That girl, Eva," he said.

"Oh," Eli said. "In that case, I approve. Bring her over, I'd like to meet her."

"Well, we've only been out once, Dad."

Eli seemed to ignore that. "I'm gonna have Pat Jorgenson over for dinner on Sunday. She's excited to meet you and Julie."

"Who's Pat Jorgenson?"

"My date from last Friday."

This took a moment to sink in.

"I'm not even sure if I'll be here," Prager said.

"You'll be here, or no car on Saturday, how's that?" Eli said, and wheeled himself back under the Ford.

Before he met Eva on Saturday morning, he had to stop by his bass player Ken Kovacs's place to borrow Ken's parents' canoe and tie it down to the roof of the car. Their house was where the Lonesome Cowboys practiced. Ken was the fifth child of five, and the last one at home, and his parents, Arnie and May, seemed eager to have his friends around. They were generous in the way of people running a garage sale who give things away to the folks who come at the end.

In the meantime he looked up the word "Moonglow" because it had been bothering him and he felt it would've been dorky to ask her. He wanted to know what she knew without her having to tell him—it seemed more manly that way—so he looked it up on the Internet. He doubted it was the Benny Goodman tune; he'd narrowed it down to either the magnolia tree or the yellow-orange heirloom tomato, and knowing her, it was probably the tomato. Did she want Moonglow tomatoes? He would buy some for her if she did. He hoped that they were hard to find, and that he'd still somehow find them and, better yet, somehow sneak them into her locker as a surprise. Romantic gifts were so much better when they were rare, personal, and unexpected. Maybe he'd fill her locker with Moonglow tomatoes and wouldn't even leave a note. (But perhaps it could wait until he knew for sure that she meant the tomatoes.) In any case, his most significant gift to her was already in progress, cost him absolutely nothing but time, and would be ready in two days, tops.

He texted her from the parking lot, and almost didn't recognize her at first when she came outside wearing a white crew-neck shirt, a baseball cap, and tan pants with a lot of pockets. Her nails were still black and she had lipstick and eye makeup on, but otherwise she barely looked like a Goth anymore.

"Hey, cool outfit," Prager said, only because he thought everything she wore looked great on her.

"Thanks. Closest thing I had to fishing clothes. Good-looking canoe!" She tossed some Whole Earth bags full of cooking supplies in the back of the car, and when she got in, they kissed, briefly, like a couple that's been going out for a while.

"So how was your Friday night?" she asked.

"Pretty mellow," Prager said. He couldn't muzzle his enthusiasm for his big personal surprise any longer. "I actually started writing a song for you. You want to know what it's called?"

"What?"

"'Steamy Night on a Steamboat.'"

Eva laughed. "How does it go?"

"Wait until it's done, and I'll play it for you," he said. He'd written a song for a girl twice before, and man oh man did those end up being some memorable nights.

"OK," she said. "Where are the poles and the bait and everything?"

"All that stuff's in the trunk. The bait we can get up there at a gas station." It'd been a while, but as a kid he'd been fishing a bunch of times, usually with uncles or grandparents. His own parents hardly used their poles; Prager didn't even ask his dad if he could borrow them.

"I can't wait to grill some fresh walleye," she said, and she touched his arm as he drove, and kept it there. The Current was playing "Fade into You," by Mazzy Star, which was incredible, and he wished the song would last forever and her hand would never let him go, even if it was really awkward for her to hold it there like that.

While on the 169 North, into pine tree country, he found himself talking about his dad's dating life. He didn't plan on it, it just happened. The idea of his dad going out on dates with people and maybe even sleeping with people was like a nuclear bomb falling on a pit of toxic waste in his brain, and if he didn't have Eva in his life to distract him and make him feel good, who knows what he'd be capable of.

"The worst thing is," Prager said, "he's not ready."

"How do you know?" She had her hand near his leg while he drove.

"You can tell just by being around him," Prager said. "He's a lot angrier. He hardly listens to me or Julie about anything. He's just going to break this stupid woman's heart."

"How do you know she's stupid?" Eva asked.

"She must be if she's dating him. In the state he's in."

"Have you met her?"

"Nope, and don't want to either. I guess she's a widow too, so maybe she's just desperate."

"People need people," Eva said. "What's wrong with that?"

That sentiment kind of pissed Prager off; it missed the point entirely. "Well, has your dad dated anyone since your mom died? I don't imagine that was a day that you circled on your wall calendar."

"He's not even my real dad," Eva said, matching his piqued tone.

Prager stared straight ahead at the road; he didn't know to respond. Unfortunately, Eva spoke next, her voice now much softer.

"I'm sorry, I don't know why I said that. Nobody knows I know that. Well, like, my cousins do. But that's it."

Prager glanced at her face. She didn't look back at him. "How did you find out?"

"I found my birth certificate the last time we moved."

"Wow. So you know who your birth parents are? Are they still alive?"

"One of them is, maybe. I don't know. I'm sorry I brought it up. I don't want to talk about it."

"OK," Prager said, feeling bad that she didn't yet trust him with that kind of personal information.

"Who's playing at First Avenue this month?" she asked, making it clear that the previous topic was off the table.

Of course he knew; he knew every band that was playing through October. Just then, he really didn't feel like naming off all the ones he'd even consider seeing, but it was clear that's what she wanted to talk about, not the stuff that was emotionally important to *her*, so he went with it, and they ended up talking about music nonstop for pretty much the whole rest of the drive.

It was a good thing that Eva was tall and strong, because they needed two people to untie that heavy wooden canoe from the car and portage it to the pier. It felt like one of the last days of summer, with just a bit of chill coming off the massive lake, and the water was clustered with motorboats and canoes. When he looked at the empty parts of the beach, he imagined that they were 1850s pioneers, paddling to find a new homestead in Ojibwa country.

It turned out that getting in a canoe was way harder than it looked. Plus, sitting on those little benches in the thing was kind of precarious. Prager forgot to bring life jackets; lucky for them, walleye were usually caught close to shore.

Eva had no qualms about digging her hand into a Styrofoam cup of nightcrawlers and piercing one of those struggling little guys twice through with a fish hook. It made him think of his mom. The handful of times they'd gone fishing as a family, she'd always baited her own hooks, even when they were using leeches. She'd been a straight-A student in her teens but liked motorcycles and baseball and dive bars and getting her hands dirty; she was awesome like that.

It was something to watch Eva's hands on his mom's old rod, doing the same things he'd only seen one other woman do before, impaling a feisty nightcrawler twice through. He got really sad all of a sudden, and it must've shown in his eyes.

Eva glanced up at him. "Don't look so upset," she said, in a half-joking tone. "It's a law of the universe. You gotta kill things in order to live."

Prager took a deep breath as he pulled a worm from the cup, going along with the pretense that it was the worm killing that disturbed him, as wimpy as that made him seem.

After an hour, they caught one gold-and-brown-striped fish that was kind of small, and they put him back. Prager swore it was a baby walleye; Eva seemed fairly sure it wasn't.

After another hour of drowning worms and losing them in little nibbles, it was almost 5:00 p.m., and supposedly the best time to catch walleye was in the evening; clearly, they were just too eager and had started too early.

Finally, around 5:30, Eva's red-and-white bobber plunked below the water, and her thin green rod bowed with an invigorating weight. It was another one of the gold-and-brown guys, beautiful and gasping, held aloft by his lips, urgently splattering the air. He was small, but still bigger than the last one, and Eva and Prager were hungry for any kind of victory. Prager couldn't speak for Eva, obviously, but he wanted to get the fishing and grilling and eating part over with so they could start making out again and he could more vigorously touch the boobs he had just sorta grazed last time.

Prager was at the ready with the blue Playmate cooler full of melting ice to meet the fish as Eva swung it into the boat, unhooked its lips, and closed the lid on their quarry. For some reason, they high-fived afterwards. Until that moment, he had looked askance at people who called fishing a sport, but the catharsis of it all made it feel like they'd somehow competed and won.

"Well, that might be big enough for both of us," Prager said. "Wanna call it?"

"Oh, come on," she said. "I think we can get more."

He was actually a little afraid that she would get super into it. They'd been out on the lake for three hours at that point and Prager figured that this part of the mission was now clearly accomplished, but she acted like they were just getting going.

"How much can we eat, anyway?" he asked.

"One more, come on," Eva said. "After all the work getting here."

• • •

In the end, the one was all they caught, and when they lifted the wet canoe out of the water, the sun was setting. They stopped a bearded guy in a vest who was lugging a large cooler across the parking lot and asked him where they could grill their fish. He asked how many they had, and Prager showed him.

"This a walleye, right?" Prager asked.

The bearded guy looked as if you'd just asked him whether Kirby Puckett was a man or a woman. "Nope," he said, "that's a yellow perch."

"Is it edible?"

"Oh sure," the guy said. "It's a panfish. Great eating."

The guy directed them to a nearby park in the city of Isle with outdoor grills. It looked like an awesome place to have sex for the first time, because it was free, and had trees and a view of the lake, but there were a ton of people there. Prager decided he'd get to work on the fire, as Eva dug a pan and a steak knife out of her grocery bag.

"Good thing I just learned how to fillet a fish," Eva said. "The one thing I could really use though is an actual fillet knife."

"Where'd you learn to fillet?" Prager asked, shoving balled-up newspaper between the charcoal briquettes, like his dad taught him once.

"At the Steamboat."

"Oh, really?"

"Yeah, it's awesome. Everyone there is super nice. They let me help with a whole bunch of stuff. Prime rib. Lobster. Walleye."

"How many times have you been there?"

"Not counting the time with you? Three more times."

"Did they hire you to work there or something?"

"I'm sort of their kitchen intern, which is awesome. Everyone there is teaching me a bunch of stuff. There's this one cook, Maureen O'Brien, she's super nice. She's letting me do all of her prep work."

"How much are they paying you?"

"I said I would work for free—I offered."

"Sounds like slave labor."

"No, it's not. They give me dinner—that's more than fine with me. And I get to take home food for my dad. And Jobe said he's going to try to get me a real kitchen job, if not there, then somewhere really cool. He says I have a once-in-a-generation palate."

"I think he's just trying to get in your pants, is what I think."

"You know what, fuck you," Eva said.

Prager almost felt like he'd lost his balance. People had said this to him before, but this was different. He had hurt somebody, and she had hurt him back. But he was still right, he was sure of it.

"I'm just saying, he didn't pay any attention to *me* last Thursday."

"He's with somebody, for your information."

"That doesn't matter. Men don't care about that."

"And you would know that how?"

This was totally sucking ass. He wanted to make her apologize for not telling him what she was up to, not finger himself as the unfaithful pervert that Jobe probably was. "How come you didn't ever tell me you were going down there?"

"You never asked. You never ask me what I did yesterday, or last night, or anything. I ask you about your day, and then you go off on a tangent about it."

"No I don't," he said. "I've asked you how your day was tons of times."

"That's not how I remember it."

"Well, I have. Totally."

"Have it your way, then," she said. "How's it going with the fire over there? I need to heat the pan up before I put the oil in."

• • •

The perch fillets were lightly breaded and spittin' in the pan before Prager realized that he was the one who had better apologize if he was going to get so much as a kiss out of this whole sorry day. She accepted the apology, but when they sat next to each other on the picnic table and ate their pan-fried yellow perch in the dark, she was quiet.

"This is way fresher than anything you could get at the Steamboat," Prager said at one point.

"Actually, it's about the same," Eva said.

"Really?" Prager said. "They're right on the lake where the fish is from?"

"Why'd you stiff the waitress on our date, by the way? Jobe says you left her like a dollar."

"I left her every dollar I brought."

"If you knew where we were going, you shoulda brought more."

"Well, I didn't know you were gonna order such expensive shit."

"It's getting late," she said, shoving the rest of the fish in her mouth. "We should get back."

She fell asleep in the car on the way home. Prager tried to tell himself it was because she was just that comfortable with him. But when he dropped her off and she just hugged him, he felt like an eighteen-wheeler had driven off a cliff and landed on his heart.

He went home and turned off the lights in his room and put on the song "Why," by Annie Lennox, the *MTV Unplugged* version, the one he got on a mix CD from one of his ex-girlfriends, and put it on repeat, he felt that fucking sad. He stared up at the Radiohead poster on his ceiling and felt the lyrics echo in his heart like a penny tossed down an empty well. Why was this boat sinking? They had barely even started rowing. But it was.

He needed to text her, and apologize again, but it was 12:20 at night.

Finally he thought he should just see if she was up, and if she was, he'd apologize. At 12:22 he texted You up? and stared at the little screen on his flip phone waiting for her response until 12:45, when he finally plugged the phone back into the charger and turned the ringer off and closed his eyes.

The next morning he was woken up at noon by his dad grabbing his foot.

"You forgot to take the canoe off the car," Eli said. "I had to drive it to church and back with a canoe on it."

"Oh," Prager said. "Sorry."

"Pat's coming over for dinner in five hours. Have the canoe off the car by then. And dress yourself nice."

Vik Gupta was over at Ken Kovacs's house, jamming in the garage they used as a practice space, when Prager drove there to give the canoe back. Vik and Ken were deeply unimpressed with him when he told them the story of his fishing trip with Eva.

"You blew it," Vik said. "You had a woman on a boat, even, and you didn't execute."

"Have you been in a canoe?"

"Anywhere where two people can fit, they can have sex. It's the law."

"So what the fuck you gonna do now?" Ken asked. Prager had known Ken for longer, and Ken was a little more invested in Prager's emotional life journey.

"I don't know," Prager said. "I already called her today and left her a message, and left her a text both last night and this morning."

"Maybe call her again, and apologize again."

Vik got up from his drum stool. "Ken, weren't you listening? He got hugged at the end of a second date! Hugged! I wouldn't wish that on anybody! Seriously, you'd rather get slapped in the face than hugged!"

"Yeah, that's true," Ken said. "You can work with getting slapped in the face. There's a lot of emotion there, you just have to flip the dime."

"Prager, here's what you should do tomorrow. Flowers. Chocolate. And another gift, something personal, something only the two of you would know. And have you written her a song yet?"

"Yeah, I started."

"Well, get on it tonight, master it, play it for her ASAP."

"What if I have to skip band practice again tomorrow?"

Vik and Ken glanced at each other. "This is an alt-country band," Vik said. "All this heartache is *comme il faut*. Jeff Tweedy would kill for a week like this. You might get a whole album of lyrics from just yesterday alone."

Ken nodded. "Go get 'em out there."

Prager was in his bedroom practicing "Steamy Night on a Steamboat" when his dad knocked on the door. Prager had lost track of time; it was 4:56.

"She's here," Eli said, smiling. "Come out and say hi."

No way was this woman thirty-five. Maybe fifty-five. She had thick legs, wrinkles around her eyes, and gray hairs sprouting from her hairline. She was smiling, but Prager could totally tell it was a fake smile just to be polite. She had a large orange ceramic baking pan with her covered in cellophane, and there were two more unfamiliar dishes on the dining room table already.

"What is all this?" Prager said.

"Pat's made a home-cooked meal for our entire family," Eli said.

It was disturbing enough to walk out into the living room on a Sunday afternoon in the fall and not hear a lurid NFL game chundering from the TV, much less to feel a cheerless, significant silence, and to see this strange woman, and all of her food, and all of its invasive smells, filling the empty spaces in their raw home.

Pat Jorgenson extended her hand. "So nice to meet you, Will," she said. "I've heard so much about you."

"Yeah, OK," Prager said.

"Only the good things," Eli said, patting his son on the back, which he pretty much never did ever. "Julie!" Eli shouted.

"Just a minute, Dad, God!" came a girl's voice from behind a closed bedroom door.

Eli glanced at Pat as if to say, *Teenagers.* "Please, be seated. Pat, may I get you something to drink? I bought a bottle of Chardonnay."

"Just water for now, thank you."

"Will, if you want any white wine, help yourself. I hear it goes with seafood."

Prager had never heard his dad say anything close to those sentences in his entire life. "OK, where's the seafood?"

"Pat made tuna casserole. In the orange pan."

"You know I'm a vegetarian, Dad."

Pat looked at Eli, but avoided his eye contact. "Oh, I'm sorry, your father didn't tell me."

"You just went fishing yesterday," Eli said, "you can't be that much of a vegetarian. Just pick out all the fish if you have to."

Julie came out of her room wearing a Minnesota Vikings jacket zipped all the way up, pink hot pants, and a Lone Ranger mask.

Eli shook his head. "Julie."

"This what I wanna wear."

"Nice jacket," Pat said.

"I don't care what you think," Julie said. "Why is she sitting in Mom's chair?"

Pat looked at Eli. "I should switch chairs with you."

Eli didn't move, except to look Julie in the face. "At least take the mask off."

"If the mask goes, I go."

Pat touched Eli's hand. "It's fine."

Eli said, "We should say grace."

"We don't say grace in this family, Dad," Julie said.

"It's OK, Eli," said Pat.

Prager lifted his wineglass. "*L'chaim*," he said.

"So what is all this repugnant garbage?" Julie asked.

"Julie," Eli said. "Be nice."

"Why? I don't want to be here."

"Remember what I said? No sports for a week?"

"Sounds like a deal to me. Can I go now?"

"No, just five minutes. Just tell Pat something about yourself. She's heard a lot about you guys and wants to get to know you better."

"I just got my first period last month," Julie said.

Prager laughed; he couldn't help it. Pat pursed her lips as she passed around the au gratin potatoes she had made.

"Julie."

Julie twisted a slotted spoon around in a casserole dish."What's this?"

"Au gratin potatoes," Pat said.

"Rotten potatoes? Looks like it."

Prager laughed again.

Eli pounded his fist on the table. "Julie. Both of you."

Pat looked up. "She can leave if she wants."

Julie immediately got up from the table. "God, thank you."

Eli pointed to her. "Don't leave your room."

Julie slammed her bedroom door and put on the song "My Neck, My Back" by Khia, and turned it up real loud. Prager started to laugh again. Eli almost got up from the table, but Pat restrained him.

"Don't," she said. "Just ignore it."

"Will, tell Pat about your country music band," Eli said.

"I'm actually really busy writing a song tonight," Prager said. "For a girl."

"Well, you should get to it after dinner."

"Mind if I go and just work on it right now? I'm kinda in the zone."

"Sure," Pat said. "I'll make you a plate."

Prager was going to say, *That's OK,* but she seemed so eager to get Eli's unpleasant children out of the dining room, she had piled up the tuna casserole, boiled string beans, and potatoes au gratin on his plate before he could object.

Prager didn't look at his dad when he took the plate and left the dining room. Pat said something like "Nice to meet you," which he didn't respond to, and the first thing he did when he got to his room was dump the plate in the garbage.

It was actually real hard to write a song on the acoustic guitar with that dirty hardcore rap song playing in the background, but Prager wasn't about to declaw his sister's protest. For a moment, he tried to think of a day when he'd felt closer to Julie, when he'd loved her more, and only the day of their parents' accident came to mind.

An hour later, his dad was still somehow eating dinner with that woman, and Prager was starving, but he'd also finished "Steamy Night on a Steamboat," and was at last ready to play it for Eva.

Her cell phone went straight to voice mail. He took a deep breath and tried her house phone. It rang a long time. Finally, her dad answered. He sounded wasted.

"Yeah?" Jarl said.

"Hi, this is Will Prager. Is Eva home?"

"Nope," Jarl said. "She's working that restaurant job."

Seemed weird, for that late on a Sunday evening. "OK, can you tell her to call me as soon as she gets home?"

"Yeah, sure," Jarl said. "Are you the guy whose band plays Jimmy Buffett tunes?"

Will was dismayed at Jarl's memory of their brief interaction, but he wasn't in the mood to have this particular conversation. "Yeah," he found himself saying. "And I gotta go, I gotta get to practice."

"Next time you play, make me a VHS tape of it so I can see you guys," Eva's dad said.

"We will," Prager said for some reason, realizing that he had no idea how he could make that happen, even if he wanted to.

"I'll tell her Jimmy called," Jarl said, and laughed before he hung up.

Prager stopped her in the hall before fifth period. Her hair was up, she wasn't wearing any makeup, and she looked tired. Even the white T-shirt she was wearing, which read LARK MANAGED SERVICES and looked like a promotional giveaway shirt from a company picnic or something, seemed out of character.

"How come you haven't returned any of my texts or my calls?" he asked her.

"I was going to, I've just been super busy."

"Too busy to even return a text? What's up with that?"

"So, what do you want to tell me?"

"I want to play you the song I wrote you."

"I don't know if I have the time for that today," she said, leaning against the lockers in the hallway. "I gotta work at the store after school every day this week."

"Well, maybe after you get off work, then. What time is that?"

"Seven," she said.

"I'll call you at seven-fifteen. Why do you have to work every day? Are you trying to avoid me or something?"

"My dad got fired from his job," she said. "So I gotta pick up all the shifts I can. It's not about you at all." She glanced at the doorway to their history classroom. "I guess we'd better get to class."

He sat in the front row for an hour, watching Killer Keeley talk about the French and Indian War, and tried to think of his next move. Vik Gupta would know exactly what he should do, but he couldn't talk to Vik until after school. She was obviously not so excited to see him, like she used to be, but one thing was still certain. If he could just figure out a way to play "Steamy Night on a Steamboat" for her today, she'd fall in love with him in a second. By the end of class, he'd decided that this was the only plan that would work.

At 7:15 p.m. and nine seconds, Prager called Eva's cell, and once again it went straight to VM. He tried her apartment, and no one answered; a machine didn't even pick up. He tried again, three minutes later, and got the same result. He tried one more time at 7:25, and nothing had changed. It rang and rang, eleven, twelve, thirteen times.

He threw his guitar in his dad's car and drove south toward Prescott. The Built to Spill tape was still in the tape deck, and he just let it keep going; it might as well be the damn soundtrack to everything.

He didn't know where the Steamboat Inn's kitchen was, so he went inside and asked the headwaiter, a young fat blonde woman with a ponytail, who said that he could either get there through the EMPLOYEES ONLY door by the bathroom or through the door on the side of the building by the employee parking lot. He said thanks, and while he was standing there he noticed the waitress from his date standing by the bar, putting cocktails on a tray, and he went up to her and put a ten-dollar bill between the drinks.

"Sorry about last time," he said.

From the look on her face it didn't seem like she even recognized him.

Prager picked up his guitar from the backseat and walked around back to the employee lot and saw that the black wooden door to the kitchen was swung all the way open; between Prager and the kitchen, there was just a heavy-looking black metal screen door, and even from a distance he could see a lot of what was happening inside. It was really bright in there, a stark, hospital white from above, and way less fancy than he would've guessed a kitchen like that would look. There were big silver basins and spigot heads on long snakes and black rubber mats on the floor with holes in them. There were maybe six or seven people in there, all wearing white, all terribly busy cutting meat, tossing salad, peeling fruit.

He saw Eva in there, in her new style of a white T-shirt and pants with a lot of pockets, standing next to a woman he didn't recognize who was dressed exactly the same way—maybe that Maureen O'Brien person—and they were peeling something over a silver bowl and laughing. It was too bright in there for them to see clearly outside, and no one so much as looked in his direction.

He walked to his car, put the guitar in the backseat, and got the Sexy Gran'pa beer koozie out of the glove box where he'd left it for good luck. He came back to the screen door, and quietly crammed the beer koozie in around eye level, in the space between the frame and the screen.

She found him the next morning, before school, by the vending machines.

"Let's go for a walk," she said.

"How did you know to find me here?" he asked her.

"Your friends told me this is where you hang out," she said.

They walked outside, past where all the heavy metal dudes smoked cigarettes, all the way to the highway, almost.

"Well, I got your message of sorts, last night."

"Yeah."

"So is that it, are you done with me?"

"I'm assuming you're done with me. You tell me you're gonna be home at seven-fifteen and you're not. That's totally shitty."

"The restaurant called me and wanted me to come in."

"You could at least call me and tell me that your plans have changed."

"I admit, that was careless of me. And I'm sorry. But part of it is that I just don't know if I can handle you right now."

"What's that supposed to mean?"

"I don't think you're ready for what you want," she said.

"How would you know?"

"You know, maybe I don't. But either way, you're like the most intense guy of all time, really. It's a lot, OK? I'm just saying, take it easy. I'll be here."

"You'll be here?"

"But in the meantime, let's just be friends."

Prager had heard that one before, and pretty much learned to turn off what a girl said after she said that, because it was all bullshit.

He didn't talk to her before fifth period or sit next to her during seventh period anymore, but they still said hi when they passed each other in the halls, out of politeness, he guessed, but that was it. To other people in class, no one could probably tell they'd ever kissed, that he wrote a song for her, and that she'd been the last thought on his mind every night.

At home, meanwhile, Eli, Julie, and even that awful Pat who was around all the time now, they all knew what was up, and he didn't try to hide it from them either, mostly because it made it easier for him to be curt and disagreeable without being hassled. He had to quit listening to Built to Spill, Neutral Milk Hotel, Annie Lennox, Mazzy Star, Soul Coughing, and all of the other bands that reminded him of her even a little bit, but his own band got more of his time, and they even scheduled a gig for December, at the Rec Center where he used to see Smarmy Kitten shows.

Alone in his bedroom, he helplessly ruminated on what she said, specifically the phrases "not ready" and "I'll be here." As the weeks passed, with this in mind, he remained calm and respectful and not intense. By mid-November, he and Eva were even in the same eight-person group in history class, pretending to be delegates from the four southern colonies. And the day before Thanksgiving, she even touched him on the arm twice. He talked to Vik Gupta about it over Thanksgiving break and the first Monday back in school he went in twenty minutes before the first bell to wait by her locker. He couldn't wait another second.

He'd only been there a few minutes when Eva, surprised to see him, smiled and said, "Hey." She was wearing her winter outfit of a thrift-store duster and floppy black stocking cap, no makeup, no painted fingernails.

"Hey," Prager said. "I just want you to know I'm ready now."

Eva looked at him, a little puzzled. "OK. Ready for what?"

"You want to go on another culinary adventure this Friday?"

She looked at him for what felt like thirty seconds, and then down at the floor, and then back at him.

"I'm moving," she said.

"Oh," he said. With each second that her words, and everything they meant, were hanging in the air, threatening to be true, he started to feel like she was taking the school apart brick by brick and throwing the bricks at his heart. "When?"

"This weekend."

Prager could feel he was losing all ability to remain composed in the face of these words, but his mouth kept trying. "Where?" he asked.

She looked at the ground and continued talking. "Maureen moved to a restaurant in the Cities and she can get me a full-time job there."

"Full-time job," was all he could say.

"Well, my dad lost his job here and can't find a new one, so it's kind of my family's best option."

"So what high school are you going to?" He surprised himself at summoning such a long, coherent sentence.

"I figure I'll get a GED. I don't need to waste my time in high school anyway, it's not like I want to go to college or something. No offense if you do."

"Oh," he said. It sounded nuts to him. Who didn't go to college? The nonsense of this idea emboldened him a little. "So you're just going to be a chef in a restaurant."

She didn't seem to respond. He noticed just then that she wasn't taking out her books and materials for one class, but rather was emptying out her entire locker into her backpack.

"It was illuminating, Will Prager," she said, looking at him. "I think of our steamy night on a steamboat often."

"You do?" he asked. She nodded.

"Well," she said. "Later."

He watched her pull the heavy black backpack over her shoulders and walk down the hall, her smooth brown hair and black stocking cap drawing his stare until the very end, until she turned a corner toward the exit, when old Mrs. Colwell, who'd just exited her freshman English classroom, turned and stared at him, forcing Prager to glance away. When he looked again at the space where Eva last was, she was gone.

He needed to get out too, right now, but he couldn't leave by the same doors. Head down, he walked to the other end of the hall and left, pushing through a busload of underclassmen who were no doubt staring at his red eyes filling with tears.

Prager made it outside, face and body in the cool, clammy, forty-degree late autumn air, and kept walking across the grass and soft brown leaves and concrete, and was off school grounds for almost half a block, passing a squat yellow house with an American flag out front, before he realized that he, unlike Eva Thorvald, had left the building for no real purpose, and had nowhere to go, and nowhere else to be in the world besides the place he just left.

He turned back toward the school, thought of the lyrics to "Reason to Believe"—the Tim Hardin song made famous by Rod Stewart—and stood there, waiting in the cold for his feet to move, and sooner or later they did.

GOLDEN BANTAM

While parked down the street from her boyfriend Mitch's town house, waiting for his wife's car to pull out of the garage and leave for work, Octavia Kincade stared at the plastic pink flamingos sticking out of the snow in his neighbor's yard and had what her former therapist would've called a moment of clarity. It was all Eva Thorvald's fault, she realized.

All of it. Not just the fact that she was freezing to death in a godawful Pontiac Aztek with a busted heater, but her frustrating lack of commitment from former Bar Garroxta executive chef Mitch Diego, her two kids with Adam Snelling, her marriage to Adam Snelling, the breakup of the Sunday Night Dinner Party, even what happened to Lacey Dietsch—Eva's presence had set all of this in motion. As she awaited the text from Mitch's second cell phone, which he used just for her, she looked through her frosty windshield at the snow falling for the second time that April and, like those stupid ironic flamingos, felt imprisoned by the cruelty of circumstances beyond her control.

It wasn't any colder outside the car, so she figured she would maybe wait outside, maybe even lie down in the snow by the flamingos without her jacket on. Was it possible to die of hypothermia in April? Probably, if it was still below freezing out. Maybe she would be the first. As she lay down in the clammy snow, and felt it soak the back of her jeans and wool sweater and hair that she'd just spent over twenty minutes on, she was sure that whether she survived or not, it would send that bastard a message: *Look at what you drove me to do.*

. . .

Five years ago, Octavia would have known better. For starters, she should've known not to extend a warm, welcoming hand to a helpless creature like Eva Thorvald. But Octavia was a nice person with a big, generous heart who felt sorry for outsiders and tried to help them. And people like her never get any thanks for their selflessness. They are not the ones with the hardness to make others wait; they are the ones left waiting, until their souls are broken like old bread and scattered in the snow for the birds. They can go right ahead and aspire to the stars, but the only chance they'll ever have to fly is in a thousand pieces, melting in the hot guts of something predatory.

It was the last July weekend of 2009, in the deep sticky bulge of summer, and Robbe was having some people over at the house near Lake Calhoun that he'd bought on a short sale and then exhaustively modernized. The kitchen was outfitted with marble countertops, a center island, two recessed refrigerators—each with a glass door—a hatch in the floor that led to the basement wine cellar, and a painfully tasteful version of every necessary or desired piece of kitchen hardware.

Octavia, who was twenty-six at the time, didn't know anyone else around her age with such a pimped-out kitchen, but Robbe Kramer was unusual among her friends. He was twenty-nine, shaved his face every day, and had graduated from Carleton back in 2002, the perfect time to join a mortgage loan firm and start slinging subprimes to the masses like pancakes at a charity breakfast. She didn't know him back then, and had a hard time believing that the collection of Châteauneuf-du-Papes beneath her feet were purchased on the backs of foreclosed blue-collar families and fixed-income seniors. She asked him about it once, in those terms. He just replied, "Were you there?" and looked at her as if she'd just flipped off a mall Santa in front of the children.

By 2009, that revenue model no longer existed, of course, but Robbe had already cashed out. While he watched his bosses get taken to court, he got a Realtor's license, took cooking classes, and sold the treatment for a memoir called *An ARM and a Leg: One Young Man's Ride on the Bubble*.

Robbe's life and home were truly impressive, but she wasn't going to embarrass herself gushing over every little magnetic knife rack or hobnailed sand iron tetsubin. When Octavia first walked into the kitchen, Robbe was literally explaining a pressure cooker to a young, gawky tower of a girl, and she was acting shamelessly super interested, as if she'd never ever seen a pressure cooker before and Robbe was the genius who invented it. Women look their stupidest when they have a crush on a guy who's out of their league, and Octavia suspected that was what she was seeing.

"Hi, I'm Eva," the tall girl said when she noticed Octavia watching her. Upon closer inspection, Eva was big, in both the right and wrong places—not fat, per se, but proportionately large, awkwardly assembled on a towering frame. Her awful white T-shirt and cargo pants were a nonstarter, but the subtle lipstick, chipped nail polish, and messy long hair all vaguely evoked something more feminine than Eva might have intended; she was obviously careless and unrefined, but even then, one could see the potential. She reminded Octavia of a Greek statue in progress, before all the extra marble had been chipped away.

"Hi, I'm Octavia," she said, arm outstretched as she angled around the center island. Octavia liked to be the prettiest woman in the room whenever possible, and it was no contest here. Especially when she was wearing her canary yellow Betsey Johnson swing dress (she was one of the few women she knew who could truly pull off canary yellow), her gold and lapis lazuli earrings, an ethnic-inspired, chunky coiled snake bracelet, and two big, showstopping lapis lazuli cocktail rings, one on each middle finger.

Robbe asserted himself between them. "Octavia's a fixture at the Sunday dinners I was telling you about."

"Cool beans!" Eva said. That kind of enthusiasm was grating, but Eva was probably still young enough to correct it later. "What do you make?"

"Oh, nothing crazy, a little of this, a little of that," Octavia said.

"She's dissembling," Robbe said. "She makes, let's call them, sexy versions of old-school comfort food. Remind me what they were, I don't remember."

Octavia said, "Black truffle oil mac and cheese with bacon and smoked gouda. Gnocchi gratin with pecorino cheese. Walleye casserole with homemade cream of mushroom soup."

"Real cool," Eva said.

Robbe looked at Octavia as he nudged Eva with his elbow. "This one works in the kitchen at Bar Garrotxa."

Octavia was actually impressed. BG, as everyone called it, was the hottest tapas bar in the Cities. Anderson Cooper had recently been spotted eating there. Joe Biden brought his party there after an afternoon fund-raiser in 2008. And several of the most influential local food blogs had ranked it among the best in Minneapolis/Minnesota/the Midwest. All of this conspired to make its dashing executive chef into a budding star, and what this gawky work in progress was doing there made Octavia mighty curious.

"You work for Mitch Diego?" she asked Eva.

"With him, yes."

"And how old are you, if you don't mind me asking?"

"I just turned twenty."

"Wow, you're a baby," Octavia said. That explained a lot. Now Octavia wondered if she should just feel sorry for her. "What exactly do you do there?"

"I'm a sous-chef. For now."

For now. Octavia couldn't believe the little ingénue. Like anyone her age could possibly do better. "Well, what an impressive place to work," she said. "What's he like as a person?"

"Mitch? He's OK."

"That's all? He's OK?"

Eva shrugged. "When he's in the kitchen, he just kind of puts the finishing touches on everything. I don't talk to him that much."

"But to work with his food every day. You must love everything on the menu."

"Given the ingredients, it's all right. I do my best to help it along."

Damn. *Given the ingredients, it's all right?* If she'd said that in front of Mitch, Octavia believed, Eva would never even boil pasta in this town again. Baby girl needed to get spanked, big time. "Well," Octavia said, "I'm sure he appreciates whatever it is you do."

Octavia sat in Robbe's lush backyard, in a Crate & Barrel deck chair next to Robbe's Honeycrisp apple tree, while her bitchy, judgmental ex-roommate Maureen O'Brien smoked a cigarette and ashed it onto the lawn. *Christ,* Octavia thought. Why did Robbe still invite Maureen to his parties? Because she worked at a cool restaurant? Because he wanted his parties to look busier? It couldn't be because he actually liked her. It was too bad Maureen wasn't a lesbian, with the buzz cut and the truck driver paunch and the sirloin-thick hands. She even held her cigarettes down at waist level, palm downward, like a dude, instead of arching her elbow and wrist, palm toward the sky, cigarette tip pointed downward, like a woman of a refined caste.

"So what's your friend's deal?" Octavia asked. "She's inside forcing Robbe to explain every single item in his kitchen. I hope to God she doesn't *like* him."

"Eva's awesome," Maureen said, not looking at Octavia. "Leave her alone."

"How'd you meet someone so young and relevant?"

"We worked together at the Steamboat before it closed," Maureen said.

"Why'd they close? Breaking child labor laws?"

Maureen sucked on her cigarette and blew its plume toward the ground. "That chick has the most sophisticated palate I've ever seen."

"But can she cook?"

Maureen looked down at Octavia and extinguished her cigarette against the side of the apple tree. "Like you wouldn't believe."

A few days later, when Octavia saw that Robbe had added a seventh e-mail address, Eva Thorvald's, to the Sunday Night Dinner Party e-mail chain, she felt that she'd have to bring her A game to show the newcomer what's what. On Wednesday, when everyone had to disclose what they were making, Octavia waited for everyone else to chime in before making her announcement.

Robbe: Open-face Kobe beef sliders. Chipotle mayo.

Sarah Vang: Termites on a log (hemp seeds on hummus on celery)

Lacey Dietsch: Jell-O salad! ☺

Adam Snelling: Corsican-style Paris-Brest

Eva Thorvald: Caesar salad

Elodie Pickett: Cabernet Sauvignon (Walla Walla) [for sliders]; Sauternes
     (France) [for Paris-Brest]; Vermentino (Sardinia) [for Caesar salad]

Octavia: My famous summer heirloom tomato casserole, bitches!

Elodie (me again): Sangiovese (Umbria) [for tomato hot dish]

They'd only been doing the Sunday Night Dinner Party every other Sunday for three months, but this was looking like a typical menu. The idea was, everyone was supposed to put a new twist on a familiar item, but the only people who consistently did that were Octavia and Sarah Vang, who usually brought something cheaper and easier to make than what Octavia brought. Robbe came up with the idea for the theme but routinely ignored it, instead just making whatever he wanted to eat. Adam, who worked at a bakery in Lyndale, always only brought bread, and Elodie, the aspiring sommelier, came through with wine pairings.

There were a few problems with Octavia's high school friend Lacey Dietsch. First of all, she was the mother of a newborn—a little bald, bug-eyed girl named Emma—that she brought to all of the meals, strapped to her chest like a parasitic twin. If Octavia had known in advance that Lacey would insist on being with this creature all of the time, not once leaving the baby home with her husband, she'd never have extended the invite. No one else at the Sunday Night Dinner Party had kids or was even married.

Also, Lacey either didn't get the spirit of the theme or outright ignored it, bringing cloying, straight-up comfort food right out of a Lutheran grandma's cookbook. She was first invited in March, after Octavia noticed on social media that she was working as a part-time server at Hutmacher's, an old-school, old-money bistro on Lake Minnetonka, close to where they grew up. It was sad to confirm that a person could work at Hutmacher's and have none of the class or talent in its kitchen rub off on them at all, but Octavia liked her—they were on the volleyball team together back in the day—and held out hope that Lacey would one day bring something competent or edible. The following Sunday Night Dinner Party, as it turned out, would not be that day.

"Hey guys!" Lacey said, her naturally curly red hair glowing in the evening's golden hour, the sunlight bedazzling the red cellophane over a glass bowl of wobbling green strangeness. Lacey was a glow of color and happiness that no one besides her husband ever wanted. She was upbeat and harmless as an educational toy, and it was never insincere—in fact, she was a one-woman plague of sincerity, the Patient Zero of earnest zeal. Though one could imagine it might have helped her career as a waitress, in social situations her personality made you hate the world and hate life.

"I brought Jell-O!" Lacey said. "With shredded carrots on the top!"

"And that's a new twist on comfort food how?" Octavia asked.

Lacey shrugged. "It's comfort food, with carrots," she said, and brought it into the kitchen.

Robbe, dressed in skinny jeans and a black polo shirt with a popped collar, which all somehow worked for him, smiled at Octavia as he brought them each a Pimm's cup with muddled cucumber.

"Hey, good news," he said. "An old business associate of mine just bought investment property in Bali. Seems like a good place to hole up and pound out the memoir, you know?"

She didn't remember putting her hand on her heart, but it was there. "Oh. When would that be?"

"He's gonna renovate it first, so maybe late September."

"What about when you need to interview people, or fact check, or do research?"

Robbe shrugged. "I don't need to do any of that. It's a memoir. However I remember things is the truth. That's what's so great about it."

"How long will you be gone for?"

"I don't know. If I like the place, maybe years. I'll rent this place out and live on the proceeds."

"Oh my God." She was still processing all this, and didn't know what to say. "Everyone will really miss you."

Robbe winked at her. "Then we might as well party."

At that moment, there was a knock on the door, and Elodie opened it to find Eva standing there in a plain white sleeveless blouse and tan skirt, holding a wooden bowl and a canvas bag. She had a smile of relief.

"Wow, I'm glad I remembered the house," she said.

• • •

Octavia helped Eva carry her stuff into the kitchen, where Octavia's summer heirloom tomato casserole was keeping warm in the oven. Eva sniffed the air and smiled.

"Smells delicious," she said.

"I know, doesn't it?" Octavia said. "I based it off a recipe from *Petite Noisette*. I made a lot of my own tweaks, though."

Eva looked blankly back at Octavia at the mention of the hottest new underground food blog in the relevant world. Octavia loved that Eva hadn't heard of it.

"Oh nice," Eva said. "What kind of tomatoes did you use?"

"Early Girl," Octavia said. "They're my favorite early growth heirloom."

"Early Girl isn't an heirloom. It's an intentional F1 hybrid."

"No, it's an heirloom."

"No, it's owned by Monsanto. They're fine tomatoes, but if you want an early growth *heirloom,* I like Moskvich. They're exactly the same size, same globe, same indeterminate vine, everything. Heirloom Johnny Lao has them right now at the St. Paul Farmers' Market. They grow up here in zone 4b just fine, you just have to plant them in warm soil. And I'd start the seeds indoors in bisected eggshells."

Octavia had quit listening after "Monsanto," and Eva finally noticed this.

"Sorry," Eva said. "I'm rambling."

"Well, you sure know your tomatoes," Octavia said. "I used to grow San Marzanos myself because they were the best for paste."

"I used to grow them too, as a teenager down in Iowa," Eva said. "And I quit for probably the same reason. Aren't there much better paste tomatoes now? You got Jersey Giant. Opalka. Amish Paste. Isn't it a huge relief that the reign of the San Marzano is finally over?"

"Let's go see what everyone is doing," Octavia said, leaving the kitchen.

• • •

Robbe didn't have chairs for his dining room table, he had two long benches, so there was no head of the table, just people sitting across from each other, like in a school cafeteria. At this dinner, Octavia sat across from Robbe, Eva sat across from Elodie, and Adam Snelling, a pearl-snap-plaid-shirt-wearing guy who was kinda cute, but too quiet, and Sarah Vang, who wore loud colors and had an obvious knockoff designer handbag, sat across from each other. Because they were now seven, Lacey sat at the end, facing no one, her swaddled child flung across her chest.

Eva insisted on preparing the Caesar salad at the table, which seemed to Octavia like an ostentatious demand for someone at their first Sunday Night Dinner Party, but Robbe confirmed that this was the way the first Caesar salad in history was prepared, so Octavia let it slide.

Eva rubbed the sides of the wooden bowl with bisected cloves of Porcelain garlic and prepared the dressing, a mixture of Koroneiki olive oil, warm coddled free-range brown egg yolks, Worcestershire sauce, freshly ground Madagascar black peppercorns, one freshly diced Porcelain clove, and a bit of Meyer lemon juice. She placed single whole romaine leaves on everyone's plates and drizzled the dressing over them, topping each with four homemade sourdough bread croutons.

"Wait," said Sarah Vang, who until this point had watched in awe. She was tiny and had cute clunky hipster princess glasses but canceled out her demure appearance with her loud, squeaky voice. "Where's the anchovies and the cheese?"

Robbe leaned forward over the table. "Caesar Cardini's original Caesar salad didn't have cheese or anchovies," he said.

"Obviously, Eva knew that already," Octavia said. She saw Eva smile to herself briefly.

"Well, I know it's not everyone's favorite version of the Caesar," Eva said, "but yeah, it goes back to the 1920s." Octavia saw that Eva looked at the floor as everyone took their first bites.

"Oh my God," Elodie said. "This is insane."

"Damn," said Sarah, licking her fork.

"Wow," said Robbe, his jaws full of romaine and croutons, his lips shiny with thick Koroneiki oil. "It's official. She's coming to every dinner."

Everyone else concurred. Eva smiled and thanked them softly.

Remembering Eva's snotty tomato lecture and previous sharp talk about Mitch Diego, Octavia wasn't buying the humble act. Inevitably, one day Eva would overreach and expose her inexperience and vulnerability in devastating fashion, and Octavia would decide then whether to swoop in and rescue her, but until then, she was forced into the exhausting task of helping her village correctly raise this arrogant child.

"It's a real nice salad course," Octavia said, at last. "I imagine it's easy to make a great salad with such expensive ingredients, though."

Robbe looked from Octavia to Eva. "Those aren't expensive ingredients. I would know. Did you see her make it? It's freshness, proportions, timing, am I right?"

Eva shrugged and nodded.

"I almost forgot the wine," said Elodie, rising, and returned from the kitchen with an open bottle of Vermentino. "Don't finish your salads yet!"

For most of the table, it was too late.

Although Sarah Vang valiantly initiated a heated argument about the quality of food trucks, offering as her sole evidence the popularity of a single gourmet food truck in Los Angeles, the conversation kept looping back to Eva's ridiculous salad. With each course that came out that night, somebody made some reference to why the dish wasn't prepared at the table or where were the Madagascar peppercorns. Octavia's famous summer heirloom tomato casserole barely even got a mention.

By the time Lacey Dietsch's unappealing Jell-O salad came out, which looked like congealed aquarium water with the dead goldfish shredded on the surface, no one was hungry for anything except more chatter about that stupidly basic Caesar. Then something happened that made Octavia want to cut herself; on her way to the bathroom, she glanced into the kitchen and saw Robbe kissing Eva on the cheek. It was on the cheek, but it was a kiss, and Robbe had his eyes closed, and Eva did too.

Eva did not deserve this. Robbe had had a dining room full of attractive, smart, tipsy women—women close to his age, who had accomplished something with their lives—at his place for the last three months, and *this* smart-ass tomato girl is who he chooses? Worse, now Eva would be driving home tonight imagining herself cooking meals in Robbe's kitchen, making pie from the apples in his backyard, lounging with a cocktail on his white midcentury modern sofa, making love in his four-poster bed, the feel of his smooth lips lingering on her face until the moment her eyes closed on the memory.

Yes, Octavia could obviously see what Eva saw in Robbe. Aside from the money and the superficial aspects, he was quite literally a gateway to a more sophisticated, adult world. Were people Eva's age having dinner parties like this one? Hardly. The Sunday Night Dinner Party was, except for poor Lacey Dietsch, a carefully curated assemblage of experts who were at the top of their respective games. Not even Maureen O'Brien was ever invited, and not because she was petty and unattractive—it was because she didn't do any one thing well enough. Eva must've understood what a privilege it was to receive Robbe's invitation. And now that she'd also been handpicked from among more worthy adversaries for the affection of the most desirable bachelor Octavia could ever dream up, well, that girl must be melting like sugar on his tongue.

What Robbe got out of it was harder for Octavia to figure, and it would be a while before she realized that he hadn't chosen Octavia or Elodie or Sarah because to choose an equal would be a sign of maturity, and this boy did not want to grow up, at least not yet. Octavia hoped Eva would be his last roll in the hay before he finally realized that these young girls had nothing to offer but ignorance and demands.

Octavia, who had grown up in Minnetonka around people with both money and taste, who had degrees in English and sociology from Notre Dame, whose dad was a corporate lawyer and stepmother was a model turned pharmaceutical sales rep, was meant to marry a man like Robbe Kramer. She didn't even want a better life than the one she grew up with; she didn't need to be wealthier, just comfortable, with a husband like Robbe who valued the same lifestyle. She would be happy, she knew, being his plus-one to political fund-raisers and charming the less intelligent wives of his prospective business partners. She'd even learned to play golf, knew how to make twenty-seven cocktails, and could watch a Minnesota Vikings game and understand it without asking questions. She knew how to be around rich men, and it was heartbreaking to see Robbe waste himself, for now, on some wide-eyed, guileless little no-name kid.

"Think I'm going to call it a night, you guys," Octavia said.

She badly needed to decompress after that dinner. When she went home, she did something she'd never done before; she took a few hits off her housemate's bowl. That April, Octavia wanted to move some-where closer to her job in Uptown, so she rented the second floor of a house from a divorced twenty-nine-year-old woman named Andrea who worked for a theater company and smoked up while watching HBO. From the first-floor kitchen, which they shared, Octavia glanced into the living room and saw that Andrea had left her weed and pipe on the coffee table, for the first time since they'd lived together.

It was clearly meant to be. It was like her housemate knew.

The following week ended up being just about the worst five-day stretch of Octavia's adult life to that point. There was a random drug test at the children's educational nonprofit where she worked, which she failed, because she'd done drugs for the first time in years just thirty-six hours before, and was immediately put on administrative leave without pay, which pretty much meant that she was fired. As a result, her dad cut her off financially, saying he wouldn't give her another check until she checked into Hazelden and tackled the drug addiction he claimed he'd always suspected she had.

"You fucking bastard," she said to her dad on the phone, and hung up, tears in her eyes.

To his credit, he'd left her alone after that, but now with no job and no money from home, Octavia Kincade was financially screwed.

She was still in enough of a foul mood that when the e-mail came around asking for everyone's menu contributions for the following Sunday's dinner, Octavia waited for Eva to respond, which she did, with "Sweet Corn Succotash." Octavia pressed delete on that e-mail.

Octavia believed that morality was a learned social construct, as was responsibility, humility, and even generosity. Humans were born evil, as little sociopaths intent purely on slaking their own impulsive desires, and many never learned to be good, or evolved traits like empathy or compassion, instead remaining selfish, destructive small children for life. Eva Thorvald, that unrepentant, arrogant crowd-pleaser, was the most devious of all the small children Octavia knew and, ergo, would only be corrected into a life of humility through being broken.

Octavia arrived at Robbe's house at the exact same time she always did, a green ceramic bowl under her arm, and walked in, without knocking, as usual.

"Oh, hey," Robbe said, entering from the kitchen. "You're early."

"What's that in the bowl?" Eva asked, following him. She had beaten Octavia here somehow.

"Sweet corn succotash," Octavia said.

"Ha, that's funny. I made that too."

Robbe looked annoyed. "Didn't you see the e-mail?"

Octavia shook her head. "I never got the e-mail."

"Well, if you don't get it, you need to text me or call me," Robbe said. "Now we're gonna have a shitload of succotash."

"I may just dump mine in the trash right now," Eva said. "After your awesome tomato hot dish last time."

Octavia didn't recall Eva praising her heirloom tomato dish last week; in any case, it was much too late for her to put on a show of false humility. "I'd hate to see you do that," Octavia said. "After witnessing your magic Caesar."

"I have an idea," Eva said. "Let's put each of them in bowls of Robbe's so we can't tell who made which one, how's that?"

"Whatever floats your boat," Octavia said, though secretly she liked the idea.

The problem was, you could tell one from the other at a hundred feet; one had diced organic red pepper (Octavia's) while the other had French-cut Blue Lake string beans (Eva's). The corn in Eva's was also whiter.

"Why did you do yours with green beans?" Octavia asked Eva in the kitchen as their succotash was being transferred, for no good reason now as Octavia saw it, to their more anonymous new homes.

"I often use okra. But green beans are in season locally."

"What kind of sweet corn did you use?"

"I think it's Northern Xtra Sweet bicolor."

"Oh, nice." Octavia smiled. In her research over the last two weeks, she'd learned that Northern Xtra Sweet was an extremely common variety of corn; you could get it anywhere. "Where'd you get it?"

"Oh, I drove to Mr. Xiong's farm down in Dakota County this afternoon and got some right off the stalk."

"Just today? Before you got here? How'd you pull that off?"

"It wasn't a long drive. What kind of corn is in yours?"

"I got heirloom Golden Bantam. From a woman who sells herbs at the St. Paul Farmers' Market."

"Wow, never heard of it," Eva said. "Who's the herb vendor?"

"Anna Hlavek. But she doesn't sell it to the public, you have to ask." Octavia had the inside track; she'd heard about it from a friend of hers who'd dated Anna's son Dougie the year before.

Octavia knew she had won this round. With American cornfields at close to 90 percent GMO corn, and all of the numerous crosses and hybridizations and so-called improvements made to corn even before genetic intervention, Anna Hlavek at the farmers' market was growing something almost unheard of: an open-pollinated corn variety that hadn't changed a bit in more than one hundred years. From what she was told, Anna had inherited the seed stock from her grandfather, who'd bought it from a catalog when Burpee first introduced Golden Bantam 8 Row back in 1902. This was the exact corn Octavia's great-grandparents ate at their farm near Hunter, North Dakota—old-fashioned plump, firm, milky kernels that burst in your mouth and were so sweet, it could've been served for dessert. No one, not even Eva with the fancy ingredients, could've gotten hold of this sweet corn; you had to know someone to make sure you were getting the real deal, and Octavia, as luck would have it, did.

"Can't wait to try it," Eva said.

The seating chart had devolved a bit from the week before. Adam Snelling still sat across from Sarah Vang, but now Eva sat across from Robbe and Octavia sat across from Elodie. Octavia did get to sit *next* to Robbe, however, which in a lot of ways was really better than sitting across from him. Lacey, meanwhile, sat at the tail with her baby, facing no one again.

"Why do I always have to sit down here?" she asked. It was rare for her to complain; Octavia felt that Lacey should be happy just to be there, and figured that she had been.

Everyone stared down the table at her. "It's just the way it turned out," Robbe said.

"Can someone switch with me?" she asked, and looked at her friend, the woman who had invited her. "Octavia?"

Octavia shook her head. "I need to be here, I'm handling one of the early dishes."

Robbe shook his head. "You don't *need* to be anywhere, Octavia."

She was stung that he didn't seem to want to be next to her as much as she wanted to be next to him, but put on a smile. "It's easier to distribute from over here. Her dishes always come at the end."

"Fine," Robbe said. "Well, sorry, Lacey."

Lacey nodded and sighed. She used to have a perfectly nice place to sit, across from someone and everything—at least until fancy Eva showed up—and was probably doing the math in her head just then, figuring that out. "You know, I'm gonna go," she said, and stood up.

"All right," said Octavia.

"Why?" asked Adam Snelling. Adam was super nice like that.

"You guys don't like my food, you make me sit here at the end of the table by myself, you never talk about anything I know, and you never even ask me any questions about myself."

"You shouldn't wait to be asked," Robbe said. "I don't." This, from Robbe, passed for empathy.

"Well, see ya later," Lacey said, and stomped to the kitchen, coming back out with the Tupperware bowl of ambrosia fruit salad she'd made with canned fruit cocktail and Cool Whip. Her baby daughter had started to cry from all of the jostling and Lacey had to shout over the child's wail. "Have a good dinner party," she said, standing in the open doorway. "Bye."

After she closed the door, hard, the remaining six diners sat in silence for a moment before Robbe stood up and cleared Lacey's wineglass and silverware.

"I think in the future when we invite a new person, we should run it by the whole group first," he said as he walked into his kitchen.

Eva, the newest person, and invited by Robbe's decree—not run by the group at all—had the nerve to speak up. "I know someone who I think might like to come," she said.

"Looking forward to hearing about them," Robbe said, setting the two white bowls of succotash on the table.

Octavia tried Eva's first. She hated to say it, but it was exquisite. The green beans and corn were each just slightly firm, the bacon was fragrant and not too salty, and the nearly diaphanous white onion pieces were in that Goldilocks zone of piquancy, neither overbearing nor nominal.

Then Octavia tried her own. Her corn was firm and starchy; she didn't know when Anna picked it—Octavia had just bought it the morning of the day before—but the kernels hadn't kept their sugar. Some of them even felt like loose teeth in her mouth. She looked around the table and saw people spitting into their napkins.

"I'll have more of the one with the beans," Elodie said, and Adam quickly concurred.

That bitch Anna Hlavek. It should be required for a sweet corn vendor to post the exact date and time of their harvest to avoid these awful mistakes. Eva, of course, had used corn that was probably only four or five hours old at that point; *that* had made all the difference, not what damn varietal it was.

"Whose was whose?" Sarah asked, with her loud, disharmonious harpy voice.

"I brought the one with the red pepper," Eva said. "It was really good a day ago. I don't know what happened."

Before Octavia could even gather her thoughts, everyone started talking.

"The sugars in sweet corn can turn to starch really fast," Sarah said. "You're still so amazing for someone your age. So amazing."

Eva nodded. "Thanks. I know I still have a lot to learn."

"This might actually be my favorite thing you've ever made," Elodie said, looking at Octavia. "This could win awards."

Adam nodded and smiled, mouth full.

"Octavia is back, ladies and gentlemen," Sarah said.

Robbe, who'd seen the women transfer their succotash into his bowls, said nothing. He just stared at the side of Octavia's head, the way someone stares at a theater curtain in the moments before the play begins.

"Thanks, everyone," Octavia said, watching as Adam gathered everyone's plates, mounds of her Golden Bantam succotash sitting, lightly touched, on every one.

The next day, Robbe insisted on meeting Octavia for drinks at Horseless Carriage, his favorite old-man bar, for 5:00 p.m. happy hour. Though Octavia was busy updating her résumé—she was going to leave off her previous employer altogether and just tell people that she'd been volunteering with children the last two years—she obviously agreed to meet him.

When she arrived, he was halfway through a martini already, sitting under a backlit sign advertising a Prime Rib Special, playing with his cell phone. The place smelled like stale popcorn and Bar Keepers Friend, and the handful of other people there were hunched over pull tabs at the bar or watching baseball on silent TVs.

Robbe looked up from his phone and nodded when she entered, but did not put down the phone, much less rise from his seat like a gentleman.

"I'm kinda seeing Eva," Robbe said. "I just wanted to tell you."

She'd suspected this travesty was under way, but actually hearing it hit Octavia in the heart with a cast-iron skillet. "Why did you need to tell me that in person?" she asked.

"Because I know you like me."

"Well yeah, as a friend, I like you as a friend."

"Have it your way," he said. "I actually did think about sleeping with you at one point, but you seem like the type that would get all psycho afterwards."

Octavia took a deep breath. "I'm so glad we skipped all that. I have been meaning to ask you, though—how come you didn't say anything about the succotash during the dinner yesterday?"

"What do you mean?"

"You saw us put our succotash into bowls. You were there in the kitchen."

"I don't remember that. But I'd had a few."

"All right." She got the bartender's attention and ordered a Long Island Iced Tea, which was wildly passé, but Christ, she needed it, and it wasn't like anyone in this bar knew her.

"So what's going to happen to you guys when you move to Bali?"

"What's going to happen to who?"

"You and Eva."

"I don't know. Maybe she'll come with."

"What kind of woman would just drop everything and run off with you?" Octavia knew she would've skipped town indefinitely and left for Bali with Robbe at any moment, at least until maybe five minutes ago.

"Have you been to her place?"

"God, no."

"She lives in a totally sketchy apartment with her dad off of Lake Street. I was there a few days ago, and when I was waiting for her to come down, I seriously thought I was going to get shot. If I were her, I'd get the hell out of there first chance I had."

"So that's it. You think you can rescue her."

"Who the hell knows," Robbe said. "But do you know who she's bringing to the next dinner? Mitch Diego. Nobody will have to bring anything. He's going to make all the food. How do you like that?"

"I'm intrigued," Octavia said.

• • •

For the dinner with Mitch Diego, Octavia wore her best dress, a chocolate BCBG jersey dancer dress with a plunging neckline, cinched at the waist with a red wool belt. It wasn't a summer color—the dress was from the fall 2008 season—but it literally stopped men on the street, so screw it.

Mitch Diego looked like a slightly heavier version of the pictures on his Web site, but he still had a look that Octavia lusted after: a beard of silver and charcoal, with slick, curly obsidian hair and dizzying brown topaz eyes. She even loved the black chest hair popping up from the neckline of his white pearl-snap shirt; not a trendy look, but she admired men who ran with it. He looked Octavia up and down but didn't introduce himself, so neither did she, but she caught him looking so many times she started folding her arms in front of her chest.

Eva stood in the corner of Robbe's kitchen, next to his Kitchen Aid mixer, watching Robbe and Mitch from a distance. Robbe touched her every time he passed by her, and she touched him back, rarely speaking to him or Mitch, but obviously happy to be along for this ride, in an exquisite kitchen with a rich handsome man-friend and a legendary local chef.

Adam Snelling froze when he walked into the kitchen and saw Octavia. "You look real beautiful," he said to her face, in a way that seemed like it was involuntary, like he just *had* to say it, which was nice, and took a cigarette out of his pocket. The clean white cylinder shook between his fingers.

"Give me one of those," Octavia said, and led him out to the backyard. For some reason, Mitch Diego followed them.

"Bum a smoke?" he asked Adam.

Adam held out the pack for Mitch. "You don't need to be in the kitchen?" Octavia asked, preemptively crossing her arms in front of her chest.

"Dirty little secret," Mitch said. "Eva has saved my life. She does everything I can do and people can't tell the difference. I'm actually writing a book now, I have time to write a book."

"What's it called?"

"*Tapas Girls and Bottomless Sangria: Hot Times in Spanish Kitchens.* You know anyone who can help me with a book proposal?"

Robbe sat across from Eva at the end of the table, then Sarah across from Elodie, and, in a new twist, Adam across from Octavia at the other end. She was hoping that Mitch, who'd be in the Lacey Dietsch position, would sit next to her, but when Mitch saw the table he left the room and came back in from the study with a desk chair, which he put at the head of the table. Octavia wondered why no one had thought of that before.

"Tonight's menu," Mitch Diego announced, "is summer corn chowder, made from Golden Bantam sweet corn. Main course is slow-cooked organic pork shoulder tacos with mint, black beans, and Wisconsin feta cheese, and salsa made from Nebraska Wedding and Cherokee Purple heirlooms. Dessert is Paula Red apple crisp."

Everyone applauded, and Octavia watched as Eva rose and disappeared into the kitchen.

The meal that Eva made and Mitch Diego took credit for was predictably incredible. People begged for leftovers, Sarah Vang demanded that Mitch Diego open a food truck, Robbe claimed that it was the best meal he'd ever had in his home.

The diners lingered over the extra salsa, a beautiful blend of yellow and purple heirloom tomatoes from Heirloom Johnny Lao at the St. Paul Farmers' Market.

"Why do you buy from him?" Mitch Diego complained to Eva in front of everyone. "He's too expensive and he's an asshole."

"He's always been nice to me," Eva said.

• • •

It could've been the ninety-degree weather, and the surfeit of Elodie Pickett's amazing wine pairings, and the fact that Sarah had to leave early to pick someone up at the airport, but the remaining three women and three men found their way into pairs and were dancing in the living room, touching each other's sweaty bodies and then draped on them, sitting on each other's laps during breaks.

Octavia recalled lying across Adam's legs, her head arched over the armrest of the sofa, looking upside down at Elodie, Mitch, Robbe, and Eva dancing on the hardwood floor to "Kids," by MGMT. The smile on Eva's inverted face was so unrestrained and beautiful, Octavia actually felt herself feeling happy for the stupid girl. She still couldn't watch Robbe kiss her, but she was starting to feel OK about how things had turned out, maybe.

Octavia was also surprised that she'd begun to find Adam attractive; he wasn't her type at all—gangly, with a cheap haircut and stubble and a love of cheap short-sleeved plaid shirts—she'd hardly spoken to him at all for the first few months they'd shared these meals together in this house. He hadn't even registered to her as a sexual being. Now, all of a sudden, she wanted to lead him behind the toolshed and let him take all of her clothes off, and she wasn't even sure exactly why.

If the afterglow from outdoor sex hadn't lingered for the next few days, it would've been another horrifying week in Octavia's life. First of all, how was she supposed to know that the stupid dashboard alarm on her BMW was telling her that her coolant tank was empty? Now she needed to replace the radiator and a bunch of hoses, and she didn't have that kind of money anymore.

Also, she got a phone call on Monday afternoon from her high school friend Jessica Mitchelette, who was a fellow front line on the volleyball team. She said that Sunday night, Lacey Dietsch was walking through her neighborhood, pushing her infant daughter in a stroller, when a guy in a pickup truck made a right turn and hit her, dragging her under the truck for a hundred feet before he stopped. Her stomach was split open and her intestines were prolapsed onto the asphalt. She died before the ambulance even arrived. The stroller somehow wasn't hit; they found it half pushed onto the center median, the baby soundly sleeping inside.

Later that week, Robbe announced that there was going to be just one more Sunday dinner before he and Eva moved to Bali, and it was going to be a big one—a Labor Day wine and cheese fund-raiser to raise money for Eva's dad's medical care and nursing home fees, to take care of him for the length of time that he and Eva would be away. They would charge a hundred dollars a plate, no exceptions, but figured that people might pay that much for an all-day, all-night party of wine and appetizers by Bar Garroxta's famous executive chef, Mitch Diego.

Octavia showed up early, in a sleeveless ivory dress (last chance to wear white in 2009!), having driven over in Adam's Honda Accord, walking with him to Robbe's front door arm in arm.

"Have you paid in advance?" Robbe asked at the door. He was wearing a tie and holding a clipboard.

"Paid?" Octavia asked. "We're your friends, we get in free."

"No one gets in free," Robbe said. "Eva's dad has lots of medical bills and needs a full-time home health-care nurse. That's what this is about."

Since when did Robbe Kramer get altruistic? "Wow, your girlfriend must have a magic pussy," she said.

Robbe frowned at her. For a famously blunt guy, he hated perverse or immodest conversation; he felt coarseness was blue-collar and beneath him. She supposed that every man, or even a four-year-old in a man's body like Robbe, had to have a code.

Octavia stared at him. "You know I don't have that kind of money. I've been unemployed for a month. I can't even afford to fix my car."

"I can spot you," Adam said, because he was so nice.

"No, you work at a bakery, you can't spend two hundred dollars on appetizers."

"Yeah, but it's for our friend's dad," he said.

"Not really. It's so this one can run off with his twenty-year-old girl-friend."

While they were talking, a large Jamaican-looking guy ambled up the sidewalk behind them. "Hey, I paid in advance," he said. "Ros Wali from Simple Space Solutions."

Robbe checked the clipboard and waved the guy in. From the look of the list, it didn't look like they were going to have any trouble making money and didn't need to soak their friends.

Robbe turned to Octavia and Adam. "If you guys need to run to an ATM, we'll be going for a while."

"Screw it," Octavia said, turning her back. "Come on, Adam."

She never saw Robbe Kramer again.

She saw Eva Thorvald three more times. The first time was at a popular café in Loring Park, a block down from the apartment that Octavia could no longer afford. It was two weeks after Labor Day, and the leaves weren't changing color yet, but there was already a soft bite in the breeze, and the outdoor tables were full of Minnesotans plundering the final days of summer. Inside the warm brick-walled building, full of young people on laptops and cell phones and well-dressed couples noshing over breakfast pastries, Eva sat at the thick wooden table farthest from the windows, under a vintage French poster for Lillet. Her hair looked even crappier than usual, and her face was red and blotchy.

"Thanks for meeting me," she said.

"Sorry again about not making it to your fund-raiser. We couldn't afford it."

"It's OK. Have you heard from Robbe?"

"No, not in weeks." For some reason, Eva looked crushed when Octavia said this. "I thought you guys were leaving for Bali."

"He left," Eva said, putting both of her hands over her face. Octavia watched her body shudder with deep breaths.

"Robbe left for Bali already? I thought you were going with?"

Eva wiped her face. "I can't go with. We only raised sixty-seven hundred dollars. It's not enough for everything. I can't just leave my dad here. I just can't."

As someone who hadn't even spoken to her own dad in more than two months, Octavia was touched and confused by Eva's loyalty to someone who apparently hadn't done her much good and was a total money pit besides. And, more important, she also felt like she'd seriously dodged a bullet with Mr. Kramer.

"Sixty-seven hundred dollars, that's gotta pay for . . ."

"We still owe forty grand for my dad's liver transplant," Eva said. "Plus, my dad needs someone to cook for him, and give him his insulin shots on schedule, and help him do the laundry and dishes. It's a lot."

"It's still almost seven grand, that's gotta help."

Eva shook her head. "Robbe stole half of it. He said he earned it."

"What? That shithead. He doesn't need your money. Sue him for it."

Eva held a brown paper napkin against her wet eyes. "That's a stupid amount to hire a lawyer for. Not like I can even afford a lawyer."

"But it's the principle of the thing. And maybe you can get damages."

"It's gone. He stole it."

"You know what? Have another fund-raiser."

"For the same thing? Two weeks after the last one?"

"Then don't call it a fund-raiser, just call it a fancy meal."

"But there's nowhere to even have it."

"Well, have it anywhere, have it outside somewhere. When the weather's still nice. Get Mitch Diego to cook again and you're golden."

"He didn't even show up to this last one."

"But you still raised almost seven thousand dollars? And people were happy?"

Eva nodded, wiping her face.

"Then screw Mitch Diego. I don't like him anyway."

"You know, what's funny is, I think he really likes you. He talks about you all the time."

Such interesting food for thought, but at the time, Octavia was happy and wasn't interested. Adam had even started biking to work so she could have his car while she looked for a job. And that was his idea, not hers. It was something to be around people who thought like that. "I'm with somebody," she said. "A nice man."

"Well, I gotta go make lunch for my dad," Eva said, finishing her water. "If you hear from Robbe, let me know, I know you guys were close."

What a sucker, Octavia thought as she hugged her. Of course Robbe didn't actually love her; he had robbed her and fobbed her and tossed her aside to be stuck in Minnesota with her sickly dad while he wrote his memoir in Bali. Robbe had goals, and therefore he knew who could help him and exactly how long to keep them around. And here were Octavia and Eva, thousands of miles from him, broke, and cursing his name.

The second-to-last time Octavia saw Eva was actually just three weeks later. Elodie Pickett, whom Octavia hadn't heard from in forever, e-mailed that she and Eva had a business proposition and asked if she wanted to meet up somewhere. Octavia had just gotten a part-time job on Lake Street working as a discard counselor for Small Space Solutions—she had been hired by a guy named Ros Wali, who claimed to have been at Robbe and Eva's Labor Day fund-raiser. She went into people's homes and told them what they should get rid of, which she found she had a talent for.

Eva's apartment is right nearby, Elodie texted. Let's just meet there.

Eva's apartment was arguably worse than even Robbe had implied. The whole place smelled like beef stock and mold, and the one place to sit was occupied by a fat man whom Octavia assumed was Eva's dad. He was watching one of Octavia's favorite shows, *Cater-Mania with Miles Binder,* the episode where Miles and his crazy staff try to throw a Thanksgiving party for a hundred people on three hours' notice. A classic.

Eva kissed her dad on the head. "What are you watching this for?" she asked him.

"It reminds me of you," he said.

She laughed. "This show annoys the hell out of me."

He glanced behind him at Octavia. "Who is she supposed to be?"

Octavia, now feeling violently awkward, and not wanting that gross man to look at her, stepped into the small kitchen. It was the only room that was somewhat generously appointed, and it was crammed with beaten appliances and kitchenware—stacks of pans and pots were piled on each of the stove's burners—but before she could really take it all in, she was pulled into the unit's one bedroom, which was Eva's.

The bedroom was as spare as the rest of the house, and except for a few of the dresses and blouses hanging in the closet, there was not much to suggest it was a girl's room, with its plain white bedsheets and white particleboard nightstand. Instead of a dresser, stacks of transparent plastic tubs held her underwear and socks. The most interesting features were the worn posters for the Smiths and Bikini Kill taped on the walls, and the stacks of cookbooks piled on the floor, many with bookmarks sticking out of them at all angles, and tags on the spines from library sales.

For lack of anywhere better everyone sat on top of the bed, like college kids. This made Octavia feel uneasy, but not as much as the apartment did in general. Was this poverty? She'd never seen people who actually lived like this. It was almost like the apartment from the movie *Trainspotting.* It made her nervous, like she was holding on to the edge of an inner tube in a current, and the slightest shock might suck her down into this standard of living, with these people. Now she realized why even though poor people had the numbers, they could never start a revolution; they feared and despised the people one step below them, and for good reason.

"So what's up?" she asked. "I can't stay long."

A voice from down the hall rattled the women's bones. "Eva!" the man's voice shouted. "When's dinner?"

"I'll be right there," Eva said, and scrambled off of the bed. "Sorry, guys, I'm making my dad a rosemary-shallot beef stew, I gotta go see if it's done."

That explained the beef part of the smell. "No worries," Octavia said.

"I'll get her up to speed," Elodie said, and looked at Octavia. "How are you?"

"Good. How are things at the nonprofit?"

"Chugging along. They promoted Sammy to take your job."

"Ha. He can't even write a cover letter."

"He's learning." Elodie shrugged. "Anyway, Eva and I are going to start doing epicurean dinners around town and we just wanted to tell you that we could use your help."

"What do you mean, epicurean dinners around town?"

"Eva said it was kind of your idea. Just sort of throw dinner parties at random places and charge people a flat rate of, like, a hundred dollars, for a really fancy meal, and make it kind of exclusive."

"Why not just open a restaurant?"

"Your idea's way better. We don't have to rent property and pass safety codes and get a liquor license and that kind of stuff. We don't have to be open on a Tuesday when there's like only two people eating. We can just move in somewhere for one night and move out. Are you interested in helping us cook and make the menu?"

"I don't know, I already have a job." After being unemployed for two months, it almost felt ostentatious to say that.

"Well, this would just be like once or twice a month. We already have, like, thirty people coming to the first one this Friday. That's at least three thousand bucks that we'd split three ways."

"After expenses."

"I suppose, yeah, but that wouldn't be a lot. And I'm paying for the wine out of my share."

"I don't know, it sounds like a lot of work." This was sounding to Octavia like a lot of labor and expense, and without Mitch Diego's name attached, and Robbe's money and connections, could they be sure that even thirty people would show up? They were talented chicks, sure, but it takes so much more than that; from where they were starting, in a small bedroom in a crappy apartment, sitting on low-thread-count sheets, it looked like they were going to take a bath on this one, and Octavia didn't need any more shame in her life at that point.

The volume on *Cater-Mania with Miles Binder* got substantially louder from down the hall. Eva appeared in the doorway. "Hey, can you guys please keep it down? My dad says your conversation is bothering him."

Elodie looked behind herself at Eva. "Was the door closed?"

"Yeah, but he said he could hear you through the door. I just don't think he's used to people being over."

Octavia nodded. "You don't say."

"Anyway, you guys want any beef stew? It's almost ready."

Octavia got up from the bed. "I should get going."

Eva watched Octavia as she passed through her bedroom doorway. "Did Elodie tell you about our dinner party on Friday?"

"I'm going to have to pass, guys. I just got too much going on."

Eva looked sincerely disappointed. "You're seriously one of the best chefs I know. Seriously."

"That's nice of you to say," Octavia said.

"And we don't want you as an employee or something, we want you as an actual partner."

"I know, and I'm flattered. But thank you."

Eva and Elodie gave each other a *What do we do now?* look that Octavia saw; it was actually kind of touching that these two kids thought so much of her. At least, they did once.

"You should at least come by and eat for free and let us know what you think," Eva offered when Octavia was on her way out the door.

Octavia and Adam totally forgot about it by the time Friday rolled around, and neither of them even heard about how it went, so Octavia assumed it had gone poorly and those girls wouldn't ask anything of her again.

The last time that Octavia saw Eva was four years later, in the produce section of the Seward Co-Op. Octavia was there because it was her lunch break and it was cheap and she'd taken to buying things in bulk for the family she now had with Adam, which included a three-year-old and a one-year-old.

"Octavia?" she heard a woman's voice say.

Eva Thorvald no longer resembled the awkward ingénue she'd first met in Robbe Kramer's kitchen; she'd evolved in every possible way. She was now a grand, luminous twenty-four-year-old with tree-limb arms, Angelina Jolie lips, scarred chef hands, cinder-block feet, generous breasts, and the kind of ass that rap songs are written about—she hadn't grown into being a woman, she had become a woman with an exclamation mark, the sort of hardy feminine brute of the Pleistocene from which all women, great and frail, are descended.

Octavia was relieved to see that this forceful, glowing Eva was dressed the same as ever—although in a clean, nicer version of her stock outfit—but with what looked like an expensive hairstyle, tasteful makeup, and brand-new New Balance shoes.

"How are you?" Eva asked. Octavia found herself taking a step backwards when Eva spoke. "I've seen your blog, it looks like you're doing well."

Octavia's blog, where she exhaustively documented her children's lives every day, had been named one of the Top Ten Mom Blogs in the Twin Cities by the Minneapolis paper, and had garnered her a bit of attention. She was occasionally stopped by a stranger who knew her from the blog, but she never would've guessed that someone like Eva Thorvald had read it; in fact she'd pretty much forgotten about Eva Thorvald altogether. "Thank you. I just hope other new mothers get something out of it. We're all in it together, you know. How are you doing?"

"Same old, same old. Just buying some emergency ginger, you know."

"How are *you* doing, are you working in a restaurant?"

"No, no," Eva said. "Still doing the dinner party that we started back in October of '09. It's been very labor-intensive."

"Is Elodie still with you?"

"Nope, no, Elodie moved on, she and her partner opened a wine bar in Uptown. It's doing good. It's right next door to where Bar Garroxta used to be."

"Oh yeah," Octavia said, like she'd heard of this. She hadn't been able to afford a nice meal out regularly in over four years, and was out of the loop. "What's it called?"

"You'll like this. She named it 'Dietsch,' in honor of our old friend Lacey. Once a year she holds a fund-raiser barrel tasting for Emma Dietsch's college fund. You should swing by, Elodie would love to see you."

"And the dinner party's going well? You still getting around thirty people?"

"No, no, it sounds crazy, but we're actually averaging a hundred and fifty, but we're trying to scale it back to around twenty and have the events be more unusual."

"How much are you charging per dinner, if you don't mind me asking?"

"Right now, about five hundred bucks."

"A hundred and fifty people paying five hundred bucks each? How often?"

"About once a month. None in December, twice each in August and September. But now we're starting a new reservations system, expanding the staff, and hosting dinners in way more exotic locations. It's going to increase our overhead like crazy. You don't even want to know. We're going to have to raise our price a whole lot immediately, which I didn't want to do. It's a giant risk. But it might be really amazing if it works. So we're in a major state of flux right now."

Octavia had no idea how to respond. She didn't know anyone with these kinds of problems. "Cool," was all she said.

"Speaking of, I gotta bounce. I have a meeting with a loan officer at three."

"All right, good luck with that," Octavia said. "But hey, you ever hear from Robbe Kramer?"

Eva froze as if a stranger's toddler had just grabbed her leg. "I did, about a year ago, I did."

"I saw his house got foreclosed. I also heard that he's living in Thailand with a twenty-two-year-old."

"Yeah, I heard that. They were here visiting and they tried to get into one of my dinners for free."

"What did you do?"

"I didn't let him in."

"You didn't beat him up? Slash his tires?"

"No, he has what he deserves already," Eva said. "Good to see you. Don't be a stranger."

In the parking lot afterward, Octavia saw Eva walk to a shiny Honda Odyssey minivan and waited for her to drive off so she wouldn't see Octavia get into her beat-up old Pontiac Aztek that she'd bought used from Craigslist.

She sat in the car and took out her cell phone and did the math. Five hundred bucks times a hundred and fifty people was $75,000. That times thirteen was $975,000. That divided by three was $325,000. She could be making $325,000 a year right now instead of the $29,000 she was making as a discard counselor. More than ten times as much, if she'd remained sitting on that crappy bed in that shitty apartment four years ago.

And also, what was Eva doing driving a minivan if she was pulling in mid-six figures? It blew Octavia's mind. It was like Eva was afraid to be rich, or didn't know how to be.

In the days since, in her head, Octavia would often spend the $325,000 she could've had. She'd spend it while standing in line at the post office, at a checkout at Wal-Mart, while making French toast for her husband and eldest daughter, while riding in Mitch's ten-year-old Mercedes with the dented fender, while lying in the snow outside his place, watching her phone, waiting for him to text.

Her phone buzzed. NOT TODAY, the words said.

Not today? That old washout didn't get to tell *her* not today. After putting a popular restaurant out of business, Mitch Diego was lucky he had a mistress at all, let alone one as beautiful and interesting as Octavia Kincade.

She snapped to her feet and stomped out of the snowbank to his front door, her clothes dripping wet snow onto his welcome mat. She could see a light on upstairs; he was certainly home. The door was locked, so she pounded on it. He didn't answer, so she pounded on it again. With both fists she pounded on it.

Her phone buzzed. LEAVE OR I CALL THE COPS, it read.

LIKE YOU WOULD DARE, she texted back, and pounded with her open palm this time.

She took a break and texted him, IF YOU DON'T OPEN YOUR DOOR, IT'S OVER and watched the door. Nothing happened. She pounded on it again. She pounded and shouted. She took another short break and then pounded again.

She didn't hear the car park in the street, the sound of a driver's side door slamming shut, or the footsteps of the man who walked up behind her. "Ma'am," he said. She didn't turn around. "Ma'am," he said again.

VENISON

It used to be, if Jordy Snelling could change one thing about his life, it would be that rifle season went a week longer and didn't overlap with bow season. Now here it was, two days from the opener, and he hadn't even cleaned his goddamn Mauser yet.

His brother Adam had come by early to visit their mom, and he brought his new lady friend Eva with him. For some stupid reason they didn't wake him up when they got there, and now here he was getting up and they were about to leave. Also, his right hand was swollen up like a turkey drumstick and the knuckles were scraped raw. It had hurt from the moment he woke up, but his nose and face felt fine. Did he get in a fight? Maybe he won.

"Hey," Eva said, smiling, when Jordy walked into the living room. Eva was real tall, seemed pretty nice, and supposedly had a job as some kinda fancy chef or something. This was only the second time he'd ever even seen her, but he was already 100 percent sure that she was way, way better than Adam's snotty ex-wife Octavia, who nobody ever liked anyway. "What happened to your hand?" she asked.

Jordy laughed. "Hell if I know," he said, crossing the room to check on his mom, who was sleeping, fully reclined in her easy chair. Since she became so bony and pale, he could never look at her body for very long. "How's she doing?" he whispered to Eva.

"Good," Eva whispered back. "She was up earlier."

"We were waiting for you to get up so we could go," Adam said. His brother looked tired, but he always looked tired, because he worked at a damn bakery for some reason. "Eva's got her cousins coming into town tomorrow and she's gotta get her place ready."

It was 11:00 a.m., and the hospice nurse, Mandy, should've come by now anyway. He didn't like to be alone with his mom for too long, especially when she needed her meds. What if he fucked something up? Her breathing was heavy again. She slept all the time now, and she didn't get out of her recliner too much.

On their way out, Adam hugged him, and Eva hugged him, kind of firmly for someone he didn't know too well, and they told Jordy that he'd be fine and to call them if he needed anything. Between them, and the neighbors, and his aunt Melanie up in Inver Grove, someone was usually around, at least.

After they left, he checked on his mom again—still sleeping—and went out to the second-floor apartment's balcony, the only place where he was allowed to smoke. Outside, they were cutting the forest across the street to make room for new condominiums. Trying to get it done before it started snowing. It meant that all of the deer in those woods were going to be flushed out into streets and backyards just in time for mating season.

What people don't understand about deer is that they're vermin. They're giant, furry cockroaches. They invade a space, reproduce like hell, and eat everything in sight. A few adult deer can eat an entire garden in a couple of hours. And not just the vegetables, but the stalks, the leaves, the roots, everything. Leave you with nothing.

And worse. Four years ago, Jordy lost his high school buddy Matt Dubcek to a fucking deer. Dubby had just gotten his motorcycle license like the week before. He was out on his 350cc Honda—not a big engine, but more than enough bike for a newbie. Not a lot up front, though; no fender, no windscreen, no front fairing. It was night and some buck walked out on the highway right in front of him. He didn't even have a chance.

Jordy tried to imagine that he'd have reacted differently, that his reflexes were good enough that he'd have jumped off to the side or even laid the bike down. Anything better than hitting the flank at sixty miles per hour. When they found Dubby, he was basically beheaded.

He had just gotten married to this chick Lisa who'd done a tour in Afghanistan. Last he heard, she was up in Lakeville, pregnant with some other dude's kid, and working at the new Cracker Barrel they got up there.

The intercom bleated; someone was in the lobby. He crushed his cigarette into an empty Keystone Light can on the deck. The nurse. He tapped the intercom to buzz her into the building, then stopped and looked at his reflection in the hall mirror. There was no helping what he saw in the time he had.

The apartment door opened; it was Dan Jorgenson. "Hey man," Dan said, his hand rooting around in his greasy tan Carhartt jacket. "You forgot your phone charger in my car." Dan handed it to Jordy. It was sticky from God knows what. "Thought you might want it," he said.

"Hey, thanks. I had no fuckin' idea I even lost it."

"Dude, you were beyond fucked up last night. You fuckin' punched a hole in the wall of Scotty's dad's garage."

"That explains it," Jordy said, holding his swelled hand up to Dan's face.

"Looks better today than it did last night," Dan said. "Hey, can I come in for a beer? Or is your mom sleeping?"

"Yeah, but the nurse'll be here any sec," Jordy said, turning from the doorway.

"Cool." Dan smiled, taking off his Carhartt stocking cap and his black steel-toed boots on the mat by the coat rack. He followed Jordy

down the hallway in his chunky gray socks, and turned left at the dinette, while Jordy walked into the living room.

Jordy patted his mom on the shoulder. She was up, and had turned
on the TV. A *Storage Wars: Texas* rerun was on, and a tiny brown-haired
woman and a big guy in a cowboy hat were arguing over other people's
stuff. Jordy didn't know what would happen to all his mom's stuff, but
he sure as hell didn't want strangers touching any of it.

"Was that the nurse?" his mom asked.

"No, just Dan."

Jordy's mom turned and looked over her shoulder, seeing Dan just as
he cracked open a Coors Light. She waved at him and said, "Hi, Dan."
He raised the can and smiled.

"It's already eleven twenty," Jordy's mom said. "I hope that's not your
first beer."

"Sorry to say it is, Linda. A little hair of the dog."

"You look after this one," she told Dan, pointing at her son.

"I sure try to."

Jordy was embarrassed. "Come on," he said, leading Dan toward his
bedroom.

Dan sat in the chair at Jordy's desk, next to his Acer laptop, which was
softly playing a Tool song through the attached external speakers, while
Jordy sat on his mattress on the floor and drank from a bottle of Early
Times.

"It smells like dirty laundry in here," Dan said.

"That's because I got a fuckin' ton of dirty laundry," Jordy said. "So
what happened? Did I get in a fight with someone?"

"No, but you were getting real chippy. That's why Scotty locked you
in the garage."

"I don't remember none of that."

"Yeah, and like at three in the morning, we were like, oh shit, what about Jordy, because by then you were locked in there for, like, three hours. And you were passed out on the floor of the garage next to the snowblower. And there was a big fuckin' hole in the side of the garage. Like in the drywall."

"What was I supposedly getting chippy about?"

"I don't even know. I was downstairs playing pool. Scotty said you just went off. I don't think you hit anybody or anything. But Micayla got me and was, like, Scotty wants your help with Jordy, and you were pounding the walls and shit, and Scotty was afraid you'd break something, so we locked you in the garage."

"Shit. Is Scotty pissed at me?"

"Ah, he'll get over it."

They heard a knock at the door. Dan glanced in the direction of the sound. The nurse was here; someone else must have let her in through the security door downstairs. Maybe because she was recognized around the building. Of course, the residents here knew Dan, too, but no one's opening doors for that guy. Jordy capped the bottle, chucked it into his laundry basket, and put an Altoid in his mouth.

Jordy opened the door. Mandy was standing there in her usual outfit: a short-sleeved white button-up shirt and tan slacks, and carrying a blue canvas shoulder bag of medical supplies. He agreed with Dan that Mandy was pretty hot. Some people might say she wore too much makeup, but to Jordis P. Snelling the Third, she wore exactly the right amount, and she smelled like how chicks smell at prom all the time.

When she was there, caring for his mom, it bothered him to stare at her tan arms and curly brown hair, and he never looked down her shirt when she was bent over; no matter how hot she was, doing that kind of shit felt out of line. The weirdest part was that she was twenty-four, a year younger than him, and was so perfect with his mom, like she'd been doing this job for a million years. How does someone that young get to be such a great hospice nurse already? Maybe if you don't fuck up your life too much, anything's possible.

"Hi, Jordy," she said. "You hangin' in there?"

"Yeah, I guess."

"You all ready for hunting season?"

"Ha, no. Still gotta pack and clean my rifle and stuff."

"How's your mom today?" She always said "your mom" to Jordy when talking about her. It always hit him a little.

"Watching *Storage Wars: Texas*," he said, moving aside to let her in. "My brother gave her her meds already."

She stopped on the mat and took off her white tennis shoes. "OK, good, your brother was here." She seemed to trust Adam more than Jordy, and, well, who could blame her?

"I'm Dan," Dan said, moving his beer to his left hand and extending his right.

"I remember," she said, watching as he lowered his hand. "Sorry I'm a little late, Jordy. I've been having trouble with my car."

"The Jetta?" Jordy asked.

"Yeah. It just turns off sometimes when I'm stopped at intersections."

"Could be your throttle cable. What year is it?"

"A '92. Pretty old, I know."

"Y'know, there's this thing on your throttle cable you can adjust to set the idle."

Mandy laughed. "I don't know how to do that."

"Before you go, I'll do it for ya."

"OK, thanks. That's really sweet." She touched him on the shoulder. Jordy thought she kind of stared at him in a way that was a little vibey, but he could've been imagining it. As she passed them, Jordy noticed, she avoided touching Dan.

Mandy announced her presence as she approached Jordy's mom from behind and leaned over her. "Is there anything I can get you to start off? A glass of water?"

"A margarita," Jordy's mom said.

Mandy laughed politely. "I don't know if we can do that!"

"Why not?" Jordy said, taking a white plastic Twins cup from a kitchen cupboard.

"At this stage of care, we focus on pain management," Mandy said, as if reading from a brochure. "And we don't recommend mixing alcohol with this level of pain meds."

"Why?" Jordy said. "It's not like she's gonna operate heavy machinery."

Jordy's mom nodded. "You got that right."

Jordy put on his jacket. "I'm gonna run out and get her some margarita stuff."

"Well, I can't control what you do when I'm not around."

"Come on, Dan," Jordy said, and then looked Mandy in the eyes. "Don't leave until we're back."

Jordy's mom held up her left hand in a little weak wave. He'd fuckin' get that woman the best margarita money could buy.

There were only two liquor stores in Farmington, and they were both owned by the city, but they still had a decent enough selection. Jordy and Dan had to go to the one out on Pilot Knob Road because Jordy's ex-girlfriend Kaylee worked at the one downtown and he still owed her money from when he bought his Glock and there was no way they were having that stupid conversation today.

There wasn't a ton of variety in the margarita mix section. Jose Cuervo, Mr. & Mrs. T, Margaritaville. Hard to tell which was the best.

"Hey," Jordy asked the guy working the register, a fat old townie named Russ Arnsberg who used to manage a sit-down pizza place that went out of business. "How's this Mr. T mix?"

"It's good enough for who it's for," Russ said. "That being people too lazy to make it themselves."

In the refrigerated section, Dan found a twenty-four-ounce glass bottle that read N. W. GRATZ'S ARTISANAL MARGARITA PREPARATORY AMALGAMATION, 100% OREGON TILTH CERTIFIED ORGANIC, GMO FREE, CRUELTY FREE. It was less than half the size of the other bottles and cost four times as much. "What's the deal with this stuff?" Dan asked.

"Wouldn't give ya a nickel for a case of it," Russ said.

Jordy waved his left hand at the row of mixers. "Well, what do ya fuckin' recommend, then?"

"I recommend ya make yer own at home. One, one, three, that's the ratio. Easy enough a blind pig could do it."

Jordy picked up a bottle of Margaritaville brand mixer, which was the most expensive variety in a halfway decent size and had a "Chef's Best Taste" award on the label. He yelled to Dan if he'd found the Patrón.

"Nope," Dan said from the beer section.

"Patrón's behind the counter," Russ said. "But if you're making margaritas it's a waste of money to buy Patrón."

Dan walked over, his old-fashioned flip phone in his hand. "Hey. Goldie's having people over after he gets off work tonight."

Jordy saw a white plastic container of margarita salt at the end of the row and took it. He might as well go all out. "Do you have any limes?"

"People don't buy 'em here and they get moldy. They got 'em at Lou's Red Owl."

"Goddammit," Jordy said, putting the mixer and salt on the counter by the register. "And gimme the Patrón. The green box."

"How's your mom doin'?" Russ asked, scanning the items.

Jordy shook his head. "Not good. Got the hospice nurse over there right now."

"Sorry to hear that."

"Well, whatcha gonna do?" Jordy said. He just hoped Russ didn't go into the God talk like a lot of people did.

"She was a good woman," Russ said, like she was fuckin' dead already. "You may not know this, but she was a hell of a bowler. Back in the early eighties we were in the same league over here. She always kicked our ass."

"Huh," Jordy said, because what the hell do you say to something like that? He wasn't there.

Russ pulled the handles of a thin plastic bag around the bottles and salt and handed it to Jordy. "Yeah, well, tell her hi. And take it easy. Don't do anything I wouldn't sit on."

Back home, Jordy spread the Margaritaville mixer, the Patrón, the salt, and the limes from Lou's Red Owl on the kitchen counter. Mandy ignored him from the moment the alcohol came out of the bag, which was about the time that Jordy's mom took notice.

"Whoa, you didn't have to get all that," she said from her chair.

"We're makin' you a margarita."

Dan cracked open another Coors Light. "It's gonna be the best one you ever had, Linda. How do ya like it, blended, or rocks and salt?"

"Well, blended, usually."

"Blended," Jordy repeated. He opened the doors of all the cabinets, finding cups, plates, coffee mugs, breakfast cereal, a red plastic tub of Folgers, a big thing of Bailey's, some port, and a bottle of Galliano they'd had forever. After about the fifth cabinet door, a part of him wanted to yell, *So where the fuck is the blender?* But he couldn't, so he just muttered it, then took a deep breath and looked out toward the living room.

"Hey, Mom. What cabinet is the blender in?"

"Next to the oven," she said, as loud as she could.

As Jordy fumbled with the components of the Black & Decker Crush Master, Mandy walked into the kitchen with Linda's empty water glass. "Have you ever made margaritas before?"

"I thought you were against the whole idea," Jordy said. "Anyway, they got instructions right here on the bottle. Six ounces mix, two ounces tequila."

"We can put in more tequila than that," Dan said.

"Yeah, fuck this," Jordy said, looking at the bottle.

Dan pulled the cork on the tequila bottle and started dumping it into the blender. "You figure about halfway?"

"I am not here, I did not see this," Mandy said.

"Now just fill it the rest of the way with the mixer?" Jordy said, unscrewing the top and pouring in a green fluid that reminded him of conventional antifreeze.

"You guys," Mandy said. "You haven't even put the ice in yet."

"Shit. Ice, I don't even know if we have ice."

Dan opened the freezer. "You got, like, one tray."

"Well, dump it all in there."

With the entire tray of ice, the faint green contents were nearly up against the lip of the blender's pitcher.

"Shit," Dan said. "Fluid displacement, dude."

"We hardly got any of the mixer in there."

"Maybe if we grind it up, it'll make room."

"I have no fuckin' clue," Jordy said, trying to put the lid on the blender.

Dan was confused by the Crush Master's settings. "Smoothie? Maybe Pulse?"

Dan pressed PULSE, the lid flew off, and as they watched, ice chunks, sugary green mix, and tequila splattered over everyone's shirts and faces and hair.

"Fucking shit!" Jordy said.

"Great, great," Mandy said, looking down at the front of her blouse. "Great."

"Dan, just back the fuck up, OK," Jordy said, tearing two paper towels off of a roll and handing them to Mandy.

"Geez, dude, sorry," Dan said, grabbing several paper towels off of the roll.

Mandy dabbed at her shirt with a paper towel. "I gotta go to my next patient in, like, ten minutes."

Jordy glared at Dan as he wiped himself off. He never should've let Dan near the blender. Ever since Dan was a kid, he was an absolute shitbrain with any object that had moving parts or required thinking. He didn't even get his driver's license until the fourth try, and that was probably because the folks at the exam office didn't want to ever see him again.

"Sorry, man," Dan said again.

"You ruin fuckin' everything," Jordy said, wiping off the counter.

"I got another shirt down in my car I'm gonna get," Dan said, and left the kitchen to go put his boots on.

"You can fuckin' stay down there," Jordy said.

"If I can just for sure get the smell out," Mandy said, dabbing her shirt by the sink, acting like she ignored the exchange. "I don't have time to go home and change."

"Maybe she's got a shirt you can borrow."

"It'd be better than nothing."

Jordy walked quietly into the living room and touched his mom on the shoulder. "Mom, can Mandy borrow a shirt of yours?"

"Of course," Jordy's mom said. "Go into my closet. Anything you want."

Mandy sighed. "Thank you. I'll bring it back."

Jordy pointed down the hallway. "My mom's room is back there."

"Thanks," Mandy said, and disappeared around the corner.

While she was changing, Jordy finished cleaning up Dan's goddamn mess and went back to the job, holding the lid down on the blender, adding a little more mix, even though Dan was wrong, grinding up the ice did not make more fucking room, and sliced a lime with his Buck knife to garnish three glasses. He wasn't sure how to salt the rims of the glasses but figured that part could wait.

He was just pouring the margaritas when Mandy walked back out, wearing a long-sleeved blue denim shirt that Jordy remembered his mom wearing to the last family reunion two years ago, when she had a stage IV malignant tumor on one of her ovaries that was about a week away from being diagnosed.

She was supposed to be going in to get her liver checked out. "The doctor's gonna tell me again to quit drinking," she said at the reunion, "so first I'm gonna drink up." His mom had a total blast at the Knights of Columbus Hall with her sisters and cousins, at one point standing on a table with her sister Melanie, singing "Mustang Sally." They were so happy, and nobody knew there was anything wrong. That shirt was in a thousand pictures taken that day and night, framed on people's walls, all over everyone's Facebook pages, all of that. She'd never worn that shirt since.

"Is this OK?" Mandy said, standing in the living room for Jordy's and Linda's approval.

"Yep, looks all right," Jordy said.

"You look beautiful," Jordy's mom said. "You should keep it. Really. Keep it."

"Thank you, but I can bring it back next time, no problem."

"No, please. It looks perfect on you. Keep it."

"Thank you," Mandy said. "Now I better get going."

Jordy walked over to the living room with a tray of margaritas and set them down on an end table near his mom's chair.

"Hey, what about your car?"

Down in the parking lot, Jordy lifted the hood of Mandy's 1992 Jetta. He'd noticed that Dan's car was gone; the clumsy fuckup got the hint, at least.

The forty-five degree early November afternoon smelled like cold water and dead grass, even with the metal and oil of the engine rising to his face. Jordy hoped it was going to snow before Saturday—it was way easier to track deer in the snow—but it didn't look like that shit was going to happen. Though it was promisingly overcast today, Friday's forecast was for partly cloudy skies and highs in the mid-forties. Just painful.

Mandy sat in the front seat of her car with the driver's side door open, as Jordy messed with the throttle cable of the Jetta until it seemed like the idle wouldn't give out.

"Oh, and look," Jordy said, calling her over to her chunky-sounding idling engine. "Your intake manifold isn't sitting correctly. It's not sealing the intake. You gotta get that looked at."

"I don't know when I have the time to do that," Mandy said. Jordy knew that she probably didn't make a lot of money and maybe couldn't afford to fix the car, but to lose the car would mean losing the job.

"Use my car tomorrow. I'll just get a ride up north tomorrow morning from my dad or something. Then leave your car here and I'll take a look at it Monday when I get back. The only problem with my car is that the horn is kinda fucked."

"You don't have to do that."

"You're taking care of my mom, so."

"I know, but it's my job." Neither of them said anything for a moment. They just looked at each other. He stared at this little mole behind her left ear. He decided he liked that mole. "Well, thank you," she said, at last.

"Oh, hey, and if you're free tonight and want to go to a party," Jordy said, not knowing why he was saying this, "a guy I know is getting some people together at his place here in town. If you're interested."

"Yeah, maybe. Text me the address." Jordy thought for a moment and realized that yes, he had her number in his phone, because of his mom. Jordy looked at her, in his mom's blue shirt, while her idle ran high and her intake manifold was tweaked and the air smelled oily and cold. This was as perfect as things were likely to get.

• • •

His mom had finished off one margarita and was starting on a second as Jordy took his boots off in the doorway.

"Mom, you were supposed to wait," he said.

"This is the food of the gods," she said. Jordy sat across from her and picked up the one drink remaining. Even a foot from his face, he could smell that it was the strongest margarita he'd ever had.

"This is," his mom said, smiling at him, "the best margarita in the world."

He held his margarita in his left hand and rubbed her bony back with his right hand as they watched another episode of *Storage Wars: Texas,* which seemed to be on a lot.

"Christ, a lot of people abandon their shit," Jordy said.

"Mandy sure is nice," his mom said. "You should get married to her."

Jordy laughed. "I'm not even going out with her."

"She likes you, I can tell. Just ask her, I bet she'd say yes."

"OK, whatever, sure." Jordy put the margarita down. "Can I get you anything else right now?"

"Venison meatballs," his mom said. "Gotta get a deer so you can make us those venison meatballs."

"Can you still even eat them?"

"Don't tell me what I can't do."

"OK, then," Jordy said, looking out the living room window onto the parking lot, hoping they'd be able to shoot a deer. He thought that maybe he'd stay out in the woods all week until he did. "Maybe I can get Adam to come down. And Melanie. We can have a big dinner with stuffing and mashed potatoes and all that stuff. I'll get some of that wine you like, that White Zinfandel. What do ya think of that?"

Jordy's mom was asleep.

"I think that sounds pretty nice," Jordy said real quiet.

● ● ●

Jordy's friend Goldie, the host of that night's party, lived in town, in a house near the bowling alley. He shared it with an older guy named Cliff Fuzzing who was super into home microbrewing and made a really hoppy IPA that he was always forcing on people. Goldie had been living there since he got out of the navy. Now he worked security at Treasure Island, spending all day watching busloads of bluehairs spend their children's inheritance on slot machines, and at night tried to make his house the party capital of Dakota County.

As Jordy pulled his Buick into a parking spot on the street, he saw Mandy and a cute friend of hers, though not as cute as Mandy, walking toward Goldie's house. He couldn't believe she'd actually showed up. He tapped his car horn to get the girls' attention. Then he remembered that it was busted. The girls turned and saw him. The horn went *Blrnnnnn-nnnnnnnnn*. Mandy, smiling at first, frowned as the horn continued to blare. The other chick never smiled at all.

"What the fuck's your problem?" the other chick said.

Jordy rolled down his window. "It's fuckin' busted," he shouted, pounding on the steering wheel with his fists. The horn stopped. Then started again, *Blrnnnnnnnnnnnnnn*, without Jordy even touching it. He reached behind his seat, grabbed a socket wrench, and whaled on the steering wheel until the mindless whine finally died.

The other chick turned to Mandy. "Red flag," she said loudly, as Jordy ambled in their direction, a twelve-pack of Coors Light under his arm. He was trying to act relaxed and cool, which for him was pretty much impossible anyway, but really fucking hard after beating the shit out of something.

"Hey, how's the Jetta?" he asked Mandy.

"Holding up, thanks," she said, smiling. "How's your mom?"

"OK," Jordy said. "My aunt Melanie's over."

"Oh, hey, this is Emilee." The other chick gave Jordy a halfhearted wave.
"Hey," Jordy said.

"Oh, and hey," Mandy said, reaching into her purse, pulling out his
mom's shirt, which was rolled up like a burrito. "I washed it and everything."

Jordy pushed the shirt back into her hands. "No, it's yours. My mom
wants you to keep it. Seriously."

Jordy could hear that EDM shit blasting from Goldie's house. He
hated EDM, but chicks liked it, so whatever. Emilee said she was just
gonna go ahead and go in. Mandy said, no, I'll go with you, put the shirt
back in her purse, and said thank you to Jordy.

Goldie was slumped across a beanbag chair but rose to his feet when he
saw Jordy and the girls enter, and he introduced himself to them as
Mark Goldsmith, like he was a Realtor or a pastor or someone respect-
able. Cliff Fuzzing entered from the kitchen when he heard the wom-
en's voices. He was dressed in his usual faded Pink Floyd T-shirt and
was drinking from a brown bottle with a home-printed sticker that said
CLIFF'S EDGE IPA. He told Jordy that Coors Light was not allowed in his
house. Then Scotty's hot but annoying girlfriend, Micayla, walked up to
Jordy and asked him straight up if he brought any of his mom's Oxy.

"I'm not giving away my mom's fucking pain medication," Jordy said.

Then there was Scotty, drinking from a red plastic cup, standing
outside the closed bathroom door. "You owe my dad six hundred bucks
for the garage," Scotty said. "Fuckin' psycho."

Jordy's head hurt real bad. There was a ringing sound. He had a hard
time breathing through his nose. The air smelled like blood. There was
that ringing sound again. He felt like he was in his bedroom at his
mom's place. He was. He rubbed his eyes. There was dried blood on his

hands. That ringing sound again. It was his phone. On the edge of the desk by his head. It said DAD. His ride north.

"Oh shit," Jordy said.

"I'm downstairs," his dad said. "You ready to go?"

Jordy looked at his phone. It said 8:26 a.m.

He'd called his dad yesterday to get a ride up to their hunting grounds on Uncle Hobie's land in Pine County. And here was Dad. Picking him up.

"Oh, shit, give me five minutes."

"Did I wake you up?" his dad asked.

"Yeah, sorry. Just give me five minutes, I'll be right down."

"Take your time," Jordis P. Snelling the Second said. "Hobie's gonna be mad we're late for lunch. But whatever pisses off your liberal uncle is OK with me."

"I'll be right down," Jordy said, and hung up.

At least all of his hunting gear and his Mauser were in one corner of the closet. He put his right foot down and felt something. Dan Jorgenson was sleeping on the floor next to his bed, curled up on his side, in his jacket, dirty jeans, and holey white socks. Dan must've brought him home again. He didn't even remember Dan being at that party.

Jordy slid off the foot of his bed and walked straight into the attached bathroom, but didn't turn on the light. He had dried blood around his lips and his nose. A big bruise on his goddamn cheek. Christ, his arms hurt. He took a piss and wiped the blood off of his face with a black bath towel and piled up all his hunting gear into a black garbage bag and grabbed his rifle and cell phone charger.

His brother Adam was sitting at the dinette table, typing on his laptop. He said he'd come down every weekend during deer season so Jordy could go hunting with their dad and uncles. Jordy wasn't presently working himself, which meant he could be with their mom a lot, but it was crucial to have a break. The first day of opening weekend was the best day of the year.

"Holy crap, what happened to you?" Adam said when he saw his brother.

"I have no fuckin' idea. I gotta go, Dad's downstairs, he's givin' me a ride to Hobie's."

"Christ, you look like shit," Adam said.

"How's Mom? Is she up?" Jordy asked, looking in the direction of the easy chair. His mom's weird CPAP mask was on, and she was snoring softly.

"She's sleeping." Adam winced, looking at him. "Are you wearing one of her shirts?"

Jordy looked down at himself for the first time that morning. He had on his mom's blue denim shirt over his clothes from last night. There was blood on the front of it. "Fuck," Jordy said, taking the shirt off. One of the buttons was missing and it was ripped near the collar. "I gotta get it fixed and cleaned," he said.

He put the shirt into the garbage bag with his hunting gear, and then dragged his ass back into the kitchen and started mixing up some Gatorade powder with Mountain Dew instead of water.

"Eva's not here?" he asked.

"No, her cousins are in town. They're prepping for one of her big dinners next weekend. But she says hi."

"Does she know you're going through a divorce?"

"Yep, she knows all about it."

"Has she met your kids?"

"Nope, not yet," Adam said, not looking up. This was probably a sore subject for him. Even though he was the one who got cheated on, Octavia had hired an expensive lawyer and got a restraining order against him. It was some real bullshit, what she did to him. Jordy figured it was because Octavia came from money and those people can never be kind to poor people for very long, not in Jordy's limited experience.

"Christ, my fuckin' head is fuckin' killing me." His left hand, his shooting hand, also still hurt, but not worse than yesterday. Between that and his head, though, he felt almost too fucked up to go hunting.

"You should take one of those, ha," Adam said, pointing to their mom's pills on the table, the OxyContin.

"I don't know." He knew how huge these pills were in the local party scene. It wasn't really his thing, though. He'd never even tried it once.

"One won't kill you."

Jordy opened the bottle. "She only has like eight left."

"I'll get it refilled today," Adam said. He was a kind, responsible guy; if he said he'd do something, it would happen.

"I guess, then," Jordy said, took a pill, and washed it down with his Mountain Dew and Gatorade mix. He walked over and checked on his sleeping mom, then set his car keys down on the dining room table by Adam's computer. "Hey. I told the hospice nurse she could use my car. Call me if she comes by and picks it up."

"OK," Adam said, not looking up from his computer screen. "Oh yeah, and Aunt Melanie told me to tell you that she drank the rest of your margarita mix last night with Mom. But she'll get you a new bottle." Melanie was nice about coming down on nights when Jordy went out so someone would at least be there. Often she crashed on the couch because she was an even bigger lush than his mom.

"OK, later." Jordy threw the garbage bag over his shoulder, picked up his rifle case, and hauled ass down to the parking lot, his head throbbing.

Jordy threw his stuff into the backseat of his dad's black Chevy Silverado and brushed a bunch of empty Marlboro Red packs to the floor of the car before he sat down in the passenger seat. He lit a cigarette of his own.

"Whoa. How's the other guy look?" his dad asked when he saw Jordy's face.

"I have no fuckin' idea who the other guy was," Jordy said. He noticed the dome light and the car horn were missing; where they used to be, there were just open holes with a couple of wires. "What happened in here?"

"It's where the government puts sensors, in your dome light and car horn. For tracking."

"Ah," Jordy said.

"Did you get that e-mail I forwarded you? If you don't consent to live in a police state, you should take yours out."

"Well, I took out my car horn."

"Good. You gotta think for yourself."

"I don't know what I fuckin' think."

Jordis turned on his radar detector and turned up the volume on his AM talk radio, where some guy on *Off the Grid with Buzz Morgenstern* was saying something about the connection between drug abuse and gun control, of all things. "Then listen to this," his dad said. "What they're saying is the truth. The pharmaceutical industry is working with the government to keep us doped up and docile. And who's for gun control, besides weed-smoking hippies and doped-up seniors and worried moms on antidepressants? Think about what's in that stuff. Think about it. Makes sense."

"Can't rule anything out," Jordy said.

The painkiller rolled over his brain like waves of sunlight. The armrest set into the passenger door began to tingle beneath his fingers. He took a long shot of whiskey from the flask in his pocket, and his head slowly lifted, for the first time in a long-ass time, into a place where he didn't hurt anymore.

• • •

Rifle season in Minnesota begins at sunrise on either the first or second Saturday in November, and for the past thirteen years, ever since he was twelve years old, Jordy had been waking up at 4:30 a.m. on that day so he could be in his deer stand, locked and loaded, when first light rose over his uncle Hobie's farm.

Jordy had the entire ride north to fuckin' stress out about how he packed his charger but not his phone, and got no sympathy from his dad, Aunt Trudy, or his uncles Hobie and Langford, most of whom didn't even have mobile phones and saw no truck in them, as Langford put it.

"What if you break down on the side of the road?" he asked them over Friday night's pot roast.

"You fix it," Hobie said.

"You don't travel with tools?" Langford asked.

"I traveled with a tool," his dad said, pointing his thumb at Jordy.

He slept for maybe five hours, and not just because Hobie and Trudy's downstairs bedroom smelled like cat piss, or because he was freaked out by the giant picture of a younger Hobie and Trudy posing with Bill Clinton in 1992. He went over and over in his head what he remembered from Thursday night, which wasn't fuckin' much. He remembered Mandy looking at him with grave concern and saying, "Look at me," while holding both his shoulders, but he wasn't sure whether that happened or if he just imagined it. One thing he didn't remember at all was how he came to be wearing his mom's blue shirt over his clothes. That's what bothered him the most. Dan could tell him what happened, but he didn't know Dan's number by heart, so he couldn't even call him from his uncle's house phone. He wondered if Mandy ever came and borrowed his car. Adam hadn't called yet, but he would.

• • •

Jordy had made the ladder to his deer stand himself about ten years ago by nailing some flat pieces of pinewood into the side of a tree. It was just light enough out that he could see it without a flashlight. He climbed the fourteen feet to his stand and settled in. Mandy must've come by to pick up his car, he figured. Adam probably just couldn't find Langford and Trudy's phone number. Adam never once came hunting, or ever came up to Hobie's farm without the rest of the family, so no way he'd know it. Jordy put his ass down on the cold wood and waited, with nothing else to think about.

Deer are nocturnal, so there was a real good chance of getting one if you were out early enough on opening weekend. And sure enough, maybe fifteen minutes in, Jordy heard a *blam* and a *blam* from north of his position. Hobie.

Everyone met at Hobie's mark. Beautiful eight-point buck. Trophy rack, no points broken. First shot was by the book; behind the shoulder, into the lung. Second was a Texas heart-shot, up the ass, which Hobie said was a mistake. Langford asked him why the second shot, and Hobie said that the deer took off, and he's not chasing a blood trail for a mile. In other words, he was just being lazy.

"And at least now the deer won't suffer as much," Hobie added.

"Bleeding heart," said Jordy's dad.

Langford laughed, and even Hobie did a little.

Jordy didn't see what was so damn funny. "It's probably gonna ruin the meat," he said, and that was definitely a possibility.

Once the lungs and guts were removed and tossed aside, where they'd probably be gone in twelve hours, due to coyotes or maybe black bear, the rest of the guys dragged the buck to the ATV and trailer they kept parked at the edge of the woods and threw it on a plastic tarp. Trudy came out to the garage, helped them lay cardboard on the floor, and watched as they strung up the buck by its hind legs. His dad and Langford argued about farm subsidies before commencing their usual feud about how long the deer should hang before processing. Langford always insisted on at least a week, but this wasn't his year; it was still too warm out, and it wasn't supposed to get below freezing again until Monday. This deer and any others they shot today would hang a couple days, tops.

A few flakes of snow were starting to fall. Even though it melted when it hit the ground, this was like sleigh bells on a roof on Christmas Eve. There was something about the first snow that made deer freak out and get real about mating, which meant that they'd be out in force. Jordy said he was going to go back out before it got too bright. He'd only bought one tag, so might as well use it now.

He left the ATV by the garage and walked to his dad's stand, which was the closest one to the house, and the nicest, with seat warmers, a cup holder, and a wood platform at elbow level. He couldn't smoke out here—white-tailed deer could smell it from two miles away—so he drank. You had to do something.

Mandy had definitely grabbed his shoulders and told him, "Look at me," with grave concern at some point Thursday night. He was sure of it now. She hadn't seemed angry, more worried. He didn't remember what he said next, or what she did next, or anything. But there was at least a moment where she was concerned and not mad.

A snowflake landed right on the tip of his left thumb. It seemed to look back at him as it dissolved. Behind it, directly behind it, in the distance, there was a fluttering. He lifted his binoculars. It was a doe, walking toward him. How much closer would it get before it picked up his scent? He was fourteen feet up, and the wind was to his face, so he could stand to be patient. He checked to see if he'd chambered a round; yes he had. Thank Christ for that. A sound, any sound in the world, and they can just take off. This one kept coming, like it was being led to him, and even paused broadside to his stand. He lined up its shoulder in his sight, just as it raised its head and looked straight at him. It couldn't see him. He knew that. Their vision was terrible. But he saw its eyes as he pulled the trigger, and the vermin doe stumbled and ran. He'd nailed it.

He chambered a second round before climbing down. He found the doe only a few hundred feet away from where he shot it, skinny rear legs twitching. He was lucky; often they go much farther. As he took out his knife to cut its throat, he felt like he was being watched. But from where? If it was his dad or his uncles, he would've heard the steps. Then he saw it. A little guy. With little nubby horns. Why hadn't he seen the fawn before? It was right in its mother's footsteps. It just stood there, looking at him, and then down at its mother. It didn't know any better.

Jordy would've shot it. It's technically legal to shoot fawns. He just didn't have a second tag. These things were rats. This little guy would grow up and eat gardens and kill motorcyclists. He knew that.

"Get!" Jordy said. Instead it came closer. It sniffed the back of its mother's head. Maybe he could shoot it and ask his dad for his tag. His dad would hate wasting his tag on a fawn, though.

He took out his Buck knife to start field dressing. The little guy was watching him. Jordy decided he didn't want the fawn to watch while he slashed its mother's throat. Vermin or not, it creeped him out. He raised his hands above his head and yelled, *"Raaaahhrrr!"* and finally the little guy ran off a few yards.

Jordy groaned, got to his knees, and got to work. He looked up at one point, and saw the little guy watching him from about twenty yards away. Jordy roared again, but the little guy didn't move.

He heard footsteps behind him, and saw it was Hobie.

"Aw, shit. The one other guy that's used his tag."

"Why, you see another one?" Hobie asked.

"Straight ahead," Jordy said, pointing to the fawn.

"This his mother?" Hobie asked. "What the hell you shoot her for? She's got a little kid."

"I didn't see him."

"Look at him. He's tiny. Late in the year for something so tiny."

Jordy didn't look up as he tore the mother's lungs out. "That's what I thought."

"Won't last long, probably. On his own."

"That's what I was thinking. I woulda shot him, but I obviously just used my tag." Jordy continued to cut and stopped at the deer's nipples. "Aw, fuck, her milk sacs are full."

"Well, that's some sad stuff," Hobie said, staring at the fawn. "Let me help ya drag her outta here."

Langford and Jordy's dad commented on the beautiful doe as Hobie and Jordy dragged it into the garage. Langford laughed and said these two deer musta been a married couple. Jordy didn't say anything about the fawn and neither did Hobie.

"Adam called," Trudy said. "You need to call him back immediately."

"Finally," Jordy said, and took off his boots in the garage before going inside.

Hobie and Trudy still had one of those old rotary dial phones, the kind with the big chunky plastic handle. It was full-on morning and the kitchen smelled like Folgers and burnt toast. A napkin holder on the table, made out of black iron, had the inscription *Although you'll find our home a mess / sit down, relax, converse. It doesn't always look like this / sometimes it's even worse,* and Jordy stared at those words as he heard the phone ring at his mom's apartment.

Adam picked up on the third ring. "Hello?"

"Adam, what's up?"

"She's gone."

"What?"

"She's gone, she's gone."

"What? You mean Mom?"

"Yeah, she's gone." He was crying. "Like half an hour ago."

"What? No. No fuckin' way. She was fine. No fuckin' way."

"We just helped her move to her bed—"

"You and who? You and Mandy?"

"No, some other nurse. Casey. Casey, she's still here."

"Fuck!"

"And she just started breathing real heavy—"

"Fuck!" Jordy ripped the phone out of the wall and threw it at the kitchen sink. He grabbed the stupid black iron napkin holder with the stupid fucking quote and broke it in half and kicked over the fucking table and then Hobie came in there and grabbed him and said what the hell are you doing and Jordy swung at him but when Hobie grabbed his arms and he couldn't move, Jordy felt all the fight leave his body, and all of his internal structures gave way, and it fucking sucked, but there was nothing he could do but fucking lose it right there on the cold, dirty brown linoleum floor.

He didn't have anything to eat that day until he was on the way home with his dad. They stopped at a Subway attached to a gas station. When he placed his order for a foot-long meatball marinara with extra cheese and no vegetables, he wondered if the sandwich artist could tell that his mom had died.

. . .

The only person who didn't want his mom cremated was his dad. As far as Jordy and Adam were concerned, he gave up his vote when he divorced her. His mom's doctor said that her cancer was so bad, the only thing they could donate from her body was her corneas. Everything else had to go. They cremated her and split the ashes between them and their mom's sisters. Jordy got his in a black film canister that had Scotch tape holding down the lid. There were white bits of bone in it.

Melanie planned the wake and the funeral, so they were way up in Duluth, where that side of the family was from. Of course, by then it had snowed a ton, and it was snowing that day, slowing down all the cars and the old people. He was a pallbearer, but didn't have a black suit because he had never needed one before, so he had to borrow an old one of his dad's, which was wool and smelled like a wet sock. Everyone told him how nice he looked, and that they were sorry, but otherwise people just stood around and looked at the ground and talked about the snow, clearly just waiting for the whole thing to be over.

In the church basement after the funeral, some old lady told him to eat something, and gave him a tiny ham and cheese sandwich on a Styrofoam plate. He sat down at a table with Dan Jorgenson and ate the meat part as he looked around the room. Despite the weather, a lot of people were there, under the drop ceiling and fluorescent lights, sitting at tables draped with cheap white tablecloths, drinking coffee and eating seven-layer dip and little sandwiches like nothing devastating had happened. He'd taken four Oxys over the course of that day and they were the only things that kept him from losing his shit.

. . .

He never would've admitted this to anybody, but almost the whole time he was thinking about Mandy. He did get a card from her, a beautiful white card that said *With Deepest Sympathy* on the front. On the inside, she signed it, "Love, Mandy." But she didn't come by the apartment like some people did, and didn't return any of his calls or texts, ever. Jordy thought that was extremely fucked up. But he kept the card in his coat and looked at it sometimes.

Jordy didn't want to stay at the apartment anymore, even though it was paid up to the end of the month and he would've had the place to himself, so he moved all of his stuff to his dad's place in St. Paul. The only problems were that his dad never had anything good to eat and the TV was always on Fox News, which was boring as shit.

"We gotta figure out what to do with all your venison," his dad said in his kitchen, five days after Jordy's mom died. "If you don't want to eat it, give it away."

"Food banks probably don't take raw deer meat," Jordy said, taking the frozen, vacuum-sealed red blocks out of his dad's noisy old Hotpoint freezer. His dad had inherited the super-old house from *his* dad, Jordis P. Snelling the First, who inherited it from *his* dad, Langford Hobart Snelling. It was in an old part of St. Paul that was now considered historic. Which meant that it had no dishwasher and old fixtures and appliances that were always humming and buzzing, not like the quiet, newer machines at the apartment.

He stacked up the deer meat on the tiled kitchen counter and put them in plastic bags from under the sink, which his dad was probably saving for when he walked his dog, but he didn't say anything.

"Why don't you give it to Adam's girlfriend?" Jordy's dad said. "She's a chef."

This sounded fuckin' awkward. Was he just supposed to knock on her door, and be, like, *Hey, I met you twice, here's an entire dead deer?*

"How do you know she even wants it?"

"Because I called Adam, and he asked her, and she said yes." His dad often liked to introduce topics for debate after everything had already been decided.

"So, she's expecting it, then?"

"Yep. I think she's real excited."

"Maybe I'll wait for Adam to get off work first. And he can come."

"Don't be a wimp about it," his dad said. "She knows you. Just get it over with."

Jordy didn't really want to get off his ass and get in the car and schlep a shitload of venison to some chick his brother was dating, even if she was nice, but it did seem like the best way to get rid of the stuff.

Eva lived in a kinda fancy white two-story house on DuPont over by Lake Calhoun. It was right near a famous rose garden that some chick dragged him to one time. He liked the big old trees that lined the street; even with their leaves gone, they gave the neighborhood a sense of safety and reliability. As he lifted the cold, heavy bags of frozen venison from the trunk of the Buick, a totally hot female jogger ran past, staring straight ahead, wearing what looked like brand-new workout clothes, and all of a sudden he felt a million miles from home.

Eva answered the door, smiling. He took an involuntary step back. It hit him that he hadn't been smiled at in a while. Why she seemed so happy to see him, he had no fuckin' idea.

"Jordy, come in," Eva said. "I heard you might come by today."

The house smelled like coffee and burning cedar, and the big, wide-open living room with the fireplace and the clean, new-looking furniture looked way nicer than any place he'd seen in a long-ass time. Two people, a stubbly-faced, tattooed man with black hair, and an intense-looking blonde woman—both probably in their thirties, hard to tell, but definitely adults—were on one of the sofas, each on their own laptop, and a young teenage boy sat on a brown rug and played with a smartphone. They all looked at him when he entered, and although they didn't seem unfriendly, he felt like he was in the way. "I gotta get back on the road in a minute," he said.

Eva hugged him, hard. "I'm so sorry about your mom," she said.

"Yeah," Jordy said back, patting her back once. He was surprised at first that she knew, but of course she did. "Thanks."

"It's really tough, I know. My mom, she died when I was fourteen."

"Wow," Jordy said, because what do you say to that? It probably sucks even more at that age. Looked like her mom's death didn't ruin her life or anything, though.

"Oh, hey," Eva said, keeping her hand on his back as she pivoted to face the people in her living room. "Everyone, this is my friend Adam's brother, Jordy. Jordy, these are my cousins Randy and Braque, and Braque's son Hatch."

Braque raised her eyebrows. "*Friend* Adam?" she asked Eva.

"Shut it," Eva said, pointing at Braque.

Braque touched the kid Hatch's back with her foot. "Hatch, look up from your phone for a second and greet our guest."

Hatch glanced up from his phone and waved once.

Braque turned to Jordy and gave him a *What can ya do?* look. "The kid has loved those fuckin' things since literally before he was born."

"I hate it when people misuse the word 'literally,'" Eva said. Jordy noted that the grammar was corrected, but the swearing went unremarked.

"What's in the bags?" Randy asked, standing up to get a better look. He seemed like a guy who'd been through some shit; Jordy could just tell.

"Venison," Jordy said.

"Sweet," Randy said. "I love venison."

Braque didn't take her eyes off of Jordy. "Eva doesn't even have a picture of Adam. I was starting to wonder if he even existed."

"No more questions about his brother," Eva said.

He was curious why Eva apparently hadn't told these people much about her relationship with Adam; Jordy knew a fair amount, and he wasn't the type to hit his brother up for details. Adam had told him that he and Eva met like six years ago at a dinner party, so they'd known each other for a long time, but then like two months ago she came to his bakery to get bread for some event, and they'd been hanging out ever since. It was nothing covert or weird or anything. He didn't know why Eva was being so secretive about it, but maybe she was just a private person. If so, he respected that.

Eva smiled at Jordy, who hadn't moved. "Sure you can't take your coat off and stay awhile?" she asked him. "Lunch is just about ready."

"I don't know." He could eat, he figured, depending.

Braque looked right at him again. "Listen to what your brother's girlfriend is making," she said. "A Savoy and Mammoth Red Rock cabbage slaw with homemade Spanish peanut oil dressing, and a vegan aloo gobi with Purple of Sicily cauliflower and heirloom Mercer potatoes. Oh yeah, and every ingredient was grown on property she owns or by local people she knows. How do ya like that?"

Jordy hated to admit it, but he was a little confused. His first thought was, why all the trouble? Does she make such crazy stuff every day for lunch? Must be fuckin' exhausting.

"He doesn't need to know all that," Eva said. "It's basically just coleslaw and a spicy potato cauliflower stew. Just beta-testing some stuff for the dinner this weekend."

"Cool," Jordy said, not taking his jacket off.

Braque grabbed Eva's hand. "Hey, I'm gonna ask him," she said, and then turned to face Jordy. "OK, Eva just got a huge offer to take over for Miles Binder on *Cater-Mania*. Do you watch that show?"

"Heard of it," Jordy said.

Eva shook her head. "Not in a million years will I do that show, or any show."

Braque motioned around the room. "Everyone thinks she should fuckin' do it."

"Well, I'm *not*."

"You're being such an ass-clown. All the big chefs have TV shows. You should have a show, and a cookbook. You should have a shitload of cookbooks."

"I have way more exposure than I want already," Eva said. "Maybe I'll judge another baked goods contest next year. That's actually fun and easy. This other stuff isn't."

"You don't even have any pictures or recipes on your Web site," Braque said.

"That's right, I don't," said Eva, smiling.

"I hate arguing with this fuckin' chick," Braque said, shaking her head.

Randy laughed. "The trick is, don't disagree with her."

Braque looked at the new stranger in their house. "What do you think, Jordy?"

"I don't know," he said. It made him fucking anxious to have all these people looking at him when he had nothing to say. "I think I gotta get going."

He glanced back into the living room as he opened the front door. Randy and Braque looked really bummed, as if Jordy was a star player quitting a baseball team or something. He supposed it was nice that they wanted him to stick around for some reason, but he hardly knew these people, and their arguing and questions were making him edgy.

Braque sat up. "Well, say hi to your brother from us. I hope he's half as cute as you are."

He nodded once, hoping in that moment never to see that Braque woman again.

Eva picked up her purse from a rack by the door and followed Jordy out to her front step, closing the door behind them. "How's a hundred?" she asked.

"What?" he asked. His face was flushed with the cold outdoor air, his nose free of the warm smells of a strange home, and he hadn't noticed that she'd followed him out.

"A hundred bucks for the venison. I hope that's enough."

Jordy was about to say that he didn't need any money for it, but then for some reason he didn't. "A hundred's OK."

Eva handed him the money and hugged him again. "If you need anything—anything—let me know, all right?" She looked him in the face. "I'm thinking of you."

"Yeah, OK," he said. She was a good person, and maybe even meant what she said, but he had no idea how to respond. "Thanks," he said. He'd never said that word so much before this week, when he learned how perfectly it could shoot down further conversation. This woman had tried harder than most, and probably deserved better.

In the car on the way home, he wondered if he could have got more than a hundred. He always fucked up every kind of negotiation. But whatever. It was a hundred more than he had thirty minutes ago, and he needed it for more pills for when his mom's ran out, which would be real soon. He would just have to figure out where to get them. He had some ideas. He was good at that kind of thing. Or was going to have to be. Because this was another four-pill kind of day today. He could just tell already.

BARS

Who doesn't like bars? That's what Pat Prager wanted to know.

Pat sat in her kitchen and made a list in her head of all the people she knew who loved bars, whether they were light and crunchy Rice Krispies bars, sweet and tart lemon bars, or rich and heavy peanut butter and chocolate bars. That list numbered *everyone*. Kids loved bars, teenagers loved bars, Pastor Evan loved bars, and even Pastor Evan's wife, Jenni, who always made such a show of skipping the bars—Pat had seen her in her car, eating them, after everyone else left Bible study. Cops loved them, firemen loved them, teachers loved them, her first husband, Jerry Jorgenson, now in God's kingdom, loved them, and even her second husband, Eli Prager, who, between work and writing for that Minnesota Vikings blog on the Internet, always came up from his man-cave to sneak more bars.

Everyone knew that Deer Lake made the best bars in the county—one of them had won the Bars division of the County Fair Bake-Off six years in a row—and everyone knew that the best bars in Deer Lake were made by the women of First Lutheran Church.

Pat didn't like to toot her own horn, but her peanut butter bars had won the blue ribbon for Best Bars five of the last six years now. Still, she couldn't rest on her laurels, because there were some really darn good bars out there. Like Sandra Bratholt's cherry coffee cake bars, Frances Mitzel's sour cream raisin bars, Corrina Nelsen's lemon bars, and Barb Ramstad's Kraft caramel bars:

1 bag caramels

5 tablespoons cream

¾ cup butter, melted

1 cup brown sugar

1 cup oatmeal

1 cup flour

½ teaspoon baking soda

¼ teaspoon salt

1 cup chocolate chips

½ cup nuts, chopped (optional)

Preheat the oven to 350°F. Melt the caramels and cream in a double boiler. Cool slightly. Combine the butter, sugar, oatmeal, flour, baking soda, and salt. Mix until crumbly. Press half of this mixture into a 9-by-13-inch pan and bake for 5 minutes. Remove from the oven and sprinkle with the chips, the nuts, and the melted caramel mixture. Sprinkle with the remaining crumbs and bake for 15–20 minutes more at 350°F. Don't overbake. Cut while warm. The caramels and cream may be melted in a microwave.

How are you gonna beat that? If only there were two blue ribbons to hand out. But Pat knew that wasn't realistic. To top a bar recipe like that, you needed a better one, and so far this was it:

2½ cups crushed graham cracker crumbs

1 cup melted Grade A butter

1 cup peanut butter

2½ cups powdered sugar

1 cup milk chocolate chips with 1 teaspoon Grade A butter

Mix together the graham cracker crumbs, melted butter, peanut butter, and sugar. Pat into a greased 9-by-13-inch pan. Melt the chips and butter and spread them on top of the bars. Set in the refrigerator until firm. Cut into bars.

Didn't get much simpler than that, did it? Pat had been making that recipe for twenty-five years, and it was the one that won her five blue ribbons and one red ribbon in the six years since she had finally given in to the extreme public pressure and entered it in the summer County Fair Bake-Off. This year's was just a week away now, and the deadline to submit a recipe and entry form was tomorrow.

That evening, Pat would meet the other women in the Fellowship Hall of First Lutheran Church for the "dry run," where everyone who was considering entering the County Fair would make a full batch of their bars, just for the other church women, and they would have an anonymous vote among themselves to determine who would be encouraged to submit. Now that the First Lutheran women had asserted themselves as a force to be reckoned with, it was important that everyone put her best foot forward.

The TV interrupted one of Pat's all-time favorite movies, *Lawrence of Arabia,* to declare a severe storm warning for the area. Pat called everyone to ensure they would make it; they were Minnesotans, and a little thunder and lightning wasn't going to hold them back. Only Frances Mitzel, who was sixty-two and, in her words, "not the best driver," expressed some hesitation.

• • •

Pat got to the church early to turn on the lights and set up the tables with plates and napkins. She parked her old Honda Accord in the minister's spot and saw before getting out of her car that the Fellowship Hall's lights were on already. Maybe the Cub Scouts had left them on. That wasn't like them. She retrieved her nine-by-thirteen-inch pan of peanut butter bars from the floor of the backseat and walked with it under her arm to the front door, which was propped open. The air smelled like ozone and a tall gray thunderhead rose over the corn farms on the edge of town. There were no sounds but the engines of passing cars and the warm breeze pushing through the willow trees on the edge of the parking lot, touching Pat's face, pushing her bangs straight up in the air.

In the Fellowship Hall, a skinny woman in an impertinent white summer dress—no sleeves, low neck, and cut above the knee—threw an ivory cotton tablecloth over a folding table.

"Hello there," Pat said, smiling. "I'm here with the women's group. We'll be using this room tonight."

"I know," the woman said, her pretty face, with its sharp chin and wide brown eyes, earnestly smiling back. She looked as elegant and sophisticated as a TV anchorwoman. "Evan and Jenni said that I could come early and help set up."

She didn't even call him *Pastor* Evan.

"I'm Celeste. Celeste Mantilla. My family's new here."

"Wow. Well, welcome to First Lutheran. I'm Pat Prager."

"Oh my God," the skinny woman said, taking the Lord's name in vain in the Lord's house. "You're Pat Prager. *The* Pat Prager?"

"Yep," Pat said, removing the cotton tablecloth from the folding table. "Well, first thing is, we save the nice tablecloths for funerals and

214 J. RYAN STRADAL

other public functions. 'Cause it's just us tonight, we'll use one of the disposable paper ones."

"Oh, yes, I'm sorry," Celeste said, helping Pat fold the tablecloth. "Wow, I've heard so much about you. Six-time blue ribbon winner."

"Just five, actually."

"Oh, it'll be six by next week, I know it. You know, I brought something tonight, but I'll feel lucky if I'm just picked to enter."

"Who told you about all this?"

"Oh, Barb Ramstad. We bought the house two doors down from hers."

"Oh, that big one?"

"I know, right? Too big for us. Cleaning one bathroom is bad enough, but try four. There goes half your day. And I don't even want to think of the heating bills in the winter. But it's nice being close to the Ramstads. I got a boy in middle school who's the same age as their son."

This woman had a teenage son? She didn't look a day over thirty. And that thinly disguised bragging about her giant house was so ignorantly prideful. Pat had just met this woman and she could already tell that her loose attitude and freespending, big-money ways were going to cause problems for everybody. "Oh, nice," Pat said. "So where'd you move here from?"

"Fort Myers, Florida. My husband got a job at 3M, so we moved up here for his work."

Probably a rich engineer. "There's ELCA churches in Fort Myers? I thought you'd be more Missouri Synod down there."

"No, there's four in Fort Myers. We're sure blessed to have this one up here now."

Pat could see the skinny woman's bra when she bent over. To dress like that in a church, even in the Fellowship Hall! Maybe in Florida they sang hymns in their bikinis, but that wouldn't fly up here. "Well, we're surely blessed to have some new faces in our congregation," she said.

As they unfurled the cheap white paper over the table, Pat did start to feel bad in her heart about cutting this woman down. Celeste was a stranger in a strange land and here in God's house it was Pat's duty to be welcoming and think of how she'd want to be treated in that situation. Besides, it wasn't as if Pat's family didn't have its complexities. After all, her son, Sam, was apparently the biggest pot dealer in the high school, which wasn't exactly something she'd put on a bumper sticker. Even so, it's not like he was a total waste like his cousin Dan Jorgenson down in Farmington. Sam was getting a 3.4 and his freshman-year teachers said that he showed promise. There was no punishment that would change him; he swore that he never tried any worse drugs, the pot sales were saving them money on his future college loans, and the stuff would probably be legal in a year or two anyway. Besides, he did the right thing and tithed.

Pat heard Sandra's heavy steps in the hallway and turned to see her with Barb right behind, each of them carrying a pan of their signature bars, then Corrina, running in last, holding an umbrella, with her bars already cut up and piled in a mint-green Tupperware bowl. Why had they agreed to send only three to County this year? Pat wished she could vote for them all. She was waiting to see Sandra and Corrina size up this skinny newcomer, but apparently Barb had introduced Celeste to them already, at some event or happening that Pat hadn't been made aware of.

"I like those capri pants, Barb," Celeste said, pointing below Barb's waist at the pork-chop pockets and drawstring hems.

"Oh, thanks. Got 'em at Kohl's. Originally fifty dollars, cut down to twenty-nine, but I got 'em for nineteen with a coupon."

Everyone nodded in admiration at the good value.

"The blouse was an even better deal," Barb continued. "It's Guess brand, originally seventy-nine dollars, but I got it at T.J. Maxx for eighteen."

"Wow," Corrina said. "Every time I go there, I never see anything like that."

"Well, you gotta know when to go to these places."

"How was the drive into town?" Celeste asked.

"Wind's pickin' up," said Sandra, who, in her faded XXL Twins T-shirt and knee-length denim shorts, was eager to end the fashion conversation. "We better make this quick."

"Where's Frances?" Pat asked.

"She didn't want to drive in the weather," Corrina said.

"Well, I don't want her to miss out if she made bars."

"It's OK, Pat," Barb said. "She said she knows her bars aren't going to win anyway."

"So it's just the four of us for three spots?"

Celeste looked over the group. "I made some," she said, reaching down to pick up a large canvas sack sitting against the wall. Thunder rattled the light fixtures again as she produced a nine-by-thirteen-inch pan containing a dark brown and stark white concoction. "These are my Mississippi mud bars."

"Do you have the recipe?" Pat asked, and Celeste pulled a piece of cardstock from her Louis Vuitton bag on the floor.

"Yes, right here," Celeste said, handing the card to Pat:

4 eggs

1 cup Grade AA butter, softened

2¼ cups sugar

1 teaspoon vanilla

1½ cups flour

½ cup cocoa

1 cup chopped nuts

7 ounces marshmallow crème

Preheat the oven to 350°F. In a large copper mixing bowl, at medium speed, beat the eggs, butter, sugar, and vanilla until light and fluffy. Add the flour and cocoa. Beat until well blended. Fold in the nuts. Spread in a greased 9-by-13-inch pan. Bake for 40–45 minutes.

Immediately place spoonfuls of marshmallow crème on top and spread until smooth. Let cool for one hour.

Frosting:

⅓ cup Grade AA butter

½ cup cocoa

2½ cups powdered sugar

⅓ cup heavy whipping cream

1 teaspoon vanilla

Melt the butter; stir in the cocoa. Cook for 1 minute. Add the powdered sugar, whipping cream, and vanilla and mix until smooth. Spread on top of the marshmallow crème. Freezes well.

"Looks like a crowd-pleaser," Pat said, handing the card back.

"It might be a tad rich for some," Celeste said. "But yes, kids adore it."

"Pat, should we even serve yours?" Sandra said. "You know the rest of us are just fighting for two spots here."

"Well, I definitely want to try them," Celeste said.

The rain came in at an angle and began to pummel the windows. It sounded like people, bad people, throwing pebbles at the church. Pat went to the glass and saw pea-sized bits of ice jumping in the lawn.

"It's hailing," she said.

"Oh, jeez," Barb said, and started slicing her bars.

While Pat was eating one of her own bars, just for comparison, the fluorescent lights flickered out, and almost immediately the chilling wail of that awful tornado siren kicked in from three blocks away. As if they needed a siren to tell them that their lights were out. The elapsed time between the lightning and its thunder was getting shorter; the storm was directly over them now.

"How exciting," Celeste said, smiling.

"Well, even if we're stuck here," Sandra said, slicing herself a Mississippi mud pie bar, "at least we won't starve to death."

"Oh my," Corrina said, taking a bite. "Celeste, these are incredible."

Sandra looked at her own tray of bars and shook her head. "Well, I don't have a shot this year. Celeste, if we don't finish 'em all here, I'm gonna steal them and take 'em home."

"Thank you," Celeste said, looking down at her feet. "It's just an old family recipe, nothing special."

"Why a copper mixing bowl?" Pat asked Celeste.

"Oh, for the egg whites," Celeste said. "It stabilizes them. Don't ask me how."

Barb looked at Pat. "You didn't know that?"

"I actually don't separate my eggs for bars. When I'm making a soufflé or sponge cake, I add a little cream of tartar to my egg whites, and that does the trick for me."

The other women nodded.

"Don't get me wrong, though. Who wouldn't love to have a copper mixing bowl," Pat was quick to add. "But we just gotta work with what God gives us."

"I use a copper whisk," Barb said.

Sandra, finishing her Mississippi mud pie bar, licked her plastic fork. "I think we have our winner right here. What do you think, Pat?"

Pat nibbled at her Mississippi mud bar. When she raised it to her lips, she saw that Celeste's bar left a thick stamp of greasy oil on the paper plate. In her mouth, she literally felt granules of sugar wash around; her fillings cried out in protest. She chased the thick buttery slab with a glass of water, which she swished around in her mouth before swallowing.

"Definitely one of our final three, yes," she said, smiling.

• • •

When the rain receded enough for all of them to drive home safely, Pat got in her rusty old Accord, which didn't look like much, sure, but got a person from point A to point B reliably and had been loyal to the family through so much abuse. Not even Eli's ungrateful daughter Julie could destroy that car. The problem, on days like today, was that one of the rear windows didn't go all the way up, and even though they had taped up a Hefty bag to cover the gap, the storm had blown it right off the car. Now part of the backseat was sopping wet and would have to be dried later so it didn't get full of mold.

Why was God testing her like this? With the storm, the wet seat, and, most painfully, the soul-breaking trial that was Celeste Mantilla. Maybe, Pat thought, God felt that she was having it too easy with the blue-ribbon-winning bars year after year. Maybe He felt that she needed a challenge. And so He had sent this demonic force, in the form of a beautiful woman with these ridiculously sweet bars, to oppose her, to put things in perspective, to remind her of what was really important. Like He said in 1 Peter 1:7, "The trial of your faith, being much more precious than of gold that perisheth." Which was true. But why were the most pious always the most severely tested?

Don't answer that, Lord, she said as she turned onto her street, and whispered a brief prayer of apology. She also forgave her friends, for the Mississippi mud bars proved that their spirit might be strong, but their flesh was weaker than ever. One day they would see the error of their ways; but when the time of their contrition came, she would be gracious and forgiving to them and *not* say that she had known from the first that Celeste was pure evil, because no one likes to hear an I-told-you-so.

At home, the power was still out, so there was no opening the garage door. Pat carefully stepped up the wet concrete stairs to her front door with her one-quarter-empty tray of bars and trudged up to the kitchen. Her husband, Eli, and son, Sam, were drinking milk and eating Schwan's mint chocolate chip ice cream in the candlelight, watching distant lightning from the kitchen window.

Wiping her face and head with a paper towel, Pat looked at Sam's huge bowl of ice cream without saying anything.

"Mom, it'll go bad otherwise. With no power to the fridge."

"Did you save any?" Pat asked.

"A little," said Eli, eating the ice cream out of the box, tilting it to her eye level.

"So, Mom, who else besides you is going to County?" Sam asked, squirting more Hershey's chocolate syrup on his ice cream.

"Me and Barb, and this new woman, Celeste," Pat said, setting her tray of bars down on the kitchen counter.

"When the power went out," Eli said, putting his empty glass of milk in the dishwasher without rinsing it first, "I was six hundred words into a blog post about an injury in our secondary. Then, blam! All gone."

Sam looked up at his stepdad and said nothing. Pat's son from her first marriage wasn't a Minnesota Vikings fan, or a fan of any sports, really, and neither was Pat, but that didn't prevent Eli from telling them each about everything he wrote on his blog.

"And I was *juuuust* about to save it and shut the computer off."

Pat removed a milk glass from the dishwasher and rinsed it out in the sink. "Anyway, this new woman Celeste's a piece of work," she said.

"Well, they don't even have the results of the guy's MRI yet. But I knew we should've picked a safety in the draft. We switched to a Tampa 2 D and we have *one guy* who's a Tampa 2 safety. And so guess who goes down today in practice."

"And her bars. Basically fat bombs. Of course, you-know-who just loved them."

"And there's no decent free agents this time of year. Blew our chance there."

"They don't realize how embarrassing it's gonna be to enter those bars in a County contest. You have to be more nuanced at the County level. It's not like the judges are a bunch of eight-year-old boys."

"Maybe we can move one of the corners to safety. That's what I was proposing."

"And you should see her. You can bet she doesn't even touch these bars. She looks like a model."

"Who looks like a model?" Eli asked.

"The new woman at church, Celeste."

"You should invite her over sometime," Eli said, opening the freezer. "What else we got in here?" He pulled out two flat brown rectangles wrapped up in cellophane. "What are these things?"

"My edibles," Sam said. "Brownies. They go for forty each."

"Edibles. Is this a felony amount in here?"

"No, felony's one and a half ounces. Way less than that in those things. An ounce each, tops."

"You should only sell these, then."

"I don't sell. My friends sell. I grow and manufacture."

Pat stepped out of the kitchen without looking back. "I don't want to know any of this," she said, walking into her separate bedroom. "Help yourself to the bars."

The day of the County Fair Bake-Off, it always made sense to carpool, so Pat agreed to meet Barb and Celeste at Celeste's house over on the lake. The five-bedroom, four-bath stone house was the nicest, most expensive place in town; it used to belong to a personal injury attorney and his family. Pat had never been in the house before and was a little curious about it. Sure seemed like a lot of space for a couple with two teenage kids. What were those extra bedrooms for? Maybe they were hoarders.

Pat rang the doorbell and heard it echo through the vast space inside, like a lonely voice in an empty tomb. She thought of 1 Timothy 6:9—"Those who desire to be rich fall into temptation and a snare, and into many fool-ish and harmful lusts which drown men in destruction and perdition."

A man who looked like a younger Peter O'Toole answered the door. For a moment, the excruciatingly handsome man stared at Pat, with a look that said, *What are you doing here?* but in a sexy way.

"Yez?" he finally said, in a heartbreakingly warm accent.

For a moment, Pat couldn't move or speak. She looked at his head of wavy light brown hair, the clean-shaven jaw, the shocking blue eyes, and the buttons on his white dress shirt that showed no strain near the na-vel; though she had never seen "washboard abs" up close in person, she was sure this guy had them. Pat found it necessary to quickly remind herself that she loved Eli with his scarred face and scratchy beard. In fact, that's what attracted her to him—the promise of a big, full heart that needed healing, beneath that rough, tough-guy shell. She com-posed herself, met the handsome man's eyes, and spoke. "Hi, I'm here to see Celeste? She's driving us to the fair."

The man looked past her. "Ez that your car?"

She turned and looked back at her rusty Accord with the fresh black Hefty bag hanging in the rear window.

"Yep, sure is."

"Do you mind," he said, thoughtfully touching his strong chin, "mov-ing it down a house or two? We just moved here and I don't want to give our neighbors the wrong impression."

"OK," Pat said.

"I'll take this in for you," he said, relieving her of the tray and setting it on the floor, near the shoes.

"Thank you. Be right back," Pat said, walking down their driveway, thinking about what he had said about giving the neighbors the wrong impression, succumbing to unkind thoughts about these people and their evident, vulnerable pridefulness.

After moving her car two houses down and coming back to the front door, she found Celeste waiting.

"Did Oscar make you move your car down the street? I'm so embarrassed," Celeste said.

After Pat picked up her bars from the floor by the doorway, Celeste led her through what Celeste called the "lawyer foyer" into the main living room, which was clean and spartan and arranged with that horrid midcentury modern furniture like the kind that Pat's parents had in the 1960s. That style was supposedly making a comeback, but it only reminded her of uncomfortable groping from disrespectful boys and awful family game nights, when her dad got drunk and swore at everyone.

"I'd love to give you the tour," Celeste said, "but I'm afraid Barb says we have to get going. Registration got moved up to 9:30 a.m. So we better make tracks."

The doorbell chimed and there was Barb, standing at the door with her bars. "Let's go, ladies!" she said.

On her way out, Pat saw something pink and slender descend the staircase behind her, and turned to see a teenage girl in a low-cut spaghetti-strap top, with straight bangs like that Zooey Deschanel, mope her way down the stairs, her angelic face downcast in teenage-girl frustration.

"Mom!" the pretty little nymph said. "What the fuck did you do with my fucking iPad charger?"

"I left it in your room, honey," Celeste said, setting down her tray of bars as she put on a pair of red-bottomed heels in the doorway.

"Which one? My bedroom or my study room?"

"Your study room."

"God, Mom. How many times do I have to tell you, don't touch my shit."

The girl turned and saw Pat watching her. Pat was disturbed by the language—it reminded her so much of Julie before she finally left—and the teenage girl grinned at Pat's disapproving expression.

"Hey," the girl said, absolutely unembarrassed. "You Sam Jorgenson's mom?"

"Yes, yes I am," said Pat, unable to look the girl in the face.

"Tell him to text me back, OK?"

Barb tugged on Pat's arm and whispered for them to go. Celeste kissed her daughter on the cheek, shouted a goodbye to her husband, adjusted her Ray-Ban sunglasses, and followed Pat and Barb out onto her driveway.

"Wow, nice shoes," Barb said. Barb was the most brand-conscious of the Deer Lake ladies, at least until you-know-who breezed into town. "Are you sure you want to wear Louboutins to a county fair, though? There's, like, cow and horse poop everywhere."

"Oh, these are knockoffs," Celeste said.

There was some discussion over whether to take Barb's Jeep Cherokee or Celeste's Mercedes GLK, but after a short discussion it was decided that they would take Celeste's car because Pat had never been in a Mercedes before. Barb sat up in front to help Celeste navigate the long, lonely rural roads to the County Fairgrounds, and Pat sat in back, to keep an eye on everyone's bars.

As they drove past the lake, Celeste caught Pat's eyes in the rearview mirror.

"I think my daughter Madison has a huge crush on your son Sam," Celeste said.

"Oh my," Pat said.

"She met him at that coffee shop, Professor Java's. He works there, right?"

"Yeah, not nearly enough."

Celeste laughed. "Apparently he's playing hard to get."

"Well, he's got a busy life."

"What else does he do?"

Pat wanted, just then, to tell Celeste that Sam was the biggest drug dealer in the entire high school, knowing that it would permanently put the kibosh on any future relationship between her child and Celeste's little demon-spawn.

"Well. He's holding down a 3.4 GPA. He's vice president of the skate-boarding club. He's into music. A typical teenage boy, I guess. What about your daughter?"

"Well, she's a National Merit Finalist. But she had a private tutor to teach her all the tricks on the test. She got in the IB classes, barely. Varsity volleyball, dance. She's done with Cotillion, thank God for that. For college, she wants to go to NYU, but that girl is going to college in New York City over my dead body. Oscar and I are going to make her go to Michigan—it's closer. And Oscar likes their football team."

"Neat," Pat said.

"Our son, meanwhile, never leaves his room," Celeste said. "He's probably just, y'know, doing his thing, but I hope he's not looking at anything weird when he does it."

Pat decided that she had nothing to say on the subject.

"Any other kids?" Celeste asked.

"Well, Eli has two kids from his first marriage. Will and Julie. They're grown up, both of them live outside of Chicago."

"Cool. That must be fun to go down to visit them."

"They don't really talk to us."

"They side with the mom in the divorce?"

"No, their mom died, that's what happened. They still side with her, though. They can't stand me. Never could."

"That really sucks. You helped raise these kids, you put them through college, right? How old were they when you met Eli?"

"Sixteen and thirteen."

"Wow, you never had a shot. And not even a thank-you, for what you've done."

"It was hard at first, but now . . . I try not to take it personally."

"Well, if it's any comfort to you, I'm sure my own kids are gonna be just as bad. I know for a fact Madison's only going to call us when she needs money."

A snore burst from Barb's face. Pat and Celeste both withheld laughs as they looked at their friend, zonked out in the passenger seat.

"I wondered why she wasn't chiming in," Pat said.

"Know what I like about you, Pat?" Celeste said. "You're real. I think you're the most real person I've met here. There's not one fake or pretentious thing about you. I can't tell you how much I love that."

"Thanks," Pat said.

Celeste glanced at her dashboard GPS and turned left down a country road. "I'm glad we're friends," she said.

Because they were participants, they got to park in the free lot close to the main food tent, where all of the judging contests were held. By 9:15 a.m. it was already eighty degrees; it was going to be a scorcher.

They stepped onto the grass and followed an old man in a bright yellow vest to the tent for registration and to hand in their bars. It was important to do this fairly quickly, so the bars suffered no adverse effects in the heat.

Upon entering, Pat's senses were overcome by a fog of cinnamon, ginger, chocolate, vanilla, and buttery pie crusts. The long tent was filled with more than a hundred people, mostly women, many holding fresh baked goods, with a few pies still softly steaming from their vents and folds.

Celeste, of course, couldn't believe it. "What a place," she said at last. "What an honor to live in a part of the world that loves good old-fashioned baking."

"My mom used to say, have a house without a pie, be ashamed until you die," Barb said, and they walked forward, through the boys setting up folding chairs, toward the registration table at the far end.

. . .

"Well, I don't know about you ladies, but I could go for some food after this," Barb said, once they found out what line they were supposed to be in.

"Can you save my spot? I want to go see who the judges are this year," Pat said.

Barb looked at her as if Pat had just suggested they run across the fairgrounds, take off their shirts, and streak the demolition derby. "Knock yourself out," she said.

Pat never cared much for that phrase, but decided that now was not the time for her opinions, so she just stepped out of the line and said she'd be right back.

"Hey there, Pat," she heard a young woman's voice say as she entered the tent.

Pat turned around and saw it was Susan Smalls, a real nice young woman from church. They had just talked recently because Susan was married to an Afghan War vet who was medically retired and still looking for a job. Eli was trying to help them out by getting her husband an interview at UPS, where Eli had worked since his machine shop went out of business in River Falls and they moved to Minnesota—maybe the company that had saved their family could save another. So far, sadly, their prayers hadn't been answered, and Pat had been trying to avoid Susan until she had something good to report.

"Sure is a warm one out," Susan said, smiling. A three-year-old boy twirled between and around her legs, and Pat admired the young woman's short, practical haircut and modest makeup on her pretty round face.

"You can say that again."

"How's the family? Are they here?" Susan asked.

"No, this year it's just me and a couple of friends. What about yourself?"

"Oh, my husband's here. He got a job at the mini-donut stand."

"Oh, which mini-donut stand?"

"The Lutheran one."

"Well, of course," Pat said, and the two women laughed.

"Say, I hate to pester you about this, but you heard from Eli's boss at UPS yet?"

"No, not yet. But I'm sure we will any day now."

"You think it's rude to send the résumé again? In case it got lost the first time?"

"I don't suppose it could hurt." Pat touched the corner of the pan under Susan's arm, eager to change the topic. "So what are you entering this year?"

"Something new. They're called Resurrection rolls."

"Resurrection rolls?"

"Yeah. What you do is, you put marshmallows in melted butter and then roll them in cinnamon sugar. Then ya wrap 'em in crescent roll dough and put them in the oven for twelve minutes. Then—this is important—while they're baking, read John 20, verses 1 through 18."

Pat tried to think of what it was. She didn't know John 20 off the top of her head.

"'Now on the first day of the week Mary Magdalene went to the tomb early, while it was still dark, and saw that the stone had been taken away from the tomb,'" Susan said. "And the same thing happens to the marshmallow. You take 'em out of the oven, break it in half, and the marshmallow is totally gone. He is risen."

Pat smiled. "Resurrection rolls. Now that's a shoo-in."

"Well, I'm not gonna lie. I sure could use the first prize in Miscellaneous Baked Goods. This year it's a Target gift card worth fifty dollars. The way this one is growing, and with my husband between jobs, well, it would be a help."

Pat nodded. That fifty-dollar gift card was no small potatoes, but the first prizes in each of the Bars, Pies, Cookies, and Cakes divisions were Target gift cards worth seventy-five bucks. The big leagues.

"Well, good luck, Susan, I'm pullin' for ya."

"I'm glad I'm not competin' against you, Pat," Susan said. "God bless."

Now at the far end of the tent from registration, Pat angled to sneak a look behind a partition at the judges' table. The judges were never announced ahead of time, and were different every year, to prevent corruption, but they were always present for registration. She took in the six faces, all of whom she knew, and then she took a deep, sad breath, swallowing the hard fact that God had saved His most difficult test for last.

The judges were:

Victor "Sexy Venison" Strycek: An unmarried, twenty-eight-year-old firefighter born and raised in the town of Deer Lake. Three years ago, to raise money, the firefighters had published a "hunks" calendar; Victor's page (November) featured him shirtless, at a grill, frying up venison steaks. It was not an unattractive photo, but since then, all of the young people called him "Sexy Venison," and now he even answered to it. There was absolutely no chance he'd vote for anyone but Celeste Mantilla.

Sister Lois Freehold: A Catholic nun from Deer Lake, Sister Lois was on the judging panel every six or seven years, and the only year she'd been on the panel since Pat had been entering her bars was the one year Pat got a red ribbon instead of a blue one. A strong Catholic entry from St. Boniface in Deer Lake, or St. Elizabeth Ann Seton in Deer River, would get this woman's first-place vote, no question.

"Aunt" Jenny Sjoholm: Aunt Jenny was the bulwark of central Minnesota's baking community. She'd been the chairwoman of the Baked Goods Judging Committee since 1976. An enthusiastic supporter of Pat Prager's bars.

Clarence Peterson: Eighty-year-old Clarence Peterson was a legendary local mechanic who could "fix any damn thing without a heart or a computer," or so he said. There were two big strikes here against Pat: She and

Eli never brought anything to Clarence for repair, and he'd never been a judge on a baked goods panel before. Those types, especially the men, always went for pretty faces and rich treats.

Ross Peterson: Make that three strikes against Pat. Ross was Clarence's mentally handicapped grandson, who was a savant at small engine repair—a Rain Man of riding mowers. Another thing: They were both Methodists, so even though First Lutheran Church in Deer Lake had dominated Bars for the last seven years, a strong entry from Calvary Methodist Church would now have two automatic first-place votes.

Miss Minnesota Runner-Up Rachael Bauer: Now things may have been looking up. Everyone knew that skinny girls didn't like buttery sugar bombs that made them fat and ruined their complexion. But then Pat recognized the immodest dress on the person talking to Rachael. Celeste and Rachael were talking and laughing! They knew each other! Celeste just moved here, for Pete's sake. How could this have happened?

Also, what kind of baked goods judging panel had three men on it? One was fine, but three? This was obviously a P.C. overcorrection to last year's six female judges. And of the three remaining women, one was Catholic, and one was somehow friends with that horrid Celeste. This was bad, this was real bad.

Pat got in line behind Barb and Celeste at the registration table, where two old women in floppy sun hats took their names, their recipes, and their bars.

"Celeste Man-teeya?" one of the old women asked, pronouncing Celeste's last name in what Pat would later learn was the proper Spanish style.

"No, Mantilla, like vanilla," Celeste said.

"Where you from originally? It's such a pretty last name."

"My husband's from Florida."

"No, originally, originally."

Celeste sighed. "He's half French, half Cuban."

"I knew it," the old woman said. "Being from Florida."

"Are you going to ask for their family trees as well?" Celeste said, glancing at Barb and Pat. "Go ahead, we have all day."

"Just asking," the old woman said. "My husband and I had our honeymoon in Cuba in 1955. Beautiful place."

"Well, we wouldn't know."

"Guess we better get this line moving." The old woman looked up at Pat. "Next."

Despite Barb's earlier request for some food, she first wanted to show Celeste the 4-H Livestock Judging Area. Celeste was still whining about the racism of the old lady at registration; Pat would never admit it outright, but she got some pleasure from seeing Celeste get a little miffed. Some small thing had to go wrong for Celeste Mantilla today in order for Pat to feel that the Lord would restore a sense of harmony and balance in the world.

"What do you think, Pat?" Celeste asked her as they entered the dusty poop fog outside of the Pig Barn.

Pat was shocked to be asked for an opinion and didn't have a ready answer. "Well, you can't control other people, but you can control how you react to them," she said, because somehow it was the first thing that came to mind.

Celeste stopped walking and nodded. "Wow," she said. "That's the smartest thing I've heard in a long time."

With that, Celeste seemed to cheer right up. The three women walked into a punishingly hot wooden building that smelled something like hay, dirt, and excrement being baked in an oven. There, they winced together at the lazy, prizewinning pigs, and the incident at registration was never spoken of again.

The awards for Bars were the second of the day, at 12:15 p.m., after Miscellaneous Baked Goods at noon. Each judge had six points to allot for each entry: three to a first-place vote, two for a second, and one for a third. Three times, Pat's bars had gotten eighteen points—meaning all six first-place votes—including last year. She already knew that this wouldn't happen this year, and had set her sights on winning a red ribbon, or at least a white one. She had never been to County and not won a ribbon before. Ever.

On their way back to the main food-judging tent, Celeste and Barb stopped at a stand and ordered Hot Dish on a Stick. Pat, not hungry, stuck to a bottle of water. Pat noticed Barb's pale Nordic skin growing red under the late morning sun and gave her some SPF 50, which Barb only reluctantly accepted because she said she wanted to get tan. The results were only twenty minutes away and Pat was amazed that neither Barb nor Celeste seemed anxious.

Barb was talking about the best time to buy clothes at T.J. Maxx. "The one down in St. Louis Park is the only one in the state with a Runway section," she said. "If you get there on Tuesday or Thursday after the new stock gets delivered, you can get a Marc Jacobs dress for, like, ninety-nine dollars."

"Marc Jacobs, or Marc by Marc Jacobs?" Celeste asked.

Pat had no idea what they were talking about. "It's almost fifteen minutes to noon," she said. "We should really get to the tent and get good seats for the results."

"Marc Jacobs," Barb said. "And take it easy, Pat, we'll be done in a minute."

• • •

Because Celeste was such a slow eater—not used to food on a stick, obviously—and a slow walker in those stupidly awkward red-bottomed heels, they didn't get back to the food judging tent until 12:03 p.m., just after the results for Miscellaneous Baked Goods were announced.

"Next up is a County favorite: Bars," Sister Lois Freehold was saying into the microphone as the women entered the back of the tent. "We have our first-, second-, and third-place winners decided, and we'll hand out the prizes in about ten minutes."

Pat saw Susan Smalls on the other side of the tent, and from the look on her face, Pat knew that Susan hadn't won the fifty-dollar, twenty-five-dollar, or even the ten-dollar Target gift card for Miscellaneous Baked Goods winners. This was a woman whom Pat knew could sure use a little money. It was heartbreaking to look at her standing there, tired and sweaty, next to her clingy, quiet three-year-old boy who was dressed in too-small yellow elastic shorts and a too-large "Big Dogs" shirt with a stain on the front. Hardworking people don't dress their kids like that when they have a choice.

Sister Lois was at the mic, and it hit Pat—why was Sister Lois speaking? Aunt Jenny was always in charge of these kinds of things. Pat stood up from her white folding chair and saw a strange blond middle-aged man sitting in Aunt Jenny's chair.

"Excuse me," Pat said to Celeste and Barb as she moved past them into the aisle. "I gotta see what's up with the judges."

As Pat approached the judges' table, Sister Lois met her gaze, and looked at Pat the way a principal looks at a student who's been kicked out of school.

"Mrs. Prager, please wait for the results to be read," Sister Lois said. "Like everyone else."

"Who's this?" Pat asked, pointing at the unshaven middle-aged man in the chair where Aunt Jenny once sat.

"That's Aunt Jenny's son, Stevie. Aunt Jenny got heatstroke and her son has to fill in as a judge. Now please return to your seat."

This Stevie, whoever he was, stared straight ahead without acknowledging this exchange. This creeped Pat out even more.

"OK," Pat said. "So he judged? He voted?"

"Please sit down, Mrs. Prager."

Pat, aware that everyone in the first several rows was looking at her, retreated to her row. Celeste and Barb moved down a seat to make space for her, which unfortunately meant that Pat had to sit next to Celeste for the results.

"Hey, I know that guy," Celeste said, looking at the new guy seated at the judges' table. "He works at 3M. He's in my husband's department. Oscar's his boss."

Sister Lois Freehold walked to the microphone and spoke.

Pat's heart stuck in her throat and she clutched her knees and stared at the floor. For some reason, she remembered the time when Sam was three and tried to flush his Thomas the Tank Engine down the toilet and it got crammed in the plumbing sideways—irretrievable, unloved, pummeled with excrement. Yes, she felt like that.

"It'll be OK," Celeste said, touching Pat's shoulder.

"In third place," Sister Lois said, never lifting her eyes from the clipboard she held in her left hand, "with five points, Barb Ramstad's Kraft caramel bars."

The audience clapped politely. Pat took a deep breath. Five points were nothing. That meant that the voters were agreed on the top two bars, and whoever they were, they each got almost all of the votes, and it was probably very close.

"Barb Ramstad," Sister Lois said, "please come up to claim your ten-dollar Target gift card."

Barb smiled as she got to her feet. Celeste patted Barb on the butt, like baseball players do. Pat just said, "Congratulations, Barb," and smiled sincerely.

Pat watched as Barb walked extra slow to the front of the tent, probably just to annoy her. Sister Lois was waiting for Barb to get her prize and ribbon before announcing the second-place winner, and that took a while, because, for Pete's sake, they let Ross hand out the ribbons, and he didn't know which color the third-place ribbon was, and Clarence had to come over and correct him.

"OK now, where was I?" Sister Lois asked the audience.

Pat bit her lip and clasped her hands.

Celeste put her hand on Pat's back. It felt weird and cold, like a giant spider.

"Second place? Second place, with nine points," Sister Lois said. "Jessica Duncan's strawberry rhubarb bars."

"*Yeahhhh!*" a voice shot up from the crowd, and a healthy, plump, vigorous-looking young woman with curly dyed-red hair shot up in her seat amid a chorus of cheers in her section. She wasted no time getting to the front and collecting her prize.

Pat knew right then that she'd be going home without a ribbon. It didn't hit her as bad as she thought it would; the anticipation of this moment had been far more petrifying. Still, her chest felt hollowed out by anger. She felt a little like crying, but knew she wouldn't. She felt Celeste's body next to her and perceived the coldness, the heartless confidence coming off it. Celeste had been sent here to hurt her, and she was getting away with it, and Pat kneaded this again and again in her mind, pushing against the forgiveness that she was born into, the forgiveness that had given her the strength to marry Eli, and remain married, and withstand, together, the incredible hurt she received from Will and Julie, and the sins of her own son. The forgiveness was breaking apart in the face of losing her ribbons to this harlot.

"Wow, who's that?" Celeste said, watching Jessica Duncan jump up and down onstage after receiving her red ribbon and twenty-five-dollar Target gift card.

Pat didn't answer. She could hardly even look at Celeste right then. Luckily, an old woman behind them spoke up. "That's Jessica Duncan. She goes to the Methodist church."

Pat looked at the old woman and nodded approvingly, even though Pat obviously wasn't Methodist.

"She's going to Juilliard in the fall. The acting school," the old woman said, apparently a treasure trove of Jessica Duncan information.

"Wow, and she makes award-winning desserts too," Celeste said. "Some guy is sure gonna be lucky."

As Sister Lois approached the microphone, Pat took a deep breath.

Celeste leaned forward. "I gotta admit, I'm excited," she said.

Pat, in her brain, pushed Celeste out of a window onto a stone court-yard, and watched as dogs ate her body.

"First place, with thirteen points," Sister Lois said, "Patricia Prager's peanut butter bars."

"*Yes!*" Celeste said, raising her arms and shouting above the polite clap-ping in the tent. Before Pat could move or think, Celeste had thrown her arms around her, and when Pat realized what was happening and finally rose to her feet, meeting the smiling expressions of Sister Lois and the rest of the judges, Celeste held her in an embrace from behind, repeating "I knew it!" without a trace of envy or scorn in her voice, just happiness, the happiness that Pat was too stunned, in that moment, to feel.

Still holding her blue ribbon and seventy-five-dollar Target gift card in one hand—almost as if she was afraid they'd disappear if she set them down—Pat dished out with the other the rest of her bars, which the judges sold for one dollar a piece, for charity. As she was setting out the last few, Clarence Peterson put a dollar on the table and took one.

"I'd pay five times as much," he said. "You ever need your oil changed or tires rotated, I'll accept payment in these."

Sexy Venison put down two dollars. "One for me, and one for Rachael," he said, passing a paper plate over to the former Runner-Up Miss Minnesota. "Truly amazing, Mrs. Prager," he said, and in the sound of his voice and the sincere look in his eyes she understood why women fell for him, despite his reputation. It also occurred to her that this was her second time in a day being so close to washboard abs, but she had *seen* this fellow's abs. Rachael smiled as she accepted a peanut butter bar from Sexy Venison. Looked like she was going to be the next person to see them.

"Hey, congratulations!" a little woman's voice said.

Pat turned and saw that it belonged to Susan Smalls, extending her free arm in a half hug as she restrained her wiggly, squealing son with the other. "I'm glad one of us won something."

"Me too," Pat said, almost instinctually, and then realized how arrogant that sounded. "I mean, I wish both of us won. I wish you won."

"Can I see the ribbon?" Susan asked, and as she leaned forward, her grip on her toddler loosened, and he bolted away down the length of the tent. "Connor!" she yelled, dropping her shoulder bag at Pat's feet, muttering a quick "Watch my stuff, please," and marching after her child.

With Susan's back to her, Pat looked down at Susan's canvas shoulder bag at her feet. It was pushed from the inside into an uncomfortable shape, and had creamy stains down the sides that Susan either hadn't noticed or couldn't be bothered to remove. As the former mother of a toddler boy, Pat recalled her own vain, useless efforts to maintain a once-strict standard of cleanliness, and the liberation of surrender.

Watching Susan's back as she wrestled with her difficult child, Pat knelt by the dirty bag, placed her hand inside, and buried the seventy-five-dollar Target gift card deep among Susan's things.

• • •

In Celeste's fancy car on the way home, Pat sat in the back again with the empty and half-eaten trays of bars.

"You know what they were telling me, Pat," Celeste said. "Everyone thinks you have to take your bars to the next level."

"Oh, gosh, I don't know," Pat said. It sounded to her like a polite way of saying go out on top and give someone else a chance. Which was maybe a good idea.

"The State Fair has three separate contests for different kinds of bars, you know," Barb said. "Plus another separate one for gluten-free bars."

"Forget that," Celeste said. "Excuse my language, but fuck the State Fair."

Pat bristled at the sound of that word. Also, she liked the State Fair.

"You need to enter these bars in the *Petite Noisette* contest," Celeste continued.

"Whoa," Barb said. "That one costs forty bucks just to enter."

"Yeah, but first prize is five thousand dollars. And do you know what else? Pretty much everyone who finishes in the top three or four spots gets job offers from big-city professional restaurants."

"What's *Petite Noisette*?" Pat asked.

"It's a culinary lifestyle Web site," Celeste said. "It's the hot new thing."

"And they're local," Barb said. "They're based out of the Cities, in Loring Park."

"Oh, nice," Pat said, trying to remember where Loring Park was.

"If you win that one," Barb said, "you'll be the executive baker at some fancy restaurant in the Cities. Making sixty grand a year. Or more."

Sixty grand was more than what Eli made.

"That wouldn't happen if you just went to the State Fair," Celeste said. "It's another level altogether."

Pat tried to think of a situation in her life where she'd ever fielded multiple offers, for anything, and nothing came to mind. Most of the time it was hard to even get one person to want her for anything. Except when it came to her bars.

"Well, maybe, I guess," she said.

Eli leaned his back against the fridge, the light from the kitchen window reflecting against his shiny bald head, and took a swallow of his Grain Belt. Pat had been expecting him to be more enthusiastic at the prospect of her winning big money.

"The thing with that contest is, they should say that first prize is four thousand nine hundred and sixty bucks," Eli said. "If they're gonna charge you forty bucks to enter. That's what I think."

This wasn't helpful. "But do you think I should enter or not?"

"Heck, I don't know," Eli said.

"But also, the winners get offered jobs in the Cities that pay up to sixty grand."

"Sounds like a bait and switch to me," Eli said. "Plus why do you want to drive an hour and back every day to work in the Cities? Maybe you'll be making a nice income, but you gotta figure the cost of gas in the equation. And who's gonna be taking care of things around here? There's a lot you gotta think about."

Pat hadn't figured in the cost of gas. But it would be worth it. Especially if you were making up to sixty grand.

Eli crushed the beer can and set it on the kitchen counter. "Hey, where's your Target gift card? I was gonna go pick up some charcoal briquettes for the grill."

"I gave it away to Susan Smalls."

"What? What'd you do that for?"

"They're in bad shape, Eli. Her husband still hasn't found a job."

"Well, no kidding. The dude has PTSD so bad he can hardly tie his shoes."

"I know, but it's not his fault. I thought UPS wanted to hire veterans."

"Ones who can tie their shoes," Eli said. "And you know he can't pick anything up with his left arm? Why on God's green earth would you tell him to apply for a job where all you're doing is lifting stuff all day?"

"I figured there was maybe at least an office job."

"Look, it's not on us to care for every wounded vet in the world. I suppose the military oughta look after its people better, but it's not our responsibility to pick up the slack. No way in hell. They got their families to help them."

"You know, they also have a church, and friends, and neighbors," Pat said.

"I didn't tell him to go to Afghanistan and get half his shoulder blown off."

"Remember that story I told you about that woman in New York who was stabbed to death in public with a bunch of people watching, and nobody did anything? Remember how disgusted you were by that story? Well, that's you right now. That's you, watching, and not doing crap about it."

Pat left the kitchen and went into her bedroom, closing the door behind her. She was glad she had given that gift card away to Susan Smalls. And she'd enter this big-city contest no matter what Eli said. And she would pray for guidance, but she wouldn't ask the Lord forgiveness for swearing at her husband. That was gonna stand for now.

The next morning, on her way to volunteer at church, Pat imagined taking a right turn toward the interstate and driving to the Cities. She imagined doing something she loved, baking, and making sixty grand a year at it. And the part Eli was so mad about, the one-hour commute each way, Pat actually viewed as a blessing. Imagine, two hours a day, totally to herself, even if she was in a car the whole time. She could get books on tape or learn Spanish. And then what? With her money she could go on a one-person trip to Spain and learn how to tango dance. She'd have an instructor named Rodrigo who'd have a crush on her, but she'd stay faithful to Eli.

The more she found out about this contest, the less intimidating it seemed. The "celebrity judges" were no one that Pat had heard of: a woman who ran a "pop-up supper club" named Eva Thorvald, a "street eats blogger" named Hyannis Jackson, a food photographer named Kermit Gamble, and a woman named Sarah Vang who owned a food truck—a food truck!—called "Pho on Wheels." The really good chefs must've all said no; none of these people actually worked at a restaurant or a bakery, and one of them worked in a gosh darn food truck.

It did turn out that registering for *Petite Noisette*'s annual "Best of Bake" affair was a bit more of a rigmarole than registering to enter the County Fair, but it was nothing that Pat couldn't handle. She needed to submit the names of two people in the food or hospitality industry willing to nominate her; calls to Aunt Jenny Sjoholm and Joe Cragg, her former manager from her waitressing days at the Perkins in River Falls, before she married Eli, secured those. A week later, the *Petite Noisette* people e-mailed her to tell her she had earned one of the fifty spots, asked for the forty-dollar entry fee, and then later sent another e-mail with a registration number and event info. And that was it. She was in.

Unlike most baking contests, this *Petite Noisette* one took place at eight o'clock at night, and was at a fancy-looking hotel in Minneapolis called the Millennium, and had entertainment supplied by people with the names "Qwazey" and "DJ June Gloom." With all the attention paid to extra stuff like that, Pat reasoned, there would be less paid to the food, which would be to her advantage. In her experience, younger people didn't bake much anymore, and she wondered if she'd start a flood of

Deer Lake ladies down to win the Best of Bake contest every year, and maybe by the time she was sixty they'd move it to a more reasonable hour.

As for *Petite Noisette* itself, it seemed a little weird. Nothing she'd much care to read regularly. They reviewed restaurants and boutique hotels and seemed intensely concerned about where stuff like the cotton in the hotel towels came from or the chives on a baked potato were grown. They sourced every ingredient of every meal they reviewed and put them all on little maps. Pat assumed they weren't very trusting people.

The week before the contest, Pat decided to make her bars one more time, but with Grade AA butter, the kind that Celeste used, just to see whether it made much of a difference. She had just set the ingredients on the counter when she heard a knock on the front door.

Madison Mantilla, dressed extremely immodestly in a bikini covered up by some kind of oversized sleeveless T-shirt thing, stood in the doorway of Pat's house with a fancily wrapped box under her arm, tapping her cell phone.

"Oh, hey," Madison said, glancing up at Pat. "Sorry, Sam usually lets me come right in. I texted him, he knows I'm here."

"You just about frightened the pants off of me," Pat said.

"Sorry," Madison said, putting her cell phone in the waistband of her bikini bottom and holding out the box for Pat. "Oh, hey, this is from my mom."

She was taken aback, and forgot to sustain her offense at the girl's rudeness. "Thank you. What is it?"

"Just open it."

It was clear that Madison expected Pat to open it, right then, in front of her. Pat gently separated the tape from the folded paper with her fingernails—perhaps she could save this fancy paper to use again—and revealed a Sur La Table box with a beautiful copper mixing bowl inside.

"My mom said you should use it for the contest. And to say good luck and everything."

"I can't possibly accept this," Pat said.

Sam's voice, brazen and unstable, broke into their exchange. "Hey, what are you doin' out here?" he asked, standing where the hallway met the living room, staring at Madison. "Quit dickin' around and get back here."

Pat looked at her son. Where had he learned to talk like that to women?

"Fuckin' chill for a sec!" Madison said. "I'm bonding with your mom here."

"All right, I'm gonna get started without you, then," Sam said, and turned and walked back down the hall. *Started on what?* Pat wondered, but was afraid to ask.

"Well, tell your mom thank you," Pat said, wanting this whole exchange to be over. "I guess you'd better go see my son now." She put the copper bowl back in the box and took it over to her bedroom, but Madison followed her.

"You have your own bedroom? Cute," Madison said, standing in the doorway of Pat's bedroom, taking it in. Pat was happy with the modest little room, which was furnished with a queen bed in a hand-me-down wooden frame, a plain dark wood end table, a small IKEA lamp, and a yellow dresser.

"Yes, it is," Pat said, and moved into the doorway.

Madison picked up a framed picture of Eli, Pat, and Sam from the dresser. "Why don't you share a room with your husband? Is he totally gross?"

"I left butter sitting out," Pat said, walking from her room across the hall into the kitchen.

"Why did you put it in your bedroom?" Madison said, following Pat back into the kitchen with the copper bowl, setting it on the counter.

Pat looked at the bowl. It was gleaming and perfect and would be, by far, the most expensive thing in her kitchen. "I don't know," she said.

The girl leaned against the counter and sighed. "My parents should get separate rooms," she said. Pat glanced at her and thought of a pea-cock at rest. "I don't know why the hell they're even still together," Madison said, out of nowhere.

Pat wondered for a second if Madison was a spy from Celeste, sent to draw out her real feelings, but no—Madison seemed sincere about this. Maybe she just didn't have any other adults in her life to talk to, someone with the benefit of perspective like Pat. Pat considered all of this when she, at last, replied.

"Because it's what you do," she said, facing the girl. "You make a vow before God, it should mean something."

"Not to a lot of people, it doesn't," Madison said.

"It's work," Pat said. "And the work never stops."

"But why even stay together if it's no fun and all work? My parents don't do anything fun anymore. The only time my mom has fun is when she's out with you."

That was interesting for Pat to hear, but she decided to let it go unre-marked upon. "Because it's not just work," she said. "It's family."

"My mom should at least get her own girl cave when I move out," Madison said. "I told her she could have my office."

"That's nice of you," Pat said.

"And by the way," Madison said, pointing toward Pat's room, "you should girl it up more in there. Maybe get some shabby chic French provincial furniture."

"I don't know." She did not intend to say more, but heard herself con-tinue. "There are other spending priorities at the moment."

"Well, maybe when you win that big contest."

"Maybe then." Pat squared her body to look at Madison, wishing to end the conversation. "Thank you. And thank your mom."

"What? Oh yeah, for the bowl. Duh. Well, nice talkin' with ya, Sam's mom."

Pat heard Madison knock on Sam's locked door, waited for the door to open, and waited, finally, for the sound of the door locking behind them, before she could breathe and focus. Standing at the counter, over her plain ceramic mixing bowl, she drove everything that upset her into her hands, and put those hands to work making something delicious for everyone to enjoy. God did not make her a vengeful person; God made her a giving person, and even in this house of people who could be so hateful and hard, her one skill, she knew, was to serve them and make them happy, the way even an unwatered tree still provides whatever shade it can.

The day of the *Petite Noisette* contest down in the Cities, Pat couldn't find any of her friends to accompany her. Everyone had family in town, or was out of town, or had just come back from being out of town and weren't settled yet. Finally she convinced Sam to join her by offering him unlimited use of her car the last week before school started; she would walk to church or get a ride. Some mother-son bonding time before the start of the school year. It would also be six hours of his life where he wasn't running his marijuana empire or hanging out with Madison, so that was a blessing right there.

Pat's car only had a tape deck, but Sam brought his adapter that connected his little MP3 player to her car and allowed him to play his music. He put on Pink Floyd, which reminded her of her older brother Mark, and how he had defied the wishes of their parents when he drove way out to Milwaukee once in the late 1970s to see them with his friends. Mark said at the time that he wished the trip was longer so he could spend even more time away from their parents.

Pat hoped that Sam didn't feel that way about her, but it was hard for her to tell sometimes.

• • •

Pat hadn't actually been to the city of Minneapolis in more than two years, and as she got older, each trip down there seemed to overwhelm and exhaust her before she even got out of the car. She was just about shocked out of her shoes when she saw how much it would cost to park at the hotel garage, but told herself that it was much safer than parking on those streets.

In the hotel lobby, which was very fancy and clean, if a bit spare on the décor, she didn't see many women her age, or many women who looked like her at all, and certainly nobody carrying around a glass tray of bars covered in plastic wrap. They were all the way up to the floor the ballroom was on before she even saw somebody carrying something that might have food in it. A tall blonde woman in her twenties, dressed in an immodest striped dress, with unsettling tattoos of tigers on the backs of her exposed thighs and calves, was carrying some kind of rectangular maroon duffel bag that looked like a nicer of version of what pizza delivery guys use.

Pat and Sam followed the woman to a registration table set up outside two large open doors. A sign mounted on an easel read PETITE NOISETTE BEST OF BAKE EVENT. They watched as the woman handed her large bag over to the pretty girls seated behind the table, one of whom ran it inside to the ballroom behind her while the other checked the woman's name off a list and asked her to sign some papers.

As the tattooed woman pranced into the ballroom, one of the girls at the table looked directly at Sam.

"Sir?" she asked. "What's your name and registration number?"

Sam looked blankly at the girl's upbeat face. "Huh? No, I'm here with my mom."

"Oh," the pretty girl said, then looked at Pat. "Oh, cool."

Pat set her bars down on the table. "Hi, I'm Pat Prager, and this is my son, Sam."

"OK," the girl said. "It's a twenty-dollar admission for guests."

"What? Oh gosh," Pat said.

"I got it, Mom," Sam said, opening a surprisingly fat wallet; Pat didn't even want to know.

The girl accepted the twenty from Sam, and then looked at Pat, as the other girl poked the red plastic wrap on Pat's bars with her pen. "And this is your entry?"

"Yes, these are my peanut butter bars."

"Do you have an informational card with the recipe or ingredients?"

"Ah, no, I didn't know I was supposed to bring one."

"It's OK. Are they vegan, gluten-free, celiac, non-GMO, all of the above?"

Pat looked at the girls and then at Sam. "No, I don't think so."

"Any of the above?"

"None of the above, I don't think."

"Where did you source your ingredients from?" one of them asked. "Are they local?"

"Yeah," Pat said, "they're from the store about a mile from my house."

One of the girls behind the table laughed. "Sorry," she said.

Pat was so confused. "Well, they are. I maybe even have the receipt in my purse."

"No, that's fine. Go on in, peer voting just started and will go until eight-thirty. Get your ballots at the red table."

"Have them sign the release forms," the other girl said.

"Oh, yeah, sign these. This one's to consent to video- and audiotaping, and this one basically says that you are responsible for what you eat and supply to be eaten, and it waives *Petite Noisette* from any damages."

Pat never heard of anybody suing the organizers of a bake-off before, but she already knew she wasn't dealing with the usual crowd here. Being a good sport, she and Sam signed everything and stepped into the doorway of the ballroom.

It was like something out of a movie. One entire wall was a half dome of glass triangles that looked out upon the dark, twinkling Minneapolis skyline. Young people in summer yellows and pale greens moved plates of cinnamon and caramel and vanilla scents across the dark carpeted floor, setting the desserts up on small cream tables tagged with black numbers. Up a couple of stairs, at the far end of the long carpeted room, a tattooed young woman in a tasseled stocking cap and a basketball jersey stood behind two laptops, as some kind of jittery music played from the speakers on both sides of her. She remembered when popular music didn't sound like a chainsaw falling down a flight of concrete stairs and actually made people want to dance.

Backing away into the doorway of the ballroom, Pat realized that she could hear the registration girls talking.

"Locally sourced ingredients," one of them said. "From the store a mile from my house. I might have to tweet that one."

"These are so weird and gross."

Pat, still standing in the doorway to the ballroom, watched as one of the girls from the desk brought her tray of bars to a man in a black suit, who brought them to a long table and scooped them out onto an empty platter labeled with the number 49.

Pat thought she was going to cry. "Did you hear that?" she said to her son.

"Yeah, fuck 'em," Sam said, and she was actually slightly pleased to hear her son swear. "They're a bunch of snobs. Let's see what the hell they think is so damn good."

Sam walked to the nearest table, where something labeled CHOCOLATE CHIP BANANA OAT CAKES—VEGAN/GLUTEN-FREE/SOY-FREE sat on a platter next to the number 3.

Pat looked at the card next to the platter.

2 cups gluten-free oats sourced from the organic, pesticide- and GMO-free farm of Seymour and Peonie Schmidt, Faribault, MN, home-processed into oat flour

½ cup regular oats, not processed (same source as above)

½ cup brown sugar, homemade: fresh unsulphured molasses, stirred into organic fair trade Hawaiian cane sugar, each purchased at Frogtown Community Co-Op

½ teaspoon ground Ceylon cinnamon: fair trade, purchased at Frogtown Community Co-Op

⅓ cup Gala Apple applesauce, homemade, apples sourced from McBroom Orchards, Hudson, WI; organic, GMO- and pesticide-free

2 medium very ripe organic bananas, fair trade, purchased at Frogtown Community Co-Op

2 tablespoons Sunrise Hills brand low-fructose Artisanal Blue Agave syrup, purchased direct from manufacturer, Taos, NM

Pat stopped reading there. Sam chucked one of the oat cakes in his mouth.

"Nothing special," he said. "Kinda weird. Kinda like eating a banana-flavored granola bar or something. Want one?"

Pat shook her head. She didn't want to know what it was like.

"I'll tell you this, Mom," Sam said. "Eli would throw a shit fit if you served that as dessert."

"These ingredients, they're so specific," Pat said. "These people make their own oat flour and brown sugar?"

"It all looks the same in the toilet the next morning," Sam said, and Pat laughed a little. Thank God for him.

A young man in tight jeans, a plaid shirt, and a bow tie walked up to Sam. Kind of a weird fashion sense, but he was smiling, and that's what counted. "Hey man," he said. "You need a ballot."

"Oh yeah, that's right," Sam said. "We have to vote."

"What's your name?"

"Sam Jorgenson," he said, glancing at his mom.

"Dylan, and that's my wife, Oona, over there," the young man said, pointing to a happy-looking young woman in yellow high-waisted pants, standing near the DJ. Didn't those kinds of pants go out of style a long time ago? Maybe they were on sale, and she was trying to save money. "You brought your mom with you, that's cool."

"Yeah," Sam said. Pat could see that once again her son was mistaken for the chef, and this time she stepped back and remained silent, remembering the last time she opened her mouth to this crowd.

"It's great to see someone so young be so serious in the kitchen. How old are you?"

"I turn seventeen next week."

"You gotta be the youngest person here. I had to come over and meet you. What's your specialty?"

"Brownies."

"Nice. Where do you buy your ingredients?"

"Well, the main ingredient, I grow myself at home."

"I love it!" the young man said, genuinely excited. "That is so awesome."

"Thanks."

"We made the Raw No Bake Chocolate Torte, number 8 over there. What about you, you enter your brownies?"

"Oh no, we got the peanut butter bars, number 49."

"Let's try 'em," Dylan said, waving his wife over. "I'll vote for yours if you vote for mine."

"Sure."

"Go get your ballots at the red table," Dylan told Sam and Pat. "We'll meet you at number 49."

"That was a friendly young man," Pat said. She looked around the room at the pretty, strangely dressed young people. Celeste had put her up to this. If Pat's bars somehow won over this crowd of picky eaters it would be because she once again met a test and overcame it. She had held on to her faith at the County Fair, and God blessed her; perhaps, in this strange land, He would bless her again.

• • •

Pat and Sam found a stack of sheets on the red table that had check boxes next to the numbers 1 through 50, and a short line for comments next to each. Pat thought it was extremely strange to have a baked goods contest where the contestants voted, but didn't want to say anything to anybody. She just wanted to skip to the end.

She looked across the room at Dylan and Oona, who were now consuming Pat's bars back at number 49 with a third person, a serious-looking, solidly built woman in her midtwenties wearing a white T-shirt and cargo pants, who stood out from most of the room because of her plain, unfashionable clothes.

"Hey," Sam said. "Sorry that everyone thinks I'm the cook."

"Well, it's OK with me," Pat said. "I think I'm fishing in the wrong pond here."

"I don't know, I think you're gonna kill. You're the only person that's made anything that anybody knows. Do you wanna go try those people's chocolate cake thing?"

"I don't know. You can."

Pat heard a voice say, "Excuse me," and turned to see the woman in cargo pants standing next to them. She was much taller up close, and her clothes, while casual, seemed brand-new.

"I'm Eva," the woman said. "Are you the people who made the bars on table number 49?"

"Yeah," Sam said. He seemed to have gotten used to speaking for them.

"I just wanted to confirm that. And you are?"

"Sam Jorgenson. And this is my mom, Pat Prager. She actually made them. I'm just here hangin' out."

"Cool beans," Eva said, and looked at Pat in a strange but warm way, as if Pat were a letter from home with money inside. "Pat, I haven't had bars like those since I was a kid in Iowa."

"Thank you," Pat said. "I don't know how old you are, but I know I haven't changed the recipe since then."

Before Eva could respond, a young bearded man in a vest put his arm around her shoulder, muttered something in her ear, and briskly led her to a table of young people nearby. As she was pulled away, Eva looked back at Pat and shrugged sadly, as if to say, *What can you do?*

As they watched Eva become enveloped in a new conversation, Pat whispered to her son, "That was one of the judges."

To pass the time, they joined a small crowd assembled around platter number 8, the Raw No Bake Chocolate Torte. Pat looked at the instructions:

Prep time: 30 minutes

Freezer time: 2 hours

She started to read the ingredients but stopped when she got to "avocado."

"What is this?" she said. "How the heck can you make a cake like this?"

She felt all of the young people crowded around the table start to vanish, and quickly, like a bunch of parents leaving a pool that somebody's kid had pooped in.

"And what does raw mean?" Pat asked. "Raw cake, what does that mean?"

"It means that none of the ingredients were ever cooked," said a bearded older man, his sandy hair thinning, pink polo shirt buttoned to the top. "Sometimes the kitchens that make raw food don't even have hot water."

"Hey!" a female voice called out, and Pat, Sam, and the bearded man all turned to see Oona and Dylan waving at them from platter number 49. "Come over here!"

Pat and Sam made their way across the room to platter number 49, where Oona had a big smile on her face.

"Wow, guys!" she said. "What's in these? They're amazing!"

"They totally taste like the real thing," Dylan said, and glanced at Oona. "What's in 'em?"

Sam looked at his mom.

"Butter," Pat said. "Powdered sugar, peanut butter, milk chocolate chips. Graham crackers."

Dylan and Oona stared back.

"Butter?" Oona said. "What kind? Almond butter?"

"No, regular milk butter. Like from cows."

"Hormone-free cows?"

"I don't know. It's just Land O' Lakes butter. It was what was on sale."

"Oh," Dylan said.

"Does their milk have bovine growth hormone?" Oona asked Dylan.

"I don't know, but I think they're on the list," Dylan said. "Are you thinking about the baby?"

"I don't know, do you think I should go vomit it up?"

"I don't know, is that worse? The bile and stomach acids?"

Pat couldn't believe what she was hearing. She felt like a pilot flying through clouds who couldn't see anything. "On purpose you're going to vomit up my bars?"

Oona, face pinched, glared at Pat and Sam. "You trying to trick people or something? By not having an ingredients card? It's not funny. People have serious allergies and dietary preferences and things."

"I'm sorry, I didn't know," Pat said. "I didn't know you were carrying." It's true, she didn't appear to be showing at all.

"Cow's milk is really bad, especially for children," Dylan said.

"It's full of a bunch of hormones and toxins," Oona said.

Pat looked at Sam. "Well. I ate these same bars almost every month I was pregnant with him, and he turned out OK."

"But that was your choice," Oona said. "It's not mine. You have to care what other people put in their bodies."

"I'm sorry," Pat said, her voice wavering. She was not raised to confront people or defend herself in a confrontation; she was raised to appease, to mollify, to calm, to tuck little monsters in at night, to apologize for things she screwed up without realizing, to forgive, to sweeten, and her bars, her bars did that for the world, they were her I'm Sorry, they were her Like Me, they were her Love Freely Given.

"You can't just blindly feed these to pregnant people," Oona said.

"I've been making these bars my whole life," Pat said, almost pleading. "My whole entire life."

"Maybe it's time to stop," Oona said. "And take a look at what you're putting in there, maybe." She looked at Dylan, said, "Come on," and the two walked away.

Everyone near them at the *Petite Noisette* affair, having either overheard Pat's devastating confrontation with Dylan and Oona or been made aware of it, quickly created a pocket of isolation for Pat and Sam and platter number 49.

Gone was the hope of five thousand dollars; gone was the job in the Cities and the dance lessons with Rodrigo. Pat had overreached; she had fallen prey to temptation, and her greed and selfishness had led to desires that had brought her to this sinful place. Her family, God was telling her, was all that mattered. Not the judgment of these people and their awful food. She suddenly felt sorry for these people, for perverting the food of their childhood, the food of their mothers and grandmothers, and rejecting its unconditional love in favor of what? What? Pat did not understand.

She stepped forward, moving toward platter number 8, parting the crowd where she walked. "How can you eat these raw cakes and things?"

she said, loud enough to be heard clearly over the music. "You weren't raised on these things, none of you were. You were raised on good desserts, not on this crap!"

"Mom, can we go?" Sam said.

Pat looked around at the crowd. Most were too embarrassed to look directly back. "Tell me," she said. "Who doesn't like bars?"

Two burly men in dark clothes walked toward Pat and Sam. They had an expression on their faces that said, *Please make this easy for yourself.*

"Mom," Sam said.

"Who doesn't like bars?" Pat said. "Who doesn't like bars?"

Pat never felt like getting a strong drink. Other than communion wine she maybe had white wine a few times a year, with an anniversary dinner or out with the ladies. But boy, she felt like a strong drink after leaving that ballroom. They'd only asked her to leave the event, after all, not the building itself, and how often did she make it to the Cities? And certainly she never got to have a fancy drink at a fancy hotel bar, which she only remembered ever doing twice, one time on a date with her first husband, Jerry Jorgenson, and another time after a wedding where the hosts didn't supply alcohol. That was only a month before Jerry died. This would be a reward for surviving this ordeal.

Sam had told her he was a little bugged out after what happened upstairs and had to find somewhere to chill for a bit. She knew what that meant. She figured her son was an expert at being covert about his habits by now.

When her margarita arrived, Pat took a long pull from the red straw and cursed Celeste in her heart. She imagined that horrid woman, even in her troubled marriage, sitting in her beautiful home, delighting at the troubles she caused for others. Celeste had set Pat up to fail and she knew it. She was furious and jealous that her bars had lost and Pat's won and had sent Pat on this awful fool's errand for revenge.

But maybe Celeste wasn't a Jezebel, Pat realized. Maybe she, Pat, was the Jezebel. The thoughts and hopes that led her here, to this place, defied and threatened her marriage, her family, her home. Yes, they were often ungrateful, difficult, and even unloving, but this escape, this escape she sought here in this building, had taught her a lesson. She had reached beyond her loved ones, beyond her duty as a wife and mother, and she was being punished for the unfaithful harlot she was in her heart. She was Jezebel, and she had just been thrown from the tower to the courtyard below.

She prayed, right at the table—let them look, she had nothing to be ashamed of—and begged for forgiveness.

She unclasped her hands and had drunk the rest of her margarita before she knew it and ended up ordering another, which was gone by the time Sam came back.

Pat had forgotten to eat dinner amid all of this; she had assumed she would eat at the event. The two margaritas hit her a little harder than she expected, but assuming her son was stoned on marijuana, she was still probably the safer driver, being that it was her car and she knew the ins and outs of it pretty darn well, at least better than he did.

With the help of the map on his phone, they found the freeway and drove north in the direction of some place that made more sense, where people loved their children and fed them real food. They put on Pink Floyd again, and to Pat, it sounded far better at night, the artificial glow of Minneapolis fading behind them, like the bright fire of Gomorrah at Lot's back, and the indigo summer sky extended the promise of darkness ahead.

"I forgot to get my tray back," Pat said, after a time.

"Forget it, Mom," Sam said.

• • •

A pair of flashing red and blue lights appeared in the rearview mirror, and the sound of a police siren followed.

Pat looked at it in the mirror, and then returned her attention to the highway lines, which looked like blurry stripes of frosting, leading them home.

"Is that for us?" Sam asked. "Oh shit."

Pat turned down the music. "What?" She looked around. No other cars were near them; the siren was for them, and only them. Pat felt her heart seize up. She felt the alcohol in her body, and behind her eyes, that slowness, that unaccustomed haze.

She had no practice at getting out of a situation like this.

"Were you speeding?" Sam asked her.

"I don't think so. I don't know."

Pat steered her old car to the side of the road, and the police car came to a stop behind them.

"Huh," Sam said, looking behind him. "It's a K-9 unit."

Pat closed her eyes and thought about praying—what to pray for in this situation? She knew the answer. A thought hit her. "How much marijuana do you have on you?" she asked her son.

Sam sat up. "None," he said.

"Don't lie to me, you smoked some tonight. How much do you have?"

"Not much."

"More than one and a half ounces, total?"

Sam stared back at her, evidently scared by the unfamiliar tone of his mom's voice.

Pat spoke louder. "More than one and a half ounces total?"

"I don't know, maybe."

"Give it to me," Pat said. "All of it. Now, right now, before he gets here."

"Why?"

"Now, right now."

Pat's voice felt as serious as it had ever been, more than at either of her weddings, more than at Jerry's funeral or her parents' funerals, even. Sam rifled through his pockets and backpack, producing a little pipe, a small bag of weed, and a pot brownie. Pat took them and crammed them in her purse just as she heard the slam of the cop's car door behind her. She resettled and took a deep breath, and felt the shadow of a man's body and the harsh beam of a flashlight fall across her as he tapped a knuckle on her glass.

Pat grabbed the handle with her left hand and took care to roll the window down calmly.

"License and registration," the cop said, his white teeth shining.

"They're right here in my purse," she said, in acceptance of what was meant to be. She held the zipper in her fingers, opened her eyes against the white light, and felt herself, a wretch misshapen by desire, submit to the mercy of her Lord.

THE DINNER

About once a month in the tasting room, a customer would ask Cindy how to make wine out of supermarket grapes. Sometimes these people were misguided hands-on types, but more often they were cheapos who came in with coupons for two free tastings and left without buying anything. Either way, she had to correct them; wine is created when the sugar in a grape breaks down into alcohol, she'd say, and a supermarket grape has a fraction of the sugar required.

If it was close to harvest and she liked the customers, she'd take them outside to the vineyard and let them eat a Merlot grape off the vine, watching their faces as they swirled the seed-plump sugar bomb in their mouths. Can't buy that in a store, she'd say.

By Labor Day, the Merlot in the vineyard had a Brix of 23, and in her opinion was ready to be harvested. It was always the first harvest of the year—the Cabs, Zinfandels, and Petite Syrahs came much later—and Cindy loved it. Other vineyards waited on their Merlot, harvesting it at 26 or 27 to make big, jammy, alcoholic varietals, and although these were popular, to her they lacked the nuance and the restraint of a grape that leaves its vine a little early. She also felt that it was a little easier on the vine, not stressing itself out and yielding its vanishing October nutrients into desiccating grapes, even though stressed vines often lead to wonderful wines.

• • •

On September 5, the first day of the Merlot harvest at Tettegouche Vineyards that year, Cindy was stuck in the tasting room. Denisse Ramirez, the sales and wine club manager, who would normally handle the tasting room by herself during the harvest, was out sick, and the job fell to Cindy, the most recent hire. She had said when she came aboard as combination sales manager and associate winemaker that she would do her part to help make another unknown operation famous, just as she had with Daniel Anthony Vineyards and Solomon Creek Winery. Whatever that entailed.

She wiped down the long black marble counter and set a single bronze spit bucket in the center, because she didn't want to have to clean more than one. She removed the glasses from the dishwasher and fit wine aerators on the freshly opened bottles for today's flight and set them in a row.

The first customers of the day were a couple who arrived right when Tettegouche opened at eleven. The woman was a young hipster princess, with bangs, a patterned sundress, and cat-eye glasses. The man was an odd match for her; he looked like someone's idea of a sportswriter, with an unshaven face, a blue baseball cap, blue jeans, and a long-sleeved checkered shirt rolled up to his elbows. He looked at least ten years older than his companion.

"Two tastings," the man said, removing a Two Free Tastings coupon from his back pocket. Even if new wineries needed these tacky things, Christ, she despised them.

"IDs, please," Cindy said, looking at the man. "Just hers, I don't need yours."

"We'll start you off with the Sauvignon Blanc," she said, getting straight to it, pouring one ounce each into two stemless Riedel glasses.

"That's OK," the man said, waving Cindy off. "The Bordeaux whites around here have too much malo." He was using winespeak for malolactic fermentation, a process by which tart malic acids in red wine (and some whites) become soft, sometimes buttery lactic acids.

"Perfectly fine," Cindy said, pouring his glass into the bucket on the counter. "Next up would be the Chardonnay."

Over the last two decades, Cindy had met thousands of male wine snobs trying to impress their girlfriends while on a sex trip to wine country. The polite thing in these cases was to be quiet and go ahead and let the guy play the expert to the woman; men really got off on that. But watching this couple now dump out most of her Chardonnay, Cindy didn't feel polite.

"Not a fan of our ninety-two-point Chardonnay, kids?" Cindy asked, to be mean. Not only had the Chardonnay not received ninety-two points from anyone, but none of their wines had received any score from any wine critic, anywhere.

"No, I loved it," the woman said. "It was delicious. It's just we have six places to go to today and we gotta pace ourselves."

"Oh, live a little," Cindy said.

"Wish we could," the woman said.

It occurred to Cindy that when she was around this chick's age, she was doing exactly the same thing, flitting into half a dozen wineries a day with a man ten years older, acting smarter than the wine pourers, but actually swallowing the wine, never spitting it out. What idiots they had been. It was a miracle they had survived, all the times they drove around absolutely shitfaced, windows down, screaming out the sunroof.

She'd left Jeremy St. George six weeks after they got to Australia in 1989. He was threatened by her burgeoning expertise; when she correctly guessed the year and vintner of a particular Australian Pinot one evening, and he didn't, and his reaction was to call her a "stupid lucky bitch" in front of everyone—well, that was all she needed to hear.

Months later, she turned down a chance to see him off when he moved to Tokyo. She figured that he would be sufficiently put off by the snub never to get in touch with her again, which was how things played out. Since then, he seldom came to mind; she'd thought of him only when she'd made certain mistakes with men in her unmarried years, and the Napa Cabs and Central Coast Pinots he introduced her to had their sentimental associations smudged away after years of repeated exposure.

Still, he had been a charismatic, talented scoundrel who almost certainly was on to a new woman after a week in Japan; there was nothing to long for or feel sorry for. Wherever Jeremy was in the world, she was sure he was fine.

"Of the seven you're visiting today, what's the highlight?" Cindy asked.

"Besides Tettegouche?" the woman asked, pronouncing it *tet-goosh-AY*.

"Tet-uh-goosh," Cindy said.

The man leaned forward. "Well, the main reason we're up here is to pick up an order from Saxum."

"Oh, very nice," Cindy said. "How did you hear about them?"

"Eva Thorvald just served Saxum's Terry Hoage GSM at one of her pop-up supper clubs up in Minnesota."

"We read about it in the *New Yorker*," the woman said.

"Oh," Cindy said, and felt herself back away from the counter.

The young woman kept talking.

That name.

She hadn't heard that name in twenty-four years.

It would've been nice to say that Cindy never went a day without thinking of her daughter, but the truth was, most days, she just didn't.

• • •

Still, sometimes an otherwise calm afternoon would be accosted by a song from the late 1980s, a menu item at some luckless bistro, the sight of a bald man pushing a stroller, or something as brutally common as the faces of girls, and later women, who would have been her daughter's age.

Now that the name had been actually spoken to her, she felt herself freeze in place, immobilized by the feeling that any movement at all would somehow give her away.

The man and the young woman stared at her, smiling mildly, like they were just waiting for her to respond, but she sensed that they knew everything, just from the way she was standing.

"You don't know her?" the man asked. "She runs a pop-up supper club called The Dinner."

Cindy's palms were sweating; she moved her hands behind her back and gripped her left wrist. "Have you been there?" she asked.

The woman shook her head. "We wish. We've already spent a year on the waiting list."

"Why?"

"Well, she only does it four or five times a year. Always in a different place. One time it was on the edge of a cliff, and the guests had to rappel down the side for the main course. Once, it was in a boat that was rigged in place at the edge of a waterfall."

The man smirked. "Our friend Kermit was going to live-tweet that one but they didn't let him."

"Yeah. They take away everyone's phones and don't give them back until they leave."

"How's the food?" Cindy asked.

"I hear it's indescribable," the woman said.

"Everyone says it's the best meal they've ever had," the man said.

"Our only hope is that she picks randomly across both her priority and regular waiting lists."

The woman frowned. "It's not random. She tries for variety."

"Yeah, that's right," the man said. "She doesn't want, like, twelve investment bankers."

The woman pointed to the Merlot bottle. "Is that next? We have to keep moving here."

"Oh, yes, sorry," Cindy said, pouring three ounces in each of their glasses.

In ten minutes, the man and woman zipped through the rest of the tasting, and then left without buying anything.

She never saw them again, never got their names or learned where they were from. Before they had even reached their car, a white BMW, Cindy had turned the sign in the window to CLOSED, locked the door, dashed to the desktop PC in the office, and, for the first time in her life, entered "Eva Thorvald" into Google.

Her memory of her daughter's face, from a time when she still went by Cynthia, had been thickly bundled for its quiet passage through unmarked time. Without a photograph, Cindy's image of Eva was that of an increasingly vague, featureless infant, and she had no apprehension of how that baby might have matured. She set her shaking fingers on the keyboard, pressed a button, and in a bright, savage instant split all of this open.

Eva had her dad's broad shoulders and big smile. And her mom's eyes, nose, and cheekbones. That was her, that was her baby, all grown up, fierce and beautiful and unknown.

She didn't know this person, she told herself, but while staring at her image, Cindy's eyes fattened with tears. This was why she had avoided ever doing this before; she was deeply afraid it would upset her, even though she never regretted leaving for a moment, not once. She hadn't even cried on the day she left, she was so confident that she and her daughter would be better off without each other.

And Cindy still honestly believed there was no way she could've been a good mother. She was thrilled, not nostalgic, never to have to go down the diaper aisle again or purée food every day or deal with literal piles of shit in clothes, on bedsheets, on carpeted floors. And frankly, the idea of even living with a teenage girl made Cindy want to jump in front of a wine tour Humvee. Teenagers were her least favorite people on the face of the earth, and she never could've lived with a bratty teen princess without appalling amounts of Xanax and fat bowls of Northern Lights. But looking at Eva, the adult, she felt something grappling with her insides.

She wiped her face and stared at the blue and black words on the white screen: "Eva Thorvald, America's bad-girl chef." "Controversial chef Eva Thorvald keeps diners guessing." "Thorvald's table the toughest to get in USA."

The reviews of Eva's food were astonishing: "Thorvald's five-thousand-dollar dinner a total-body experience." "A once-in-a-lifetime necessity for serious and adventurous diners." Cindy couldn't tell if the critics were trying to justify the ridiculous price—five thousand dollars for five courses—or if all this, at last, was true.

Eva was an amazingly successful chef; that was clear. Lars must be so proud. His love alone must've cultivated her skills and inspired the confidence needed for this level of achievement. Cindy read no mention of him, but certainly he was there, behind the scenes, perhaps running her hot line or at least plating dishes. It'd be like him to stay out of the spotlight.

Maybe if she'd been a foodie, Cindy would have heard of her daughter much earlier. She'd tried cooking around the time she met Lars, but making a great meal was too much work, and when she got into wine, it was game over for everything else. Food was best if it was easy, and with Reynaldo, her current husband, she finally had a guy who loved so-called guilty pleasure food as much as she did. She went to the gym every day, so there was nothing to feel guilty about anyway.

Cindy spent another twenty minutes entering various search queries into Google. She found no bio, no address, no interviews, no mention of a husband or children, no Facebook page; just private Instagram and Twitter accounts, several fan sites, and, of course, the reservations page for The Dinner.

The text on the Web site was stark: sixty dollars nonrefundable for priority VIP list, twenty dollars nonrefundable for nonpriority list. Cindy checked the regular list first. The next slot was number 2364, estimated wait time: 295 years.

The priority VIP list was taken through slot number 194, estimated wait time: four years. Not that she really had a choice, but if she was ever going to see her daughter, she wanted to do it from a distance, as part of a public, professional relationship, before there might be a personal one. Four years seemed like a long time to wait, but it had already been twenty-four. And in a way, it was good, because she needed time to prepare mentally. Whatever uncertainties afflicted the intervening years, one monumental event now seemed likely. She would, one day, see her daughter again.

She took her credit card out of her purse and signed up herself, Cindy Reyna, and her husband, Reynaldo Reyna, separately on the priority waiting list, each with a +1. She figured with a waiting list that long, and maximum two lifetime slots per name or credit card number, she might as well double their slim chances now.

The e-mail receipt arrived instantly. Cindy Reyna, credit card charged $120, nonrefundable, for slots number 196 (Cindy Reyna +1) and 197 (Reynaldo Reyna +1).

Cindy couldn't believe that two more slots had sold just in the amount of time it took her to enter her credit card info. She also wasn't sure how she'd explain all this to Reynaldo. Maybe it could wait.

It felt like a decade had passed before either of them heard anything.

In that time, Cindy turned fifty. Her second ex-husband, Daniel Anthony, died of a brain aneurysm while scuba diving on vacation in Thailand. One of the partners quit Tettegouche, and it failed, deeply in debt. But what pulled Cindy toward the second great course correction of her life was her husband, Reynaldo, turning fifty-two.

Every year on Reynaldo's birthday, they ate dinner at a McDonald's. Because they had money and no kids, they made it an adventure; year two of their marriage they ate at one in Paris; year three was the white colonial McDonald's in Hyde Park, New York; year four was the one below the Museum of Communism in Prague; this year it would be the famous Rock N' Roll McDonald's in Chicago. They had already decided that on year six they'd hit the world's largest McDonald's in London.

As the eastbound flight reached cruising altitude, Cindy opened the latest issue of the *Economist*—she saved her smarter reading for public situations—when she saw Reynaldo look at his reflection in the dead black screen of his cell phone and pluck at the gray hair in his beard.

"Screw the yearly prostate exam," she said. "Call the hearse."

"Yeah, I know." He nodded.

"I'm joking," she said.

"Yeah." He nodded again, staring at his reflection. He looked good for his age; he was bald, but trim, energetic, life still in his eyes. He worked in the neonatal intensive care unit at a hospital in Palo Alto and somehow he'd staved off the gray in his beard until that year.

Reynaldo felt that, since he was childless, his heart had sidestepped the empathy that would've broken it every time a neonate coded. Sometimes you could save a twenty-five-week-old through intubation, and sometimes you couldn't. Work had to go on. He could come home from the OR and watch a Golden State Warriors game like nothing had happened—a day when three neonates coded was indistinguishable from a day when he saved three lives. The emotional regulation, he said, came with time.

On the plane to Chicago, in first class, on the morning of his birthday, her husband was now as sad as she'd ever seen him.

"What you thinking about?" she said at last.

"Seventy," he said. "You know my dad died at seventy?"

"Seventy is pretty far away," Cindy said.

"It is, and it isn't," he said. "It is and it isn't."

In the cab from the Drake Hotel to the Rock N' Roll McDonald's, it came up again.

"You know," he said, looking out the rear passenger window at a darkened city park as they turned left onto Clark Street. "If I had a kid this year, I'd be seventy when he graduated from high school."

"Well, you're not having a kid this year, I can promise you."

"I'm just saying. I don't even know if I'd live to see him get his diploma."

"Well, you don't have to worry about that. Which way is Navy Pier? Did we pass it already?"

"I'm just saying," Reynaldo repeated.

"It's behind us," the cab driver said. "Way, way behind us."

"I want to find a different job when we get back," Cindy said after sex that night. "I'm thinking of being a sommelier again." Since Tettegouche went under, she'd been managing an in-town tasting room for a supermarket-level winery, which was the wine equivalent of working at a florist on Valentine's Day, every day. As such, she'd become weary of the crowds, the unoriginality, and the predictable, cheap happiness on the faces of people who didn't know any better and didn't want to.

"You can do whatever you wanna do," Reynaldo said, and turned his back to sleep on his side, facing the window.

The next morning, she was on the treadmill at the Drake's gym, listening to her treadmill mix—"Kiss Me on the Bus," by The Replacements, "Head over Heels," by Tears for Fears, "Finest Worksong," by R.E.M., "How Bizarre," by OMC, and "True," by Spandau Ballet, on repeat. Right during the chorus of "How Bizarre," which is stupid and obvious and clichéd but that's just the way life is sometimes, it hit her. She pressed STOP on the treadmill, got off, and stood for a while on the wooden floor, staring at the stupid TV mounted on the wall, her face burning.

Reynaldo was brushing his teeth in his boxer shorts when she returned to the room, sweaty in her tight yoga-style gym clothes.

"How was the gym here?" he asked.

"You want to have kids, don't you?" she asked.

"What do you mean?"

"You want to be a dad. And you want to have your own kids too, I bet, not adopt them."

He nodded. "Yeah, maybe."

"So what does that mean?" she asked. Neither had moved; they were on opposite sides of the room with the bed between them. The reflected morning gleam off of downtown Chicago's buildings glowed behind him, as he stood, puffy and bald and hairy and heartbreaking, a toothbrush sticking out of his face.

"I don't know," he said.

"Oh, God," Cindy said, and she fell on the bed. She buried her face in a pillow and pounded the mattress with her fists. It didn't matter what else was said now, her brain already knew how all this shit was going to pan out.

Reynaldo started crying and sat next to her. "I still love you," he said. "I love you, so much."

He placed his hand on her back, and although it felt like daggers of ice, she didn't shake it off. She let him think that he was comforting her, because at that moment there was no comforting her at all.

On the westbound flight home, the *People* and *InTouch* magazines Cindy bought at the airport went unread on her lap.

"And do you know what the biggest thing, the number one thing is?" she asked Reynaldo, who was slumped in his seat, drinking his second Bloody Mary. "You always said you loved this lifestyle. You always said that. You said it was your goal in life to be able to travel whenever you want."

"I do love this lifestyle," he said. "But I also want something else. As well."

"It doesn't work like that. You get one or the other. You can fly around the world and live it up like an adult or you can shack up and squirt out some kids. You don't get both."

Reynaldo looked at her. "*You* get one or the other. Because that's what you chose for yourself. And you know, that's fair. Just don't tell me how to live."

"I didn't fucking choose," Cindy said, struggling to keep her voice at a conversational tone. "Biology fucking chooses. Maybe you'd agree with me if your balls fell off at age forty."

The steward came by and Reynaldo held his empty Bloody Mary in the air. "Another, please."

The steward looked at Cindy. "Another sparkling water for you?"

"No, I'm good," she said, watching as the steward passed Reynaldo a bottle of Grey Goose and a bottle of N. W. Gratz's Artisanal Bloody Mary Mix. Cindy saw the label, emblazoned with OREGON TILTH CERTIFIED ORGANIC, GMO FREE, CRUELTY FREE, and shook her head.

"Jesus."

"It's the direction that food is heading," Reynaldo said. "You want to argue about this too?"

"No. Forget it. Where were we?"

Reynaldo sighed. "You said I'd understand you better if my balls fell off at forty and was thereby denied the choice of having children."

"Yeah. I think you'd be a lot more compassionate."

"But you never had kids and you never wanted kids. It's not like some lifelong dream was stolen from you by menopause."

"You never wanted kids either, that's what you said when you lied to me five years ago."

"I wasn't lying. It was true then."

"Oh, that's such bullshit."

"No it is not," Reynaldo said, mixing his drink. "But it'd be easier if it was."

"It's not easy either way," she said. "Not for me."

Under California law, a divorce could be finalized in six months, but Cindy couldn't wait that long to get on with her damn life. After looking exclusively at jobs out of state, because California was saturated by know-it-all kids with sommelier certifications anyway, she took an opening in the Great Lakes resort area of Charlevoix County, Michigan.

This time, she was the fancy overqualified West Coast wine expert moving to the Midwest to take a job away from a young local. The restaurant's general manager, a woman of Chinese descent Cindy's age with the intriguingly un-Chinese name of Molly Greenberg, hired her at the end of a Skype interview, and two weeks later, Cindy was uncorking fifty-seven-degree bottles of Châteauneuf-du-Pape for middle-aged couples sunburned from a day on their boat. She never met the twenty-six-year-old Level II sommelier she'd beat out for the job; he'd left town in protest, ending perhaps the best chance for Cindy to play out the balance of her adulthood as a beautiful inverse of its beginning.

She'd rented a small house in Petosky, outside the town of Charlevoix, made her own meals at home, spent mornings reading on the porch, and biked to work when the weather was nice. Every day after waking up, she'd check the Eva Thorvald blogs to see if a dinner had been held, and if so, which slot numbers were invited. Days in which numbers were called were good days, even if they were never hers; the other days she just had to get through.

One afternoon before the dinner shift, as Cindy was behind the bar putting aerators on the wines they sold by the glass, her boss, Molly, came up behind her and put her hand on Cindy's shoulder.

Cindy shuddered; it was the first time she'd been touched since she'd had her hair done the week before, and the proximity of Molly's Chanel No. 5 and the feel of her cold, bony hands freaked her out. Molly was one of those women who were both tiny and about twenty pounds too skinny; Cindy wasn't the tallest woman she knew, and kept herself in decent shape, but next to Molly she felt like a hockey player.

"Whoa, sorry to startle you," Molly said. "Just wanted to see if you're feeling OK."

"Yeah," Cindy said. "I'm fine."

"You just looked a little preoccupied, is all. Do you have a long-distance boyfriend?"

Cindy laughed. "Nope, way too old for that."

Molly leaned in to Cindy's shoulder and got quiet. "Having an affair?"

"God, no," Cindy said.

"You just seemed like you were thinking about somebody."

"Nope, just zoning out."

"Whatever's going on in your life, it won't stay secret in this town—just to warn you," Molly said, and returned to her office.

A few days later, Cindy was washing her one plate in the sink when she heard a knock on the door. Drying her hands, she gazed through the peephole and saw Molly standing there.

"Hey!" Molly said when Cindy opened the door. "I was in the neighborhood and I thought I'd drop by. Did I catch you at a bad time?"

"Not really," Cindy said, and the two women stared at each other for a moment before Cindy apologized and asked her boss to come on in.

Molly was the first person to enter Cindy's rented house; Cindy watched as Molly took in the one chair in the living room, the one chair by the little Formica dining table, and the dish rack with one plate, one glass, and one set of silverware drying.

"Wow, you sure packed light," Molly said. "Can I sit? I don't want to take your only chair."

"Uh, sure," Cindy said, coming to terms with the weird fact that her boss had just invited herself over. "It's a nice night, why don't we sit out on the porch?"

"OK. Got anything to drink?"

"Well, got some Grenache Rosé in the fridge."

"Sounds divine," Molly said. Cindy saw her stand up and walk around the living room, looking at who knows what. There was no TV to turn on, no framed photos, no art on the walls, just a couple of books and a dozen or so magazines on a small coffee table.

Why was this woman here? They would have a glass of wine and then Cindy would say that she had a 7:00 a.m. yoga class (which was true) and boy, was she tired.

. . .

Cindy came out to the porch with a bottle of Santa Ynez Valley–area Grenache Rosé and two Syrah glasses. Molly was already on the swing, so Cindy set the wine down and dragged the living room chair out.

Across the street, a little girl in a pink dress wailed as she was being pulled from the backseat of an old Dodge minivan.

"I hate you!" the little girl screamed between sobs.

"Come on, time for bed," the exhausted mother said, dragging her child up the driveway toward the front door. She shoved her daughter inside and closed the door behind them.

Molly shook her head. "You ever have any of those?"

"Nope," Cindy said.

"Me neither. Let's fuckin' drink to that."

After only a year in Michigan, Cindy started seeing reports of priority VIP numbers in the high 100s receiving invitations; they were getting close. It had been just over three years since she put down the $120 reservation; maybe there were more dinners, or more dropouts, or both. You weren't able to choose the date—if Eva Thorvald invited you to the dinner next Thursday and you weren't able to make it, well, that was it, you lost your space, no refunds. She'd also read about folks who'd lost their jobs in the interim and now couldn't afford the ten grand cost for two people. All of these circumstances helped her chances.

It was strange to think about her daughter every day in this way, after so many years of hardly thinking of her at all. Without an intense job, social calendar, or relationship to distract her, as they had all of her life, Cindy started to feel that her time in Michigan was a kind of exile or retreat, and this retrenchment, whether intentional or not, lent her a potent focus. The thought of seeing her daughter again pruned every competing impulse, and the priorities of what now felt like a former life, once so

bright and heavy, had fallen away. This commingling of obsession and sim-
plicity was a surprisingly satisfying way to get by.

"You need a man!" Molly said to her one night when they were staying
late, finishing a bottle of 2007 Château La Fleur-Pétrus that some idiot
couple only drank one glass out of.

"No, not unless he can . . ." Cindy was going to say, *Move me up the
list at The Dinner,* but stopped herself. No one in Michigan knew anything about that yet.

"Not unless he can what?" said Molly. "Refrain from drinking vodka
while mowing the lawn? Or refrain from falling asleep in the kitchen?"
Molly, conversely, was an oversharer; these were well-known traits of
her husband's.

"I'm sure it's exciting to stumble over the love of your life during his
kitchen nap, but I'd rather just masturbate and go to bed early."

"Fred and I know a guy who'd be terrific for you, just terrific. Fred
met him the last time he was in AA."

"Not now, Molly," Cindy said.

"He's cute, and not just Michigan cute either. How about I have ya
both over for eggplant parmigiana sometime?"

Kerensa Dille, the assistant manager whom Cindy liked the most,
walked up to the bar holding out her phone. "Oh my God, my friend is
giving away the cutest Welsh corgi puppies—look."

There were four little puppies, eyes closed, curled up in a wicker
basket. They were, as Kerensa said, the cutest.

Molly put her hands on her hips. "You're leaving this room with either a dog or a date. Decide now, or you're fired."

Thanks to Molly and Kerensa, Cindy had a lot of dogproofing to do the
following morning. A few months back, after Molly's first visit, she and

Kerensa had told the entire staff that Cindy had lost all of her furniture in a brutal divorce with an abusive man. Since then, she'd become a one-woman Goodwill for every manager, waiter, and busboy with an end table, rug, love seat, art print, lamp, or houseplant to give away. Cindy didn't even go to Kerensa's church, but two members of the congregation brought her an old tube television and a DVD player, free of charge. One time, a table of three brothers who spent summers in Charlevoix gave her a Panasonic stereo that was still in the box. She felt so guilty about it all, she told everybody who donated that she'd give them all a free wine class later that summer.

The first day she had the puppy, which she named Brix, was also a ridiculous day at work. Philandering Lions wide receiver Lanchester Cunningham, slutty Grand Rapids meteorologist Diana Vecchio, and lecherous frozen fish magnate Luc Provencher all had made reservations for that evening with large groups, and a representative from a Traverse City winery known for its Riesling was coming at four to do a tasting. She left Brix on a pee pad in his crate with a bowl of water, a chew toy, and some chow—she had only been a dog owner for a few hours, and it was already heartbreaking to leave the little guy alone.

The young man from the Traverse City winery arrived right on time, with branded ballcaps, T-shirts, and a few bottles of Riesling, Chardonnay, Pinot Gris, and Pinot Noir. Kerensa didn't have to be there, but she showed up anyway.

"How's it going with the puppy?" Kerensa asked.

The wine guy looked up from opening his Pinot Gris. "You just got a dog?" he asked, and off Cindy's assent, he continued. "Dogs are the best. I have nine of 'em."

"You have nine dogs?" Kerensa asked.

"I know, it's not enough, right?"

Kerensa and Cindy looked at each other again. This was his time-tested line, obviously.

"Well, I live on a farm," he said, pouring two glasses of the Pinot Gris. "Or it used to be a farm, before my dad killed himself. Now it's just a house on four acres."

Kerensa gave Cindy another look. The guy kept talking.

"Last week, my dog Eddie dug up some human bones. They were totally weird. He comes running into the house with like this femur in his mouth. I was like, oh, wow, those are human bones, Eddie. And he's smilin'. Anyway, here's our Pinot Gris. It's got a perfect balance of grapefruit, pear, and minerality, with just a touch of acidity on the finish."

"So did you call the cops?" Kerensa asked. "When your dog found those bones?"

"What?" the guy seemed genuinely surprised by the follow-up question.

"Did you call the cops?"

"Huh. How do I answer that?"

"Uh, yes or no?"

"Well . . . you know, I thought about it, and then I thought, these bones are pretty old. Whoever killed this guy probably got away with it. Whoever the survivors are got over it and moved on with their lives a long time ago. If the killer is still alive, he's probably out there, thinking about it every day, about how he killed a man. The guilt hanging over him. And isn't that enough? Why go shake up everyone's life over some bones?"

The phone rang behind the bar. It was the extension for reservations. "I'll get it," Kerensa said, and took her wineglass with her.

"Well anyway, the Riesling. Sixteen months neutral oak. No malo. Eddie's a good dog, though. If he knew that beef came from cows, he'd get depressed. Now Hecky, that one I can see killing a man and burying the body. If a murderer does walk my crooked patch of earth, ten will get you one that's it's Heckerdoodle the killer poodle. But that's the kind of dog you want guarding your weed."

"It's for you," Kerensa called out.

"Excuse me," Cindy said, and sipped the Riesling as she walked behind the bar. "You're right about the acidity. Bodes well for its aging potential." She took the receiver from Kerensa. "Hello?"

"Hey," Reynaldo said. "How's it going?"

"Reynaldo?" The blood rushed to Cindy's head. She turned her back to Kerensa and the wine guy, who were only about ten feet away and could hear everything. "How'd you get this number?"

"You're a hard woman to find these days."

"Yeah, well, I changed my cell number. So what's this about?"

"Wow," Reynaldo said. He seemed startled by her tone. "Well, I'm sorry to bother you, I know things didn't end super well between us."

"No, they did not."

"But, I got remarried, and have a baby daughter, and everything."

"Oh, nice. I appreciate hearing that you actually followed through with that. Is that all, then?"

"Well, as it turns out, I owe you a hundred and twenty dollars and I wanted to make sure you get it. That's the main thing I'm calling about."

"What do you owe me a hundred and twenty dollars for?"

"You know that restaurant reservation you made, like, three years ago? They called me and said I'm invited, and I'm going with my wife. So I figured I'd better pay you back the deposit just to make sure we're square."

That stupid bastard. She could feel both Kerensa and the wine guy looking at her, but now she didn't give a shit—this situation called for some volume.

"No, no, that's my reservation," Cindy said, raising her voice.

"Well, they called me. On my house phone."

"Look. We were still married then. That used to be *my* home number too. I was trying to save two spots so we had a better chance." At the time, she thought she was being clever by putting their shared house phone down as his number.

"Yeah, and they called my spot. And I didn't know it, but it's like a once-in-a-lifetime opportunity. Cassandra's just over the moon about it.

You know, it was her that suggested we pay you back your deposit? That's how grateful she is."

"No, *I'm going*. I made the reservation."

"It's not in your name. Why can't you just wait until your name comes up?"

"Because she's my daughter and I need to see her."

"Because who's your daughter?"

"Eva Thorvald."

"Now you're just making things up."

"I'm not."

"I thought you never had a kid, and never wanted one. That's what you always told me. For five years. For six years, actually, six years, counting the year before we were married."

"Well, I had one."

"And you what, gave her up for adoption?"

"No, I left her and her dad."

"Oh," Reynaldo said. "Oh. Oh! So her dad was your ex-husband from Minnesota. The one you never talk to. Right. OK."

"Yeah."

"Why don't you just go up to where she lives and knock on her door?"

"I can't do that, I can't do that. I'm too scared to do that. I just want to see her at a distance."

"And she's never looked for you, never searched you out."

"If she did, I never knew it. So when's the next dinner?"

"Tomorrow. Right in the middle of South Dakota. We're flying into Pierre."

"Tomorrow? And you're just calling me now?"

"It was hard to find you."

"Well, I'll be there."

"Let me talk to my wife."

"I'll be there."

She hung up, and copied his number from the phone's caller ID display onto her hand. She turned to see Kerensa and the wine guy staring at her.

"What," Kerensa said, "was all that about?"

• • •

Cindy found it hard to look Kerensa in the face when she told her whole story and chose instead to stare out the dining room window at the boats on the lake.

"I am so sorry," Cindy said to her friend.

"What for?" Kerensa said. "I can understand why you wouldn't want to talk about it. You wanted us to get to know you as you, not as the mom of some famous person."

Cindy exhaled. After decades away from the Midwest, she'd forgotten that bewildering generosity was a common regional tic. First the free home furnishings, now this. It was all lovely and weird. "Thank you," she said. "That's way more kindness than I deserve."

"Hey, we all got secrets," the wine guy said.

"I can't imagine," Kerensa said to him, and then looked at Cindy. "Let us know what she's like."

Cindy couldn't believe these people.

Later that night, when she was attempting to answer a question at Diana Vecchio's table about which Moscato on their wine list was the one that some rapper named Qwazey sang about, Molly came up behind Cindy and hugged her. It felt like it did when her mother used to do that to her as a child, come up behind her and hug her for no reason. It always puzzled Cindy when her mom did this.

"Call for you on the reservations line. Your ex-husband."

Cindy left the table immediately, without even saying "Excuse me," and ran to the phone in the office.

"Can't do it," Reynaldo said. "I'm sorry. We already bought our plane tickets and everything."

"What? I'll pay you back for the ticket!"

"I gotta prioritize my current wife over my ex-wife, that's all there is to it," he said. In the background, Cindy heard a woman say, "Tell her she has a slot, and she'll just have to wait," and Reynaldo repeated, "You have a slot, you'll just have to wait."

"Fuck you, Reynaldo," she said, "I'll see you there," and hung up.

The last-second flight from Traverse City, Michigan, to Pierre, South Dakota, was going to cost her close to two months' rent, and the 6:00 a.m. departure meant she'd have to be up by four in the morning after working until midnight. Also, she checked flights from SFO, and both her flight and Reynaldo's flight had the same connection in Denver; they'd be on the same plane to Pierre.

Cindy spotted Reynaldo from a hundred feet away at the Denver air-port, standing in line at the gate. It was weird to see him in person after three years of trying to forget about him, but it also felt a bit like only a month had passed. He was wearing a gray suit that she didn't recognize, had more gray in his beard, and looked as if he'd lost weight. He'd heard her coming up behind him and turned around. She was wearing an out-fit she thought might make an impression on him, culled from her past life of means and expensive tastes: slate gray Donna Karan pencil skirt, white poplin shirt, closed-toe ivory pumps, fitted peplum blazer, and big black Prada sunglasses, looking damn good for someone on three hours of sleep, and she could tell from his expression that he thought she looked good too. Not that she wanted anything to happen; she just wanted him to realize what he'd been missing out on, and to keep real-izing it every time he looked at her.

"You owe me for my wife's plane ticket," he said, not smiling. What-ever remote, lukewarm simmerings still lingered in her heart for him instantly vanished when he spoke. After all they'd been through, *that* was how he greeted her?

"Where is she?" Cindy asked.

"She decided to sit this one out," Reynaldo said. "She's extremely averse to confrontation."

"It was her call, not yours?"

"Correct."

"Just seeing where you stand."

Reynaldo looked at his ticket. "What seat are you?"

Cindy said, "16B."

"I've got 4A," Reynaldo said.

"Okay, then." She saw his mouth open, and Cindy hoped that he wouldn't offer to switch with somebody to move closer to her; at this point, she'd already had enough from him. "See you in South Dakota," she said, and walked to the end of the line, pulling a copy of the *Economist* from her carry-on.

The next time Cindy saw Reynaldo was at the baggage claim in the tiny Pierre airport. He had a larger suitcase than she did, which wasn't typical for him. His new wife was apparently making him fancy.

"So, where to now?" Cindy asked him. She hated depending on him for all of the information.

"I have no idea," he said. "It's one-forty. I might just go check into my hotel."

"Which hotel are you staying at?"

"ClubHouse Hotel and Suites. You?"

"Budget 5."

Just then, a young man in horn-rimmed glasses and a tuxedo walked past them, pivoted around on his shiny heels to face them, and asked if they were Reynaldo Reyna and his plus one. It pained Cindy to be "plus one" to her ex, but she nodded.

"Two forms of ID, please," the young man said, holding out an iPad, which had a credit card scanner attached to the side. "And that will be ten grand."

"You're with The Dinner?" Reynaldo asked. "I guess I could assume, but I'd better be safe."

"Of course. I'm Yonas Awate."

They each handed him everything he asked for.

"Split down the middle?" Yonas asked, holding up the credit cards.

"Yes," Cindy said. "So where is it happening tonight?"

"You will see."

"You're driving us? You work for her?"

"Yes."

"Can you take us to our hotels first?" Reynaldo asked.

"Whatever you like," Yonas said, handing them back their cards. "I will collect you each around five to arrive at the property by six."

Stepping out of the baggage claim in Pierre into the afternoon August air was like stepping into God's own dryer; Cynthia had only been to South Dakota once before, and didn't recall it being so hot, or so flat.

"Whoa, someone left the heat on," Yonas Awate said as he led them across the parking lot. When nobody responded to the comment, he shouted, "Humor!"

"I've been up since four in the morning," Reynaldo said.

Yonas motioned them toward a black Lincoln Town Car. There was tan dust on the wheels and the bottoms of the doors. A tall blond guy with sunglasses and a perfume model's jawline sat in the front passenger seat with the window open. Yonas motioned toward the man, introduced him as a dinner guest named Holger Schmidt, and made introductions all around.

"Where you from, Yonas?" Reynaldo asked once they were on the road.

"Minneapolis," Yonas said.

"No, I mean originally."

Yonas bit his lip. Cindy could tell by his expression that Yonas hated having this conversation. Reynaldo's dorky public chatter never endeared him to people as much as he thought it did.

"My parents were born in Eritrea," he said. He pointed to the climate controls on the dashboard. "Hot, cold, indifferent?"

"I'm a little warm," Cindy said, and Yonas turned on the air conditioner and passed her back a cool glass bottle of water with a white label that read BUHL R-O.

"What's Buhl R-O?" she asked.

"It's the purest water in the world. It's from a pristine deep well near Buhl in northern Minnesota. Then they run it through a proprietary reverse osmosis and ion-exchange purification system."

"Wow, never heard of it."

"It's the only kind of water Eva Thorvald uses."

"So, what's she like in person?"

"She's like this water. That's all I will tell you."

Cindy opened the bottle and held it to her lips. It tasted like thick, cool fog.

"You know, where they bottle this water, it's actually treated as hazardous waste under Minnesota law," Yonas said. "It turns out, water with all of the impurities taken out is violently solvent. But bottling it, you let some bacteria settle in, and it mellows out."

Yonas held out a bottle for Holger.

"No, sounds hideous," Holger said, with a slight German accent.

"Different strokes," said Yonas.

Reynaldo nudged Cindy. "Want to see a picture of my daughter?"

"Nope," Cindy said.

"I'll see it," Holger said.

"OK, sure," Reynaldo said, and passed his phone up to Holger. Holger looked at the picture for two seconds and passed it back to Reynaldo.

"I don't recognize her," Holger said. "I go to all the clubs in Berlin and I've never seen her before."

Reynaldo looked a little scared. "Well, I kind of hope not."

"Just messing with you," Holger said.

"How about some music?" said Yonas.

Cindy's hotel room had a fake lemon smell and a squealy AC window unit. There was a stain on the carpet the shape of Wisconsin and scratches on weird parts of the walls, out of the reach of adults or furniture. An old tube television was chained to a console by a metal wire and the remote was glued to the bedside table in some kind of plastic holder.

When she was with Reynaldo, they never would've stayed in a place like this, and with his money, they didn't have to. Now it was the only kind of place she even considered, and she didn't care. She'd had decades of luxury travel, on her own and with her second and third husbands, and it didn't matter how expensive or opulent the room was, checkout was still always at eleven, and when she walked out the hotel doors, she was still herself, and the thread count and concierge service and private pools were no longer real; they were borrowed like bodies in a dream.

What really broke Cindy's heart was when she'd see the bill and think of what wine they could've bought with that money. She believed that no hotel in the world, now known or yet to be conceived, could ever dominate your senses like a 1989 Château Margaux or pack more surprises into twenty seconds than a 2007 Les Clos Sacrés Savennières. Every aspect of a hotel room was ephemeral; a great wine stayed with you forever.

Therefore, she was absolutely OK with a hotel room that had a view of a parking lot, a highway, and a Happy Chef restaurant, all of it chastely, happily American, lacking in any glamour or pretense, apologizing for nothing.

As she watched semi trucks grumble to and from the restaurant, she begrudged all this lack of significance for one reason only: that this was going to be the place where she reunited with her daughter, somewhere out there in all this Dakota.

She lay down on top of the spongy, flower-patterned comforter, but in spite of having slept only three hours, she wasn't tired. She had the pepper in her blood of a soldier being sent to war. There was nothing like home here. Just, perhaps, something to hold on to in the absence of one.

Cindy was applying lipstick at ten minutes to five when she heard a knock at the door.

"Ms. Reyna!" a man's voice called out.

Cindy opened the door to find a scruffy guy in a plain black suit standing in the dingy hallway. He had the vibe of a heavy metal drummer; he had a lot of rings on his fingers and she bet there were tattoos under his jacket sleeves. He extended a ring-laden hand with a smile.

"I'm Randy Dragelski," the guy said. "Your car is waiting."

"Is Yonas here?"

"Yonas is now just with Mr. Schmidt. I'll be driving you and Mr. Reyna."

"Just a minute," Cindy said, leaving the door open. Randy remained outside in the hall. "You can come in, I just need to finish up."

Randy watched as Cindy finished with her lips. "Wow, damn," he said.

"What?" Cindy asked.

"Oh, nothin'," Randy said. "You just have real similar eyes to Eva's."

"Oh, what a funny coincidence," Cindy said.

Cindy was relieved to see that she was the first person to be picked up. She took the front passenger seat next to Randy, who drove with one arm fully extended to the top of the steering wheel.

"How long have you worked for Eva?" Cindy asked as she buckled her seat belt.

"I've worked with her the longest. I was the first hire when it was still just her and Elodie running things."

"How long ago was that?"

"I don't know, fall 2009, or something."

"What do you do for her?'

"I used to do a little bit of everything, but now I just do this. Guest relations. It's my favorite part."

"So, what's she like, Eva Thorvald?"

"She's amazing." The love was evident in his voice, but after a breath, he frowned. "Is this for a blog or something?

"No, I work in a restaurant in Michigan. I'm just curious. Is she a good person to work with?"

"Yeah, or I wouldn't be here." He was all business now. "She's the best and expects the best."

Cindy put on a pair of old eyeglasses, which she kept in her purse as a backup and hardly wore. "I wonder what her upbringing was like."

"She wouldn't want me to discuss it with guests," Randy said.

Cindy was surprised. "Oh. Can you tell me where she's from?"

"Same place as me," Randy said. "A place that's gone."

Reynaldo was waiting under the porte cochere of his hotel, wearing a tuxedo, which made Cindy shake her head.

He stared at Cindy when he got in the backseat. "What's with the glasses?" he asked.

As they drove out of Pierre and into the country, Cindy looked out the window. The car dipped between green hills, where clumps of trees gathered in the acres of tall grass, like lost platoons from a defeated army. They saw a sign for the Crow Creek Reservation and, later, signs for something called Wall Drug.

After a while, Reynaldo tapped the back of Cindy's seat. "So what's new in your life?" he asked.

"Not much," she said, not turning around. "Same same."

"Boyfriend?"

"Just got a dog," she said. "A Welsh corgi puppy."

"Ha, I thought you said you didn't want kids."

"What do you mean?"

"With a dog, it's almost like having a kid."

"No, it's not like having a kid," she said. "It's preferable in every possible way. That makes it like having a dog."

They turned down a paved two-lane road, and from the top of a gravy-colored hill, Cindy could see a valley lined with trees. They turned down a dirt road that jostled the car and made the fancy water in the drink holders quiver in sympathy.

A wooden and barbed-wire fence, which went off endlessly in both directions, enclosed nothing that Cindy could discern. Two men wearing suits and walkie-talkies with headsets stood by its gate, and Randy stopped the car when he approached them.

"Reynaldo Reyna and his plus one, Cindy Reyna," Randy told them, and Cindy watched as the young men relayed those names back to a supervisor. Eva Thorvald would now know that they were here.

From the car, they could see the top of a hill, with two long dining room tables covered in ivory tablecloths.

"Those are Regency tables," Reynaldo said. "Real nice. You can tell by the legs."

Cindy had no idea when or where her pediatric surgeon ex-husband had learned about dining tables. As they drove past, they could see a small, diverse staff bringing ornate chairs out to the tables.

The car stopped by an immense tent, maybe a hundred feet long or more, which looked to Cindy like an Arabian tent for oil sheiks. Next to the tent, there was a two-story bus that said WILSHIRE MOBILE ESTATES. She supposed that was Eva's private coach.

Randy opened Cindy's door. He collected Cindy's and Reynaldo's cell phones after an armed man in sunglasses patted them down. He asked them to step into the tent for tea or cocktails, and said that men's and women's washrooms were in the luxury bus.

"Is Eva joining us for drinks?" Cindy asked.

"No," Randy said. "She's very busy."

"Where's the kitchen?"

"Can't go there, ma'am."

"Can you just show me where it is?"

Randy got on his walkie. "Hey Braque, got a guest here who wants to see the kitchen."

"You got the guest's phone and camera?" Braque responded.

"Yep."

"Let me ask. Who's the guest?"

"Cindy Reyna."

"OK, one sec."

Cindy watched Reynaldo proceed into the guest tent where the drinks were being served. She wasn't able to see inside in the brief time he'd pulled the flap aside. "Is this a strange request?"

"Not really," Randy said. "People ask to see the kitchen all the time."

The walkie crackled. "That's a negative."

"OK," Randy said, then looked at Cindy. "Sorry."

Cindy turned her back to the tent. "What are you up to now?"

"I have to greet the late arrivals," Randy said, looking at the sky, where a bright yellow-and-green hot-air balloon hovered against the blue.

"Depending on what we learn about our guests, they may not merely get picked up by a car at the airport."

"May I join you?" Cindy asked. "I'm done hanging out with my ex-husband in enclosed spaces."

"You might get dirty," Randy said.

Cindy followed Randy down a wooded hill to the edge of a wide, brownish-blue river. Fallen branches, shrubs, and saplings grabbed at them; there didn't appear to be a trail, but Randy seemed to know where he was going. The last time Cindy had been in the woods was the previous summer when some of the girls from work rented a cabin upstate, and she hardly even went outside the whole time.

If they could see her now. A sharp twig scratched her calf; she removed her heels and mud rose between her toes. It was exhilarating.

She stopped near the river's edge when it started to get muddy, but Randy charged on ahead, tan streaks smearing across his black pant legs.

"There they are," he said, pointing at the river. A red canoe with two people in it was making its way across the water toward them. Randy trudged back into the woods, toward a tree with a black ribbon tied around it. How he knew where all these things were, Cindy couldn't fathom.

The boaters had landed; they were a young, fit-looking couple in jeans, plaid shirts, and life jackets, but were dirty and wet and looked like they hadn't slept in days.

"Now what?" the woman said, collapsing on the shore.

"OK, the next thing on the list is this," the man said, sitting down in the muddy grass, pulling a laminated card from his cargo pants. "It just says, 'Quiet Dog Tree.'"

The woman sat up and stared into the forest. The man continued to look at the card, repeating the phrase to himself.

"There it is," the woman said, pointing up the beach to her left. "Up there, the tree with the bark shaved off."

"No bark. Oh, that was an easy one," the guy said, and he followed the woman up into the woods near where Randy and Cindy were hiding.

The couple knelt by the naked tree and saw a laminated card that read LOOK UP.

"Welcome to The Dinner," Randy said, walking toward them. "Follow me for tea and cocktails."

The man and woman shrieked and hugged each other.

They said they'd been offered an "adventure package" when their reservation was accepted, which meant that they had to find their way here from their home in Chicago using only clues and nonmotorized transport. They said it took them just under a week.

"What are your names?" Cindy asked them.

"Will and Katie Prager," the young man said, pride evident in his phrasing, which was sweet.

"Recently married?" Cindy asked.

"Yeah," Katie Prager said. "This is our honeymoon, actually. Our friends did a Kickstarter for us, once we heard our reservation was accepted." It turned out they'd put their names on the list long ago, and had always planned to have their wedding just before the date they'd been chosen to attend The Dinner—whenever that would be.

On the way back up, Will also mentioned that he'd dated Eva "for a minute, during a really dark time" back in high school, but that apparently had no influence in moving him up the list. "I signed up the day the reservation Web site opened," he said.

"Maybe she just wanted a certain combination of people," Randy said. "But I can't speak to that."

Minutes later Randy was leading Cindy across a field to where the yellow-and-green-striped hot-air balloon was landing.

A big guy with loose cotton pants the colors of the Jamaican flag and a T-shirt that read WHERE'S THE PARTY? hefted himself out of the basket as Randy met it with a stepladder. There were a number of Jamaicans in Charlevoix, and she really liked the ones she had gotten to know, but she certainly didn't know enough to tell if this guy was actually Jamaican until he spoke.

"Whoa, that was somethin' else," the big guy said. *Nope,* Cindy thought, *American. Boring.* He helped his companion, a woman smaller than himself, but not small, out of the basket behind him. "So, this is the place, I take it? I was told to look for a long-haired guy in a dirty black suit."

"If your names are Ros Wali and Rashida Williams, yes, this is the place."

"Yeah, that's us," he said.

"Follow me for tea and cocktails," Randy said. "It's twenty minutes to the first course."

While Randy led the newest couple to the tent, Cindy snuck up the hill to the tables and peeked at the names on the place cards. There were sixteen in all, and Eva Thorvald was not among them; she didn't eat with her guests, as Cindy had hoped. Cindy had unfortunately, but inevitably, been placed next to Reynaldo, so she switched herself to the other table and put her husband next to that Holger Schmidt guy instead.

From the top of the hill, she could see both the river on one side and the sun setting on the other. She also saw two bearded men in fishing vests carrying a large blue cooler between them, and watched them as they walked the length of the tent and around the back. That must be where the kitchen was.

She started her way down the hill.

"Hey," Randy said, appearing from nowhere with a broad-shouldered, grim-faced young woman. "If you're not doing anything, can you help Maureen and me pick the corn for tonight's dinner?"

"Pick the corn?" Cindy asked.

"Maureen O'Brien," the woman said. "I'm an old friend of Eva's."

It was astonishing to Cindy to meet all of these people from different parts of Eva's life. "Going back how far?"

"I met her when she was sixteen and I was twenty-four," Maureen said. "And yeah, corn." Maureen pointed to a small cornfield, maybe sixty stalks, on a plot of land close to the farmhouse. "Eva first planted that corn four years ago. That's how long we've been planning to have dinner in this spot. Want to get to work?"

Cindy was tempted, just to ask this woman a million questions about Eva, but she'd gotten dirty enough, and she'd hated cornfields ever since junior high, when her dad got her and her brother a summer job detasseling corn. It was supposed to teach them work ethic, but the pay sucked, the early mornings were worse, and because she wore short sleeves in an attempt to get a tan, she'd sliced her arms bloody at least twice a day on the corn leaves, which cut like fresh paper.

"I was actually going to go freshen up a bit," Cindy said. Randy called for one of the security guys, a big galoot named Dougie, to accompany her to the luxury bus. The far end of the tent, where the kitchen was, remained at a distance.

At 7:30, the sixteen guests were seated for dinner. Cindy found herself between Ros Wali and a stunning black-haired woman named Asgne Fihou (pronounced *AH-nay FEE-how*, she said preemptively) and across from a couple from South Korea named Ha Man-hee and Lee Mi-sun. It was clearly an international table; Holger Schmidt was now, after Cindy's switch, the only non-American at the other one. Reynaldo, of course, expressed shock that he wasn't next to Cindy, but when Holger told him to put a lid on it, he sat without another word.

She spotted the canoe couple, Will and Katie, at Reynaldo's table; it looked like they'd been supplied with formal wear in their size, but they still had the pallid, grooved faces of people who had been awake for days.

Randy pushed in Cindy's chair, as other staff members did the same for the other guests. "I'll be your personal attendant this evening," he said. "There will be no substitutions or alterations to the menu, but anything else you may desire, please let me know."

"Is Eva coming out at all during the dinner?"

"If she does, it will be sometime after the third course," Randy said, handing Cindy a small ivory-colored vellum card. "Here is tonight's bill of fare."

Amuse

THINLY SLICED, FIRE-TOASTED *PANE DI CASTAGNE* WITH
DRY-CURED PORK SHOULDER (COPPA STYLE, FROM EVA'S
BERKSHIRE PIG, WILLIAM) & ALDERMAN PLUM
AND GINGER CHUTNEY

PAIRING: *2012 Luciano Saetti Lambrusco
Salamino di Santa Croce*

First

PAN-SEARED WALLEYE
SERVED FILLETED OVER GOLDEN BANTAM SUCCOTASH
(SWEET CORN/RED ONION/BLUE LAKE GREEN BEANS)

PAIRING: *2009 Littorai Mays Canyon Chardonnay,
Russian River Valley, CA*

Second

GRILLED VENISON
SERVED WITH GRILLED MOSKVICH TOMATOES, WILTED
KALE WITH SWEET PEPPER JELLY VINAIGRETTE (HOUSE-
MADE SWEET PEPPER JELLY & SHERRY VINEGAR &
GRAPESEED OIL)

PAIRING: *2005 Marcassin Blue-Slide Ridge Pinot Noir,
Sonoma Coast, CA*

Third

PAVLOVA WITH TODAY-PICKED SOUTH DAKOTA
BLACKBERRIES
SERVED WITH A MINI SHOT OF CHOCOLATE HABANERO—
INFUSED DARK CHOCOLATE ICE MILK

PAIRING: *1990 J. J. Prüm Wehlener Sonnenuhr Riesling,
Trockenbeerenauslese*

Finish

PAT PRAGER'S PRIVATE RECIPE DESSERT
WITH (*YOUR CHOICE*) KOPI LUWAK COFFEE, 2002 QIAN-
JIAZHAI OLD GROWTH SHENG PU'ER TEA,
AND/OR ARDBEG 1974 PROVENANCE, SERVED NEAT

• • •

Cindy had been looking forward to the wine pairings the most; she'd hoped for more reds, but it wasn't meant to be with this menu. Two dessert courses, that was a new one.

"Oh, fuck me!" she heard a man say at the other table, loud enough to make her turn to see who it was. It was Will, the canoe guy. He was staring at the bottom of the menu, a distressed look on his face.

It seemed to be a polite crowd, and the loud curse was met with murmurs of disapproval from both guests and staff. Will seemed like a sweet kid, but he needed to tone it down over there.

"What are the fuckin' chances!" Will shouted.

Holger glared at Will and said, "Shut your pie hole." God, she could propose to that man.

The *amuse* course came out; two perfectly browned isosceles-triangle toast points, thin as tortillas, framing a curl of bright pink ham, accompanied by a white ceramic spoon of pale red chutney. The Lambrusco followed, poured from a chilled decanter, which wasn't 100 percent necessary if the wine was properly stored.

"What do you do?" Ros Wali asked Cindy. "Do you work here?"

"No, I'm a sommelier in Michigan. What about yourself?"

Ros Wali motioned to the woman on the other side of him. "Me and Rashida are licensed discard counselors. We can go into your home and tell you what you don't need."

"Wow, never heard of that. Does it keep you busy?"

"Man, you wouldn't believe," Ros Wali said. "Here's my card."

He handed her a card the colors of the Jamaican flag; on one side it read *Licensed Discard Counselor: Home or Office—Live Simply, Live Well!* and a phone number; on the other, it read *USE ROS WALI* in huge letters.

"So," Ros Wali said. "Sommelier, huh. What can you tell us about the wines on this list?"

"Well," Cindy said. "The 1990 vintage of this German Riesling is supposed to be one of the best in its history. The American Chardonnay I've had a bunch of times, and it's very much to my liking; it's less oaky and alcoholic than a lot of domestic Chardonnays." Cindy realized that she was leaping down the rabbit hole of winespeak; she glanced up to make sure that her audience was still interested, and they were. "Pretty much everything from Marcassin is a home run, if a bit spendy, and this organic dry Lambrusco should be perfect with Coppa."

"Wow, OK," Ros Wali said. "I knew all that, I was just checking."

She tore the cured ham in half with her knife, and used a little plum chutney as a paste to affix it to a toast point. Is that what you were supposed to do? She saw Man-hee across the table make his into a dainty sandwich.

Before raising it to her mouth, she stared at the little pink, brown, and red bite in her hand. When Cindy had last seen her daughter, she was a whiny little alien who shit all day and cried all night out of hunger. Cindy did breast-feed her a couple of times, but she hated it; it hurt like hell, and whatever mother-child bond was supposed to explode in her heart during those moments just never happened. Now, somehow, here she was, being fed by her child.

Objectively, it was astonishing. The tartness of the chutney, the saltiness of the cured ham, and the dry, earthy wine all locked together in a happy scrum, like brothers reuniting after a summer apart. She didn't believe that this course alone was a thousand-dollar value, but she could've eaten an entire popcorn bowl full of it and not been satisfied.

She felt the woman next to her, the one with the impressively obscure name, get up and take her wineglass with her. By the time she looked up, Reynaldo was sitting down in the empty chair, putting his napkin on his lap, setting his wineglass on the table where the woman's was.

"There, that's better," he said. "Holger was hitting it off with Asgne in the drinks tent earlier, so I hope you don't mind the switch."

Cindy threw back the rest of her wine.

"Wow, some *amuse* plate, huh?" Reynaldo said. "You know we got to see Eva Thorvald earlier? She popped in to get some tea. I was looking for you but I couldn't find you."

"What?" Cindy tried to stay calm. "You got to meet her?"

"Well, not meet her exactly, but see her up close. She just said hi to everybody. Where did you go, anyway?"

"When was this? Did she say she was going to come out here?"

Ros Wali nudged her. "Hey, don't get worked up. She just came in, got some tea, said hi, and then left. It was like ten seconds. That's all you missed."

"It was pretty cool, though," Reynaldo said.

"I'll say this," said Ros Wali. "She's another type of being. You can just tell. She ain't from where you and I are from. She's from somewhere else."

The second course arrived: two glistening little rectangles of white fish on identically sized mounds of yellow and red succotash. Man-hee and Mi-sun across the table each took a bite, and Mi-sun snapped forward in her chair, clutching her head.

Ros Wali glanced at Cindy. "Maybe we should send this one back?"

Mi-sun's face lifted, and there were tears on her cheeks, but she was smiling. Man-hee was rocking his head back and forth, eyes closed, while he chewed slowly.

Mi-sun wiped her eyes.

Reynaldo tried his. "Wow. This is supposed to be the best area in

South Dakota to catch walleye, and if that's why we're specifically eating here, I'd say it's worth it."

Cindy hadn't even touched hers yet and Ros Wali's plate was empty.

"That motherfucker was insane," Ros Wali said. "But that was it? Just those two tiny pieces?" He called his personal server over, a young guy with long blond hair.

"Hey, Jordy, can I have seconds?"

Jordy pursed his lips and shook his head. "Sorry, no can do."

Ros Wali pounded his fist against the table, rattling everyone's wineglasses. "That's a fuckin' travesty, man! A fuckin' travesty!"

Rashida put her arm around him and told him to chill.

She saw that Reynaldo was closing his eyes and touching his temples as he chewed.

"Quit being annoying," she said.

"This is indescribable, indescribable," he said. "The corn, it tastes like golden sugar. The fish, it's like, it's like . . ."

"Indescribable?"

He nodded. "I just wish Ayren was here."

That wasn't his wife's name. "Now who's that?"

"My daughter. A-Y-R-E-N. It's an anagram of Reyna. Ayren Reyna. She'd love this."

Oh, God. "She's a baby," Cindy said. "She loves her own snot."

"But don't you think if she had something like this now, it could maybe change the course of her life?"

"I doubt it."

"Did you and Lars," Reynaldo said, "ever feed . . . her anything like this? Just wondering if that explains it."

"I sure didn't," Cindy said. "Maybe Lars did. He probably did."

"Proves my point, then."

Cindy poked Reynaldo's leg under the table with the butt end of her knife. "Please don't bring up Eva again."

"You're here at my pleasure, you know," he said, and stabbed his last piece of fish with his fork.

The walleye and succotash were, in Cindy's opinion, remarkable. The fish, maybe just an hour or two out of the river, was heartbreakingly tender, dissipating in her mouth like a spoonful of cream. Pairing-wise, the Old World–style Chardonnay was perfect; she tasted hints of gunflint and honey, just like a top-of-the-line Chablis. Still, this was all nothing that would make her openly swear at the table, but perhaps she was too distracted to submit to the unchecked enthusiasms of her fellow diners.

"Randy," she said, calling him over, "is Eva coming out after this course?"

"If she does, it'll be between the two dessert courses," Randy said. "She's way too busy in the kitchen until then."

The third dish, a tiny cut of venison steak, about half the size of a playing card, with tomatoes and sweet pepper jelly, was a different matter. The venison, firm enough to meet your teeth, and soft enough to yield agreeably in your mouth, revealed subtle, steely new flavors with each bite, while the tomatoes were so full of richness and warm blood, it was like eating a sleeping animal. Their pairing, the light-bodied Pinot, didn't erase these senses, it crept beneath their power, underlining them. It was about as much flavor as fifteen seconds were capable of; after one bite and one sip of wine, Cindy felt luminous and exhausted.

Mi-sun and Man-hee were both rocking back and forth in their chairs, weeping; Ros Wali was rattling the table with his fists, screaming, "The injustice! The injustice!" while Reynaldo was slicing the venison into nearly diaphanous slivers, perhaps to make it all last longer.

Yes, the dish was flawless, and the wine pairing was supernatural, but these people were out of control. Were they trying to emotionally justify the meal's price tag? Did they have too many cocktails in the drinks tent? It was a breathtaking meal, one of the best that Cindy had ever had, but the hysteria around her was making her brain red.

"And now, the first of the two dessert courses," Randy announced. He placed before Cindy a pavlova the size of a mini-donut, with five black-berry halves clinging to its tiny plateau, and a copper shot glass filled two-thirds with a creamy dark brown liquid.

"That's my personal favorite," Randy said, indicating the liquid. "Drink it immediately after you eat."

Reynaldo was trying to cut his pavlova into quarters. "You know this is the longest I've been away from my daughter?" he said. "I left home at four-thirty in the morning today. It's been sixteen hours."

"Fourteen," Cindy said. "This time zone's two hours ahead." She put the whole thing in her mouth, chasing it with half the shot of the spicy chocolate ice milk. "Whoa," she said involuntarily.

"It's still the record," Reynaldo said.

"Well, good for you," Cindy said. "I'd love to hear more about it, but I'm having such an interesting dialogue with Ros Wali over here."

Ros Wali, at that moment, was bent over his empty plate, licking a blackberry stain. "It gives life!" he shouted.

Cindy felt the staff behind her converging and murmuring among themselves; almost as quickly as she perceived it, Cindy turned and saw Yonas Awate standing alone between the tables.

"Eva Thorvald thanks you for coming to dinner tonight," Yonas said, pivoting as he spoke, looking each guest in the eye. "She regrets that she is too exhausted to join you all in person, but is so happy that you could share in what she told me has been her greatest dinner of all time. She's told me that even though you won't meet her tonight, she's telling you her life story through the ingredients in this meal, and although you won't shake her hand, you've shared her heart. Now please, continue eating and drinking, and thank you again."

• • •

Cindy couldn't bring herself to applaud with the others. What an awful, insincere, lazy cop-out! She remained staring at Yonas, her heart gushing acid into her ears and eyes.

She looked down the hill toward the luxury bus and her eyes swept the decay of protocol around her. The Korean couple was lying on the ground, like toddlers spent by their own histrionics. Ros Wali was being physically restrained by his female companion, his arms flailing, knocking over a lit candle and a half-full wineglass.

Reynaldo remained oblivious to all of this. "I still love you, you know," he said, slumping forward, belly full of alcohol and unrequited nostalgia. "My wife only let me go on this trip with you because I told her it's what I needed to do to finally get over you."

"If she believed that," Cindy said, "she's definitely too dumb for you." Looking around, she saw that the other servers, including Randy and Maureen, were occupied in helping Rashida Williams get Ros Wali under control. He was really pitching a fit about injustice; everyone was captivated.

"Your secret's safe with me, you know. Because I love you. I'll never tell anyone."

"If the last course comes, guard mine for me," Cindy said. "I gotta go." She drank the last of the spicy ice milk and got up from the table, feeling the alcohol touch her limbs as she stood and dashed down the gentle slope of the hill toward the luxury coach.

"I'll be here," Reynaldo said. "I'll guard it with my life."

Approaching the bus, she slapped a mosquito on her arm. Hearing the noise, a husky tattooed security guy halted his long oval path in front of the tent to stare at her.

"Just using the ladies'," she told him.

She stepped inside the opulent vehicle—even in the dim light, it looked fancier than almost any place she'd ever lived—and made her way past the bathrooms to the bedroom in the back. The door was ajar. It was dark and empty.

Once she got to the second floor, she could feel that the bus was completely unoccupied; in fact, it looked as if it had barely been used at all. The counters and tables were empty except for a copy of an insurance form and a rental agreement.

From the window, a small flickering light caught her eye. Sitting outside around a small fire pit behind the tent were three women; the night disguised their faces, but Cindy knew who was there.

She'd played two versions of this night—oddly, she'd always imagined it as night—hundreds of times in the intervening years between the morning at Tettegouche Winery and that evening in South Dakota. In one of those musings, she'd approach Eva Thorvald and say, *Hello, I'm Cynthia Hargreaves,* and the two of them would look in each other's eyes, and the wordless mother-daughter gravity between them would instantly break the years of silence. She'd hold her daughter for the first time since she was a baby, and after wiping away each other's tears, they'd spend all night into the morning excavating their lost memories together. Perhaps Cindy would even move to Minnesota to be closer to her daughter, and work for her impressive empire as a sommelier— everyone would be so happy, and it would be the kind of touching human-interest story that'd raise Eva's national profile—one could now add *forgiving* to her impressive list of characteristics.

The more likely scenario was that Lars had interpreted Cindy's heart-breaking sacrifice decades ago as a bad mother's selfish mutiny. That was easy to imagine. Perhaps he'd spent Eva's entire life convincing her that somewhere, her cruel birth mother still existed, as distant and unremarkable as a soldier in a foreign port. That would be how Lars would see it, and a father only needed to tell a little girl once that her real mother had abandoned her for breakable things to become unfixable.

• • •

Downstairs, she removed her heels and spied out the bus door's window, waiting for the security man's loop to take him out of sight, then darted barefoot around the bus, toward the fire.

From a distance, she could hear the three people laughing. They appeared to be drinking beer and eating. The women started laughing again, but when they sensed someone approaching them, one of them stopped and sat upright.

"Hey, who's that?" a woman's voice said.

"Hi," Cindy said.

"Hi," the woman's voice answered back. "What's your name?"

Cindy moved closer to the fire, and with each step could see all three of them more clearly. There was a short, plump older woman with glasses and short hair, a husky, broad-shouldered young blonde, and another woman, with a face she recognized from the Internet.

Cindy had never seen her own eyes and cheekbones on another living person before. They were more pronounced in the firelight, and, coupled with Lars's nose, assembled a remarkable face, from every angle. Cindy had seen that face before, when perfectly lit and airbrushed for glossy magazine pieces, but not the bags under the eyes, the smeared, messy hair, the stained cargo pants, the scars on the forearms, or the wide, dirty bare feet propped up on a milk crate. Her daughter was the most stunning human Cindy had ever seen.

Cindy had planned what she was going to say next for several years, but now that she was here, it was difficult to open her mouth. Her blood clawed at her insides as the words fell between her teeth.

"I'm Cynthia," she said. "Cynthia Hargreaves."

The three people around the fire looked at Cindy as if she had just said that the weather forecast predicted partly cloudy skies for tomorrow.

"Hi, I'm Pat Prager," the older woman said, standing up and shaking

Cindy's hand. This woman had a warmth about her; when she smiled, it seemed sincere and calm.

The blonde girl didn't move from her chair. "Braque," she said. She pointed to a teenage boy cleaning dishes in the kitchen tent. Cindy hadn't noticed him before. "That's my son Hatch over there."

"Hatch," Cindy said to herself.

"He's named after a town in New Mexico," Braque said, and slapped a mosquito on her arm. "Fuckin' organic bug spray is for shit," she said to herself.

Eva stood up and shook Cindy's hand. "Do I know you?"

"I guess not," Cindy said. Hearing this young woman's words, seeing her face, and touching her hand, she felt like she didn't know where she was, and that she was a thousand miles from home—both of which her mind knew were objectively true—but now her heart translated those opaque facts into something moon-white and cold.

"No offense," Eva said, sitting back down again. She stared back at Cindy as if studying a painting in a museum. "I meet a lot of people. And you paid today under the name Reyna."

"Married name," Cindy said, staring at Eva. Her brain, now simply overwhelmed, had somehow compelled her feet to quit moving.

The security guy appeared behind Cindy and grabbed her arms. "Come on," he said. "You're not supposed to be here."

"No, it's OK, Dougie," Eva said, and Dougie let Cindy go. "Sit down, have a Grain Belt. Cooler's to your left."

Cindy took a beer from the cooler, and because there was nowhere else to sit, she sat down on its thick white plastic lid.

"Sorry, we're out of chairs," Eva said.

Pat stood up to give Cindy her chair, but Cindy pleaded for her to remain seated, claiming she was comfortable.

"What are you eating?" was all Cindy could think to say. The food on their plates didn't look like anything they'd had at The Dinner.

"Steamed broccoli, mac and cheese, and a beer," Pat said, smiling. "We just sent up the second dessert course, so we can finally eat now ourselves."

"You don't want to miss Pat's bars," Braque said. "We drove her out here just so she could make them tonight."

Cindy was transfixed on her daughter, barely listening to any of this.

"Why are you staring at me?" Eva asked Cindy. She had the tone of someone who might have been asking that question to a small child.

"I don't know," Cindy said, and stood up. "I should go."

"No, stay," Eva said. "You've been trying to get down here since you first arrived. What's on your mind?"

"I just wanted to say, I used to know your father."

"Oh, cool beans." Eva had the vibe of a celebrity who had heard dozens of compliments and entreaties every day; this phrase had the pleasant, defensive feel of a much-used stock answer.

Cindy took a deep breath. Maybe Lars never mentioned to her who her mother was? That seemed impossible to believe. "How is he doing?"

"Well, he's better. He's in a treatment facility in Michigan."

"Oh," Cindy said. She liked how Eva was like herself and didn't bullshit—she got right to the marrow of a conversation—but this was not what she expected to hear. "Where in Michigan?"

"Marquette."

"Oh, Lars is in Marquette?"

"No, Uncle Lars died when I was a baby. My dad is Jarl."

Once again, not what Cindy was expecting to hear. She felt her hand over her heart. "Oh no. Lars died?"

"Yeah, did you know him too?"

Cindy's eyes glistened. "He was the nicest man I've ever known," she said. How could their daughter be who she was now without Lars? It didn't make sense. Lars had loved their daughter with such intensity, Cindy remembered feeling alienated and jealous. Lars was one of the main reasons why Cindy was able to leave and spend a lifetime not thinking about what she'd left. "He died when you were how old?"

"I don't know. I was a baby. I don't really remember." Cindy thought she saw tears in Eva's eyes, but she wasn't sure.

Pat got to her feet and looked at Braque. "Maybe we should start packing up the kitchen." She gathered her beer and plate, glancing back at Braque as she trudged into the kitchen tent.

Braque didn't move, saying, "This is interesting." Cindy couldn't tell whether she was being sarcastic.

Cindy didn't take Pat's vacated chair, choosing to stay on the cooler, at a distance.

"So you don't remember him, then?"

Eva shook her head.

"Was your mom Fiona?"

"Yeah."

"Where's she these days?"

"She died when I was fourteen."

"Oh my God, I'm sorry," Cindy said. Fiona had been an able and enthusiastic babysitter, she remembered, but she didn't seem to like Cindy very much. No matter, now.

"It's all right," Eva said, and took a deep breath. Her rangy posture had tightened up; she was now curled up in her chair like a child.

"Are you married?"

"Everyone always wants to know that. No, and no plans to. Not that I'd announce it if I ever did."

"A boyfriend, even?"

Eva exchanged a glance with Braque, who smiled at her. "Nothing serious."

Braque couldn't help herself. "What about Adam?"

Eva kicked her cousin's chair. "You can go help Pat clean up the kitchen."

"He's totally cute, admit it," Braque said, standing. "And he makes awesome bread."

"See ya, Braque," Eva said, and both she and Cindy watched Braque drag her ass into the kitchen tent.

"So, there's a cute guy who's good in the kitchen?"

Eva sighed. "He's very sweet. And he makes me laugh. I've always been a sucker for guys who make me laugh. That's all I'm going to say about it."

"Fair enough. And so you don't have any kids or anything?"

"Hell, no."

"You sound pretty decisive about that."

"I am. I think I would be a terrible mother, actually. Braque over there, I don't know how she does it. I look at a baby and I'm like, ugh."

"I know exactly what you mean."

"So how did you know my parents and uncle?"

Cindy had to take a breath before she spoke. She used to know what she was going to say on this night. She'd practiced it for years, as she read about this young woman, this daughter of hers, as Eva became increasingly successful and famous. It was hard for her not to feel proud that some of herself was in that extraordinary creature on everybody's wish list. Many times when Eva Thorvald came up in conversation somewhere, Cindy wanted to blurt out, *That's my daughter,* because of what it would say about her—because, of course, acquaintances and friends would regard her differently if they knew her daughter was the iconic chef behind the most difficult dinner reservation in the world.

And, having eaten her food, it was clear to Cindy that Eva was deserving of all the hype and the swooning. Until a mouth closed around a fork or a spoon, Eva fought for control of every variable; she seemed to conjure miracles from crops, animals, bacteria, fire, water, and even the molecules in the air, apparently leaving no detail unscrutinized. There were many chefs far more groundbreaking than her, many more daring with what they were willing to put on a plate, but no one else who could summon such astonishing results from their decisions. Cindy realized that the world where great and heavenly things like this can exist is only possible because everything cannot be known, and perfection cannot be experienced, but the work of brilliant people like Eva makes people doubt that, for just a moment.

Eva was a part of her, yet existed in this remarkable form because Cindy had no part of her. It would've been something to grab her daughter's hand like a mother back from the dead, and instantly fill the abyss that a mother's absence might have created in her heart. But there seemed to be no knowledge in the eyes across from Cindy that such an abyss even existed.

It was up to Cindy to remind Eva's subconscious that she'd been abandoned, and force this complex emptiness into the center of her beautiful life, whether her daughter knew of Cynthia Hargreaves or not. Cindy realized that this was the critical action beneath the reasons she was here, and one thing that was inevitable if she were to earn what her heart had desired.

"They loved you, didn't they? Your parents?"

"Yeah, very much."

Cindy exhaled. She felt her legs shaking and grabbed her knees. She looked at her beer bottle on the ground. "You could've been much worse off."

"I suppose. They did their best, though."

"No. That's not what I mean. You could've been raised by a bad mother."

"Well, I wasn't. The only bad part is that she died."

"But she loved you?" Cindy asked.

"Yeah," said Eva. "She did."

Tears blossomed and streaked Cindy's face in bright ribbons.

"Are you OK?" Eva asked.

"I should go," Cindy said, wiping her cheeks. If she was going to get on with her life, she couldn't look at this young woman for another second. She turned her head, stood, and walked away.

"Hey, nice to meet you!" Eva called after her.

• • •

Cindy sat down on the cold grass on the other side of the bus and put her head in her hands. She felt someone sit next to her.

It was Randy. "You know, she found her birth certificate when she was fifteen," he said. "But when you're like her, lots of people come out of the woodwork. Claiming to be somebody to her. People who even forge documents. You're the third Cynthia Hargreaves in two years. But she wants me to ask you. Are you somebody?"

"That's not for me to decide," Cindy said.

"Did you talk to her?" Reynaldo asked in the Lincoln Town Car, and "Did you talk to her?" Molly and Kerensa asked before work on a rainy Monday, and to all of them she said, Eva Thorvald's the most beautiful person in the world, and I never expect to see her again.

Some mornings, Cindy would be on her porch, with her dog, drinking coffee, and she'd see the family across the street wrestle with their feisty child, and wonder whether her presence or familiarity was at all provoking to Eva; if one day, that woman would seek her out, and for whatever balance of time, Cindy would have a daughter again. For now, she would return to her kitchen, wash the plate, the cup, and the fork, and just live in the world she had created, the world where the two of them existed, and nothing more.

ACKNOWLEDGMENTS

This book wouldn't exist without these people: Brooke Delaney, Pamela Dorman, Ryan Harbage, Erin Hickey, Lou Mathews, Rob Roberge, Jeffrey Stradal.

Thank you, so much, to 826LA, Angela Barton, Matt Bell, Doris Biel, Amy Boutell, Cat Boyd, Louise Braverman, Aaron Burch, Leigh Butler, Cecil Castellucci and the men and women of Nine Pines, Patricia Clark, Carolyn Coleburn, Tricia Conley, Kathryn Court, Winnie De Moya, Brian Dille, George Ducker, John Fagan, Jenni Ferrari-Adler, Clare Ferraro, Hal Fessenden, Susie Fleet, Spencer Foxworth, Gina Frangello, Joan Funk, Rico Gagliano, Kate Gibson, Nathan Gratz, Amelia Gray, Anthony Grazioso, Monica Howe, Sacha Howells, Meg Howrey, Alison Hunter, Julia Ingalls, Sarah Janet, Elin Johnson, Matt Kay, Jay and Amy Kovacs, Diana Kowalsky, Summer Block Kumar, Sarah LaBrie, Brad Listi, Michael Loomis, Brandon Lovejoy, Seema Mahanian, Madeline McIntosh, Anthony Miller, Patrick Nolan, Ana Ottman, Ashley Perez, Lindsay Prevette, Scott Rubenstein, Jim Ruland, Daniel J. Safarik, Kim Samek, Jeremy Schmidt, Roseanne Serra, Joshua Wolf Shenk, Nancy Sheppard, Connie Simonson, Jen Sincero, Olivia Taylor Smith, Aaron Solomon, Eric J. Stolze, Roger Stradal, Jacob Strunk, Dennis Swaim, Mike Tanaka, Mia Taylor, Chris Terry, Alissa Theodor, Shannon Twomey, the Westshire Drive home group, the Stradal, Johnson, and Biel families, and everyone on the hardcover and paperback sales teams at Penguin Random House.

Very special thanks to my great-grandmother Lois Bly Johnson's church, First Lutheran Church of Hunter, North Dakota, and all of the contributors to the 1984 edition of the First Lutheran Church Women cookbook, on which five of the recipes in this novel are based.

Finally, eternal gratitude to Karen Stradal for a childhood full of books, for encouraging all of my "research projects," and, most of all, for teaching me how to read at a young age. When you returned to college to finish your English degree and you read me your assignments as bedtime stories, it filled me with a lifelong love of literature and writing. This book and everything I write is because of you. You are loved and missed beyond words.